COAL GETS IN YOUR VEINS

CAT RECTOR

First printing September 2024

Written Contribution by Leslie Allen
Edited and Proofread by Ivy L. James
Cover Art by Scherville
Cover Text Design by Cat Rector
Interior Formatting and Design by Cat Rector

Further contact information for contributors can
be found at the back of the book.

ISBN 978-1-7383048-1-3 (paperback)
ISBN 978-1-7383048-3-7 (hardcover)
ISBN 978-1-7383048-0-6 (ebook)

www.catrector.com

To love and the people who keep helping me find it again.

I love you too.

ALSO BY CAT RECTOR

This Too Shall Burn

The Unwritten Runes Series

The Goddess of Nothing At All
Epilogues for Lost Gods
Threads of Fate

TRIGGER WARNINGS

This book includes individual scenes that are fictionalisations of real traumatic events that happened to or around me. Some are mine to tell, some were included by request. This book is a standing monument to things that people have suffered, and as such, please proceed with caution.

A list of these side scenes and their specific triggers can be found on my website, as well as in the appendix at the back of this book.

Death

Violence

Misogyny

Sexual content

Domestic abuse and sexual assault from a spouse

Implied sexual assault involving a minor (off page)

Homophobic slurs and bigotry

Grief and depression around loss of loved ones

Recreational alcohol, smoking, and drug use

Death of a wild animal

The evils of being a vampire

Descriptive scenes of biting and blood drinking, including in sexual scenarios

Poverty

Fire, burns, and burning buildings

Don't forget to hydrate.

Just…make sure the water doesn't have any coal in it, okay?

PREFACE

This book is the culmination of many things, but primarily it's an attempt to write what I know. What I know above all else is what it was like to grow up in the generational trauma of an impoverished ex-coal mining town, and to wish to be swept away from my troubles by a handsome brooding vampire.

And because of that, I get to introduce you to Laurel and Spencer.

I thought that would be the end of it. Book written, job complete. Laurel and Spencer's stories were on the page, and so was a collection of mostly true vignettes inspired by the goings-on of the town I grew up in. To help set the scene, you know? When I handed the first draft to some local readers, I asked them to be honest. Had I been too sharp with the way I had framed this fictional version of the place I loved? Did I need to dial it back?

They read the book, then told me I hadn't cut far enough.

They asked me to add their personal stories, and the book also became a memorial.

This book is fictional. It's a fake town with fake names and there are paranormal concepts that clearly don't exist in real life. It is, however, based on real dynamics. The point of view of Penny Harbour is what most closely resembles fact. Each scene is different and from the perspective of a fictional person who lived in the Harbour. While the details have been left fuzzy or changed altogether, each scene represents a real event that happened to myself, to someone who asked me to share their story, or to someone that I love.

There are horrors in this book, and most of them are true.

For some, the hardest part of reading this book will be believing that these things happened. For others, it will be believing that the area in question is built on a duality of loving community and deep pain.

The place where I grew up was complicated. It cared. It lifted people up. It gave everything it had to people who needed it most. It did the best it could. I met my platonic soulmate there, but I also met the people who would carve my heart out of my chest and serve it back to me in shreds. It gave and stole so much from me, and it started years before I was born, and will keep doing it long after I'm dead. It shaped me and everyone I loved, for better or worse.

When I was a teenager, I thought it was paradise. At the age of 35, I know something I didn't know back then; you can't build a town on 300 years of traumatic events without it haunting the generations to come. We now understand generational trauma to be something passed down from family member to family member, through their actions but also genetically. Trauma changes people to their core, mind and body. I look at my own family tree and I see it, clear as crystal.

The town of Penny Harbour is true and it's false and only someone who lived there will properly know the difference.

I come from a place where the sea rises up to meet you. Where doors keep shuttering, never to open again. Where the tap water can smell like rotten eggs and the people who share your blood can be your truest enemy. Where the people are deeply entwined over generations, and they're divided and hold grudges and will still build your house back up when it burns to the ground. Where neighbours walk in without knocking and put the kettle on, because they know they're always welcome. Where the town is built on top of the souls of miners who didn't make it out, and there isn't a single person down any family line that it didn't touch. Where love is hard and complicated. Where getting by is often the best you can hope for.

In a place like this, the coal got in our veins for 300 years, and the trauma of it ate so many of us alive.

Yet we carry on with hope and love.

Because what else can a person do?

ABOUT COAL MINING

Coal mining was the backbone of Nova Scotia since at least the 1700s. Many towns were founded to become company towns for the mining industry. At the start of WWI, three-quarters of coal burned in Canada came from my province.

Most people know surface-level facts about mining. The quick and dirty is this: people worked long, hard days underground, breathing in toxic dust for as little as $1.50 a day. Men and children risked their lives every single day, and huge chunks of local populations died in cave-ins, explosions, poison air, and random accidents. Long term, survivors would die of coal dust in the lungs, heart failure, or mental illness. At least once, they died from gunfire when management saw fit to shoot people down.

According to the 1901 census of one town, 60 per cent of families had sent one of their working-age young boys to the mines.

The place where I grew up once had a population of under 7,000 people, and several mines per town. One specific mine was recorded as having killed 115 people during its operation. Another mine in the area killed 176 people in one accident. There were 18 legal mines and many illegal operations. The population of my town appears to have gone from 6,600 in 1861 to around 2,000 in 1921, to 606 in 1975. This is in part due to the death of the industry in the area, but more horrifically, the death of the workers in the mines themselves.

If we understand generational trauma to be something passed from generation
to generation, and we think of the way that death would have hung over
the lives of these people every single day, the effect becomes clear. While
researching for this book, very few of the miner's or their family spoke of the
effects of the mines on their bodies and minds. The ones that did spoke in the
same manner; there wasn't any choice, so we all made the best of it.

This book is my attempt to share what growing up among this trauma was like.
How the community lived and died within it. The breaking and the resilience
of a community that has been pushed to the brink of extinction by an industry
that made its money on the health of its workers.

PROLOGUE

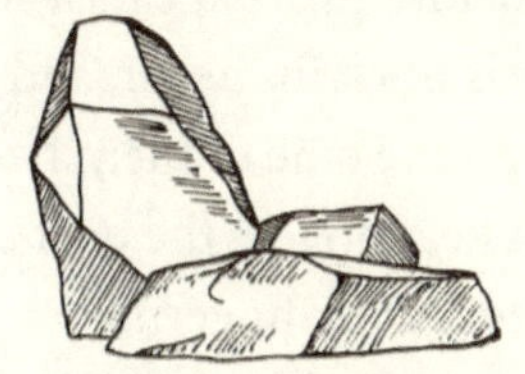

Nova Scotia
1721 to 1992

The crack of dawn came early for the miners of Umberlee #2, just the same as it did every other morning. The chill of maritime air was visible on the breath of the men and boys as they walked down the main road in the frigid winter cold. Each had a tin can in one hand: lunch made by a sister or wife or mother. Snow crunched underfoot as they made their way up the dirt road, dressed in stained slacks and heavy coats.

Dougie Bougois—Dougie Boy, most men called him—was creeping up on his fifth year of employment in the Umberlee. He was eighteen, and more man than boy by that time, especially with five years in the pit. Five years of getting in that blackened coal car and sliding slowly into the depths of the earth with dozens of others just like him. His comrades. His family. And maybe, if he was unlucky, the people he'd share his grave with.

As smooth and routine as automation, Dougie found his way to the lockers, where he stashed what few things he wouldn't take down into the dark with him: his matchbook, his good coat, and the nice new mittens his sweetheart had made him. It would be chilly for a bit, before he went down into the ground, but the pit would be hot and sweaty soon enough. With all that stowed away, he followed the others to the lamp cabin, saying his hellos and good mornings along the way.

Old Benjamin saw him coming, gave him a growl as a hello, and handed him a lantern. One that would stay unlit until Dougie knew it was safe. The mines were full of gases, and he had lost too many friends to methane, cave-ins, and explosions.

A boy learned a lot about death in a place like the Umberlee.

Dougie made his way to the tracks that would lead him underground. The night shift were saying their goodbyes amongst themselves, and the morning shift were climbing into the coal cars as they emptied out. The smell of coal and gas and sweat was thick in the air, and a layer of dust covered everything—especially the men. Some of them he'd recognize anywhere; others were coal black from head to toe, the dust coating their clothes, lost in their hair, and driven up under their fingernails.

One man coughed violently, and Dougie would've sworn he'd coughed up a cloud of black.

Dougie climbed into the coal car, the first layer of dust finding its way onto his body. A yawn rose in his chest, and he fished around in his breast pocket and pulled out a can of chewing tobacco. He'd already had a cup of tea, but maybe some chew would wake him up proper. He stuffed the brown paste between his gums and his lip. The bittersweet flavour coated his tongue, and as he waited for the cars to start moving, the nicotine did its work. It would keep his mouth wet while he was down in the deep dark, and keep him working on through the twelve hours ahead.

After he put the can of chew back, he checked his lunch tin. His sister had put together a good lunch that day: a potato, some bread rinds, a thin slice of ham, and a cup of tea in a thermos. She'd even packed him a clean handkerchief. He didn't like getting the coal in his mouth when he could avoid it, but they had nowhere to clean up down there, same as there was no toilet neither. A man did what he had to do, and that meant eating coal with his lunch.

The car shifted, drawing Dougie out of his thoughts. The whole line of cars was filled with the men of his town, some younger than him and some much, much older. Each of them crept closer and closer to the yawning maw of the mine, and so did he. It was black inside, darker than dark. No black was deeper than what was at the bottom of the pit, and they drew closer a little at a time as the cart began to slope.

The Umberlee was fifteen kilometres deep at its lowest point, and the mine manager hoped to go at least another fifteen. There were rumours, though, that the manager was runnin' the tunnels too close together. That they were in for another bump. Everyone felt it coming, but it wasn't as if anybody had much of a choice. A man didn't work, he didn't put food on the table. Wasn't as if there were better jobs around anyhow.

As Dougie's cart approached the mine opening, he turned and gave a little wave to Harvey, who was manning the switch. The boy was ten years old, and Dougie tried to be a little extra kind to him. Mining was a scary thing sometimes. For little boys, that was. Not for people like Dougie, who was half a child himself, but thought himself a man. He remembered being scared too, in the years before.

Sometimes he was still scared shitless, but he never told nobody about it, not even when the nightmares stole his sleep.

None of the other men talked about it, so Dougie figured he shouldn't neither.

The car passed into the dark, and the world faded away. The dim lights from above faded out quickly, and soon Dougie couldn't tell if his eyelids were open or closed. There wasn't any difference at all. What little light they had down there would come from lanterns, but not until later, if no gas was found in the mines, but that first few kilometres of slow track downhill sometimes got under his skin.

Sitting in the dark, he wondered what he couldn't see. Rats, absolutely. Always rats. But maybe something else. Maybe something worse. How was he to know? He couldn't see a fucking thing.

He'd go for a drink later, that was for sure. A Friday shift deserved a drink. So long as he made it out alive again to get one.

CHAPTER ONE

Laurel

Nova Scotia
2023

The shrill blare of a single set of bagpipes was loud enough to be heard all around town. It was the same old song on the same old instrument, one that sprang up a few times a year in most any Nova Scotian town. Even though my thoughts had been drifting for a while, it was hard to focus on any of them over the screeching. Not a bad screeching, though. Bagpipes stirred something in my soul when I heard them. They were part of the blood in these parts, and they were welcome—at least when they happened for a few minutes at a time and not more than once a month.

I shivered. My thick camouflage-printed coat should have been enough to keep the winter chill out, but my body heat had faded a half hour ago. We were all sitting in the open air, and the breeze kept snapping at my exposed skin. I pulled the fur-trimmed hood tighter around my face. We'd all been sitting in hard plastic chairs for long enough that my ass had gone numb, and it was starting to grate on my nerves.

The miners' memorial was important to Mom, and I figured that meant it should be important to me too. As the music continued, the town mayor stood solemnly in front of a tall statue of a man in a miner's helmet, lantern in hand. The base of the statue held the carved-out names of over a hundred men and boys. Some of them were from long before my time, and some of them had been alive—and dead—in Mom and Nan's days.

I'd always had a hard time keeping the history straight. It wasn't something I was proud of. There'd been so many mines, and so many accidents, in Penny Harbour and the towns around us. The memorial that day was for the anniversary of the Umberlee #2 Bump—or I was pretty sure it was, at least. Bumps weren't things I lingered my thoughts on for long. I'd seen diagrams of a mine bump before, and my imagination had made it far too vivid for my liking. I could practically see the ground shifting around the mineshaft, the floor rising up to meet the ceiling like a mouse trap snapping shut. People crushed in seconds, or trapped behind the blockage. Choking on poison air. It sounded like something from a horror movie, except it wasn't. At least four bumps had happened in local mines since my nan was born, each in a different shaft.

All those relatives stuck down there…

Just thinking about it made my skin crawl.

The song died out, and the mayor cleared his throat. "Thank you, everyone, for coming today. I know it's not the best weather for this kind of thing, but we try to commemorate our family and friends on the day of their death. Which is a Tuesday this year, as you can see by all the empty seats." The ten other people present on the snow-covered lawn gave a chuckle, and he carried on. "All right, folks, go on home. Thanks for coming, and we'll see you in July for the Dorothy Explosion memorial."

I could deal with a few memorials a year. God knew we'd had more accidents than the town could stand to remember. Thousands of people over three centuries.

We only gathered for the big ones.

A sniff came from beside me, and when I looked, Mom was wiping a tear from the corner of her eye. That was the most emotion I'd ever gotten from Mom over any of these events. That woman wouldn't even talk about what happened. I barely knew who she was crying over, let alone the details. But it was that way with everyone in town. A thousand tragedies, big and small, and each one of them held tight to people's chests like talking about them made them real.

Now, if one of the Joneses up the road was caught cooking meth, you'd know about that before lunchtime. That was different. That was *good gossip*. No one talked about pain, though, not in a small place like Penny Harbour, where everyone knew everyone's lives and had done so for the last three hundred years.

I gave Mom a little nudge with my elbow. "You all right to go?"

"Hmm?" Mom looked up, blinking away her tears. "Oh, yes, let's get out of here already." She stood, pulling her purse tightly against her black vinyl coat. Her cheeks were pink with the cold, her pale skin flecked with age spots. A white hand-knit hat covered her blonde bob, the ends sticking out around the edges. "Thanks for coming with me, honey."

"No worries. Bob Peters cancelled his window replacement on me for today anyways, so I had plenty of time." I trudged through the snow beside Mom as we made our way off the lawn and toward the parking lot across the street. "You coming over for supper this weekend?"

"No, no." Mom shook her head, digging her car keys out of her pocket. "Nancy asked me to go to one of them painting nights where you drink and pretend you can do art. I'm gonna go and be foolish with her for a few hours. Might even sleep in on Sunday."

"Good, getting out of the house suits you." I gave her a smile. She'd been getting more and more distant the last few years. It was good for her, really, finally having friends and fun. Mom had been struggling to have a social life for years, ever since Dad fucked off when I was a teenager. It seemed like men were a curse in our family; Pop had gone and died on Nan years too soon, Dad had disappeared and never came back, not even a phone call, and I…I had Greg.

Parked next to Mom's SUV, my old black truck looked monstrous. We stood in front of the cars, doing the dance of who was leaving first. A chill wracked up my body and I quickly decided it would be me this time. I leaned in to hug my mother and cut things short. "All right, you have fun now. Send me a picture of whatever it is you paint."

Mom hugged me back, squeezing just a little longer than usual. "I will. Say hi to Greg for me."

Her casual use of his name made me pause and catch my breath. It almost always meant she was about to start asking questions I wouldn't want to answer. "Yup, sure, will do." I hurried, and before Mom could notice anything—because she always noticed *everything*—I let her go and made for the driver's side door of the truck.

The old beast rattled and coughed to a start with all the grace of a geriatric two-pack-a-day smoker. I threw it in gear, and while I wouldn't say I tore out of the parking lot as fast as I could go, I had no interest in taking my time.

It was impossible to explain to my mother or to anyone else that I simply didn't want to talk about my home life. People would always get curious, and that curiosity would inevitably end up with me being asked about my husband, which wasn't a place I ever wanted to end up. I had nothing good to say anymore, and I'd spent all my lies on the first five years of our marriage. I didn't have many left.

The drive home was a short one. In a town with a total of twenty streets, it wasn't far to drive anywhere in Penny Harbour. I passed the grocery store, the post office, the corner store, and the gas station. Another street had two little mom-and-pop restaurants right next to the school, and a mechanic or two further down the road. That was about all there was to Penny Harbour, aside from the houses that kept the 632 residents of the town sheltered. Well, more or less sheltered. I'd done enough home repairs around the area to know that some shelter was less reliable than others.

My phone buzzed in my pocket. I'd hit a rare patch of intermittent cell service on the stretch of road I was on, and when the buzzing went off rapid-fire, playing a specific little chime over and over, I didn't have to guess who it was.

Greg had been messaging me since shortly after he'd gotten to work that morning, irate at his boss again. But since cell service was spotty at best around the Harbour, I hadn't gotten anything since I'd left the house. These new messages were probably more whining. I glanced at the ancient and slightly vibrating digital numbers on the truck dash. Twenty past three. He'd be home in an hour and a half.

Then there'd be hell to pay.

My gut swirled, all the tension settling in my shoulders. In the minute since the buzzing had started, I'd basically stopped breathing. Realizing it, I inhaled long and deep, going until my lungs burned with expansion. Exhale. Repeat. Each deep breath helped bring the blood back to my head. Kept the fear from setting in. A little trick my friend Emma had forced on me, and one that I didn't readily admit to her that I'd been using.

As I pulled up to the house that Greg and I had bought twelve years prior, relief flooded over me. The driveway was empty. Sure, he wasn't supposed to be home yet, but every once in a while he was home early, not giving me a chance to get my head right before I saw him. The lack of absolute certainty always fucked with me.

After pulling the truck up into the long driveway, I habitually put it in reverse and whipped it back into its normal spot on the lawn. Nine times out of ten, I could land the tires right in the grooves in the grass.

I hopped out of the truck and slammed the door behind me. The cold nipped at my nose again, my breath clouding in the air. I jogged up the deck stairs that led to the front door of our little bungalow and pushed the door open. It was never locked. No one in Penny Harbour locked their doors unless we were asleep or going far, and we probably wouldn't until bears started using doorknobs.

The oil furnace had kept the house above freezing while I was out, but it was still chilly inside. I kicked my boots onto the mat and didn't bother taking my coat off as I rushed from the kitchen, into the hall, and down the basement stairs. I flicked on the light to reveal the half-finished room, all concrete and storage and old furniture. A couch from the 1970s was arranged next to a coffee table and a mismatched armchair, all turned toward a generously sized television. It was the place where Greg brought his buddies to drink and smoke and give no fucks.

I only ever went to the basement to stoke the fire or get something from the deep freeze. I never put myself in his line of sight when I didn't have to.

Once I'd piled kindling and old cardboard into the wood stove, I opted for the shortcut and grabbed the small propane blow torch. When the kindling lit, I tossed a couple of split logs on top, sealed the stove back up, and booted it upstairs toward the shower.

Chasing warmth, I cranked the tap as hot as I could stand it and then stripped off my coat and clothing. The familiar scent rose in the bathroom, a thin cloud of sulphur and coal. Out in butt-fuck nowhere, we had no town water system, just wells that dredged up whatever could be found beneath the house, most of it laced with things that city folk would call unacceptable.

We just called it water.

I stepped into the steaming downpour and gasped at the shock of heat. It was slightly too hot, so I dialled the knob back a bit, taking a moment to luxuriate in the warmth. It seeped into my skin, into my muscles, pushing back the bone-deep cold the Atlantic Canadian winters often brought.

The shower brought my body back to equilibrium. I washed up quickly, less dirty than I was chilled, and stepped out of the shower before I could get too comfortable. A long, hot shower would be nice, but hell was headed my way and I needed to make sure I would survive it.

I towelled off, watching myself in the foggy mirror as I did. Sometimes I wondered who exactly was looking back at me. When the skin around my eyes had started to darken. When my hair had gotten that long. I dried it, continuing to look. To ground myself in that body that was mine but that I often forgot the age of. Thirty-five, if my licence could be believed. Cream-coloured curves lined with scars from working hard and fucking up. Lean muscle bought with countless hours of installing windows and lifting concrete. I liked my body for the most part; it did right by me. It just kept getting older.

More tired.

Who would I be in another decade? Another two?

Not bothering to get dressed right away, I wrapped the towel around my head and went out into the hallway naked. The heat had kicked in since I'd gotten in the shower, and the mildly warm air felt good on my skin.

The paranoia was creeping back in, and I checked the time immediately. Quarter to four. I still had plenty of time to get supper ready, even if I felt the seconds ticking by with each beat of my heart. I started the preheat on the oven and pulled out the potato-and-vegetable mix I'd prepared and left in the fridge the night before. Two steaks were marinating in a bowl, and I set that on the counter to come to room temperature. It was a meal that Greg normally went ape-shit for, which might help me out in the coming hours.

I opened the fridge again, this time for me. Tucked in among the food and condiments was a nearly empty four-litre water jug. I hauled it out, the last bit sloshing around inside. Setting that on the counter, I stole the pint of rum from the back of the freezer. A large cup of water, a large shot of rum. Covering all the bases.

I chugged back the water and chased it with the shot. Maybe it would make this easier. God knew something had to.

Still naked, I took the empty jug and walked it down the hall to the storage closet. Inside, among a bunch of other junk, were a dozen identical four-litre jugs. Half of them were full, the other half empty. I shelved the empty and grabbed a full one. Next time I drove up to town, I'd take the empties and fill them at the freshwater pump. The lucky town people had clean water. Our well was fine for showers and dishes, but a person shouldn't even make their dog drink it, let alone themselves.

On the way back to the kitchen, I took a minute to pull on a pair of soft pyjamas and dump my towel in the hamper. A naked woman in the kitchen might please or infuriate Greg, and had gone both ways in the past. I wasn't going to risk it.

Ten after four.

I realized that for all the stress those texts had caused me, I hadn't looked at them. Instead, I'd put myself and the house to rights because I knew the consequences of not doing that. I put the water in the fridge and went back to the bathroom to clear the clothes I'd abandoned on the floor. My phone was a thick brick in my pocket, and I grabbed it before shoving all that in the hamper as well. My chest was constricting just knowing the messages were in there, waiting.

They weren't going to be good.

He might've texted me since, but I wouldn't know until I put the phone in the one spot in the house that actually got reception.

As I walked to the cell phone window, I tapped the screen.

Twelve missed texts.

> Greg:
> Fucking cunt is at it again!!
> Thinks she can send me to these Shit Jobs
> I told Lonnie to tell her to stuff it but I know he won't
> say nuthin cause he's a fucking pussy
> usless af

On and on it went.

The last text read:

> Greg:
> are you even fucking listening, what the fuck

I put the phone on the windowsill, sitting it on its little stand that lived there.
Ba-ding ding ding ding ding
Five new texts, the last of which read:

> Greg:
> Think you can just ignore me all day
> Where are u???

I'd been out. I'd told him where I was going, and since we'd both grown up there, he knew full well the reception was shit. He had no reason to behave like that.

And yet.

Twenty after four.

I stared out the window, past the phone. The sun was setting, and my truck was sitting there in the coming dark, clunky but strong. Waiting. I could get in it and drive away. I'd had the thought a thousand times before. I'd never acted on it, but this time could be different.

I could be gone before he got back.

Emma or Mary-Jo would take me in. My mother would. They'd make sure I was safe from him.

But then I'd have to admit it.

Admit they were right. Admit why I was afraid of him. What he'd done over the years. Explain that no, he'd never laid a hand on me, but that it was horrific just the same. He'd whittled me down, little by little over the years, until I barely knew myself. That it wasn't just about my feelings. It wasn't just that he made me sad or angry. He left me hollow, but I didn't know how to make anyone believe that.

And the ones who did believe, I'd have to explain why I'd stayed so fucking long.

I had no desire to try to explain.

I had survived every encounter before, and I'd survive now.

Maybe I'd have more courage tomorrow.

The stove beeped, letting me know the oven was warm enough.

Besides, who was going to make supper if I didn't?

Time ticked by under my fingers as I prepped the rest of the meal. Plates on the table, cups next to plates, forks next to steak knives. Another shot of rum. Check the veggies. Flip the veggies. Back in the oven. Ten to five. Steak in the pan. Sear. Reduce heat.

Gravel on the driveway.

I didn't look up. I kept my eyes on the steak in the pan, blood seeping up through the meat. Greg's boots clunked heavily up the steps and the door flew open, slamming against the wall.

"The fuck have you been?" Greg snarled, tossing his work bag with a heavy thud.

I still refused to look up. "I went to the memorial with Mom today. I forgot to put my phone in the window until I started supper, but you were driving by then and I—"

"Yeah, sure, you forgot." Greg left his boots on as he marched through the house, down to the end of the hall. He yelled to be heard over the distance. "And now I can't find my good fucking wrench. What'd you do, hide it on me?"

With him out of the room, I dared to look elsewhere. Greg had tracked snow and muck all through the house.

"I haven't seen your good wrench," I called back, as demurely as I could manage.

The clatter of tools came from the other side of the house, and then it was the thumping of his boots again as he came back to the kitchen. "Shit fucking day surrounded by shit fucking people." Greg kicked his boots at the wall, one after the other, and then threw the *missing* wrench into his boot for morning.

"I'm sorry you had a bad day." The steaks were done, so I plated them both and turned off the burner, as well as the oven. That was the first time I looked at him.

If it weren't for the seething rage that always seemed to come off him in waves, Greg would've been mostly handsome. Beat up around the edges, yes, but that came with hard work. He was a welder and worked long hours in town, and he bore the burns and scars of that work. But his face was made of sharp lines, and he had a closely shaved beard that kept him looking fine even when he was covered in dirt. He'd been handsome when he was young, and age only looked good on him. But the only thing that held any weight for me anymore was how he looked at me with utter contempt.

"Bad doesn't even sum it up." Greg walked past me, close enough that it set off alarm bells in my head. He'd found the pint of rum I'd been drinking, and he put the bottle to his lips to finish it off. "I need a new fucking job, one where the boss doesn't ride me for every fucking thing."

From talking with some of his coworkers at holiday parties, I knew that *every fucking thing* included not showing up to work, smoking pot on the job, and stealing people's lunches from the fridge. He'd been kicked out of half a dozen jobs since we were kids, but sure, Greg, it was always everyone else.

"You're right. I'm sure somewhere else would be lucky to have you," I said, attempting to placate him

"The one I've got should be lucky to have me. Do you have any fucking idea how hard it is to get a new job? No, you wouldn't, cause you keep working for free like a fucking moron. Maybe I could go work somewhere else if I didn't have to take care of your share of the money too."

That burned. Greg knew what to say to get a rise out of me. I tried to swallow it; I really did. "I'm sorry you don't like my job."

"Job? You have to get paid for it to be a job."

"I do get paid. Not as much as you—"

"Barely fucking anything. I take care of the bills here." Greg stepped closer, getting into my space.

Two ways. This always had the chance to go one of two ways.

"And I'm grateful you do that." I looked up at him, trying to be brave.

If today was the first day he hit me, please let me at least have the grace to be unafraid.

"Not grateful enough." He took my face in his hand and squeezed my cheeks, making sure I was looking at him. "Tell me how fucking grateful you are to sit here and live off my hard work."

I swallowed, trying to control my breathing. Running the lines in my head. "I'm so thankful that you take care of me and the house, and that you put food on the table. I wish I knew how to thank you better."

"I know how." Greg pressed me against the counter, the edge jamming into my back. One of his hands pawed at my side, groping until he found his way under my shirt.

I let out a sigh of relief, one he immediately took as enthusiasm.

This game was one I knew how to play.

I hated him, inside and out, but I also knew the cycles. He would rage until something could reset him. If it wasn't a bar brawl or a joint, it was a fuck. If I could be a somewhat willing plaything, the rage would subside.

It was fine.

A compromise I could live with.

Sex was the only thing we ever did together anymore anyway. The only time I felt anything for him other than numbness or contempt. It was the only good thing he brought to my life, because as horrible as he was, an angry lay a few times a month was better than never being touched again.

It was what had been important when we met. We were young and bored and there was nothing to fucking do in that village. Dad had just taken off and I was so *raw*. Angry. Greg and I had partied and fucked for the last few years of high school, and one day I looked up and it was ten years later. We were married and he was so angry all the time. I could hardly remember making those choices at all. I'd just gone with the flow of things, and suddenly I was stuck. Stuck in a small house and a small life with a man who made me feel smaller than I had ever thought possible.

A man who had to fuck the anger out of him in order to feel anything.

Greg took me against the counter and then on top of it, and it felt better than nothing. Better than whatever else could have come next, at least. He'd never been good at it, but I didn't know that until it was years too late and I'd listened to enough of Mary-Jo's stories to understand I'd been missing out on something. Her conquests sometimes cared that she got off.

Greg never had.

You could just end it.

Reach over.

Take the butcher's knife and be done with it.

Wouldn't that be so sweet, Little Laurel?

My hand twitched. Ached to move. To do exactly as that little voice in the back of my mind was asking me to. It would be *so easy*.

I moved my hand from Greg's shoulder, and just as I started to inch it toward the block of knives on the counter, he grabbed my hand and squeezed, pressing it into the countertop. And then the impulse was gone, thank fuck.

What kind of monster was I?

The sex was over almost as fast as it started. I fixed my clothing and plated up the veggies that had been in the oven. We both sat down at the table and ate in silence, scrolling on our phones for the latest social media gossip. I didn't read anything. I just flicked my finger on the screen and waited until I could reasonably go to the bathroom without sparking his ire. Double-checked the alarm that would remind me to take my birth control later.

After he was done eating, Greg wordlessly grabbed a beer from the fridge and went to park himself in bed with the TV. He was a predictable creature. He'd be half-drunk by the time I finished the dishes, and he'd spend most of the night in there, glued to whatever mindless thing he'd found to watch.

And I'd be left to think over how gross the encounter had made me feel. It was a terrible brew of shame, made worse by the small knot of pleasure coiled in my gut. I hated it more than I could explain.

Like clockwork, Greg was passed out by the time I'd cleaned up. I stared at him from the open doorway, the TV going on about last night's hockey game, and I couldn't imagine getting into bed next to him. It was far too early, yes. But my skin had started crawling just looking at him.

A little voice in the back of my mind asked the same questions it always did.

Do you think you deserve this, Laurel?

Does he?

What would freedom cost you, sweet thing?

What would you do to escape his reach?

I shook myself and went to the bathroom. A storm of thoughts churning in my head, I cleaned myself up before pulling on the clothing I'd abandoned to the hamper not long ago. My coat was in there too, overlooked in my rush to fend off Greg. I pulled it on and followed my panic into the kitchen, grabbed my phone, and went right out the door.

I had no idea what I was doing or where I was going, only that I needed to go. If I stayed in that house with him, I might have killed him.

Figuratively speaking

Mostly.

Night had fallen. The cold had set in harder with the darkness, but I wouldn't care once I started walking. I bolted past the pair of trucks on the lawn and down the lane, going as fast as my legs would take me.

The world around me was abandoned, the way it always was in the middle of nowhere. Homes on large parcels of land, with enough distance between each that a whole other house could fit between. Street lights dotted the distance along the single road stretching north and south, the only other light coming from the three homes I could see from the side of the road. Nothing around in the dark. Empty space and the quiet of wind in the trees, covered in white, iced-over snow.

With a quick look at the empty road, I crossed the street and headed for my neighbour's driveway. The length of it went down past the house, a straight shot into the trees. The driveway portion was shovelled, the snow piled on either side, but the lane into the woods was still covered in ankle-high powder. Snowmobile tracks and footprints tamped down a lot of it, and I walked in the long lines as much as I could, pushing forward. Running from my problems at a brisk walk.

The lane ended, the path veering to the left and right. That far back from the road, there were no street lights, so I popped on the flashlight on my phone. Better to be seen by any late-night offroad vehicles. The track, as most called it, was the remnants of an old railroad that had run through the town while the mines were still in operation. The metal tracks themselves hadn't been there for more than sixty years—what good was a railway for a dying town?—but the imprint had remained. It served as a path for ATVs, snowmobiles, and the occasional pedestrian.

Taking the path to the right, I pressed on, trying to push the nervous energy out of my body. Fucking Greg. Fucking life. How long was I going to put myself through this same thing? He wasn't supposed to have this power over me. I wasn't supposed to be stuck in a life I hated.

When was the last time you felt safe, Laurel?

Will you spend your whole life trying to anticipate his every need?

You can never prepare enough for him.

Aren't you angry?

I was. I was furious. But I'd gotten good at hiding it. I didn't hate my *life*.

My work was fulfilling; my friends were amazing; I loved my mother. I just hated Greg. I was terrified of what it meant to leave. What he might do, but not *just* of him. The change. What was waiting for me on the other side? I'd lose the house and the savings, and I'd lose the town. Most everyone liked Greg. He never acted to other people the way he acted to me. If he stole something or was crabby with people, that was just a quirk.

No one knew how aggressive he was with someone he supposedly loved.

A howl rose up from somewhere, breaking me from my thoughts. A coyote. I'd never been out in the woods alone in the dark before, because mostly I was smarter than that. Or I hoped I was. Coyotes didn't attack people that often, and bears should be hibernating. A moose wasn't going to eat me, but stumbling on one of those in the dark was a good way to not see the sunrise.

Maybe I shouldn't have followed my feet after all.

I'd find a driveway not far away that led back to the road. Five minutes at most. I'd push on that far, then leave the woods and keep walking on the side of the road. That would be a more intelligent option.

A light was shining up ahead.

It wasn't the steady floodlight of a snowmobile. Instead it was a small, flickering thing. Fire. Someone else was out there.

The track ran along the back of dozens of properties, and it was within reason that someone needed a little alone time in the evenings. It wasn't like Penny Harbour got the attention of criminals or anything. Probably it was Arnold Porter out having a drink by his lonesome.

I kept up this negotiation with my fear as I drew closer, telling myself who it might or might not be. As I drew closer, things became clearer. The light was a small fire contained in a metal bucket, and it lit up the shape of a person sitting in a ragged old chair. With their coat on and hood up, it was hard to say which of my neighbours it was.

Whether it was the light of my phone or the snow under my boots, something drew the attention of the shape in the dark.

"Hello?" they called out.

Well, there was no getting around being noticed.

"Hello," I called back, putting on my best small-town hospitality voice. "Cold night to be sitting in the dark."

"Just as cold to be out for a walk, don't you think?" The voice was masculine with an accent that was familiar and strange all at the same time. Our local accent was thick with remnants of Scottish, Irish, and British, but his sounded…pure. Faded, watered down, but untarnished Irish. Like it had come from the source but had gotten used to being somewhere else.

I stopped at the spot where the trees had been cut into a clearing. A large pile of stone chips sat in the background, a man-made hill that towered over us both. Over the years, people had dumped all kinds of things in that clearing: a beat-up washer, two bikes, and a bunch of odds and ends.

And this guy, sitting in the dark among the old trash.

"Just trying to get my steps in before bed." It was all I could think to say. Decades of casual conversation with anyone who passed by had burned this politeness into me. An easy script to follow with everyone I met, every day. Tell them just enough but never too much, and never, ever be rude. It might get back to someone else that you were.

"I see." The stranger pulled his hood down and my heart skipped a beat. He was a good-looking guy; that much was for sure. His face, illuminated by the firelight, had a porcelain quality to it. His layered blonde hair seemed windswept, a little too long to be short, a little too short to be long. And thick, too. The kind of hair a person wouldn't mind losing their fingers in. His grey eyes were wary, and the way he looked up at me was…almost hungry.

"Didn't mean to intrude on your alone time," he said, sitting back in the chair. He waved a hand toward the fire. "I'd invite you to join me, but that seems like a strange proposition for a weirdo lurking in the woods."

The honesty shocked a laugh from me. "Well, at least you're up-front about it. You from here, stranger? I don't think I know your face."

The man shook his head, patting down the front of his too-thin-for-this-weather black jacket. "I live here, but I know that's not what you mean. I came from Away, as the locals say."

"Gotcha. Used to be that no one new moved here, until all the people from Ontario started running from the cities a few years back." I cringed, realizing my mistake. "You're not from Ontario, are you? Not with that accent, surely."

It was his turn to laugh. "No, I'm not. I'm from all over, honestly. Ireland, originally. Once upon a time. But that sound is long gone, I think."

"Hmm, I'm not sure about that. It's still there, at least a bit."

He smirked. "Good to know."

I kicked the toe of my boot into the snow. This was the time to either leave or commit. He'd invited me to stay, but probably in the way people do, assuming you'll say no. And I could leave. I could go back home to Greg and lie in bed next to him, not sleeping. Wishing for something else. Or I could sit with a weirdo hanging out in the woods by himself.

The fact that I knew which was more appealing…

"You know, if you've got another seat, I wouldn't mind some company. I'm currently running from something and could use the distraction."

Clearly not expecting that answer, the man got up and gestured to the chair he'd just been sitting in. He looked around a moment and then came back to the fire with an upside-down steel bucket. He put it down a respectable distance away from my new chair. "I really didn't think you'd say yes to that."

"Me either." I settled in as best I could onto the cold, abandoned lawn chair. Sure, he could be a murderer, but in a place as small as Penny Harbour, murder was too loud a crime. Things like that didn't happen around here. Instead, our crimes were kept within our four walls, unless it was jail time for hunting moose out of season. "I suppose it says a lot about me that I'd rather sit in the cold with some random person than go back home."

The stranger pursed his lips in contemplation. "Well, far be it for me to judge someone for running and hiding. I moved here, after all. What else could I reasonably be doing?" A joke was on his voice, and for just a moment, the lilt on his voice was slightly more feminine.

"If you moved here willingly, you're either insane or on the lam. How are you enjoying the bad well water and shitty cell phone reception?" I asked. The cold of the chair was already seeping into my muscles, so I leaned forward toward the small fire.

"It's not that bad." He shrugged, and then stopped to roll his eyes. "I mean, *it is*, but it's also what I was hoping for. I needed to…slow down." He pulled a flask from his coat pocket, sniffed the contents, and put it back. His other pocket had a different flask, which he offered to me.

I waved the flask away. "Sorry, I draw the line at being roofied in the woods."

He laughed, took the top off, and had a drink. "Smart."

"How long have you been in Penny Harbour?"

It was a question that needed mulling over, apparently. "Going on two years, I think."

"Two years? Really feels like I should have run into you at the store or something by now."

"I do a lot of my shopping in town. I mostly keep to myself."

I had the urge to ask about that. Digging up skeletons was a bit of a local pastime, but I also knew small-town nosiness wasn't a quality that people from Away valued all that much. Besides, I was just as much a stranger to him as he was to me. "Well, there's no better place to sit alone than the local appliance dump. Do you know what that is?" I pointed to the pile of stones we were sitting next to.

The stranger looked up at it, the peak three times higher than he was while sitting. "I don't, actually."

"It's from the coal mine that used to be on this spot. They'd break up the stone and off-load it into piles like these. Lots of them around here, and this one's on the small side." I put the light of my phone under my chin, speaking in a ghostly voice. "Generations ago, dozens of people died on this *very spot.*"

He looked at me, an eyebrow raised and a smirk on his lips. "Really?"

"I mean, maybe." I shrugged and pointed the light away from my face again. "There were a lot of accidents. I don't know what mine this would've been, but yeah, probably. Either way, now it's just a place to put your old washer when you don't want to pay the dump to take it. We're a very sophisticated bunch."

That drew a wide smile from him, and suddenly I was smiling too. It was weird how sometimes strangers were the easiest to talk to, and in the Harbour, they were few and far between.

"I didn't want to draw attention to it, but I was already moved by how luxurious this village is." His voice was *very* flippant and sarcastic.

I pointed a finger at him. "You watch it. I'm allowed to say nasty things because I've always been here. You're still fresh meat."

A look of delight settled on his face, and I felt as if I wasn't quite in on the joke. "I understand. Rest assured, I quite like it here."

"Good. I hope you do." And I meant it. He seemed like good people, at least from first glance. The Harbour was made up of mostly good people trying hard to stay good. Wouldn't hurt to have some new blood around.

I looked at the time on my phone. The rage had melted out of my body for the moment and was being replaced by the aftershock of exhaustion. "Listen, I'm going to call it a night, but it was nice meeting you…"

"Spencer." He stood when I did, reaching a gloved hand out to me.

I shook it, giving him a smile. "Laurel. I'll see you around. Or maybe not, since you've evaded me this long."

"You've found the place I come to hide, so my days of evasion are over, I think. I'm not here all the time, but it's soothing, sometimes, to sit and just… listen." He shoved his hands into his pockets, staring down at the little fire.

"Yeah, it is nice out here," I said, looking around at the dark, peaceful woods around us. I let the rustle of branches and the crackle of the fire come between us for a moment, before setting out on my way. "Maybe I'll see you again, then."

"Good night, Laurel."

I turned out of the clearing and started back down the track. Inexplicably, I felt good. Better, at least. Like a tiny bit of hope had been injected into my life, despite that I was walking right back into the belly of the beast.

Spencer

Laurel left and I waited. I had no intention of sticking around either, but I gave the woman space. I knew from a lifetime of walking in the dark that nothing spooked a person faster than being followed down a narrow path. She'd likely pushed her bravery to the limit already, sitting with a complete stranger in the woods. If she caught me following behind her, she'd absolutely assume I was stalking her home.

In another place, in another time, she would've been right.

She would've never made it back home.

My stomach growled, a burning pit of hunger. Pulling out the flask I *hadn't* offered to her, I twisted off the cap and tipped it up to my lips. Cold, metallic life ran across my tongue. It wasn't enough to sate the hunger—the packaged stuff never was, not really—but it was better than anything on two legs that this place had to offer.

Everyone in Penny Harbour tasted like ashes, their blood gritty as sand. Like something had seeped into their bodies and set up shop over generations. I'd never seen anything like it. And, of course, that was why I'd stayed.

A person couldn't get themselves in that much trouble if they couldn't eat the people.

Laurel had gotten lucky.

The thing that didn't make sense to me was why I'd given her my name. My *real* name.

I'd given out hundreds of false names over the centuries. Lied to countless people in order to cover my tracks. So I could hunt safely. And for whatever reason, my actual name had stumbled out of my mouth. Though no one had used it in so many years that I wondered if it was even mine anymore.

Had I gotten so desperate?

Staring into the dying fire, it was hard to lie to myself. I'd gone from place to place for so long, looking for something that would lessen the grief in my chest. Keeping to myself. Years of it, until this. Then I'd settled into an old house overlooking a harbour where everyone tasted like shit, because it finally felt right. Somewhere I knew no one and nothing was coming for me, and I could be alone with the hole inside me. Two years, alone. It shouldn't have felt so long, not held against the more than two centuries I'd seen. It should've been *nothing*. A small reprieve from the world as I mourned everything I had lost. Instead, it was a tar pit, dragging me under, one agonizing inch at a time. One I couldn't stand to leave, either.

Laurel's company had been a nice change, for once, as short-lived as it was.

Who knew? Maybe I *would* see her again.

I stood and began to fill the fire bucket with snow. Surely Laurel had gotten far enough ahead of me by that point, and I could start making my way back to the house. If I was truly lucky, something to eat would pop out of the bushes on the way back. I'd been sitting there with the intention to hunt, eventually. Catch something that somehow tasted less awful than the people. But the moment was gone. We'd made too much noise for whatever might be running around in the dark. Besides, I couldn't have her stumbling onto me with my teeth in some rabbit's neck.

I started back home, stepping as softly as I could.

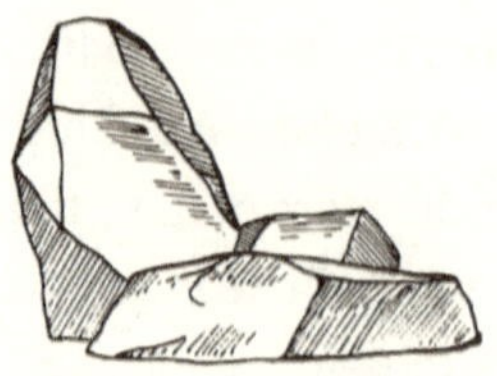

Penny Harbour

The Penny Harbour Rural Community Store was the only grocery store within a thirty-minute drive. Open from eight in the morning until eight at night, it did its best to serve the needs of the locals, no matter how many or few. And it struggled to keep the doors open; surely it did. Hours might go by without a soul inside its walls—aside from the lone cashier and a stock boy. But if the locally owned and operated shop didn't keep its doors open, no other company was going to open shop behind it. No, Penny Harbour didn't make nearly enough revenue to be considered a good investment.

It could be argued that all people needed to eat, but what did a billion-dollar corporation care about the welfare of a couple hundred people in the middle of nowhere?

Julie was thankful for the store as she walked its aisles; she hated going to town if she only needed a few things. The building had seen better days and the lights weren't as strong as they used to be, but neither were her legs or her heart. And frankly, she was the same age as the building—give or take.

She had her list, and she leaned a little harder on the cart than she would've liked to, but wasn't that the way with age? Julie was working with a modest budget, which meant her cart was full of little cans and boxes with green labels. No one could tell her food was made with the off-brand stuff anyways, and if it meant her money could spend further, she didn't mind that at all.

The store only had five aisles, but she found nearly everything she'd been hoping for. After that long, Julie knew what the store did and didn't carry. A person had to go to town—that was what everyone said when they meant drive to Hammonds, the closest actual town they had around—to get anything fancy. In fact, Julie chose recipes out of her cookbooks based on what she could and couldn't get in Penny Harbour.

She'd found one last night that called for endives, whatever in the hell an endive was. That certainly wasn't tucked between the corn and the fiddleheads, now was it?

Julie checked her list against the things in her cart, standing under the flickering fluorescent lights above her. She hadn't passed anyone in the store yet, so she was hardly worried about taking up too much space. Check, check, check. The only thing she hadn't found was fresh garlic, and so the powdered stuff would just have to do.

Ambling toward the checkout, Julie put on her friendliest smile. Colleen was sweeping the floor around the cash register, and Julie was glad to see her. She didn't much care for Donna, the one other full-time cashier, but she did her best not to let Donna know that. They were cousins, after all, and it was best to try to get along with cousins.

"How's it goin' tonight, Colleen? You keeping busy?" Julie parked her cart at the back of the register and started unloading cans onto the worn black belt.

"Oh, you know, living the dream." Which was the same as saying *fucking horrible, Julie, I work in a grocery store in the middle of nowhere and I'm bored out of my gourd, but the truck needs a new motor, so here I am.*

Colleen looked like she hadn't slept in a week. She didn't hurry back to the register, since Julie was still unloading and she was mid-sweep. Her broom collected a fine dusting of black that had found its way onto the off-white tile floor. No matter how often she swept, that black coal dust kept finding its way back inside. Colleen bent down with the dustpan, skillfully collected it up, and dumped it into the garbage behind the register. A smudge of black stayed on her pants when she wiped her hands on them.

"How's your mother doing?" Julie asked, her cart empty and the conveyor belt half-full.

Colleen had started to ring the cans through, packing them up into bags as she went. "She's been asking after you, actually. She's been doing good, but you know her. She never gets out as much as she should. Maybe sometime you could come down and play a few rounds of cards with her. All she does is work, knit, and watch *Wheel of Fortune.*"

"We miss her up at bingo." Julie took a full bag of groceries from Colleen and put it back in the cart. "I mean, we miss her, but we don't miss losing to her."

Colleen laughed, which brought some of the light back into her eyes. "I know she misses the money she got from winning all the time. I'll try to convince her to go up for a game or two, but I think you'd have an easier go of it than I would. Dinner's at five. You can come by any day after six." Colleen tapped a few keys on the cash register and a total appeared.

The total was more than Julie would've liked it to be. The total was real close to her having to put something back. She hated doing that, especially in front of people who knew her—and in Penny Harbour, everyone knew everyone.

"All right, you've twisted my leg. You tell your mother I'll be down tomorrow night." Julie tapped her card as casually as could be, as if it didn't hurt to lose all that money, and she picked up her bags. "Don't work too hard, sweetheart."

"Never do, Julie. Never do." Colleen went back to sweeping up the coal dust, and Julie hobbled outside with her bags, careful not to slip on the iced-over snow outside.

CHAPTER TWO

Laurel

Greg was already gone by the time I hauled myself out of bed the next morning. I sat up, rubbing my face with my hands, trying to decide if I had dreamt my late-night walk. It definitely *felt* like a dream. I hadn't done something that ill-advised in a long time. Not since I'd been causing trouble in my youth, and that felt like a thousand lifetimes ago.

I slung my legs down over the side of the bed and groggily made my way into the kitchen. Sure enough, my boots were sitting on the mat, still dirty.

Well. It hadn't been a dream, then.

I turned and put the kettle on the stove, the pieces of everything running together in my tired mind. I'd gone, yes. I'd met Spencer, the random dude in the woods that I'd never seen before. And was…was the rest a dream? I could remember something, but it was vague and threatening. A nightmare perhaps?

I wasn't sure.

Making myself an instant coffee, I grabbed my phone off the windowsill and took it into the living room. Reception was shit in Penny Harbour, but I could do anything that ran off Wi-Fi. Getting calls or text messages, that was a whole other kettle of fish.

My soft brown armchair was my morning spot. The place where I woke up. Once I was curled up in it, I sipped the coffee and checked my notifications. A few texts from Greg had already come through while I was sleeping. Carrying on like he hadn't come home in a rage, fucked me, and fallen asleep. It was hardly the first time, but it still pissed me off. Which was useless, it turned out. I'd tried for years to talk things out, or to reason with him, but none of it had worked. None of it was worthwhile.

And what good are useless things, Laurel?

I took a sip of coffee and swallowed that voice, along with my feelings.

I opened Tabs. It was the only social media platform anyone in the area actually used. It was the calendar, the events board, the thrift store. It even acted as the only website for most of the local businesses. If anyone was talking about this Spencer guy anywhere, it would be on Tabs.

I checked some of the easier places first. I searched for his name, and then checked the community groups. I even checked the Tabs page for the realty companies to see if it was attached to a sold house. Nothing. The name Spencer didn't show up anywhere, or at least, not with that pretty face.

Not that I was a master detective or anything, but I'd assumed it would be easier than that.

I tapped into the Tabs messenger app and hit the chat named *Sloth Survival Squad.*

Laurel:
Morning, ladies. Anyone know a Spencer that
lives here in the Harbour?

When no one started typing immediately, I drank the last bit of my coffee, left the mug on the side table, and went to get dressed.

As I went back into the bedroom, my phone pinged.

Emma:
Just Spencer Harrow. I assume you don't mean him?

Laurel:
Nope. I met a random dude in the woods last night and
he said his name was Spencer. Been living here a while, I
guess??? Never saw him before

Emma:
In the woods? Sus.

A new icon appeared, meaning all three of us were awake and present.

Mary-Jo:
Why were you in the woods at night? Trying to get eaten
:P

I typed out an explanation and erased it three times before settling on
one.

Laurel:
Greg pissed me off, so I had to get out of the house.
Went down to the track for a walk, met a dude,
had a chat

Mary-Jo:
Fuck Greg
You're pissed at him cause *he's a bad person*

Emma's response was softer, as usual.

Emma:
Please be careful, Laurel. It's not bear season yet but you
know there's lynx and shit out there.

Laurel:
I'm fine. No Spencers tho, eh?

Emma:
Nope

Mary-Jo:
No. But really. Fuck Greg

I rolled my eyes and put my phone down. I wasn't having that conversation with Mary-Jo again. She had had a decades-long string of relationships that had never turned into anything long-term. How could she possibly understand how much sacrifice it took to be married?

The phone kept pinging, and I clicked the slider over to silent. It was nearly eight and I'd told Larry Turner I'd be there by nine. He'd asked me a month ago to come over to fix the kitchen backsplash, and I just hadn't had time then.

Everyone around Penny Harbour had something that needed fixing.

It wasn't a big job, but it was going to take time. I knew for a fact mould had grown around the edges of that drywall, and I was of a mind to rip the whole chunk out, check behind it for more damage, put a new piece up, plaster the holes, and tile over it so they wouldn't have that issue again. Old houses moulded so easily, and people in ex–coal mining towns mostly didn't have the cash to be proactive about their homes.

That was where I came in.

After I'd pulled on some old navy green overalls and a ratty old blue turtleneck, I put on my work coat and steel-toe boots. A fresh powdering of snow sat outside, but the tire tracks in it told me it had fallen before Greg left for work. I pulled open the driver's door long enough to start the truck and get it warming up. After clearing the snow off the cab and the cover of the truck bed, I grabbed my giant tool kit from the shed around back. I threw it in the passenger seat and went back for a large scrap of drywall. The whole shed was a mess of leftovers, but it was an organized mess. Besides, if I didn't throw things away, I could save money on the materials I needed and charge these people less.

The drywall slid nicely into the truck bed and then it was time to leave. I hopped in the cab, which was mostly warm enough, and turned the poor old girl down the driveway.

If Penny Harbour was the middle of butt-fuck nowhere, I didn't know what to call the corner of land that Larry lived on. It was a fifteen-minute drive down a beat-up road, but the second I was outside of Penny Harbour limits, the road turned to what amounted to asphalt cobblestone. Cracks lined the road in wide circles, clearly displaying where the ground underneath had shifted since the last time the road had been paved.

Although, frankly, I'd been living in the area all my life and I'd never once caught anyone paving out that way. The last time it was paved could have been 1830 for all I knew.

A road sign that announced a 90-kilometre speed limit sat on the side of the road ahead, which was laughable. Only tourists did 90 on that road. You'd never catch me doing more than a light 50, which meant you also wouldn't catch me in a ditch either.

When Larry's house appeared around the bend, I sighed. No one had shovelled the driveway. It was good that we hadn't gotten much snow, but who knew how much ice was under there. I pulled in the driveway, the truck jimmying back and forth over the uneven gravel because its shocks were shit. The house itself wasn't looking too shabby. The outside of the old two-storey had been done up with wood shingles, which were in fine shape, but the harsh ocean air had been rough on the paint. The navy blue had chipped away in some places. But at least the shingles themselves seemed to be holding up well enough.

By the time I was out of the cab and pulling the drywall from the back, Larry was on the front porch to meet me. The man must have been in his seventies, and though he got around well enough, his back was severely arched from years of hard labour. Coal mining for a while, then logging, if I remembered right. He gave me a wave as I got closer, his olive-white skin almost translucent over purple veins.

"Well, hello, dear! Right on time, I see. Nancy put on the kettle already. Can't let you get to work without a tea, can we?" Larry's voice croaked, but his smile was bright, the lines around his face wrinkling with each motion.

"I appreciate that." Truth be told, I didn't need any more caffeine, but they'd already gone out of their way to make something. I was hardly going to say no. "How's she goin' today, Mr Turner?"

"Slowly! I'm more turtle than man these days." And it was true enough. As Larry led the way into the house, I waited on the step for him to get in through the door.

After a moment, I followed him into the mud room. He'd already started through to the kitchen in his slippers, and I set down my tool bag and drywall to undo my boots.

"Oh, you don't need to take those off, Laurel—" Larry started.

"Just long enough to get the snow off them. Don't want to track muck through your kitchen, do I?"

Larry waved a hand dismissively. "Suit yourself, then!" The kettle was already boiling, but Nancy was nowhere to be seen. "Nancy! Little Laurel's here."

I hadn't been little in years, but they'd known my parents since I was a kid, so I guess I'd always be Little Laurel to them.

Nancy came into the kitchen as I was leaning over to inspect the backsplash behind the stove. "Good morning, sweetheart!" Nancy had a little more pep in her step than Larry, and she skirted around me to turn the kettle off and start pouring water into cups. "Nasty bit of gunk on that, isn't it?"

It was, but no more than was advertised. The whole kitchen had probably last seen an update forty years before, but that was normal enough for the area. Some of the better-off families could afford upkeep. The rest of us tried not to let it fall down around our ears. Their walls needed a wash and a bit of the vibrancy had gone out of the paint. The cupboards were missing doors, as was the local style of their era. Nothing I hadn't seen a hundred times before. "I'll get that cleaned right up for you, Mrs Turner. A few hours of work and a bit of mess. That's all it should take."

As we sat down at the table, drinking tea and talking about the state of the kitchen and the world beyond it, I was reminded of why I was in the line of work I was in. They needed just a little bit of help, and that was something I could do. They'd pay me what they could afford, which wouldn't be much. Sometimes it barely paid for the supplies, forget the labour.

But someone needed to do it. Someone had to help people have a quality of life worth living. A backsplash wouldn't change much for two old people, but mould could make them both real sick, real fast. So I did it.

Greg, he'd rather I was bringing in real money. The kind that folds and buys extravagant stuff. He didn't understand why I did what I did, and he probably never would. It was also the last thing I had that gave me any real sense of purpose.

So naturally he wants to pry it from your hands, doesn't he?

Maybe he did, but sharing a tea with the Turners, it mattered a whole lot fucking less what Greg thought.

I drove home in the afternoon, and somewhere during that godforsaken drive, my phone found reception. It started pinging, and it was Greg's name that kept popping up, so I peeked at the texts.

> Greg:
> supper @ moms tonite
> home early

Fuck.

Going to Greg's parents' was almost as much fun as stepping on a rusty nail. I'd done both before, and I honestly could go my whole life without doing either again. Unfortunately, that wasn't how relationships worked, so I fucking supposed I was going to their house for supper.

Greg's truck was at the house when I pulled in, and the sight of it created a knot in my gut. I turned my truck off and sat there for a minute. I didn't really want to go in. The likelihood was that he would be fine. He usually was for a few days after he had a blowout like the one last night. He had to build that rage up again. Get to a boiling point. Until then, he'd probably just act like I was barely there, so long as everything was washed and folded and cooked.

So I mustered up the courage to get out of the truck.

He was in the kitchen when I opened the door, spreading butter over toast. His hair was wet, probably from a post-work shower, and he'd changed into jeans and a white polo. He didn't look up as he spoke. "Hey. You get my text?"

"Yeah," I said, stopping to take off my boots. "Gotta shower real quick, then I'll be ready."

"Told Dad we'd be there in an hour." Greg picked up the plate of toast and went to park himself in front of the TV. Last night's hockey stats were being read off by some old bald man whom everyone thought I was supposed to care about.

Greg wouldn't be listening anymore, so I didn't bother saying anything back. I went to the bathroom, my body dragging the whole way. I spent the next fifteen minutes scrubbing the drywall dust from my hair, but when I got out of the shower, some of it was still under my nails. Greg's family hated it when I showed up to their house unkempt.

Hot tears welled up in my eyes from out of nowhere. I didn't even remotely like those two people. I had nothing to say to Linda—who had nothing intelligent to say back—and Arthur seemed to think I wasn't good enough for his son. I hated that the thought of them brought me to tears.

I stared in the mirror, the fog framing my face. My insides felt wrong. Like there was a fissure inside me and I was one wrong move from snapping in half. Could I stop the snapping? Was I brave enough to? Or would I just let it happen?

Sometimes, when things were worse than I could manage, that little voice rose up to ask me all kinds of horrors.

Like what I'd be willing to trade for freedom from this life.

The visit was as dry and uneventful as I could have hoped for. I sank into myself for the duration. Spoke when spoken to. Linda asked questions about the house, and about Greg's job. Not my job—never my job—which was fine by me. My clients were none of her business. As usual, I shadowed Linda, helping with the cooking and the cleaning up, while Greg and Arthur sat in front of the TV, not saying a word except to curse out whoever was on the screen, usually including a litany of slurs. The whole thing lasted three hours, and by the time we left, my chest was hollowed out.

For whatever reason, Greg was happy as a clam. He chattered for the entire drive home, and though I was aware of having responded, I had no idea what either of us had said after the fact. He moved around the house, getting ready for bed, and I just stood in the kitchen. Leaned against the counter. Took long, slow sips of water.

I'd let this shit go on for long enough. Been stagnant long enough.

Something needed to change.

After the movement in the house died out, I went to look in the bedroom. Greg was fast asleep. He hadn't even said he was going to bed. He'd just gone, and he was out like a light.

What if he just…didn't wake up?

For just a second, I imagined smothering him with a pillow.

Instead, I got my boots and prepared to go for a walk.

The sun had been down for a while. Maybe Spencer wouldn't even be there. Maybe he'd actually murder me if I went back.

Maybe I was ready to be murdered if it meant not having to endure another day of my life.

The evening chill had settled in as I quietly closed the door behind me. I'd added extra layers to the ensemble and had a poor-quality folding beach chair tucked under my elbow. Something to sit on so I didn't end up with a freezer-burnt coochie. But as I walked down the path, I had the sneaking suspicion he wasn't there. I couldn't see the tiny bucket of fire, and I couldn't hear anything in the distance.

When I rounded the corner to the clearing, it was empty.

I stood for a moment, deliberating. Then I unfolded the chair, plunked it down, and got to work creating a little bucket fire for myself.

If he showed, I'd have company. If he didn't, at least I wouldn't be with Greg.

Spencer

The two-lane highway stretched out in front of me, the long, rolling hills winding through thick forest on either side. Not a car on the road other than mine. I let the car coast down one hill, just to floor the gas to get up the next, slowly weaving my way up into the pass that separated one section of the province from the next. The night was clear, the seat warmer was as hot as it would go, and the thump of the music hit inside my chest like a heartbeat.

Driving was one of the last thrills left for me, especially in a place like the Harbour.

For a county that was as impoverished as it was, every fifth car in the area seemed to be a sports car. Which meant *I* could have something resembling one and still blend in. Now, the definition of sports cars varied; some were Mustangs and Chargers, but most…most were souped-up Honda Civics. An affordable fast car, half a dozen in every parking lot in town. Most of them driven by young men and teenagers, the outsides covered in vinyl decals.

My baby was a blue four-door among a sea of them. Still thrilling enough to drive, but never something that anyone would take notice of, and *gods*, was I glad to have her. She let me *fly*, even just for a little while.

The thick guitar of the rock track ended and a '90s club song began. I tapped my fingers on the steering wheel and bobbed my head to the electric beat, waiting for the lyrics to begin. I'd danced to that track in a bar in Copenhagen nearly thirty years ago, on a rare night when I'd gone out alone. As the music poured out of the speakers, I sang along, practically able to taste the delightfully eager man I'd drunk from that night in the bar's back room. Half a lifetime ago, but a savoured memory all the same.

I'd been free once. Roaming the world with more love than I knew what to do with, gorging myself on alcohol and blood and bodies, one party, one town, one adventure after the other. Everything I could have ever wanted. An endless feast that would have made the old gods proud.

Now all I was left with was a car and some music, and the things I was running from.

The sinking feeling had been coming for me since the moment I'd woken up, ready to pull me under. When the music was that loud, when I was racing into the mountains with the night all around me, nothing could touch me. Not even the pain of losing them. Not if I could just keep going a little longer. Just keep running until daylight.

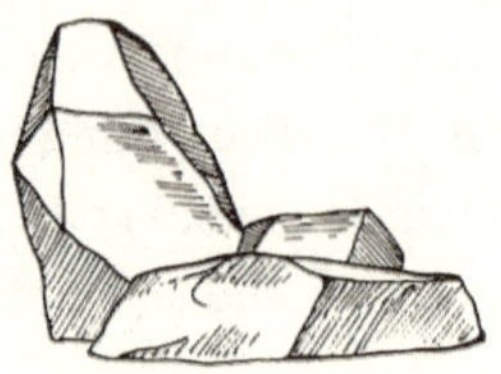

Penny Harbour

Even a place as small as Penny Harbour had two parts of town: a town centre and everything outside it. Away from the centre, streets languished in each major direction, sprawling out in large plots of land with generously sized homes. Not all were pretty and not all were faded. Some were shaped like trailers, while others had been built into spacious farmhouses. Fields ran along their backs, some full of hay, others full of cattle. And in the middle of everything, the harbour sparkled in the sun, a distant piece of the Atlantic Ocean.

In one of those homes sat a little girl named Tammy.

Her home had a basement and a middle and an upstairs. Big air ducts carried wood heat along the house, and sometimes they made it easy to hear what other people were doing in other rooms.

As Tammy played with her toys—a stuffed bear and a pair of big-eyed dolls—she listened to her parents in the basement. They thought she couldn't hear.

"But we can't afford a second car, Margret," her father said. "There are too many repairs to pay for here already."

"You don't think I know that?" her mother replied, her voice full of sadness. "But they're offering me a job in town, for more money. Couldn't we take on the extra for a little while?"

The wind blew on the house, a strong gust that shook the walls. Tammy looked up, and she heard the quiet *shhhh* of dust falling off the walls and into the sheet plastic that kept it from raining down on her. It sounded like one of the toys at school. The rainmaker, with the rice inside.

Even with the plastic there, the dust still fell to the floor and scattered out across it. It was grey powder. Old drywall, from when the house had been built nearly a hundred years back. Tammy swept it away from where she was playing.

As she did, her parents kept arguing. About money, and resources, and time. About who deserved to be allowed to go to work, and what would happen to Tammy if they both were out of town all day. Good opportunities, bad opportunities.

Tammy didn't understand most of it, but she did understand that her parents were so, so unhappy. She didn't notice as the fine black powder floated up from the ducts and into the air in her bedroom. As she breathed it in, it settled in her lungs. Just a bit. Just for now.

She had so many more years to fill to the brim with it.

CHAPTER THREE

Laurel

Staring out the window with my morning coffee, I let out a long sigh. The snow was gone and it was raining, all the water collecting in puddles along the roadside. By the look of the forecast—freezing rain late in the afternoon, because of course it was—there'd be no outside work and no late-night walks for me.

I sent a text to my client of the day.

Laurel:
Hey Alex. It's going to be too rainy to do that shed repair today. I've got time on Sunday at 10 and the weather looks good, so I'll come by if it's cool for you.

I took a long drink of my coffee and looked around the house. A pile of laundry waited in the bathroom and I had chores I could do. Small repairs I'd been putting off. With a free day, I could sink myself into those thankless jobs and finally get ahead on things. Greg was never going to do them, and frankly, he only noticed I wasn't doing them when things started to really inconvenience him.

I hit Tabs messenger.

Laurel:
Timmies run?? No work today.

Emma:
GOD YES

Mary-Jo:
My break is at 11, see you hoes there

The drive from Penny Harbour was thirty minutes of winding back roads. An enormous forest separated the village from the rest of the world, including the town of Hammonds, which most of us just referred to as *town*. The trip could be horrific in bad weather, and it wasn't all that uncommon to find a car in a ditch a few times a year. But even pouring rain in winter wasn't enough to keep most people from taking a trip to Timmies.

It wasn't that the coffee or food was good. In part, it was that the Harbour had absolutely nothing in it, and in part, it was an affordable tradition for the dirt poor. A force of habit, even. I mean, what the fuck else was there to do in town, honestly? *Shop*? With what money?

I wound the car through the roads to town, my eyes on the ditches. Not for cars. For deer. A person might get lucky and see a head poking out from below the road line. Deer were stupid fuckers. If someone got too comfortable driving, that was exactly the time a deer would spring out of a ditch and ruin your truck and your year. Maybe kill you in the process.

At least it wasn't bear season.

When I arrived, Emma's baby-blue Yaris was parked on the side of the building. We could've carpooled from the Harbour, but she'd insisted she had other errands to run while she was in town. I parked my beat-up old truck next to her little clown car and went inside.

Timmies was moderately busy, as always. It was the local watering hole for anyone over fifty. Men with grey hair tucked under ball caps with sports logos and hunting slogans sat in most of the booths. A sea of long-sleeved plaid shirts with people inside them. Emma waved from the back corner and then pointed at the drinks on the table.

"First round is on you, eh?" I said, laughing, as I approached and sat down in the booth, opposite her.

"It's not like you ever change your order." Emma stuck her tongue out at me.

Emma looked as tired as I felt. A dedicated child of the '90s, she still wore her shirts in layers, a lilac tank top over a pastel pink one. Her hair was layered and piecey. Some of it came down past her chin, while tapering off at the back of her head, all a mix of brown and blonde highlights. Her skin was always too pale—except when sunburnt—and whenever she was tired, the grey circles showed under her eyes.

"What if I did want something else?" I teased. "What would you do then?"

She slid the French vanilla cappuccino across the table. "I'd make you drink it anyway."

I quickly checked my phone, but no notifications had popped. "Any word from Mary-Jo?"

Emma shook her head, partway through a sip of her potent-smelling green tea. "I guess her boss isn't great at letting her start her breaks when she's supposed to. I'll be happy when she finds a better job."

I rolled my eyes. "You know she's never going to do that."

The look on Emma's face could only be described as weary patience. "We all come to our own changes in time, right? You know that as well as anyone."

Emma had gotten way too introspective since she started her psych degree.

"Don't give me that look." I scoffed, still somewhat bitter from yesterday's comments via Tabs. "And I know you both think I'd be better off without Greg. MJ certainly doesn't make any effort to hide it."

Emma's lips became a thin, hard line as she clearly shoved some feelings back down her throat. "Mary-Jo loves you and she's concerned. That's all. You're a big girl. I trust you to take care of yourself."

I crossed my arms over my chest. "At least you don't hound me about it."

Emma reached out and took my hand. "If and when you want a change, you know we're here for you. *Besides,* you can't say much about either of us. I don't even think *you* like Greg."

A dark laugh bubbled up in me. She had me there.

"Well, hello, strangers."

Mary-Jo strode over to the table and plopped down next to me. Two versions of Mary-Jo existed, one of them more socially acceptable than the other. The version that sat next to me was dressed for success. Her long brown hair was tied up in a severe bun, not a strand loose anywhere. She took off her black wool coat, and underneath was a white-and-black pinstriped blouse and a black pencil skirt. Seeing Mary-Jo on a workday was like seeing someone's Good Doppelganger, considering how she dressed the rest of the time.

She exhaled dramatically and slid down the seat.

"How's it goin'?" I asked.

"*Fucking great.* Don't be a secretary when you grow up." Mary-Jo took the Timmies cup that Emma was offering and took a long inhale of the dark roast inside. She craned her neck to look at the line of people at the cash. "Fuuuuuuck, I'm going to kill so much of my hour in that line—" But in the time that she'd turned around, Emma had pulled a hidden takeaway bag out from the seat beside her and put it in front of Mary-Jo. "Is that for me? I swear, someday I'll have your babies."

Emma put a hand up, waving the idea off. "No thank you. I already have more baby than I can handle."

"Where is Logan today?" I asked.

"Mum took him." Emma watched Mary-Jo dig ravenously into the BLT bagel that had come out of the bag. "Bless her, because if she didn't step up from time to time, I think I'd be toast. Hubby is back on the road again, probably another week before he's back. Between trying to keep the house clean, studying for this psych exam, and taking care of Logan, I'm basically not a person anymore."

Emma had decided a few years ago that she was going to be Penny Harbour's first and only psychologist. Unfortunately for her, that also meant she had to go from having just a high school diploma to becoming a thirty-year-old university student. She and her husband had also had a baby partway through that, as if she was determined to do things the hard way. Emma had a tenacity I never had, and I was pretty proud of her for it.

"I don't know how you do it," Mary-Jo choked out from behind a bite of her bagel. She swallowed and took a drink. "I couldn't function with the lack of sleep you get."

Emma gestured to herself. "Generous of you to call this functioning."

"All I'm saying," Mary-Jo started, "is that if it had been me, I'd have been either a student or a mom. There's not enough MJ to go around. There's barely enough of me now. The boss wants more every day and yet he *never pays more."*

Mary-Jo had been working for a local construction company for nearly five years, making the trip back and forth to town five times a week. Some of the employees often acted like complete lechers and her bosses weren't inclined to correct the behaviour. So she'd increased the amount of fabric she wore to work, and in her off hours, she'd started leaning hard on beer, scratch tickets, and bar fights. Though she'd promised to cool it with punching people in their "stupid drunk faces" since I'd had to drive up and rescue her from the drunk tank a year back.

"So did you ever find that Spencer guy you were looking for the other day?" Emma asked.

"Not since the first night, no. I went back out to the woods looking for him, but that was, like…a week ago." I took a long drink while their reactions came through.

"Dude, you should not be wandering around the woods alone at night," Mary-Jo chided.

"You don't even know him," Emma followed up. "What if he's not from here?"

I shrugged. "He's not. He said he moved here to be a hermit basically."

"This is some city girl shit that you're up to." Emma was not impressed. She even put on a prissy little voice. "*I think I'll just go into the woods at night alone and talk to strangers and get eaten by coyotes.* You know better."

"Now, now, let's not be too hasty." Mary-Jo wiped mayo from the corner of her mouth. "If she starts fucking this rando, maybe she'll finally have a reason to leave Sir Gregs-elot."

I gestured to her in dramatic irritation. "Are you serious right now?"

"Oh, I'm always serious, girlfriend." Her smirk was borderline evil.

Emma rolled her head back to stare at the ceiling. "Just last week you promised to lay off the Greg thing."

"And I will, as soon as she lays on some Spencer."

I looked at Mary-Jo. "I hate you."

"I know." She kissed my cheek and ducked away from the false swing of my hand. "It's a star-crossed love between you and me. Frenemies to bros story arc, I promise."

I rolled my eyes. I did love her, even if she drove me nuts. "You read too much smut."

It was her turn to scoff. "What else am I going to read? Literature? If I don't read smut, I'll lose my entire sex drive to those construction workers and their weird fucking comments."

"What was the last book you were telling me about?" Emma asked.

"Mmm." Mary-Jo swallowed excitedly. "Potato shifters. But I didn't read that 'cause it's sexy; I read it 'cause it's ridiculous."

More than an hour later, I was staring out the front window of the truck again, the wipers clearing the rain away. Back on the road, back toward home. I found my chest tightening the closer I got. I would get there, and then it would be a handful of hours before Greg would arrive, and it didn't seem to matter anymore how long I was without him. The thought of him coming back *at all* left me wishing he never would.

It was getting harder to tell myself everything was fine, and I knew no one else believed it either.

Just like I'd run to town in order to escape my life for a little while, I was tempted to take off into the woods in the pouring rain on the off chance that Spencer would be there. That little speck of shiny new hope that had appeared out of nowhere in the shape of some blond stranger. But no sane person would be out in the muddy, cold, wet woods. Especially once the temperature dipped again overnight and the whole world turned to ice. I sure as hell wasn't going out in that, so surely he wouldn't either.

So back I went, into the cage that had been made for me.

Or had I made it for myself?

Spencer

Sleeping in for a vampire meant getting up at nine at night—at least in Canadian winter it did; summer was another thing entirely—but it wasn't as if I had responsibilities or people to hunt. So it didn't matter that I rolled out of my soft queen-sized bed at almost one in the morning. Freezing rain pinged off my windows like little pebbles, coating the wet ground with ice.

Absolutely not.

My stomach growled and I sighed. I shouldn't have put off hunting the night before. Even if I had the will to go out there, almost everything would be hiding. Besides, it hadn't gotten easier to return to room temperature since I'd lost my pulse. It wouldn't kill me to be that cold, but it would be damn uncomfortable.

I trudged to the kitchen in my pyjamas, rubbing my eyes. I pulled a double boiler from the space below the stove—nearly the only thing in there since I didn't eat—and put it on the stove with water in the bottom. Inside the fridge was a collection of hanging medical bags, each filled with deep crimson blood. Too apathetic to be bothered with scissors, I grabbed a bag from the fridge and bit down on the top corner, piercing two clean holes through it. With a steady squeeze, I emptied half the bag into the double boiler. Low heat, and wait. Thirty-six degrees was all I needed. If it got much warmer than that, it would start to cook. Cooked human tasted almost as wrong as the locals.

As I waited, the thoughts started to creep in. Thoughts that would turn into remembered screams if I let them. I went to grab a book from the coffee table. A compact little thing about Paris in the 1850s. Violet had loved Paris. As I read, waiting for the stove to creep steadily warmer, I stopped seeing the words describing the architecture and the social movements. I saw her—I saw us—

The four of us ran through the narrow streets, laughing. Sirens and shouts rang out from the distance. We were far enough away that nothing mattered. We'd gone at least five blocks and no one had come looking for us. I stopped first, staring back at the way we'd come from. Waiting for something else to happen. For the consequences to arrive, as they sometimes did. But no one had followed, not that time.

I tried to let go of the worry, if only because my loves had none.

Violet passed me, holding the collar of her new mink coat to her face, delighted. Her blonde hair hung in loose waves around her cherub cheeks, bobbing as she ran. "I love it!"

It was Astra who went to her, slipping inside Violet's arms until she too was inside the coat. Astra was taller, and she held Violet against her, lifting her into the air to spin her before setting her down again. "It was a fine choice," Astra said, pressing a kiss to Violet's hair. "Too bad we weren't quicker. I'd have killed to see you in that black evening gown."

Willem approached, a grin on his stained lips. He was nearly a head taller than me, so I had to crane my neck up to look him in the eyes. His trim beard framed his jaw in a very dashing manner. Princely, which was ironic for a devious rogue like himself. He slid his palm across my middle, resting his hand on my hip. "Don't fret. No one's coming, love."

And he was right. No one was coming. No one would be able to touch us for decades, but I didn't know that until later. I feared it constantly. Feared that if I were too in love with my life, it would disappear. Feared that because I fought so hard for it, it was fragile and limited. That someone would steal everything from me if I didn't guard it closely enough.

I reached up to slide my thumb against his lip, my skin staining red. "You've got someone on you," I whispered, arching my neck up for a kiss.

Willem obliged, the taste of his mouth both savoury and sweet, the way young drunk lovers often tasted when we ate them. The kiss was deep, his hands running up my sides, pulling me tight—and the memory of that kiss blurred my vision and brought me back to the cold of the kitchen, the smell of blood in the air.

Hot tears streamed down my cheeks. I threw the book and it crashed against the wall in the other room. I could still feel his lips on mine, still hear all their beautiful laughter. We'd gone home after that. Lain curled up in bed together, drinking wine and telling the story of the night over and over, until the details were exhausted and daybreak was threatening to sneak in from behind the curtains.

Gods, I'd loved them so much.

I wiped my tears away, frustrated at myself. It had been *so many years!* Wasn't I supposed to be better by now? Over it?

I scoffed, just to break the overwhelming silence of the house around me.

Over the greatest love of any of my lifetimes? *Sure.*

I fished around in the cupboards for the large, faux-shattered wine glass I kept on the top shelf. I filled it to the brim with warm blood and tossed the pot in the sink with a violent clatter. Tears leaked out the corners of my eyes as I went into the living room and turned on the speakers, navigating the songs on my phone. Something dramatic and sad, that was what I needed. The music poured into the room, loud and alive, and I swayed, drinking as I did.

The pain hollowed out my chest as I danced in silken, sultry movements, the wine glass held delicately in one hand. Self-indulgent and desperate. Trying to drown out everything I'd lost. The lyrics dripped out of the speakers, and I sang them back.

You're dead as dead can be; you won't feel a thing.

I laughed—a choked, evil noise. "Darling, you have no idea."

A long drink of blood, and as I moved past it, I scooped up the open bottle of rum I'd been working on three nights prior, along with three shot glasses. I set them on the coffee table. A glass each, for Violet and Astra and Willem.

My parents and my people had taught me to honour the dead with drink and song, but that had been so, *so* long ago. Old habits, I supposed, pouring them out a drink. But there'd be no joy, not from me.

I was going to get very drunk and sing sad songs until the cat began to croon with me.

I drank back the rest of the blood, my lips wet. Stained red, like his had been.

"To the past," I whispered, and set the glass down.

Penny Harbour

Sandy dreaded the news.

Every night at six, the TV would come on and her father would sit in front of it and start to yell. The subject would change, but the message was always the same. *You're wrong; I'm right; go fuck yourself.*

It seemed to be one of his favourite things. He'd sit in that armchair, staring at the thing and waiting for it to say something he didn't like. Over the years, Sandy had listened from different places around the house as her father gave his sermons into the universe, full of rage and slurs and contempt. It was impossible not to, really. The only way to block it was to drown it out with music, or to not be in the house at all. His voice *carried*.

Maybe he thought no one was listening. Maybe having everyone hear him was the point. No matter what his purpose, it drilled fear into Sandy. With every viewing, she learned more about what she could and couldn't be, who she could and couldn't love. What friends she could and couldn't invite to the house. Not Sarah, because she was Black. Not Avery, because she was Indigenous. Ben had long hair and Dad hated hippies, but he also hated the Harper family, so Nathan and Aaron were out.

Her father yelled and her world got smaller, one broadcast at a time.

Every month, every year accumulated, until she had gathered so much secondhand hate that it felt suffocating. Dangerous. As if she was one step away from being the target of that anger at any given time if she dared show up at the house with someone like *them*. And *them* seemed to amount to everyone.

After a while, the perpetual one-sided screaming match felt like a nail gun, adding a new bolt into her private personal coffin one at a time. Trapping her inside, away from the world.

These fucking foreigners!

Thunk.

The government just wants to keep us down.

Thunk.

They think they're so much better than us!

Thunk.

It wasn't until she was sixteen that she started to notice the comments that *really* ate at her. It was all hateful, yes. But over the years, some had started to feel personal. She tried not to notice, because to notice was to admit she might just be one of the people her father hated so much. And that…that was dangerous.

Fucking faggots.

Thunk.

What the fuck do they need to be married for anyway?

THUNK.

Disgusting. Absolutely disgusting. Buncha' fucking queers.

THUNK.

Sandy disconnected. Admitted how hard it would be if he meant *her*. Was grateful that it *couldn't* be her. And she let the coffin shut on her because it was the safest thing to do.

It would be *years* before Sandy looked up and realized the box she'd been nailed inside wasn't a coffin at all. Out in the world, far from home and all the trouble home had brought, she noticed things through the cracks. Pretty women and trickles of feeling and regret. So much regret. She'd been in that box for *so long*. Trapped in the dark with no air, black dust settling in her lungs and grit coating her skin. She had mistaken her trap for a pine box. But it wasn't.

No, not at all.

Her father had ever so slowly pushed her into a closet and nailed it shut.

CHAPTER FOUR

Spencer

When I woke the next night, it was with my face in the pillow, a minor throb in my head, and a parched tongue. The drinking and dancing had continued for *much* longer than was advisable, and I was paying the piper. A ball of warm fur was curled against my side. Spectre, the stray cat who had wandered into my life after I'd moved into Penny Harbour. I pulled her closer to me, seeking out that warmth. She mewled in protest but started licking my chin.

I must have fallen back asleep, because when I opened my eyes again, the clock read an hour later than it had been, and Spectre was gone. The hangover had abated just slightly, enough to compel me to slide out of bed and back into existence.

Pulling on my red satin pants, I dodged the haphazardly thrown-off clothing from the night before and made my way downstairs. Spectre was waiting at the bottom, *screaming* to be fed. As she led me to the kitchen, I took stock of the mess I'd made.

Music was still playing from the speakers, although at a more reasonable volume than it had been most of the night. One glance at my phone told me it was almost dead. The bottle of rum was empty and abandoned on the coffee table next to a wine glass with the slightest tinge of dried blood in it. An empty bottle of wine sat next to the sink, and another half-empty bottle sat open on top of the fridge. I'd probably drunk enough to tranquillize a horse, but that was one of the many perks of the living dead. You could *just keep going.*

As I reached for Spectre's food, I caught a glimpse inside the open cupboard where I normally kept the corked wine. Empty. I'd polished off the whole fucking cupboard.

I groaned, set Spectre's dish on the floor, and checked the time. If I wanted to make it to the liquor store before it closed, I'd need to get my shit together. Not that I *needed* more wine, but if I *wanted* it, my options would be sorely limited after nine at night.

It was better to have something in the house for when the memories came flooding back than force myself to sit through it without.

After having a cold breakfast and a quick shower to wash the alcoholic musk off, I went outside to find *snow*. The driveway had a few centimetres on it, enough to need attention. I reached for the shovel with a groan and went to start the car.

"Fucking winter," I mumbled, pushing the snow in quick lines across the width of the driveway, piling it up along the side. "Settle in the middle of nowhere, Spencer. It'll be quaint and peaceful, Spencer. Stupid."

Once I'd cleared the snow down to the road, I went back to wipe off the car. It had heated enough for the job to be easy, and within a few minutes, I was making my way down the road to the one place where someone might *actually* recognize me.

The Penny Harbour liquor store had very clearly been a house, once. The only things to tip a person off to it being a store were the large bay windows in the front, the accessibility ramp, and the big neon sign that said *Liquor Store*. I parked next to the building and went up the steps, stomping the snow off my boots at the top. When I pushed my way through the door, a bell jingled, and the cashier looked up.

"Oh, hello there! Enough snow for you?" Sandra sang, a neighbourly smile on her face. I knew her name because it was on the tag she wore, but she only knew my face. It didn't seem to matter who else came through the door, though, because she had a name for everyone.

"Any snow is too much snow, Sandra," I answered in kind, giving her enough response to be friendly, but nothing she could carry on a conversation with. I picked up a basket from next to the door and headed to where I knew the good stuff was.

The store was a single room. An old living room at best. Fridges of beer were built into the back wall, and two long rows of shelves sat in the centre, each containing the smallest selection of alcohol that could be found anywhere. The wine section was made up of six types of red, seven white, and two rosé, but some wine was better than none. I picked up what seemed to be a *new* bottle, miracle on miracles, and started to read the label.

The bell above the door let out a little jingle and I looked up. Two people stepped in, heavily dressed for the winter. The first in the door was a man with a sour face. Handsome enough, but it was difficult to find underneath the scowl. And behind him—

Laurel.

I stared for a moment. The feeling of seeing a familiar face in the Harbour was a new one—well, aside from the woman behind that counter, who likely knew me only as *the raging alcoholic.* Laurel had her bare hands cupped over her mouth, blowing warmth into them, and her eyes fell on me across the tiny room.

She froze.

I didn't look away. I'd had the experience a thousand times while hunting: someone would find me striking and I could use it to my advantage, or the rare few would see me for the threat I was. But this wasn't the same. Laurel had stared at me only for a moment, and she wasn't keeping her eyes on me.

She was keeping them on the man she'd come in with.

"Hey, Laurel. Hey, Greg. How's she goin'?" Sandra chirped from behind the counter.

Greg.

Laurel clicked back to life. "Oh, tickity-boo, Sandra. You know how it is."

I'd never heard that phrase before in my life, but it seemed safe to say it meant *fine,* which, according to her heart thrumming across the room, she was not.

Laurel put her head down and headed for the back wall, where Greg was pulling a case of piss-flavoured beer out of the fridges. Since she wasn't making a point to say hello, I went back to filling my basket with French reds and rosés.

"Get what you're getting," Greg mumbled as he and Laurel walked toward the front half of the store. Her mouth moved, but her voice only gave off a meek *all right*, as if she was afraid to be heard.

Laurel walked into the middle aisle with me, only a few steps from where I was standing, and picked up a bottle of brown rum. With that in her hand, she looked up, directly at me. She held my gaze for a moment and I saw a hint of something on her face. Sadness? Embarrassment? I wasn't sure.

"Hi," I said, and I heard the immediate skyrocket of her heart, beating like a galloping horse.

Greg was by her side so quickly that he *had* to have been keeping an eye on her. He put himself between us and started to stare me up and down, a scowl set on his lips and hatred in his eyes. I knew what he saw. A man who was taller than he was, prettier than he was, and a touch too dainty for a place like the Harbour. Too confident. In need of being taken down a peg, just to see what happened.

It was hard to tell if he was a bigot or just jealous.

"The fuck are you looking at?" Greg snarled. "Move along."

I raised an eyebrow at him and didn't budge. *Greg* didn't scare me, but catching Laurel's expression, he sure as hell scared *her*. "And if I don't? What then, *Greg*?"

He kept staring, as if taking my measure. So many men, when push came to shove, knew when they'd met their match and would back away with their tails between their legs. Others, well…they sometimes left in body bags.

In a smart move for his health, Greg waved me off. "Come on." He grabbed Laurel by the arm and urged her to move around me.

"Damn it, Greg, stop," she muttered. Her protest was shallow and cowering, but by the red in her cheeks, it also *really* pissed her off.

Her heart hadn't stopped hammering.

Greg paid for their booze and stomped out to the truck with Laurel not far behind him. She kept her eyes on her shoes and her hands in her pockets, not even looking up as they drove away.

So. That was what she was running from.

Laurel

The second Greg started snoring that night, I was out the door and on my way to the woods.

I didn't have anything to prove. *I didn't.* But it bothered me in a way I couldn't quite name. Like an itch inside my chest, sitting under thick coils of nerve and muscle. It was fucking mortifying, having some stranger see that. Spencer probably thought I was some poor battered woman, just because Greg was acting out of line. Not to mention how *embarrassing* it had been, watching Greg talk to him like that just for saying hello.

I needed to apologize to Spencer, but also to tell him that things weren't the way they seemed. That it wasn't what it looked like. Everyone else looked at me with pity. I saw it all the time. I didn't want that from him too.

Maybe he would believe me.

Maybe *I* would believe me.

Yes, girl.

Lie to the pretty boy.

Lie to yourself.

When it all comes crashing down, it will only taste that much sweeter.

The night was clear as I strode across the road and down the track. The snow had covered the path down the main trail, and when I hit the intersection of it, a single set of footprints led down toward where we'd met before. It didn't mean it was him, but how many other people had come down that way? Hardly any, ever. Not by foot at least.

The little fire illuminated the clearing from between the winter-bare trees, and when I rounded the corner, Spencer was sitting there. He had a book open between the fingers of one hand, with one ankle up on the other knee. Without looking up, he said, "Should I say hello, or do we think that would be a problem?"

My voice caught in my throat. For all the things I'd thought of saying to him, it had all been a monologue. I hadn't thought about what he'd say *back*.

When I didn't answer, Spencer marked the page and put the book down. He gestured to the seat I'd left there and had never come to retrieve. "So that's Greg, hmm?"

I hesitated a moment before I sat on the edge of the seat, too tightly wound to relax into it. "I'm sorry he acted like that. It's not okay."

Spencer scoffed. "Oh, darling, I don't give a shit about what he said to me. I've had worse said by much more interesting people. You, however, looked like you were terrified."

I looked away. "He's not that bad. Just kind of an asshole, I guess."

"Laurel." Spencer waited until I looked up. "We don't know each other, but I know men like that. He's not *just* an asshole, is he?"

I didn't know what to say to that. I'd come out to the woods to try to convince both of us that Greg hadn't mortified me in front of other people, but apparently Spencer wasn't going to be convinced.

Maybe I couldn't be anymore either.

"It's not my business unless you make it my business. But you did come all the way out here, so I'm assuming you have something to say." Spencer's stare was so intense and I couldn't bear to hold it.

I let out a dark laugh. "I had a whole speech ready, but what's the point? Apparently you've got me all figured out."

He gave me a look that could only be described as tired. "I don't know a thing about you, Laurel. You told me you were running from something and it's clear who that person is. And it so happens I'm running from my own problems, so far be it from me to judge you."

"Yeah, I don't think you get to," I snapped, familiar with this kind of conversation. "I can handle myself."

The space between us had grown chill so quickly. It hadn't been my intention, and the defensive irritation quickly melted in the face of Spencer's soft, sympathetic expression.

"Sorry," I muttered.

Spencer let out an audible breath from across the fire. "Stay here, then. For a bit. You don't have to go running back to the lion's den right away, do you?"

I let out a light laugh. He was taking pity on me, but maybe I needed it, even for just a second. "Greg's asleep."

"So? Even better reason not to be there."

An odd silence fell over the clearing, interrupted only by the noises of the night. What did either of us know about each other? Except for my darkest secret, of course? I found myself grasping for something to ask, just to kill that silence.

"What are you reading?" I asked, pointing at the paperback in his lap.

He picked up the book and tossed it to me.

I caught it, barely. It was a ratty old copy of a popular '90s horror novel. "I read this in high school. Pretty good stuff back then, but I don't know if it holds up today."

"It doesn't." Spencer sat forward in his chair. "It's vaguely racist around the edges."

"Of course it is." I tossed it back and he caught it easily. "What else do you read?"

"Anything. I've come into a lot of free time since moving here, and I've stopped being selective about books." Spencer tucked the little paperback into his coat pocket. "Classics, science fiction, contemporary. Doesn't matter."

"What *don't* you like?"

"I have…" Spencer took a moment to gather his thoughts. "I have a complicated relationship with historical nonfiction. Some books are fine, but others are more fabrication than truth."

I laughed. "Oh, so you know better than historians now?"

"Sometimes," he answered without a hint of humility. "About certain places or times."

"Oh, yeah? Like where?" I sat forward, elbows on my knees.

He shrugged. "I have a thing for Irish history and Europe after the nineteenth century."

I raised an eyebrow. "You said you were from Ireland, didn't you? What's that like?"

Spencer's gaze moved off toward the trees, a little smirk on the corners of his lips. "Beautiful. Rolling green hills as far as you can see. Old stone castles and churches. Steep cliffs over churning waves. I've been gone a long time, but I still get that ache every once in a while, you know?" His eyes met mine again, dreamier than he'd been a minute ago.

I scoffed. "Actually I don't. I've never lived anywhere but here. Not even for college. I just took a trade and drove back and forth to the school every day. Penny Harbour is the only place I really know."

"That's a shame," Spencer answered, and it sounded like he really meant it. "It's a vast world out there. So much to taste."

I looked down at the ground, kicking the snow beneath my shoes. "I mean, it sounds nice, but that's not how things turned out. I've had one set of friends, one boyfriend who turned into a husband, a couple jobs. A life in *the vast world* isn't what I was given."

"And are you content with that?"

I took a long breath, debating on how candid I wanted to be. But he already knew the worst part of me. What was a little more? "I don't think I am. It's like…it's not about leaving or staying here. I just feel like I picked wrong, or maybe I…never chose anything. Maybe I let it all happen around me."

Spencer adjusted in his chair, stretching his legs out to cross them at the ankles. "The good news is that you aren't dead yet. Plenty of time to take risks."

"Like what?" I asked, a bit sarcastically. "Sitting in the woods with a complete stranger?"

Something flashed behind his eyes and it was clear I was missing part of the joke. "Yes, exactly like that." He reached inside his coat and pulled out the same flask he'd had the first night I met him. "Do you want a drink this time, or still opting to pass?"

"Fuck it." I held my hand out. "What's the worst that can happen?"

Spencer tossed the flask. "Plenty, I suppose."

I caught it and opened the top. A quick sniff told me it was rum. "Could it be worse than what's waiting for me at home every day?"

"That would be debatable." Spencer's eyes narrowed, watching as I took a drink.

I had a second quick sip, capped the flask, and tossed it back. "It's your turn now. You know my big secret, so what are *you* running from?"

"Oh, no," Spencer said, laughing. "Darling, there isn't enough alcohol in that bottle to spill secrets like that." The *r* in *darling* had a slight roll to it, exposing the depth of that watered-down accent of his.

His smile lit up his face in a way that drew me in. Made me comfortable. He might not have wanted to spill his secrets, but something about him made me want to tell all of mine.

"Fine," I sighed. "What do you do for fun?"

"Sit in the woods and be sad, apparently." He gestured to the woods around him with an effeminate flick of the wrist. "But I also like to be sad at home."

"And what do you have to be sad about?" I asked.

He leaned forward, his smile suddenly sharp and coy. "*Sad things.*"

I snickered. "You're a real thrilling person, you know that?" Oddly, this dark banter was exactly what I needed at the moment. "Like pulling teeth."

"Oh," he said, taking a drink. "You have no idea."

We carried on shooting the shit for a long while. Spencer never got all that candid with me, but he was easy to talk to. By the time the cold had gotten too far in my bones, we'd shared our favourite movies, a long tirade about several obnoxious books, and he'd given me a speech about the lack of good bars in the city. And as much as I wanted to stay, as relaxed as I'd started to feel around him, I deeply needed a hot shower and a few hours of sleep before work.

I said as much and stood to leave, and Spencer stood too.

"Wait." Spencer got up and walked toward me. He was *so* much taller than I was. He held his phone out to me, open to the contacts page. "Add your number. If anything…happens, you can text me."

I held his phone, staring up at him. We'd been so relaxed with each other that I'd half forgotten what had brought me out to the woods in the first place. "Why would you offer that? You don't know me."

Spencer laughed, and it seemed a little annoyed. "Honestly, I'm not sure. Maybe because I don't like little men who live to make others feel small. Or maybe because this has been a nice change of pace."

After a brief moment of hesitation, I slowly punched my number into his phone and hit save. "There's no reception out here, so you'll have to send me a text when you're back home. Can…can I text you about non-emergencies? Like books?"

"Yeah, we can talk about books," he said, looking down at me with the slightest smirk on his face. "I work nights, though, so don't expect much during the day."

I handed him the phone. "Okay then. Well…have a good night, Spencer."

He put his hands in his pockets, shifting his weight to one leg, looking far too content with himself. "Safe travels."

As I turned and walked back down the track toward home, I had a deep feeling in my gut that I'd done something wrong. Greg would lose his fucking mind if he knew I'd given my number to some guy, *especially* anyone as good-looking as Spencer. And just a tiny part of that guilt felt good. Like a long-deserved bit of spite in a single action.

Spencer was just a guy. I knew that, but I also knew how much bigger a deal it would become if Greg ever found out.

He could be my little secret. A friend in the dark.

Someone other than that gnawing voice that kept whispering tainted thoughts.

Silly girl. What do you think this stranger has to offer you?

Don't let him lure you in with pretty words.

He can't understand you. The dark things that make you up.

Let him run, lest you turn him to dust.

Spencer

Laurel had stayed in the woods a lot longer than I'd expected her to. She'd told me about her day, and about her worthless fucking husband—though not with such strong language—and her work. She had told me a little about the town we both lived in, and shortly into that, she'd started to yawn. And I'd watched her walk off, vastly more curious about her than I'd been before.

I waited until the sound of her departure had faded before making my way back home. The short walk passed peacefully, the wind moving the trees, the sky an endless canopy of stars. The woods turned toward the street, and the street led me home, not another soul in sight.

The house was on top of a little hill, with the harbour and the town in the distance below. Even though my original home had been more than two centuries ago and an ocean away, sometimes the view reminded me of that place. A stretch of countryside dotted with homes and fields and yards. It was no Ireland, to be sure, but the ghost of it sometimes appeared in the corner of my eye.

The house was a two-storey, 120-year-old building that sat away from the road, tucked behind a few trees. It didn't get much direct sunlight, which served me well. It meant no one could see inside, either. Whether it was just how the town was or if it was because I was hidden away, I couldn't say, but they left me alone. Just like I wanted.

I wriggled the key into the lock and shut the door behind me. As I took my snow-covered black boots off, I heard a light thump from further inside the house. By the time I'd taken my jacket off, Spectre was under me, staring up patiently.

"Were you waiting for me, my love?" I picked up the dark grey cat and nestled her into the crook of my arm, belly up. "How was your evening?" I peppered her little head with kisses as she squeaked at me. Her meows were never proper ones, not unless she was hungry.

Hungry.

I could hear her small heart beating its quick little rhythm underneath her fur. Her pulse under my fingertips, her warmth calling out to me.

I put her down and went to the fridge.

One bag was already half empty. I opened a cupboard and took out one of the mismatched mugs inside. It said *Too Pretty To Die*, which I had personally found amusing enough to buy. Too impatient to warm the blood, I emptied the bag into the cup, the metallic tang filling my nose. My whole body responded to the scent, alert and aware. Waiting to strike.

But it was just a cup, and I was just a mostly retired killer, so I took a sip and let it slide over my tongue. Since there was no one to hide from, I let myself go. My fangs slid down from the gums as I drank half the glass at once and took the rest with me to the couch.

It wouldn't be enough. It never was.

We were meant to drink people. Whole people, if we wanted to. Most humans had more than four litres of blood in them. Drinking a literal cup of blood was like trying to survive on lettuce.

I'd need to hunt something soon to tide over the hunger.

The living room was as I'd left it. Sadly, it wasn't as if Spectre was going to clean up after me. I'd made the space as comfortable as I could, all things considered. Late-night swap-and-sell purchases on the Tabs app accounted for most of the furniture: a soft couch from the '80s, a handmade wooden coffee table in front of it, and an outdated smart TV on the wall above a shelf that held a gaming console. A stack of books sat on a coffee table next to the couch, and on top of that was my laptop. A set of long speakers sat at either end of the TV, and I used my phone to put on a playlist of '90s alternative rock, just as a little background noise.

The house was already quiet enough with no one else in it. I didn't need to fill it with silence on purpose.

I brought the glass with me as I changed back into my silk pyjama bottoms and a pink plush sweater. Matching only mattered if there was someone to see you. Cosy at last, I went back to the couch. After setting the glass on the table, I scooped up the laptop and lay down with it on my thighs.

I'd spent a small fortune on the little beast of a machine, so it started up quickly. I opened up the browser and went directly to Tabs. The front page flashed with their slogan *Keep Tabs On Everyone You Love*, which I'd always found a bit off-putting, to be honest. A lot of modern technology was off-putting. But I'd known too many vampires who refused to learn how to use a cell phone or get an email address. They'd been left in the dust, and I wasn't about to stay there with them.

One thing I'd learned about social media was that you could look up anyone and learn more than you bargained for about half of them. So from my account—Steve Turner, whose profile photo was a sunset—I entered *Laurel Penny Harbour*. It wasn't hard to narrow it down. The area had three Laurels—at least with Tabs accounts—and only one had her face.

Click.

Laurel's account seemed to be set to private, but I could see a few public posts. Photos of her with Greg, and in some of them, he was cleaned up—objectively fuckable, if you didn't know anything about his personality. A few were from other accounts that had tagged Laurel in them. Friends and family. A few posts about local events or fundraisers. A photo of Laurel smiling ear to ear, holding an enormous stack of books, captioned *Winner of the All You Can Carry Book Giveaway!!!*

I scrolled a little further, and an image sank my heart into the ground. Laurel was younger in the photo, with two other women. One blonde, one brunette, and all three of them were happy beyond words. Laurel was in the centre, her arms around the necks of the others. They were clearly at a bar and dressed in sequins and glitter.

The photo brought back unwelcome memories. A club in Spain in the '80s that had been serving enormous glasses of tequila sunrise. Violet, Astra, Willem, and I had had far too much to drink. We'd been bad at hunting that night, and we'd gone mostly hungry, but it had been worth it. We'd danced all night, and we'd shared the veins of a young man before leaving him on a bakery doorstep. We'd had to run from the sunrise. The blood had only made us more intoxicated, and the four of us had gone back to our haunt to lounge and caress until we fell asleep midway through the day.

I slammed the laptop shut and tossed it onto the couch, tears clouding my vision. I fumbled for the glass of blood and drank back what was left. I let it linger on my tongue, trying to distract myself from the explosion of grief in my chest.

I missed them.

I missed them so fucking much.

I leaned over and sobbed, my hands raking into my hair. We had been everything, once. Friends, lovers, soulmates—if such a thing were real. Inseparable and perfectly separate, denying ourselves nothing. That was what we had promised each other when they'd found me and taken me in. That in death we would have everything we'd been denied in life. And we had.

Until they were gone.

And I was the only one left.

Cruelly, by the time I'd stopped crying, the grief had only increased my hunger. Refusing to think, I stormed into the kitchen and tore a bag of blood from the fridge. I bit directly into the plastic, fully aware that I would drink the whole thing, rationing be damned. It was cold and I wished it wasn't, but it still tasted like ecstasy. It tasted like relief and forgetting, and someone who had a deep affinity for salt.

I drank it back the way I'd once drunk people in alleys, as if someone would catch me at any moment.

Then it was gone. Empty.

And I would be short an extra night's worth in the long run.

I'd have to go out hunting each night, hoping for something to step into my path. I'd been intending to do exactly that in the days before, but the distraction had thrown me off.

Laurel.

Evened out but exhausted, I threw myself back on the couch, staring up at the ceiling.

I hadn't talked to anyone authentically since I'd lost my loves. Luring food didn't count. Nothing was *authentic* about the hunt. Speaking with Laurel as easily as I had…that was new and strange. In some ways, it was refreshing. In others, it felt like a betrayal. My mind had been nothing but *them* for so long that nothing else really fit.

Laurel wasn't all that different than I was, though. She was sad and tired. In pain. Maybe that made us good company. And if she tasted half as bad as anyone else in Penny Harbour, I wouldn't have to worry much about accidentally wanting to eat her.

It felt silly and impossible, and it would require a disturbing amount of subterfuge, but in theory, I could have a little human at the periphery of my life. She could never get close. It would only complicate things. But maybe I didn't need to be *completely* alone.

Only as alone as I decided I deserved to be.

A flash of fur landed next to me and crawled up onto my lap. Spectre craned her head up. She sniffed at my mouth and licked the corner of my lips clean before curling up on top of me. Her purr thrummed into my skin, which brought a smile back to my face.

"You're right, darling. I'm sorry." I ran my hand down her fur. "I've always got you, at least."

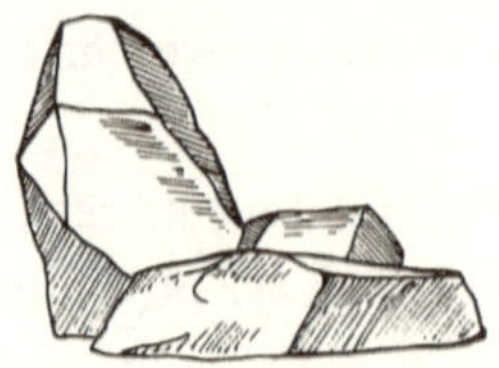

Penny Harbour

Penny Harbour happened in waves. When the industry was booming, thousands of people lived there. Toiling and laughing and making the best of things. Steady work wasn't always good work, but such was the way of things for longer than could be remembered. So the people had come in droves and set up everything a town would need. Groceries and farms and trading posts and hotels.

And then the coal stopped and so did everything else.

And a place couldn't exist with no work to exist upon.

Between the lives the mines had stolen and the people who left to chase their livelihood elsewhere, Penny Harbour got smaller and smaller. Hardly anyone moved there; people only seemed to leave and come home again.

So when Ron told his parents he was moving back to the Harbour, they sighed and welcomed him back again. They knew it was hard out there too, beyond the borders of the village. So many came back again, eventually. It got hard to look people in the eye and know they had no idea what was in a person's soul. To know they hadn't seen the same horrible things.

Ron knew the house he moved his family into; he'd driven past it all his life. They'd rented it out, sight unseen, because it was a place to start. Better that place than no place at all. And it was cute on the outside. A little dollhouse, perfect for him and his wife and the two young ones.

And then he opened the door and his heart sank to his knees.

The air was thick with the smell of rotten eggs.

He could've guessed, but a turn of the tap set his mind right. It was in the water. The well had to be full of sulphur, and it would be impossible to get it out of that house.

No wonder the place had been renting for so cheap.

Ron could see it in his family's eyes. They had followed him back to this place, this village that wasn't theirs, only his, and he had brought them to a home like *that*.

It would do. It would have to. Until they could find better.

The little dollhouse with the noxious smell and the bedroom roofs so low a person had to hunch over to walk in and the basement so full of black dust it wasn't worth stepping into.

Their luck would change, thought Ron.

It had to.

CHAPTER FIVE

Laurel

When I checked my phone the next morning, the first message I found was from someone outside of my contacts list. The preview notification gave me a pretty solid idea of who it was. When I opened the conversation, a picture appeared, one of Spencer's paperback in a trash can.

> Spencer:
> Horrible.
> If this was considered good a few decades ago, I'd hate to
> see the shit literature.

The messages were from three in the morning. He had really burned through the end of that book. I started typing.

> Laurel:
> Or maybe you just have high standards :P

Considering how late he'd been up and how he'd said he worked nights, I didn't bother sticking around to wait for a response. Besides, I had a gig twenty minutes away and not a lot of spare time. I was out of the house and down the road as quickly as I could manage.

Mark had been overdue for a chimney clean for a while. It was the kind of thing that a person could keep sweeping under the rug over and over, but left long enough, it would back the smoke up into the house and potentially kill everyone inside. So when he'd called, I'd made time. Sometimes if you told a person no after they had the guts to reach out to you, you'd never hear from them again. I wasn't going to be the one responsible for whatever came of *that*.

By the time the job was done, I'd managed to cover myself in a thick layer of black soot. It should've been a cleaner job than that, but things had gone sideways, and, well, there I was. When I got into the truck, I checked my phone on the off chance I'd gotten any reception anywhere. No missed messages. I checked the selfie camera and laughed. I looked like a raccoon, or maybe a shitty ninja. So I took a picture and sent it off to Emma and MJ. Then, feeling a little daring, sent it to Spencer too.

> Laurel:
> You wanted to know what I did for work
> You might wish you hadn't asked XD

They'd all send somewhere along the way home, or maybe once the phone was securely in the cell phone window.

It wasn't until I was home, showered, and fed and the sun was going down that Spencer replied.

> Spencer:
> Are you a Victorian chimney sweep?
> Ugh good luck getting that out of your hair

The text was followed by a picture of a new book on a bed. From the angle, he was clearly still in bed, the sheets unmade beneath the book. It was a popular modern classic I'd seen in the bookstore last time I'd gone.

I went to grab my e-reader, opened the cover to show the book I was reading, and sent a photo back.

"Laurel!" Greg yelled from the other room. "Where's my work pants for tomorrow gone to?"

The lightness in my chest from the texts fled in an instant. I hid my phone in my pocket as quickly as I could manage. "In the dryer. I'll get them. Hold on."

If anything was as bad as getting caught talking to cute men in stores, it would be getting caught texting them. As soon as I was in the basement, standing in front of the washer with my eyes on the stairs, I changed the settings on my phone. A new PIN, face recognition, and no more message previews.

It was underhanded, sure. But it would keep me protected. Whatever little joy this was going to bring me, I wanted to keep it all for myself, no matter the risk.

Spencer

The snow was soaked in blood, steaming against the cold.

The deer had run. It had stumbled upon me in the woods, barely aware that I was sitting and waiting for it. And when it *had* smelled me out, it had tried to bolt. I'd managed to slow it down, breaking one of its legs, but it hadn't stopped the thing from running out onto the trail. I'd leapt on it, pushing it to the ground before I'd torn a hole in its neck with my teeth. I'd drunk my fill, far too messily, and now, sitting next to the carcass, covered in blood, I realized how much of a massacre I'd left behind. Even when I hid the body, it would look like a crime scene until the snow melted.

Luckily, in a village of hunters and coyotes, no one would blink an eye.

Taking a breath, I gathered myself. I didn't expect anyone to come across me, not in the dead of night in Penny Harbour, but stranger things had happened. So I peeled myself off the ground and dragged the deer into the bushes, far enough back that no one but the animals should find it.

When I got back to the house, I closed the door behind me and started to strip. My clothing was soaked in both melted snow and blood. I brought it in a bundle out to the kitchen and opened the door into the little laundry room behind it. Cold water, a bunch of soap, and a prayer to all the old gods. The danger of loving my clothing and dealing with blood was that some of my favourite pieces ended up in the trash.

I needed a shower, but on a quick glance at the window, my phone's little notification light was flashing.

Considering all of three people had my number, it was safe to say Laurel had sent something.

I swiped up and found a picture of her e-reader, the book cover distinctly familiar. Taking the phone with me, I walked into the side room, found the complete series of the same book on my shelf, and sent a picture. Placing the phone back in the window, I started upstairs to the shower. Some of the blood had gone through my clothing, and a sticky film of red coated the left side of my stomach.

After making my way into the bathroom, I turned the tap on as hot as I could stand it and waited for the water to heat up. In a house as old as this one, it took its sweet time. I glanced at the mirror, wondering what stains had been left on my skin, but of course no one looked back. I'd have to find out the hard way, when the water stopped running pink.

Stepping into the shower was pure bliss. With no heat of my own, it was one of the few times I got warm to my core. I stood under the showerhead, hands on the wall, and let the water run down my back. I let out a sigh, the near-scalding heat getting deeper as the minutes passed.

The taste of the deer was still in my mouth, a gamey copper that couldn't stand up to the depth of human blood. But it felt *good* to be full for once, not just subsisting on whatever rations were in the fridge. Unlike the people, the gritty aftertaste was hardly present in the animals. Whatever it was, it was diluted down far enough to drink.

Not for the first time, I had to wonder what had happened in that town that had filled the people with ashes. I'd eaten enough people over the centuries to know blood could taste like illness. The people around the Harbour had been soaked in coal dust for hundreds of years, getting sick by the droves. Coal had gotten inside their chests and took up residence there, killing them slowly. The damp, the lack of sun, the poverty…some things stayed in the blood long after they should have been gone. Generations, even.

How long could coal dust live inside a person?

How much of it lived in Laurel?

With the thought of her came the thought of waiting messages. I hadn't even begun to wash, too busy basking in the heat, but my curiosity had started to bubble up. Was there anything waiting on my phone for me?

It was a small thing, getting a text from her. But that little bit of contact had rubbed at some long-disused part of me. Despite the last years hiding away, I'd once loved having an excuse to be social. Having a reason, no matter how small, to *talk* to someone again…it felt both odd and like coming home, somehow.

I cleaned up quickly, shut off the water, and grabbed the towel from the rack. Not bothering with clothes, I went downstairs, still rubbing my hair dry with the towel.

Three missed messages.

> Laurel:
> Holy shit, you have the whole series??
> *I'm almost done with book one and don't have two*
> *If I promise not to dogear the pages, can i borrow it*
> *tonight?*

I couldn't help smirking. Laurel might have been quiet on the outside, but a little fucking book nerd lurked under that mousey exterior.

> Spencer:
> I suppose I can lend it to you, since you asked so nicely

I'd already hit send when I realized the flaw in the plan. The track was covered in blood and I couldn't precisely drag her down there to either get suspicious or to be attacked by the predators that had surely found the carcass by then.

I looked down, standing stark naked in my living room, then around at the low-level chaos of the house. Then I laughed at the irony of inviting a human into *my* home. Oh, how the tables had turned.

> Spencer:
> I have to stay close to home though, on call for work

God forbid she ever asked in any detail what I did for work. I didn't have much of a lie prepared beyond *remote IT guy,* all based on a job listing I'd found online. The facade would fall apart quickly if she asked even a couple questions. I could use a laptop, but it didn't mean I knew a fucking thing about how it worked inside.

I sent my address to her and swallowed back the odd sense of insecurity. She was harmless, yes, but no one had come inside this little cave of mine *ever*. It was risky. Opening the fridge was enough to destroy things, let alone if she asked for something to eat, or interrogated my lack of normal kitchen fare. Hell, if she looked hard enough, she might notice I didn't own *sunglasses*.

But what was the worst that could happen?

At best, I'd kill a few hours with someone tolerable after years alone.

At worst, she'd be another body to bury in a shallow grave in the woods.

The knock came a half hour later. I hadn't heard a car pull up, and the noise startled me. Luckily I'd had enough time to get rid of the empty bottles and get dressed, which hopefully would give the impression that I wasn't an unhinged maniac.

Just a bloodthirsty killer, but who was keeping track of that?

I opened the door to find Laurel with her hands jammed in her pockets and her coat zipped up past her chin. The air outside was frigid, and I let her in quickly.

"Jesus fucking Christ, oh my god." Laurel was shivering as I closed the door. "Good fucking thing you weren't any further from the house or I might've turned into a popsicle."

I looked out through the curtain. "You didn't drive?"

"Nah, I'm just down the hill." Laurel had started to unzip her coat. "Turns out we're basically neighbours. This makes a lot of sense, though."

I cocked my head at her. "Makes sense how?"

"You live in the old Murray house."

I looked down at Laurel, surprised. "How could you *possibly* know that?"

Laurel bent over to untie her shoes. "Because my mother's friend was married to the brother of Daniel Murray, and when he passed away, his wife went to live in the old folks' home in town. They had a hell of a time selling the place 'cause no one had kept it up, and then suddenly they had a buyer. Mom said they bought it sight unseen and the person was from Away. I never heard anything about it after that."

I baulked at her like she were some kind of fortune-telling machine. "Jesus Christ, that made almost no sense."

Laurel shrugged. "Small town shit, that's all. Word travels fast and everyone knows everyone."

I shifted my weight, looking at her incredulously. "Well, since you know so much about it, I assume you don't need me to show you around."

"Nah. I don't actually know the Murrays; I just know *about* them. Again, small town shit."

The thumping of little feet came from further in the house, and by the time I looked up, Spectre was racing toward us.

Laurel's face lit up. "Oh! Who is this?"

I bent down and scooped the cat into my arms, holding her like a baby. "This is Spectre. She *would not* stop screaming outside my front door until I took her in. She loves to be scratched on the chin, if you're so inclined."

Laurel closed the space between us to scratch Spectre's chin, and the scent of her skin filled my senses. She smelled mostly of floral shampoo and lightly of perspiration.

"She's beautiful." Laurel looked up at me, smiling. A blush rose in her cheeks and she looked away quickly. "Oh, she's purring."

Spectre's purr hummed through my chest. Aside from music, it was the closest sensation I'd ever have to a heartbeat again, and it never failed to make me feel odd inside. Content to know how happy she was, and also hollow at the same time.

Pushing back that well of feeling, I put Spectre down. "A tour is in order, then, I suppose."

Laurel gave Spectre a last scratch on the head. "Lead the way."

I gestured to the room. "This, as you can see, is a living room."

Laurel pointed to the couch. "That's a couch. That's a TV," she said, pointing at the TV with a shit-eating grin on her face.

I glared at her.

"What? I thought we were naming obvious things." Her eyes were mischievous.

I let out a deep, playful sigh but couldn't help smiling along with her. "All right, be sassy. I'll have you know I do all my best lazing on that couch."

As Laurel took in the room, I found myself keenly aware that I'd never really hung anything on the walls or added all that much character to it. Sort of like most of the rooms, actually.

I led her to the doorway on the right. "This is the kitchen."

Laurel let out an interesting little noise, her brow furrowed.

"What?"

"Oh, nothing. I just—well, it's my job to notice things about houses. I fix people's homes for a living. Your cupboards are going a bit wonky over there." She pointed to the set above the stove, and indeed, they'd seen better days. They seemed to be separating at the corners, as if something was pushing the pieces out of alignment. Whatever the previous owners had done when they'd built the place, not all of it was standing up to the test of time.

I laughed. "Are you going to critique everything in my house?"

"I've already counted six things I'm itching to fix, if I'm honest. But that's a me problem. I can't help but see the work." She tapped her temple. "Can't turn it off. It looks nice, though. Love the colour."

The kitchen was compact: a fridge on the left, a stove on the right, and white cupboards in between. The countertops were a grey marble, and the walls had been painted a pale blue. Considering I only used the kitchen minimally, it did actually look like something a person would be reasonably happy to cook in.

I opened my mouth to offer her a drink, but swiftly closed it again. Very old habits died hard, it seemed, and I could neither open my fridge for her to see its contents, nor offer her a glass of fresh coal-laced tap water. All I had that was potable for a human was wine, which might come off as a ploy for a dozen things. I'd personally used it plenty in order to get someone pliable enough to taste.

Instead, I held out my hand toward the door. "Onward."

Laurel led the way back to the living room and waited as I passed and took her down the hall leading off of it. "The bedroom and bathroom are up there," I said, pointing to the staircase. "And *this* is the star of the show."

The library was the part of the house I did care about. The room was relatively large and was wall-to-wall bookshelves. I'd only filled half of them, but it wasn't for lack of trying.

"Holy shit." Laurel's mouth was wide open as she walked into the room, seemingly pulled by magnetism. She slid her hands along the shelves and, when the wall ended, circled around to feel the fabric on the ratty old velvet lounging bed I'd once rescued from the side of the road. "This is all beautiful."

Most of the bookcases held novels of all ages. Some were old and musty, but most of those were ones I'd read decades ago and had wanted to revisit. A fair few had been found in thrift stores that were open late in the winter months, when I could visit and peruse for a few hours at a time—which was an option closed to me in the summer. Then I had to rely on online purchases that would arrive and torture me from the other side of the door, bathed in sunlight during delivery hours. But I wasn't bitter about *that*, no.

"What's this? Is that—?"

"That's my collection of cassette tapes. I have over two hundred." A fact I felt justified in being rather smug about.

Her face was incredulous. "But…why?"

I shrugged. "I don't know. I like them. I've always loved it. There's something visceral about their delicacy, and the way we interacted with them in their time. Rewinding them with pencils and recording over them in layers to make new mixtapes. Stealing things from the radio in a time when it was the only way to hold on to songs. Knowing that if we didn't act fast enough, we may lose out on it forever."

"God, how old are you?" she said, laughing.

I laughed as well, until I realized she was actually waiting for an answer. "Thirty-one," I lied. It's what I'd been, once. Before I died.

Laurel moved on, seeming satisfied with the answer. And why shouldn't she be? It wasn't as if she were going to guess the unlikely truth. "Right on the cusp of the end of cassettes, like me. I had some, but not a lot. CDs fixed that issue." She ran her hands across a large cassette player that sat on one of the shelves, clicking eject on both tape decks and closing them again. "So you don't have a music streaming service, then?"

I scoffed. "Of course I do. I'm not a purist. But I like to make my own tapes for the car from time to time—don't look at me like that. My car is from this century. I've just got an adapter. These—" I gestured to two shelves in the middle. "—are all ones I made myself. The rest are whatever caught my eye somewhere."

Laurel looked up at me, curiosity in her eyes. All she said was "Neat," but I felt she actually meant it.

She went back to scanning the books, likely on the hunt for the sequel to her precious fantasy book. I let her look, marvelling in the fact that someone stood in my home for the first time since I'd moved in. It felt like a dream. I'd chosen the solitude, yes, but some days were easier than others. Sometimes it dawned on me how truly alone I'd made myself.

I deserved to be, though. To be in hiding, mourning what I'd lost. So much had gone wrong, and so much of it felt like my fault. On the good days, fault wasn't the right word. Guilt. As if I could have done things differently. Spoken up, made different choices, *anything*. And some days were so full of grief that it was hard to imagine anything else. But they were fewer than they had once been, and some part of me had been lonely enough to invite this woman into my home.

Perhaps I should've kept playing it safe. Shouldn't have let her come over.

Maybe I should simply eat her and get it over with.

She was right there. It would be so easy. Break her neck, drink her, and go back to the darkness.

"Oh my god."

The haze of my wicked thoughts parted and I came back to the present, where Laurel was holding up the book she'd been searching for.

"Here it is." She was staring so intently at it, flipping through its pages as if it were lost treasure. "Oh, it's so much prettier in person."

"You're the one who reads ebooks like some kind of monster."

"Do not start. Not all of us get a whole library, Spencer." But she already had the book tucked under her arm and was back to browsing the spines like she was at a bookstore.

"Well, now you have access to an entire library, so long as you don't dip my books in your bathwater." The words were borderline sultry. *Flirting*. It came on so naturally, the way it always had while I was hunting, but without that expectation of violence at the end.

Laurel gave me a mischievous grin. "I promise I'll just set my coffee cup on the cover."

"Oh my gods, don't you dare!" I scolded her playfully. The smile slid onto my lips too quickly.

No wonder I was acting like such a fool with her. She made it easy.

Kindness. She was looking at me with kindness and gratitude, and she had no idea how deep my pain went, or how many people I'd killed, or how I'd just debated her continued existence a few minutes ago.

What a darling woman.

Laurel looked at her phone. "Oh, shit, it's getting late. I should go. Thank you for this, though. I'll send you a photo of my shelves. Maybe there's something you want to borrow in return."

"Lovely," I said, trying to ignore the feeling of loss at how quickly she had come and gone. It had been nice to have some life inside the walls for once. The steady rhythms of breath and heartbeat and conversation.

I walked her to the front door. She had my book tucked under her arm, and when she set it down to start putting her coat and boots back on, I caught the quiet smile on her lips. It was such a stark contrast to the fear I'd seen there when Greg had grabbed her. She bent over to lace her boots and it occurred to me just how defiant she was being, putting herself in the same room with me. How much of a risk she might have been taking.

It was hardly my place to ask. Not even my concern, really. But I could respect the amount of courage it must have taken just to show up at my door.

And then I realized I'd been staring, and she was about to leave.

She stepped toward the door and looked back.

"Safe travels," I said, forcing a smile.

"Thanks again," she said, and closed the door behind her.

The house fell into silence again, the quiet symphony of her body gone. I stared after her, feeling the well of emotion rising to the surface again. The loneliness, the grief, the isolation.

I turned the music on to drown it out.

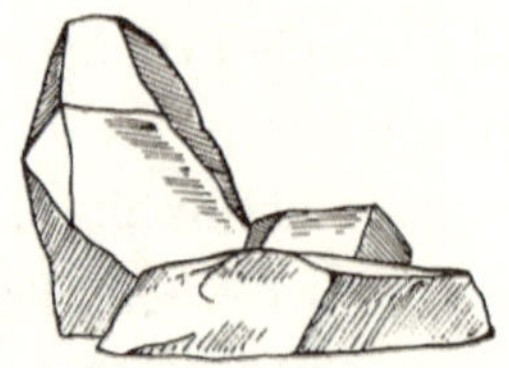

Elsewhere, Before

Emily was painting when the call came.

Her mother had sent her away for the afternoon. It was Valentine's Day and her parents had wanted to spend the day together. Which was fine by Emily because she loved painting with Aunt Heidi. Aunt Heidi would sit her on a stool so high she couldn't touch the ground and teach Emily how to paint multicoloured flowers with a single stroke of paint.

When the phone rang, Aunt Heidi got up to answer it. She went to the wall and picked up that old corded telephone—cell phones hadn't been invented yet, that would be years down the road—and stuck it to her ear. "Hello?"

Emily could hear her mother's voice from the other side, even from the kitchen counter. "Heidi, bring Emily home. He's leaving."

"Fuck." Aunt Heidi's face was lined with worry, but Emily didn't know enough to be worried herself. Adults had adult problems. Her mother was also very good at hiding things, but Emily wouldn't learn that for many more years.

Aunt Heidi spoke in a whisper, huddled over the phone, and then hung up. "Come on, sweetheart. We have to go home early."

"What's happening?" Emily asked, pulling another brush stroke across the page. She'd tried to load the colours like Aunt Heidi had said, but it never turned out as pretty. It wasn't her fault, though; she was only eleven.

"Mom just wants you to come home early; that's all. Come on, boots on." Aunt Heidi pulled the stool out from the kitchen counter and waited for Emily to hop down.

They put their coats and boots on together, Aunt Heidi stopping only for her purse and keys. They hopped in her car and pulled away from the house.

Emily didn't know it would be the last time she would visit Aunt Heidi. And if she didn't notice that Aunt Heidi was driving faster than she should have, Emily couldn't be faulted for that. She was only a child.

When they pulled up to Emily's house, Aunt Heidi brought her to the door. Mom had been crying. She was standing in the kitchen, her cigarette lit, her hand shaking as she smoked. Aunt Heidi left Emily's side and went to hug Mom.

"Are you all right?" she asked.

"No," Mom answered. "He's upstairs packing. Just…just go home. I'll call you later."

"Are you sure?" Aunt Heidi asked, rubbing her hands down Mom's arms.

Mom nodded. "I can't do this with you here."

And Aunt Heidi did as she was told. She left.

Emily didn't understand what was happening. "Mom? What's wrong?"

Mom took a last drag from her cigarette and put it out in the ashtray on the kitchen counter. Her long, curly hair was a mess around her face, and she had started to cry again. Mom crouched down in front of Emily. "Your dad is packing his bags and he's leaving, sweetie. I don't know what to do." She wiped the tears from her cheek. "He saying he's going to drive back home and—"

A door slammed upstairs and feet began to thud, stomping toward the stairs.

Mom stood up and pulled Emily out of the way. The thudding continued, and quick, so quick, Emily's dad was out the door, a suitcase in one hand.

Emily was so surprised she could barely speak. Everything had been fine, hadn't it?

But her mom was crying again. "Emily, go outside. Please. Maybe if you ask him to stay, he will."

She could do that. Of course she could. If she asked, Dad would have to stay. Wouldn't he?

Emily would only learn years and years later that he had never been capable of choosing her, not in that moment, and in none of the moments after. She would learn that it hardly made her special; she was one of a handful of secret siblings, and that man had never been able to stick by any of them.

Emily pushed open the screen door and walked the ten paces to the driveway. When she got there, her dad was lifting his suitcase into the open trunk of his car.

"Dad?" Emily whimpered.

Her dad cursed under his breath, shut the trunk, and looked at Emily. He didn't say a word.

"Please stay, Dad. You don't have to go." Emily started to wring her fingers together, knowing she couldn't do something as vulnerable as trying to hug him. She'd always been set apart from him, though she didn't quite know why.

Her dad stared at her, keeping his distance. His face was a rock, all hard grooves of anger. His eyes were so dark she could have sworn they were black, like he was full to the brim with it. None of that softened for her. And after standing there for a moment, he simply said, "I have to go."

And he got in his car and drove away, leaving Emily alone on the driveway, sobbing.

Emily would learn later that her dad had gone back to Penny Harbour. The place where he had grown up and learned to be hard and distant and unable to choose anyone but himself. Where he learned to take the scars given to him and pass them on to his children, bit by bit.

Part of Emily would stay standing in that driveway for decades. When she and her mother followed her father to Penny Harbour in an attempt to try again. In the moments when he kept not showing up for her. When she graduated and earned diplomas and moved to new places, and he opted to stay home. She would be stuck in that driveway when she chose new relationships with people who *also* weren't capable of choosing her and she couldn't figure out *why*. Just as she could never figure out why none of those people ever felt like they had both feet in the door.

It would be three more decades before she met the woman who made her feel safe enough to finally step off that driveway and leave it behind for good.

But Emily didn't know any of that yet.

All she knew was that her dad was gone, and she was alone, and she wasn't worth staying for after all.

CHAPTER SIX

Laurel

After a week, texting Spencer had become a habit. I'd wake up to some almost-morning message about how good or bad his latest book or movie was, I'd text some nothing about my work day, and for a few hours at night, we had a small overlap in our schedules. We didn't always have much to say, but it felt like the smallest escape between work and Greg and the chores that each took up so much of my time.

When Friday night hit and Greg had fucked off to his friend's place, I started to itch. Emma had an exam and MJ was out of town, but I felt like it might be the opportune time to harass Spencer into leaving the house.

Laurel:
Want to take a drive tonight?

I didn't have to wait long for a reply.

Spencer:
What do you have in mind?

Laurel:
I bet you've never been out to the cove
Be ready in fifteen, you're driving

When I arrived at his house, the car was already warming up, the thick layer of frost on the back window melting away in thin stripes. Spencer was just coming outside as my feet hit the gravel driveway, and he looked up.

"Couldn't have picked a colder night for this, could you?" he teased.

"And you couldn't have picked a thinner jacket."

He pulled at the bottom of his brown wool coat, which could at best be called fall attire. "Sometimes style has to come before comfort, darling."

I looked away. I seemed to do that every time that *darling* rolled off his tongue. "We'll see what you're saying in twenty minutes when you're next to the ocean with nothing to protect you but a cliffside."

Spencer gestured to me as he walked around to the driver's side of the car. "At least I won't look like a stuffed animal."

My coat was definitely a thick, overstuffed blue pillow, but we'd see who was laughing soon.

Spencer got in the car and I followed after. It was like any other Civic I'd been in: black interior, sporty cut, and not a lot of space in that back seat. But it was immaculately clean. Not a fast food wrapper or discarded paper straw in sight, unlike the cars of most men I knew.

"And where is *the cove,* princess?" Spencer connected his phone to the car and the start of an unfamiliar dance track came pouring out of the speaker. He turned it down and looked at me, waiting for a response.

"Princess. Yuck. Head into town, past the grocery, and up the hill. One right and then we're basically going to drive straight until we hit ocean."

"All right, I suppose I have no choice but to trust you," he teased. Spencer turned to look over his shoulder, despite the backup cam, and pulled out onto the road.

Spencer's driving was smooth. Careful but full of speed, somehow. Not taking corners quickly, but enjoying the space between them while he had the chance. He shifted gears like he enjoyed the feel of the car under him. Of course, if I were driving something that wasn't from 1992 and on its deathbed, I might have enjoyed driving that much as well.

We passed the store and were on our way up the hill when Spencer looked over. "You're awfully quiet."

"You know, it's occurring to me that I don't know what to ask you." I watched the road in front of us carefully, looking for the turnoff. "Like, yes, we've been talking, but not about *much*, you know?"

"Wait, I know this line from TV." Spencer put on a mocking imitation of a gruff man's voice. "*How was your day, sweetheart?*"

I laughed. "Fucking mediocre. I installed a new gutter on someone's house in the freezing cold, cooked dinner like I do every night, and watched Greg fall asleep in front of the game."

Spencer gagged. "No thank you. All of that sounds wretched."

"How was *your* day?"

That made him laugh. "Darling, I just woke up. My day was you telling me I had no choice but to go out to *the ocean* in the middle of February. I might be living a nightmare."

"What *do* you do? You've never said."

He shrugged. "IT for a company in Europe, which means having backward hours. Easier just to become a creature of the night than to get up that early."

I gave him a look of disbelief. "*You* work with computers?"

He looked back, mocking my expression, the fingers of one hand sitting dramatically on his chest. "Why would you think I *can't*? Are you stereotyping me?"

"I mean, I guess I am?" I admitted. "The few IT people I know are introverted gamers. You're a different kind of IT guy—oh, take this right coming up."

Spencer hit the blinker—not that there was a single soul around—and took the right turn. He started to speed back up, which was a mistake.

"I wouldn't—" But the car had already hit the bumpy fucking concrete and was jostling around like a paint shaker.

"What in the fuck—?" Spencer slowed down immediately and the car evened out, hitting the dozens of potholes with a bit more grace.

"Sorry, I should have warned you. This whole stretch is crap."

"It's like *cobblestones,* Laurel. Has no one ever paved out here?"

"I mean, they clearly have paved it exactly one time and never again."

When I looked over, Spencer was smirking, but his eyes were glued to the road, trying to find the best path through.

Eventually the shaking stopped and smoother pavement appeared. Spencer breathed a sigh of relief. "Thank the gods. My poor car."

"It'll be worth it, I promise." I pointed ahead. "Down this hill, and once we hit the bridge, pull off the road and park."

"As you say." He slowed the car as it coasted downhill and found a clear spot on the shoulder to park.

I fished a compact flashlight out of my pockets and put my mitts on. "Time to explore," I said, climbing out of the car.

Spencer got out and followed me across the completely deserted road. Out in the ocean air, the cold was so much worse than it had been when we got in the car. The difference was frequently ten degrees colder at the cove than it was in the Harbour. Underneath my shivering, the crash of waves could be heard all around, but I couldn't see anything more than ten feet out toward the ocean. The black ate up everything out there. I knew where to go, and the flashlight would keep me from breaking an ankle.

"This way." The slope down to the beach was steep, and I took it at a sideways slide, awkwardly galloping down the red-brown dirt. Everything in the bay was red-brown, the colour from the clay seeping into the water until it was the same murky colour and potent enough to stain clothing.

I cleared out of the way and turned to shine the flashlight on the path for Spencer. He seemed to be weighing his options, and after a moment he decided to jump down instead. It wasn't a choice *I'd* have made, not with how high up it was, but he landed just fine.

"You didn't tell me I stood a chance of dying out here," he said snarkily.

I made a face. "*Technically*, a decent number of people *have* died out here. We have the highest tides in the world." I pointed into the dark, where the outline of the cliffs sat in our path. "If we walk too far that way at the wrong time, the tide will press us up against the cliffs until we freeze or drown."

The smile dropped from Spencer's face. "And how long is that exactly?"

I checked my phone. "We've got three hours until the tide turns toward us, so it'll be dangerous in, like…eight hours. We've got more time than we need."

Spencer groaned. "Why is this whole area so fucked up?"

"Your guess is as good as mine." I shone the light toward the ocean. The waves were relatively close, and the sand was wet where the tide had receded in the last hour. We'd have plenty of room to walk along the cliffside. "All I can say is never fuck with the tide. Come on."

I started walking, and it took a moment for Spencer's boots to follow. Then he was beside me, his hands stuffed in his pockets, eyes ahead.

"So," I started, trying to dig up the conversation from the car, "what else should I know about you, other than that you're in IT? Have you got family? A boyfriend?"

Spencer chuckled. "That's one way to ask if I'm gay."

A knot of guilt coiled in my stomach. "Sorry. You don't have to answer."

A thick coal seam was in our path, and Spencer stepped over it carefully. A foot high, the black rock jutted out of the ground, running from somewhere under the cliffs and straight into the ocean in an endless, jagged line. Seams like that littered the beach and ran in strange diagonal lines in the cliffside, each layer a story about a chunk of history going back almost as far as the dinosaurs.

"It's not offensive, darling." Spencer eyed the coal seam for a moment as we walked away, but then turned his attention back to me. "Kids these days call it bisexual. I like people of all flavours."

"I see." I wasn't sure if I'd expected that answer. "Sorry, I know *some things* but the Harbour isn't exactly a ringing endorsement for diversity. I have a friend who's bi, but there aren't a lot of men running around admitting to liking men."

"It's a problem I've noticed, yes." Spencer opened the top button of his coat to reveal a knit sailor sweater. "I don't *actually* like wearing these; I just make sure I wear something from my straight male clothing collection when I go anywhere here." He buttoned the coat back up, adjusting his grey scarf around his neck. "And what are you, if you had to put a name to it?"

"Greg-sexual," I replied, not missing a beat.

Spencer scoffed. "You're what?"

I shrugged. "Greg was my only serious boyfriend and we ended up married. I've never spent time thinking about other people, because what's the point? I'm already trapped. So I don't know, not really."

Spencer gave me a curious look. "Have you ever looked at a woman and thought, wow, she'd be good to kiss? Even for a second?"

"I—I—well, look—" I flushed, unable to stammer out a real response.

"Excellent." Spencer tugged the front of my winter hat down over my eyes, blinding me for a moment. "That's all I need to know."

Flustered, I straightened my hat, stammering for something else to say. "You didn't answer my question. Who's in your life?"

He stopped smiling, his gaze trained on the tops of the cliffs. "No one."

"Oh." When he had said he was trying to be a hermit, I hadn't thought he'd meant it quite so intensely. "Is that…something you want to talk about?"

"Maybe someday. Not today. It's…" His voice was soft. Pained. "It's not a good story, darling. I had everything, and now I don't."

I walked beside him, letting the crashing of the waves take the place of words. The cadence of his voice was far too familiar to me. Some things no amount of words could fix.

Spencer stepped over a long piece of wet, jutting rock, and before I could warn him that he was stepping onto seaweed, his feet had gone out from under him. He landed on his back on the slippery, icy green slime, teeth gritted and hissing up at the sky.

I froze. It felt immediately like so many of the moments with Greg. The calm before the outburst. The moment just before I'd discover how deeply everything was my fault, and how much I was about to suffer for it.

Then Spencer started to laugh.

"What the *fuck* is wrong with this place!" Spencer stayed where he was, his palms over his face, howling in frustration.

I took a breath in relief. That reaction. A *laugh*. He was frustrated, yes, but not *at* me. And suddenly I could breathe again.

I carefully stepped around the seaweed, onto the steady rocks, and leaned over him. "Are you okay?"

His hands moved down his face so he could see, and his eyes were wide with shock. "Am I okay? I'm on my back on the freezing ground, covered in salty slime, in a place that will *soon be underwater*. I'm *peachy*."

I laughed and held a hand out to him. He took the help and peeled himself off the ground with a minimal amount of grace.

He turned his back to me, trying to peek over his shoulder. "How bad is it?"

The coat was soaked, and in some places, bits of seaweed clung to the fabric.

"Stay still." I started to pick the bits off with the flashlight as a guide.

"You're going to have to wash this. Ick."

Spencer groaned. "Listen, this has been nice but I'm officially demanding we turn around. I smell like the ocean and I'm *cold*."

"Yeah, no, let's turn back." The chill was getting inside my coat as well. Going to the ocean at night in the middle of winter wasn't a comfortable choice, but I couldn't say I regretted it either, not with that display I'd just witnessed. "I respect you needing to pack it in."

"I didn't say I needed to *pack it in*—what an odd turn of phrase, this place, honestly—but I'm done with the ocean for a while." He started to turn back, walking at a much faster pace than we'd come in.

By the time we made it back to the car, I was glad we'd turned around when we did. I'd started to shiver pretty hard. The windows had frosted over since we'd left it, and Spencer climbed in to immediately start the engine, cranking the heat up.

"Shit, shit, shit—" He hit the seat warmers for both of us and cupped his hands over the driver-side vents. Then he sat forward, looking at the gunk on his seat from his coat, realising what he had done. "I'm going to have to burn this seat to get the seaweed off it."

I laughed, taking off my gloves and putting my hands over my face, trying to warm my cheeks with my breath. "I feel like you have bigger problems. You look like an icicle." I put the back of my hand on his cheek, testing his temperature. "*Jesus Christ*, you're frozen. Do you even have a pulse?"

Spencer let out a dark laugh. "That would require me to be alive in the first place." He looked in the rearview mirror. "Nothing a few blankets and a movie can't solve."

"Oh, yeah. Well…" I stumbled over my words. The time on the dash read quarter past eight. I wasn't particularly ready to go home, especially knowing Greg would still be awake somewhere. But if Spencer was finished for the night, it wasn't like I was going to stay out by myself. "Maybe we can do something next week."

He looked at me. "You can stay for the movie if you want. No need to rush home to *Greg*."

"Oh. Okay." My cheeks flushed. I felt stupid, both for wanting to ask in the first place, and for wanting to stay at all. It should've been easier to ask for what I wanted, but by experience, I knew asking rarely got me anywhere good. "If you're sure."

"I'm sure, Laurel." Spencer turned to look at the back window and sighed. "Hold on. I'll clear the windows and we'll hit the store. I've got less than nothing to offer you in the way of food."

"Sounds good," I said as he climbed out of the car, grabbed the ice scraper from the back seat, slammed the door, and started to scrape the frost from the windows. The sharp tearing sound of ice peeling away made an appropriate backdrop to the confusion sitting hard in my chest.

With Emma and Mary-Jo, I knew what those relationships were. We'd been platonic soulmates since we were kids. Those bonds were tested against all the hardest things we'd ever lived through, and I knew that for what it was. With Spencer…I didn't have new people walking into my life, not ever. Something at his core was broken, but that was familiar to me. Companionable. It was how easily he laughed that felt strange. So quick-witted and snarky, and I wanted more of that.

Maybe if I tried to keep him around, I'd learn how to be that too.

Spencer

Laurel was quiet as we drove back to the Harbour. Whatever had gone on in that head of hers when I'd mentioned going home, she was still sitting with it. Her mood had gone sour, which left me frozen out for the time being as she stared out the window. I was tempted to ask, but she had let it go when I didn't want to talk about *them*. I owed her the same.

Besides, if nothing else, it didn't take much imagination to think she didn't want to go back to *Greg*.

When we pulled up to the grocery store, I stopped the car and grabbed my wallet from the console. Laurel hadn't moved. "Coming in?" I asked.

Her face flushed and she looked down. "Greg's cousin works a lot of the nights here and she's a huge fucking gossip. If I go in there, Greg will know what I'm doing the second she gets cell reception."

I stared at her. "And she really couldn't conceive of the concept of *friends*, could she?"

"Doesn't matter if she can." Laurel looked up at me, searching my face for something. "You look good; you know that. Greg took one look at you and saw a threat. Vonnie is going to see the same thing."

"Infuriating." I reached for the handle of the car. "Any requests then?"

"Hot chocolate and sugar donuts." She started to dig for her wallet.

I climbed out of the car, shutting the door before she could offer me anything.

The community store wasn't a place I was terribly familiar with, since I rarely felt the urge to *eat*. I pushed my way through the front door and into the violently fluorescent lighting. A small collection of carts and baskets sat at the front, and I snatched up a basket. The whole shopping experience felt odd. A modernization of something I hadn't really participated in for more than two centuries. Sure, I sometimes needed a light bulb or a new nail polish, but groceries were a step too far. As I walked down the aisles of the mostly empty store, I tried to remind myself how things were organized. Fresh foods in one place, freezers at the end, all the factory-made food somewhere around the middle.

Donuts. Where *the fuck* would donuts be?

With the cookies? Near the sweets?

How had I circled the entire store and not found them?

I'd managed to fill the basket with snacks and bottled water by the time I stumbled on the donuts *next to the bread*. Fucking humans never made a lick of sense. Laurel had probably started to think I'd gotten lost by that point, so I made my way to the cash register. The woman there—Vonnie, presumably—rang everything through without a word, snapping her gum as she went. I tapped my card, grabbed the bag, and returned to the car.

After tossing the bag in the back, I got in to find Laurel staring, a little smile on her mouth. "I almost went in looking for you, but I didn't think it was worth the risk."

I started up the car and pulled out of the spot. "So if I hadn't come back, you'd have just taken the car and run?"

"Pretty much." A slight bit of her frigid exterior had thawed while I was gone.

"My life is safe in your hands, obviously." I gave her a smirk and pulled out of the parking lot.

A few minutes later, we were back at the house. The second we were in the door, I set the furnace higher. "I'll get some blankets. You—" I almost told her to go put the kettle on, just in time to remember the blood hanging in the fridge. *Fuck.* She was getting under my skin, making me lower my guard. "You can choose something to watch. I don't care what. I'll take care of the rest."

Laurel pulled off all her winter gear and hung it on the hooks near the door, kicking her boots onto the plastic mat. Then she was on the couch, first digging through the bag of snacks I'd bought, and reaching for the remote next. "Good choices, Spencer."

From the kitchen, I looked back to see Laurel cramming a chunk of donut into her mouth. What a perfect example of a lady. It was oddly endearing, however, watching her flick through movie options with her cheeks as full as a squirrel's.

I put the kettle on the stove, pulled down two mugs—checking them carefully for dried blood—and went to fetch the comforters from the bed. Spectre was curled up on top of them, so I tossed her onto my shoulder, rolled up the blankets, and brought them with me.

Once I was back downstairs, Laurel spotted the cat and reached out with both hands, fingers wiggling. "Oh, gimme, gimme." I let the blankets fall and then put Spectre in her waiting arms. The cat immediately began to purr, probably because she wasn't used to her cuddling companion being *warm*.

I tossed the blankets over them, stole the hot chocolate mix, and quickly returned from the kitchen with two steaming mugs. True hunger was creeping in, but I couldn't risk trying to sate that with Laurel around. The last thing I needed was to scare off the one good thing I had going for me.

"Did you pick something?"

"You have two options." She scooted back on the cushions, legs folded underneath her and the cat on her lap. "Mindless action movie starring local celebrity The Rock, or this sci-fi Western."

I squinted at her as I curled up on the couch next to her, pulling my side of the blankets up and *praying* some of her heat would come my way. "*Local celebrity.* You are full of shit. I didn't think you were a liar, Laurel."

She waved a hand at me. "Look it up."

I did. And sure enough.

"His family's from here, even if he's not," she said, reaching for her mug on the coffee table. "We take what we can get."

"Fine, that movie, then. We can both appreciate how well he's aged." I moved to reach for my cup and shivered so deeply that Laurel noticed.

"Spencer, Jesus. You catch a chill or something?"

I cupped my hands around my mug. "I always run a bit cold. Normally it doesn't make a difference, but…"

Laurel nodded her head in a *come on* gesture. "Sit closer. I won't tell."

I moved closer, forsaking the hot chocolate and pulling the blankets up to my neck. Despite that she was also probably cold, she felt like an electric blanket to me. I should have felt guilty that I wasn't going to help make her any warmer, but I wasn't stupid enough to protest.

"Here." Laurel set Spectre on my lap, her tiny little body giving off so much heat. She pressed play on the movie and then leaned her head on the back of the couch, relaxing.

None of that should have moved me in the slightest. They were just moments. Small things, minuscule gestures. I'd slept in castles, run in the streets during revolutions, been loved so thoroughly that its absence had hollowed me out. Such little kindnesses shouldn't have left me staring at her, wondering where she had come from.

She had no idea who I was, and maybe that was *why* she was being kind. She didn't know about the monster in my chest that could end her without a thought if it had a *very* bad day. It felt like it should have been easier for her to notice that about me, considering how bloodstained my hands were.

Or maybe she was used to watching out for different kinds of monsters.

Penny Harbour

In the middle of Penny Harbour was a large plot of land, tucked in the centre of four long, sparse roads. It was a beautiful plot, covered in trees and full of squirrels and deer. Wild. Abandoned. And it made a good place to run, if a person was young enough to still find running a good way to pass the time.

In the winter, it was exceptionally good. The plot was hilly, covered in piles of stones taller than anything around. Megan and Wendy loved it there when it snowed. They could crawl their way to the top and stand higher than the houses across the way, their cheap snowboards in hand. Once they'd caught their breath, they'd adjust their snowsuits, kick their feet into their stirrups, and toss themselves down the hill. The wind in their faces for a moment, the snow whipping up around their pink, frost-touched faces. Screaming and laughing, and crawling back up for more.

Free as birds.

The land had seen so much blood that it hardly knew what to do with a pair of sunny children.

The stone had come up from under the ground a hundred years back, piled as high as it could go. The coal had come too, once. And then the holes had been filled in. The place had been left for dead. Left by everyone but those little girls.

The girls, and the twelve souls who never came back up.

CHAPTER SEVEN

Laurel

By the time a month had passed, Spencer had quickly become a ritual. The texting grew more frequent—still interrupted by his backward sleep schedule—and we made an effort to meet once a week for a movie or some other mundane thing. He seemed to have more free time than I did, and a flexible schedule, which left me grasping for straws about the shape of his job. But mostly I looked forward to seeing him.

In a sea of suffocating days with Greg, Spencer was a breath of fresh air. Just thinking of him made me smile, and how long had it been since *that* had happened?

I tried to put him out of my mind as I drove to my next client. Doug Furlough had called asking for help. Something had gone wrong with the frame around his window and their wood heat was pouring out into the cold. He'd patched it up as best he could until I could make it out to him, but that patch job wasn't going to last.

Problem was, Doug was in a tight spot. He's been in a tight spot for a long time. He'd promised to pay for my time, and I could honestly have used the cash. The cell phone and internet bills were coming due soon, and even though I often took a loss on supplies, I did try to get paid *something*. I just hoped he was being honest about it.

He wasn't always.

Doug was there when I arrived, which was a good sign. His house looked all right on the outside. Small blessings. It had vinyl shingles, which would last a hell of a lot longer than the wood ones, but it wasn't hard to spot the window frame that had rotted out, even from the truck. When he took me inside the house, I was certain his temporary fix was actually an attempt to do the work himself before he gave up and called me.

"She looks mighty rough, Doug." I scratched my head. He'd tried to pry some things away from the wall and left a lot of marks in the paint. Not to mention that some parts of the wood that shouldn't have moved had done exactly that.

"I know, I know. I made it worse. But you can smell it's bad wood, can't you?"

I could. A musty odour hung in the air. Who knew how long that window had been leaking water into the walls?

"All right, Doug, I'll get on it."

I worked for a few hours before Doug took off to get smokes. It was another hour before I realized he hadn't come back yet. Four more hours and a completed job later when I realized the motherfucker wasn't coming back at all.

Sure, he wasn't exactly going to be good at hiding from me. I knew where he lived, and I could camp in his driveway until he got back if I wanted. But it wasn't going to matter; if he was hiding on me already, chasing him down wasn't going to get my money. He didn't have it to begin with.

He's cheated you.

What a dirty thing to do.

Don't you deserve better than that, Laurel?

What if it just…burned?

Now those were some *ugly* thoughts.

Fuming, I packed up my truck and hauled ass out of the driveway. I'd skipped lunch and it was already mid-afternoon. Half an hour later, I was home and rage-texting Emma and Mary-Jo as I undressed for a shower.

Laurel:

It happens. I get it. He did what he had to do. And still,
I didn't even get comp'd for the materials, let alone paid
for my time. I wish he'd have just told me the truth

I'd have figured out a way to get it done for free

UGH!

When I got out of the shower, the message was still unread.

They were busy, or out of cell range, both of which were normal, but I was still livid.

I tried Spencer, sending the same message to him and asking what he was doing. But considering how fucking early it would be for him, I already knew it would be a fruitless endeavour. Still, I'd kind of hoped the buzzing of his phone would have woken him or something.

I got dressed, and even after that, no answer came. Not from Mary-Jo or Emma or Spencer. So instead of waiting, I grabbed an armful of bribery snacks, a dusty bottle of homemade wine, threw them in a bag, got in the truck, and drove the ten houses up the road to Spencer's place.

The feeling of stupidity chased me the whole way, but Spencer was more likely to be home than Emma or Mary-Jo in the middle of the week. He might not have been *awake* but he would *be there* at least.

I let that feeling chase me right to his front door. I rang the bell, staring at the curtain-covered window in the door and waiting for a shape to appear in it.

A sharp buzz sounded next to me, making me jump out of my skin. "Just leave it at the door," a groggy disembodied voice demanded from a tiny black speaker on the door frame.

I leaned in closer. It was one of those bell systems with the intercom and shit.

I pressed the only button on it. "It's Laurel. Wanna go for a walk?"

"Laurel?" Spencer groaned, the kind that comes with a stretch and a sigh from on top of a comfy mattress. "What are you doing here? It's the middle of the day."

"Yeah," I said, button held in. "I know it's not ideal timing for you, but I could use an ear and, like…here I am."

He fell into silence for a moment, and I thought I'd lost him.

"I'm coming down." A final click sounded, and then all I could do was wait.

After a small eternity, the lock clicked and the door opened slightly. It didn't move further, and I took it as an invitation, despite it being an odd one.

City people were weird like that.

When I got inside, the room was dark. The curtains were all closed tightly and Spencer was a shadow in the kitchen, tossing something into a garbage can under the sink.

"Don't clean on my account." I closed the door and waited for Spencer to finish in the kitchen.

He shuffled into the living room. His blonde hair was dishevelled, curling around his ears in a way that could only be described as adorable. It was clear he'd thrown on whatever he could find, and his pyjama bottoms were a wine-red silk number, while his top was a tight-fitting cropped black tee featuring an alt-rock band from the early aughts. The bottoms hung low on his hips and the top only came down to his ribs, showing off part of his stomach. It was a whole lot more feminine a getup than I was used to seeing men in, but it brought a flush to my cheeks.

He looked *good*.

"I hope I didn't interrupt any good dreams," I said, to break the silence.

He rubbed the sleep away from his eye with the back of his hand. "You did, actually. I was raiding the closet of a princess and found, like, thirty pieces I was going to steal from her. Felt a lot like a fond memory I have."

I laughed. "Well, I'm sorry to interrupt your thieving but I'm an anxious mess and I was thinking maybe we could go for a walk."

Spencer put his palm up to cover a wide yawn. "I can't. I'm exhausted. I only went to sleep a few hours ago."

I looked at the time on my phone. "You stayed up that late?"

"Yeah, Laurel, I did." A tinge of annoyance was in his voice. "Normally no one comes looking for me in the middle of the day and I don't need to worry about it."

I sat down on the arm of his couch. "I'm sorry. I don't want to bother you. I'm just having this really shitty day and I could use the company. But if that's not the kind of thing we've got going on here—"

"That's not what I said," Spencer interrupted.

"I realize I'm probably asking for this huge favour, and you'll be tired for work…I just…A job went sideways today and I was really banking on *not* being completely in the hole this week. Greg is going to be furious when he finds out, and I don't know…" I looked up at Spencer, whose face had softened as I spoke. "You've been kind of this safe harbour for me in the last month, so maybe it's overstepping, but I'm asking to call in a favour today."

Spencer sighed, his shoulders sagging. "Laurel…I can't go out there with you. I could—"

"No, it's fine." I stood up, feeling furious at myself. All the years with Greg had taught me not to ask for anything, and I was stupid to think it would be different with Spencer.

He doesn't care about you, Little Laurel.

You were just a bit of fun for him; that's all.

Something to kill time.

In what world could a pretty thing like that want anything to do with you?

"I'm going to go," I said, turning for the door. "This was a mistake."

"Laurel, you don't—"

I opened the door to walk outside, letting the light into the darkness of the house, but was stopped short. A scream had ripped from Spencer's throat from behind me and I turned to find him on the ground, backed into the shadows and curled into himself.

It hadn't been the sound of someone who had been startled by bright light in a dark room. It was pain, *real pain.*

Spencer was holding his arm against his chest, hissing, tears running down his face as the fresh burn on his arm smoked. He had thrown himself against the wall, out of the way of the shaft of light. The skin on his arm was charred and red, like he'd stuck it into a fire elbow-deep and just let it sit there.

I moved out of the doorway, heading toward him, the light from outside washing across the floor in a thick beam. "Holy fuck, Spencer, are you—"

When he looked up, his grey eyes had gone blood red, and his pained snarl had fangs.

I stopped short.

"Fuck!" He pressed himself against the wall, the light at his feet, like he was terrified of it. "Laurel," he breathed. "I—just wait. Let me explai—!" He cried out again, curling his body over his injured arm.

A burn. He'd been burned. The emergency script in my head was warring with the absolute insanity of what I was seeing. "You need an ambulance," I said, barely hearing myself.

"No!" Spencer pulled himself onto his knees, desperation on his face. "Do *not* do that. Let me explain. Please."

"What happened? I just turned around for a second…" I turned to look at the door, tracing the beam of light running across the floor, all the way to Spencer, who was trying to hide from it. The world went fuzzy around me. Like I wasn't in my body. "What's wrong with your face?"

Spencer's tongue went out over his teeth and he heaved a breath, leaning forward onto his uninjured arm. "Fuck."

Spencer

It burned. It fucking *burned*. I'd been hit by sun before and it wasn't like a person *forgot* what that felt like, but it had been a hell of a long time. I wanted to let out a litany of curses, but I knew that look on Laurel's face. She was about to bolt.

I had to keep my composure.

Her heart. It was racing. She was poised to run, and if she did, I couldn't follow her out there. Not to dissuade her, not to protect myself from whoever she might tell. It would be over. But more than that, more than the fear of what she might do, I didn't want her to *go*. I could build this temple of grief again somewhere else, but she had quietly become someone I didn't want to lose.

"You wanted a favour, right?" I breathed, trying not to let the searing pain coat my voice. Trying not to give her anything to activate her internal alarm bells. She was so deeply wired to protect herself already. "I'm asking for a favour now too. Can you give me that?"

She hesitated and I wasn't sure the words were even reaching her. "What do you want?"

I didn't know, not really. The situation was beyond lying. What was I going to tell her? That I'd burned my arm on the stove the second she turned around?

"I'm going to stay right here, and I'm going to ask you to sit in that light and just listen. Can you do that?"

Laurel stared at me, her arms wrapped around herself. Then she nodded and slowly sat down.

I glanced down at the burn on my arm and immediately felt queasy. Looking at it only made the pain more real, and no matter how many times

I'd been seriously injured over the centuries, it never made me any more willing to see the inner parts of my body.

I had to figure out how to turn on the charm enough to disarm her. I'd done it with people who trusted me less and in much worse situations, but this *mattered*.

"This is upsetting. I know that." I did my best to hide the wound on my arm without pressing it into anything, but I couldn't do much about the eyes and fangs, not while I was in that much pain. "Just think about the cove for a moment, all right? Or the walks in the woods. The movies. It's me. I'm still me. Do you believe me?"

She was staring at me, not saying a word.

"We were on that beach, and it was freezing, and I fell on that rock," I tried, practically begging her to say something. "I hated it, but it was more fun than I'd had with someone in years. And we sat on that couch together and watched bad movies, and you kept me warm. So I'm asking you to come back to me, and just hear what I have to say."

Laurel blinked several times in slow succession. "Spencer."

"Yes?"

"Tell me what happened. Right now."

I sighed. Telling wasn't sufficient. It never had been before, and it wouldn't be now. So I stayed as close to the wall as I could, and with her eyes on me, reached out for the beam of light with the same arm I'd already burned.

The pain was instant, and I recoiled, holding my hand up for Laurel to see. "That—" I huffed, the tips of my fingerings sizzling like they'd been in a frying pan. "—is what happened."

Laurel's hands had gone up over her face, only her eyes visible over her fingertips.

"I don't work in IT," I confessed. "I don't have night shifts. Those are lies I have to tell. I can't be in the sun because of *this*."

"What *are* you?" she asked, horror in her voice. "Do you have, like…a fucking allergy or something? This—no. What kind of fucking *allergy* would char you to a crisp?" Her face turned green as she said it, her mind trying to rationalize what she was saying at the same time.

I licked my lips, looking away. "Do you really want to know?"

Laurel stared at me, her face hard and unreadable. She didn't answer the question. "How? How is this real?"

I took a quick glance at my arm. Already the burn was healing, but it would be desperately slow. Two nights at least, especially if I didn't go back to sleep. I looked back at Laurel. She was watching my arm too.

"I don't know, Laurel. It just is. I wish I could give you a better answer than that."

She sat there for a long time, unmoving. Unspeaking. Long enough that the beam of sun had started creeping closer to me, and I had to shuffle carefully back. Not so quickly as to scare her, but I couldn't really afford more burns. But her heart wasn't racing anymore, and I counted that as a win.

When she finally spoke, her voice was controlled. Practised. "So the sun burns you and you only go out at night. And you have fangs."

"Yes." I swallowed. The hunger had been building since shortly after I'd been burned, and with as long as we'd been sitting, staring at each other, I was starving. I needed to drink so I could start healing the wounds. If I didn't do it by choice, eventually my body would choose for me. I couldn't exactly risk getting up, though, not with her so skittish.

"Spencer—" My name on her tongue came out like a dark laugh. "You're not. You can't be."

Finally, we were getting somewhere. "And if I was? What then?"

"I…I don't know."

I sighed, the hunger getting the better of my patience. "Here's what I'm going to do. I'm going to get up. I'm going to get my breakfast and come back to this exact spot. And you'll stay safe in the sun because I can't touch you there. Does that work for you?"

She thought about it for a moment and then nodded.

I got up very slowly, using the wall for support. Every movement irritated the burn, despite how close I kept my arm to my chest. I rounded the corner to the kitchen, reached into the fridge, and came back with a bag of blood. I debated whether or not to empty it into a cup. Would the bag scare Laurel too much, or would it convince her I was telling the truth?

I decided she could handle it.

And then I crept back to the living room, keeping myself pressed against the wall, and settled into the same spot on the floor.

"That's an IV bag of blood, Spencer," she whispered, her eyes wide, her hands returning to her face.

"It is, Laurel." I brought the bag up to my lips, then paused. "You don't have to watch." I waited until she turned her head, and then bit into the bag directly. It was a bad idea to drink as much as I'd need to heal quickly. I'd gotten more rations a week ago, but my source wasn't always consistent, and if I wasn't careful, they might disappear quicker than I could handle. I drank slowly, trying to pace myself. Willing myself to be sated before the end of the bag, as if it had ever worked before.

Laurel's head began to shift, slowly, turning until she was looking right at me. Watching me drink. Her eyes were intense, her breathing long and concentrated. The fear had become fascination, if I were to have taken a guess.

When I finished, the bag was flat, only a few meagre lines of red in the air-tight plastic. I licked my lips, then the front of my teeth. I didn't want her to see some blood-soaked monster, even if I was one. "You didn't have to look."

"I think I did," she said tentatively. "To know it's real."

"And?"

"It's real."

I took a deep breath, trying to relax just a bit. Dropping the empty blood bag on the floor, I kept her gaze. "Do you feel safe enough to close the door and come in?"

"I think so," she said. But she didn't move.

"This floor is hard on the ass, darling. I'm going to the couch." I started to get up again. "Join me when you're ready, or stay there. Makes no difference to me." It didn't, not really. But I did hope she'd choose to trust me.

I settled on the couch, lying my head in the crook between the arm and the back, my legs curled on the cushions. I closed my eyes and tried to breathe through the pain. Not that I needed the oxygen. I just had no other options. I could feel the blood working, though. It would help. Just not quickly enough.

"Ask me what you need to know," I breathed.

"Why haven't you killed me?" she asked immediately.

I laughed. "Because when I'm not hungry beyond reason, I have self-control. Which is enough, but also not the real answer."

"What's the real answer?"

"You're not allowed to take this personally."

She was quiet for a moment. "All right."

A wave of pain hit; I gritted my teeth through it and then answered. "Everyone here tastes like shit."

An awkward laugh rose up from across the room. "And why is that?"

"I don't know. I have a guess. People's blood generally tastes like their diet or their lifestyle. There are salty people, lean people, rich people. Sick people taste sick. Anyone I've tasted from too close to this place has blood that's gritty and off-putting. The animals less so." I paused, thinking better of what I was telling her. "I can be more detailed if you like. Or I can stop."

"No, that's...that's sufficient for now." Her heart had picked up pace slightly. "So you don't want to eat me because you think I'll taste bad."

"*Laurel.*" I looked up to find her standing, her hand on the front door, starting to push it shut. Staying. "I think you're good company. Maybe your blood saved you at the start, but not the nights after that. You're...I like having you here."

Laurel pushed the door until it clicked in the frame, and then slowly made her way around to sit on the opposite end of the couch. "When you were cold at the cove and couldn't get warm..."

"I'm always cold." I reached out as far as my arm would go without sitting up, letting her touch my hand. She did, and pulled her fingers back quickly.

I put my hand down and the pain jolted up as far as my shoulder. I recoiled, pressing my back into the couch, waiting for the moment to pass.

When it did, I finally felt Laurel's hand on my leg, squeezing like she was trying to offer me some kind of comfort. And her eyes. Guilt and pity and concern written across her. I looked at her, leaning toward me instead of away. Who was this foolish woman who turned *toward* monsters?

She looked down, and her mouth turned into a deep frown. "I did this to you."

I started to wave it off, but with the wrong hand, and the pain shot up my arm again.

"I'm sorry. I really am." Her eyes traced from my wrist to my elbow and then found my face. She was studying me. Taking me in like I was some exotic creature. Which I supposed I was. "I wouldn't have hurt you on purpose."

I swallowed. Her touch, her words, the way she looked at me...It was with a kindness I hadn't felt—no, one I'd stayed far away from—for a long time. It created a storm in me, and my vision blurred. I didn't want to cry in front of her. I'd never be able to explain where all that hurt came from.

"I forgive you," I whispered, my eyes squeezed shut. There was nothing to forgive, but she didn't understand that. She didn't know this pain was a drop in the bucket. Forgettable. For her, it was probably the worst she'd ever hurt someone. But I'd been burned by the sun before. Stabbed and beaten and bled through the centuries.

What she had done was nothing compared to what had been taken from me.

And if she walked away now, she took with her what little hope I'd gotten back.

"Just…" I barely knew how to say the words. How to let her in that close when so much hinged on her answer. "Just don't go."

She didn't say anything. I opened my eyes, trying to gauge her reaction. Tears had welled in her eyes.

"I won't." Laurel adjusted herself on the couch until she was mirroring me, legs up alongside mine. She pulled the blanket off the back of the couch and draped it over our legs, then leaned her head on the arm of the couch. She didn't say anything else, just sat there.

I didn't know what to say either. But she had stayed, and that…that I hadn't really expected. It hardly felt possible. Maybe she would still run, once she figured out how deep this went. How the blood bags were the tidy version of my hunger, or what I was capable of when I inevitably lost control in front of her.

If she was a temporary thing, I would enjoy her company for as long as it lasted.

I pulled my feet up onto the cushions beside her legs and settled in, laying my head to mirror hers. I don't know how long we stayed like that. Hours. Her warmth radiated under the blankets, and the comfort of that lulled me until my eyes were fluttering shut. I felt like I had dozed in and out a dozen times before I found her standing, leaning over me, her fingers gently scratching my scalp to wake me.

"I have to go," she said. "If I'm not back to deal with supper, there'll be hell to pay. Will you be all right tonight?"

I looked up at her, trying to muster a reassuring smile. "I'll be fine. I've had much worse, darling. Come back tomorrow?"

"Yeah," she whispered. "I'll come back tomorrow." She nudged me until I lay out properly across the couch, and then pulled the blanket up to my chest, my burned arm above it. Then sleep was pulling me under again.

I didn't even hear her slip out the door.

CHAPTER EIGHT

Laurel

Lying in bed that night, staring up at the ceiling, I felt removed from my body. Floating somewhere in space. Greg was snoring next to me, completely unaware of me or that everything in my life had suddenly tilted on its axis. He hadn't noticed a thing since he came home from work. I'd gone through the motions of cooking and cleaning, barely present. And if he'd clocked that I was alive at all, I couldn't tell.

My mind kept slipping back to two things, over and over.

Spencer was hurt.

Spencer wasn't human.

While I had plated dinner, I'd thought about leaving, going straight over there to find out how he was. Then I had remembered watching him empty out a blood bag like a fucking Capri Sun. I had washed the dishes and found myself wishing I hadn't left, more guilty than I had words for. Then I remembered the red in his eyes and the fear they'd struck into me.

He wasn't what he had said, and yet…he was. Nothing about how he'd been with me had changed, even if *literally everything about him* was different. He was a monster…but that hadn't made him any more monstrous *toward* me.

Unlike *other people* in my life.

I couldn't even start to think about anything past that. It was too much, too deep. What he was. What I couldn't attach a name to, because he hadn't said it

109

and I couldn't stand to breathe that to life. Everything I'd known my whole life felt like it was standing on shaky ground, ready to topple at any moment.

That was a can of worms I didn't have the willpower to open. Not yet.

I carefully got out of bed and went to the kitchen. I had no purpose being out there, but it was better than lying restless in bed. I had said tomorrow, and I needed to stay away. To let Spencer rest and to give myself a chance to catch my breath. But the draw to go over there was keeping me awake. To fix and take care of things. To get rid of the guilt that gnawed at me. I was responsible for the burn, and I felt responsible for *him*. For leaving him, especially after he'd asked me not to go.

But I needed to protect myself too. Which fucking blew, because it wasn't the literal bloodthirsty man down the road I was afraid of. It was the one asleep in the bedroom.

I went over to the phone, charging on the windowsill. I gave it a tap. A new message.

> Spencer:
> I'm sorry I scared you
> Thank you for trying to understand

Was he awake? It was two in the morning. He'd have to be awake, if he slept during the day, right?

I picked up the phone to text him, except I didn't know what to say. I stood there, staring down at the screen, willing something to come to mind. Something to break the silence with. Nothing felt right. I couldn't use the same old platitudes I normally fell back on. I didn't *get it* and it wasn't *just fine*.

> Laurel:
> I hope you're okay

A few moments later, a photo came through. He was still on the couch under the blanket, one of my books in his lap, and a glass of suspiciously red liquid on the coffee table in the background.

Spencer:
Go to sleep Laurel
I'll be just fine

And maybe…against all odds…everything would be all right, actually.

When dawn had rolled around and I still hadn't managed to sleep, I cancelled my repair job for the morning. I was prepared to tell Greg I was sick, but he never bothered to ask. He just got ready and went to work without so much as a word. I managed to sleep after that, too exhausted to do anything else. I woke up well past noon and spent the day chasing reality in circles.

I couldn't force myself to relax or change my thoughts to something else. It was an endless loop, thinking about monsters and the world and Spencer in it. But what else was I supposed to do? He'd dropped a bomb on my life. Every few moments, another question seemed to creep into my mind. It felt like a black hole I was sinking into, further and further by the hour.

After supper, with Greg glued to the TV, I sent Spencer a text.

Laurel:
Are you awake?

A few moments later, he replied.

Spencer:
Almost. I have things to tell you.

I did the dishes, yelled that I was going to Emma's, and, receiving nothing more than a grunt in response, drove up the road.

Spencer was looking better when I arrived. He had on a pair of black distressed jeans and a dark grey sweater that hung loose on one side, his bare shoulder peeking out. It was something I'd only ever seen on a woman, but it made him look delicate in a way I loved.

The sweater covered his arm, however.

"How is it?" I asked, bending to take off my boots.

"Leave them on." Spencer came over to grab his own beat-up boots. "I thought we could walk. It's a good night for it." He pulled up the baggy sleeve of his oversized sweater. His skin wasn't raw anymore, but still mottled and red. "Right as rain."

In awe, I reached out to slide a finger over his skin. The burn itself was still warm, but the skin around it wasn't. He was cool to the touch, like stone. It should have been obvious… "Incredible."

"It's quite handy, yes." Spencer zipped up the side of his boot, tucked his tight-calved jeans inside them, and put his hand on the door. "Ready?"

I nodded and he opened the door for me. I went back out into the crisp night air, my breath immediately clouding around me. And Spencer…

"How did I not notice?" I wondered aloud.

"What?" Spencer looked at himself, trying to decide what was wrong.

I forced out a puff of hot air that misted around my face. "You don't breathe."

He chucked. "No, I don't. And even if I did—" He inhaled sharply, but his exhale resulted in no cloud of moisture in the air.

"I feel stupid. Very stupid."

Spencer turned, leading me past his car and into his backyard. "Don't. Why would you notice something all of you take for granted? You have no idea how many people have been lured away by vampires far less subtle than I am. We rely on you not knowing. It makes it easy."

"Vampire," I said, testing the word. "Fuck, that is just…I guess that's a word I'm using for reality now."

Spencer laughed. "I suppose it is."

I pulled the flashlight out of my coat pocket and lit the space ahead of us. It was hard to see what his backyard looked like, but it was clear he was taking us into the woods. As we drew closer to the trees, a path appeared, and he led me in that direction.

"So, what am I allowed to ask?"

"Anything you want," he said from the shadows beside me. "Start with something difficult. Challenge me, darling."

The way he said *darling* brought a flush to my cheeks. His voice was so… light. As if the revealed secret had freed him to finally let his guard all the way down.

"If you can't eat the people, why are you here at all?" I asked.

"Mm." His lips pursed. "I did ask for a challenge…" His voice trailed off, replaced by only the sound of his footsteps. "I'm here because of what I've lost."

I tried to recall what that might have been. He'd never been forthcoming with any of it, but he'd danced carefully around the subject of friends and family. "Is this about the people you won't talk about?"

"It is," he said quietly. "I'm here, hiding in this rusty old house in the middle of Penny Harbour, because it feels like exactly what I deserve. I've lost everything I loved most, and I'm still alive, and what better version of my own personal purgatory than a place where I can't ever be satisfied again? Always hungry, always alone."

"Wow, that's…that's really dark, Spencer." I didn't know how else to follow that up.

He laughed, maybe a little too hard. "Isn't it? I cut myself off from the world, starved myself other than what blood I can get under the table in minuscule little rations, and settled down in a nest of self-pity. Downright depressing."

My body had become significantly more tense since we'd started walking, and I had to remind myself to breathe. I'd asked a *much* more loaded question than I'd expected. "What did you lose?"

Spencer's voice was pained. "The great loves of my life. Unlife. Whatever you'd like to call it." As he spoke, Spencer guided us down the path into the woods, skirting rocks and roots I couldn't even see. "But it's too soon for that question. You don't know enough yet to understand the answer."

"Then start from the top."

"From the top…well. Being turned is a dangerous thing," he said. "Without guidance, a vampire is a beast. It only knows hunger. I woke up dead and alone, and without anyone to show me how to get by in the world. I killed mercilessly. It's not something I'm proud of. People like to talk about vampires losing their souls, but that's not quite it. It's the hunger. Nothing stops it. There is no version of me that gets to stop drinking blood. I can either do it with a clear mind and choose if that person lives or dies, or I can starve myself until I tear apart the first thing that comes across my path. And once you've given in to the hunger a few times, what's the harm in drinking someone else? Moral codes vary, but once you've eaten enough people, very little feels *worse* than what you've already done to survive. There are things, though, that I will *never* do."

"I feel like this would be a good time to ask you what your moral code is." I found I was hugging myself, leaving space between us without realizing I'd done it.

"What would you *like* my moral code to be?" Spencer was definitely playing with me.

The question felt like a test. "I'd like to not be eaten, as a start."

"A fair request." Spencer hummed for a moment, thinking. "I'm not going to hurt you, and as unethical as murder is by human standards, my other crimes mostly tend to involve theft and fraud. I used to have *a lot* of fun, but now I keep my head low. I need to eat, and I try not to get caught doing it, but unlike what I was when I was turned, I'm in control of myself."

The explanation didn't do all that much to uncoil the tension in my muscles. "What changed?"

"Violet," he said simply.

"Who was she?"

He smiled slightly, a twinge of sadness in it. "She found me in a pub one night. I must have been very obvious, because she walked right over, sat down in the booth next to me, and said I was going to ruin dinner for the rest of them. I remember being shocked she knew me for what I was, but she later told me how starved I looked. How hungry. That I kept looking at the people in the bar and practically salivating. She took me by the arm and walked me out to meet the others. And I stayed with them until the end."

I stumbled on a root and started to topple, only to be caught by Spencer's hand. He put me back to rights and I shook off the lack of balance. I stopped, shining the flashlight around. We'd stopped in a clearing, and at the far edge of it was a boarded-off mine shaft. I turned back to Spencer. "That was kind of her to take you in. Was she a friend?"

Spencer laughed and looked into the darkness. "I'm going to take a risk on you, Laurel, because you've done shockingly well with me being dead. I told you I have a thing for more than just women, but that's not all there is to it. Violet and I were together, after a time, but Astra and Willem were also my partners. My three great loves. We took care of each other. They showed me how to actually *live*. I loved them more than—" His voice broke, and he stopped talking.

It was hard not to show my surprise. I was just some girl from the middle of nowhere and I'd been given *a lot* of challenges in the last twenty-four hours. Things in Penny Harbour were conservative as hell, and if anyone out there was trying to have more than one partner, the whole town would've known. It wasn't that queer people were news to me. Hell, I loved a few and maybe *I*…no, nope—I'd just never known anyone quite *that queer*; that was all.

"I'm sorry," I said, trying to gather my thoughts before I looked stupid. "But they're not here and you are."

Tears had started to run down Spencer's cheeks and he hurriedly wiped them away. "I—I can't." He curled his arms around himself, his hands tucked into the lengths of his sleeves. He seemed so small in that moment. "Another day, please. You can ask something else, but not about that. I can't…I can't always come back from that."

I racked my brain for something lighthearted to ask. Something to change the mood. "Do you like vampire movies?"

Spencer barked a laugh, clearly surprised under his trembling. "Some, yes. They can be entertaining. But so many are patently ridiculous. Like centuries-old vampires falling helplessly in love with actual teenagers. In the scheme of how long I've lived, a teenager is practically an infant." His mood was changing slightly, the topic proving to be a good distraction. "What do they even talk about? She tells him about her geometry class and he tells her about walking the streets during the Black Death?"

"What?" I teased. "You don't want a pure, chaste virgin?"

"Disgusting." Spencer's upper lip curled in disdain. "No. If the *adult* I was sleeping with happens to be inexperienced, I have no issue with that. *That's* an opportunity to share. But I'm not prowling the streets, seeking out untouched flesh like it's some kind of trophy. I'm a greedy lover. I want to get something out of it, not just teach the other person what to stick where and at what tempo. Especially if they're *teenagers*." He made a gagging face and shuddered.

I pursed my lips, trying not to laugh at his angry tirade. "I feel like you have a lot of opinions about all this."

Spencer gestured to the world, exasperation on his face. "It took a lot of fun out of it, truth be told. People weren't afraid like they should've been after those love stories got in everyone's heads. Made hunting too easy. Look at you! I'm attempting to tell you about the *tens of thousands* of people

I've drunk from and you're still out here in the woods with me. It's not particularly intelligent, even if I appreciate it. I'm a *monster* and you're just here, talking to me like we're old friends. Like this darkness isn't a fresh new hell for you."

Something about the way he said that crawled under my skin. He was being so *flippant* and he didn't really even know me. Darkness, new to me? As if I hadn't lived through decades of my own.

How dare he?

How dare he speak like you're some innocent schoolgirl?

He has no idea what horrors hold your soul down.

You could show him.

The anger was so raw when it came up, so fast and volatile. "I don't think you get to say that kind of shit about me," I snapped. "Like I'm stupid or I don't know what evil looks like. Just because my horror show doesn't come with fangs, it doesn't make me a fool. I haven't had a *single* reliable man in my life since I was born, and I figured it out, even if I had to fight for it tooth and nail. Now I'm stuck with *Greg*. Even if you're a literal monster, being around a sarcastic vampire isn't half as dangerous as what's waiting for me behind my front door—"

"Laurel," Spencer interrupted, his hands up. "Slow down. I'm not trying to say you're stupid. It was a bad choice of words, all right? But *dangerous*— darling, has Greg hurt you?" Concern was in his eyes.

"He hasn't beat me, if that's what you're asking." I stared at him, seething. Daring him. "But he's been killing me for years, from the inside out."

Spencer sighed and sat down on the nearest stump. "Laurel, I feel very compelled to tell you—"

"What? What could you tell me that I don't already know?" My blood was boiling. "I know he's a bad person. I know I should leave. And go where, Spencer? My whole world is here. I've never been further than four hours from here in my *life*. He has the savings, the house, the paying job. When people talk about Greg, they say he's just *the nicest guy*. If push comes to shove, they'll back him up. It's not like somewhere else. If I leave him, everything else goes too."

Spencer looked up at me, his elbows on his knees. "If he doesn't kill you on your way out the door."

"Yes," I replied solemnly. "And maybe that."

Spencer sighed. "It's not my place to tell you what to do. Just because you know my biggest secret doesn't mean we really know each other. Not yet. But I will tell you…as many people as we ate, as many decades as we tore our way across countries, my lovers never laid a cruel hand on me. Not once. Even we have a line we don't cross."

I didn't know what to say to that. What *could* I say? Even murderous vampires loved one another more than my husband loved me.

When I didn't say anything, Spencer kept going. "No one should have to fight to be loved, Laurel. I—"

"No? You don't think so?" I gestured toward the town. "I feel like we say that *a lot* but what did any of us get taught? That's all anyone here knows, so far as I can tell. Men get taught not to cry and to claw for every ounce of love from their parents. Then they spend the rest of their lives throwing fists to win girls that they just stand next to like hollow shells, because they've had the feelings beat out of them. Or am I wrong?"

Spencer looked away. Sighed. "No. You're right. I can't even tell you how long it took to get that out of *my* system. I was long dead, I can say that much for sure."

Fuck. The look on his face…embarrassed and guilty.

I needed to breathe. The anger was misplaced; I knew that. Spencer hadn't *done* anything. He wasn't the one with his boot on my throat.

I tried to take longer and longer breaths, listening to the dark around us. The anger just had its teeth in me so deeply.

Spencer waited a while before breaking the silence. "But you're not ready to leave."

I shook my head.

"Someday you will be. And if he needs to be fended off, well…I'm stronger than I look." Spencer stood and put his arm around my shoulder. The proximity startled me, but he nudged me to walk with him. "And for now, I'll let you off the hook. Why don't you ask me something else?"

I tried to think. He was giving me an out. A way to change the subject. But what could I ask that wasn't going to drag us back into dark places?

"What if we just went back?" I wanted to lean into him, but all the tension in my body wouldn't let me. I was so rarely physically affectionate with *anyone*, let alone someone I was still getting to know. "I feel like I'm all questioned out."

"Now that I don't have to hide the fact that I own *absolutely no food*, maybe I can go get you a snack and we can settle in for a shitty vampire movie." Spencer's voice was absolutely patronising, but I could live with that. "I'll probably have to reeducate you, after all."

I huffed. "Are you serious? I was into vampires before vampires were *cool*."

That startled a laugh out of him. "Oh, is that so? My apologies. I'm sure you'll have something to teach *me*, then."

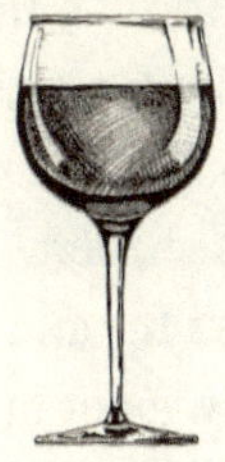

Spencer

A full movie later, I waved as Laurel and her elderly truck backed down the driveway. Something inside me was tired. An old muscle that hadn't been used in so long and had atrophied. I closed the door and locked it, and then went to the kitchen. Opening the fridge, I stared at the bags of blood inside and started to do the math. If it needed to last three weeks, divided by the number of bags…

Fuck.

I went to the phone in the window and found my contact.

> Spencer:
> It looks like I'll be needing to visit
> you sooner than normal
> A week early
> Can you make it happen?

I sent the texts and waited a moment. No reply, but that wasn't always a problem. Students had work and class, after all. And even sleep, occasionally. I put the phone away and started to drag myself up to bed.

Living on as meagre a supply as I had was going to cause issues. I could draw it out, but for how long? At some point, the hunger would start making choices for me.

When I got to the room, Spectre was right where I'd left her, curled in the unmade wreckage of my sheets. I collapsed onto the mattress and pulled her into my arms. She let out a little yelp, but then started to purr.

"That's right. Love me, little shadow. Daddy's tired."

I stayed there, curled around the cat, thinking.

She'd come back. Laurel had stayed and come back, even though I'd told her some entirely disturbing things.

She'd even been smiling when she left.

I pressed my face into Spectre's fur and breathed in the scent of her.

Everything about the last forty-eight hours was baffling. Laurel should've run. I should've been a fiery ball of ash in a field somewhere. And yet.

She'd had to go. It was late, and she couldn't have Greg noticing. But I had wanted her to stay. My phone was right downstairs, sitting in the window. All I had to do was ask if she would come back. She might have.

I groaned into Spectre's fur. "That's very stupid, Spectre. She's just a girl. A silly human woman. She's just a person who has been kind to me after decades alone, and I'm not…"

Not what?

"Nothing," I whispered to no one.

A noise sounded from downstairs. My phone.

I scooped up Spectre and ran down the stairs.

Holding the cat against my shoulder, I checked the phone.

> Laurel:
> I'll keep your secret. Good night.

I stared at the screen for a moment, unsure of what to say.

I sent back a little heart and put the phone down.

"Oh, Spectre." I nuzzled into her fur. "I'm falling apart, aren't I?"

Penny Harbour

A flick of a thumb. The hissing click of metal. The lick of flame. Brandon had stolen his father's lighter months ago. The guy had been in a fit looking for it at first, and had made Brandon's life hell, but eventually, he'd forgotten about it. It had been worth it. Dad always made Brandon's life hell, but at least that time he'd gotten something in return.

It was a snazzy old lighter. A silver Zippo where the top flipped up. It was cool to the touch, and Brandon couldn't help but touch.

He wanted the snow to melt. Every spring, when the sun made the earth warm and the fields started to grow back, burning season started. All around the village, it was burn or be burned. Anyone with land knew that.

Light the field yourself or some kid would do it for you.

Brandon hadn't lit a field before, but he wanted to.

It would be so easy.

So quick.

And maybe then…maybe if you destroyed something so completely, they would have to notice.

That voice had been there for so long, creeping into the back of his mind. Every time he went home to find barely a scrap of food in the house, or Dad asleep on the couch, or went days without talking to anyone, it came back with a vengeance.

Dad hadn't been the same since he'd been laid off. He acted so much like Grandpa sometimes. So fucking sad for no fucking reason.

Burn it and they'll have to see you.

Brandon stared at the flame in front of him, and through it, at the abandoned shed in a lost corner of Penny Harbour.

A little lighter fluid. A little spark.

Something wet was running down his face.

He wiped it away, to find that he had started crying, the back of his hand black with coal dust tears.

It was good no one was around to see that. Only pansies cried and he sure as fuck wasn't no pansy.

Brandon watched the shed burn, from top to bottom, black smoke roiling in the air, and only left when the rubble had calmed to a smoking husk.

CHAPTER NINE

Laurel

Rationing out my time became a challenge. No one knew about Spencer—at least, not in any tangible way—so it wasn't as if I could just tell people where I was. I felt like a double agent every day, hiding my whereabouts from everyone. If I told Emma and Mary-Jo, they'd assume they knew why I was with him so often. Mary-Jo would make pointed comments about sleeping with him, and I *couldn't* listen to that. And if they knew where I was, how long until I let something slip about *what* he was? How long until I made an offhand comment about his fangs or how I had to bring my own food because he didn't eat?

And then there was Greg.

Greg could *never* know.

So I'd started lying to everyone. I was sick; I wasn't feeling social; I was at Emma's or going to town. Anything but the truth. And people were irritated with me, sure. Even Mom was bugging me for a visit I never found time for, and I almost felt bad about it. But seeing Spencer felt like slowly coming back to life, and I hadn't done that in a very long time.

It had been two weeks since Spencer had taken me walking in the woods. I'd seen or spoken with him almost every day since. Mostly, we did nothing worth noting. Sat and talked, or watched movies. Listened to some band he was feeling especially passionate about. We started a co-op farm in a game and told each other stupid stories. Hours and hours, just existing in peace.

Each night I spent with him was a strange mix of things. With him, I could breathe. He was easy to be around. I didn't spend all my time desperately trying to anticipate his next move, or stepping quietly so I didn't disturb him. Sometimes, when Spencer caught me that tense, he'd do or say something disarming, and I'd try to remember where I was. Who I was with.

But with that ease came so much else. The guilt of sneaking around. The worry of being caught. The thoughts that swam through my head at being around so much of Spencer's easy queer nature. It wasn't *just* that the happiness was magnetic. It was that being around him was unravelling my life.

Ready for another session of horrible '90s movies, I pulled up to Spencer's house in the truck with a grocery bag of snacks. More than I would need for myself, in part because I liked to have options, and in part because Spencer didn't *need* to eat but had a penchant for snacking. He had definitely developed a taste for my Cool Ranch Doritos.

The door was unlocked when I arrived, and I let myself in. "Hey! I brought snacks. I—"

Spencer sat up from inside a blanket on the couch, rubbing his eyes. They were red with irritation. "Sorry. I lost track of time."

I kicked off my boots and went to the couch. The pillow he'd had his face on was wet. "What happened?"

Spencer shook his head. "Nothing."

I frowned. "Nothing new, you mean?"

He nodded, little strands of his blonde hair peeking out from under the blanket he'd draped over his head. Spencer looked like a sad little cat, and it was tugging at my heartstrings.

"Come on," I said, motioning as I spoke. "Sit up. I brought your favourite. Now get talking. Who made you cry?"

Spencer curled his legs up, leaning against the back of the couch, facing me but refusing to look at me. "I was thinking about them tonight."

I opened the blue bag of chips and passed one to him. Spencer took it and held it by one corner, like he wasn't sure he wanted to eat it.

"Do you want to tell me about them?" I asked.

Spencer didn't say anything right away. "If you want to hear it."

I curled up to mirror his position, pulling my sweater over my legs to cover myself better. The moment I did, Spencer unfurled the blanket from around himself and tossed it to cover both of us. He ate the chip and then wiggled his fingers, asking to be given access to the bag.

"I told you about how Violet found me," he started, his voice taking on a wistful quality as he spoke. "She was this daring little princess. So dainty and feminine, but she had a light inside her that could warm up a room just by being in it. Astra, they were as opposite to Violet as could be. Petite but full of wiry muscle. Stoic. Protective to a fault. Born to be a woman but more man than most I met. They *lived* for a men's suit jacket. And Willem. Sweet Willem. A rogue who was born into nothing and learned to take everything he needed. He loved roses and rich fabrics, and played the part of false aristocrat when the moment called for it." He paused for a moment. "They were everything."

"And what were you?" I asked before he could move on. "If they were going to describe you to me, what would they have said?"

A smile crept onto Spencer's lips. "The worrier, I'd imagine. I was always sure something bad was coming for us, which turned out to be a fucking *cosmic joke*." He scoffed. "But I could charm my way into most rooms, regardless of what kind of folk were inside. Helpful when we all needed strict invitations to get into any private residence."

"Oh, so that part's true!" I shook the chip bag in excitement. "You do need invitations."

"Yes, we do." Spencer reached for more chips. He gave me the most pathetic look, a handful of chips near his face, his hair mussed, and asked, "Do you still find me charming? Have I lost my touch?"

"Don't give me those eyes. You're doing that on purpose." Oddly, he was still charming, though not the way he probably meant. He looked sad, yes, but comfortable in his blanket, still wrapped in fuzzy pyjamas. Not alluring, but adorable. "So the four of you were quite a team then."

"Practically unstoppable, and *so in love*." He gave a sigh and it was so forlorn it hurt my heart. "I mean, we clashed; of course we did. Violet once stopped speaking to Willem for two months over getting us kicked out of the hotel we'd been languishing at." His face was soft as he spoke about the memory, his grey eyes glistening. "But there was never any doubt of our commitment to each other."

Commitment? What a joke.

You know as well as anyone that nothing lasts forever.

What made them so deserving of love when you are not?

Envy rose in my stomach like poison. What a stark contrast to my own life, where Greg couldn't be bothered to know where I was, so long as I was still his property. "I wish I knew what that was like."

Spencer gave me a pitying smile. "Don't you have that with your friends, at the very least?"

"With Emma and Mary-Jo? Yeah, I suppose so. When they have time." I licked the ranch dust from my fingertips. "But I leave them and go back home to the cavernous maw of Greg, and that warmth may as well not exist."

Spencer didn't say anything about that, and it was the kind of silence I knew all too well. No one ever knew how to pry you from the grip of the person you needed to leave.

"What happened to your people?" I asked.

Spencer closed his eyes, his legs curling closer to his chest. "It was 1982. We'd been in Switzerland for months, cutting our way through villages. We stopped in a place not far from the Italian border. Some of the towns in the mountains hold on to their folktales *very hard*. I remember thinking we had overstayed our welcome, but Violet loved being out there. It was hard not to do things for her. She had so much gravity.

"We'd all gone to sleep hours ago, drunk on wine from the bar below the room. Astra had wrapped her arms around me as I'd dozed off. Violet and Willem were across the room in the other bed. When I woke up, the room was full of smoke and flames." The first tear rolled down his cheek, followed by another. He still hadn't opened his eyes. "The room was as bright as the sun, flames licking the walls. Violet was screaming. The bedpost had fallen on her, and she—she was burning—"

I took Spencer's hand and he squeezed back with alarming strength. I hissed, a dull ache in my fingers, but he didn't notice. He just kept telling his story.

"Astra leapt over me to help her. She was stronger than any of us by far. We—we tried to find a way out. The doors to the room had been boarded shut, and by the time we broke them down, the building was threatening to collapse. It was the middle of the day. There was nowhere to go. People were cheering outside. Watching like it was a sport.

"I lost them in my panic to escape. I never found them again. Something knocked me out, and I was buried under the rubble for a week. I've been over that night thousands of times. They knew, I think. The town. They waited, and they drugged us, and they considered the bar to be the cost of keeping their families safe. Gods, I can't even blame them! We didn't make a habit of draining everyone dry, but when a whole town develops a suspicious amount of anaemia, some people catch on." Spencer's grip loosened. "But it doesn't change that they're gone, and I'm alone."

"You're not alone," I whispered, squeezing his hand again. Though I had a feeling nothing I could offer him would touch what he'd lost.

His eyes finally opened, and he gave me a sullen smile. "I appreciate that."

"That's a lot of time between then and now. Where did you go?"

"Everywhere. Nowhere. The first decade is a blur. I did anything I could not to be sober. Not to live without them. I looked everywhere for some kind of relief, but nothing came. And eventually I just…landed here. I couldn't run from it, so I decided I'd let it swallow me whole."

I waited a while to see if he would say anything else. He didn't. He just sat, staring at our hands, drawing circles on mine with his thumb. It felt deeply intimate, but I didn't stop him. He'd given me the most intimate part of him that he could: his pain.

When the silence went on for longer than I could bear, I cleared my throat to get his attention. He looked up, responding with a questioning little *hmm?*

"Do you want to watch the movie now? Take your mind off things?"

He nodded slightly and then shifted to lie down, his feet curled up next to my legs. I reached for the remote and turned on the TV, while he continued to try to get comfortable. When the movie was playing and he still hadn't settled, I grabbed his feet and urged him to stretch out over my lap. "Stop wiggling." I put my feet up on the coffee table and leaned back to watch, offering him the bag of Doritos again.

He didn't argue, and the wiggling ceased. His calves were cool against my thighs, even with the clothing between us, but I had a feeling he'd get warmer before long. He scooped out a handful of chips, staring straight ahead. The life had gone out of his eyes in a way that broke my heart.

Spencer

Telling Laurel about the others had been inevitable. Telling her how intensely, maddeningly hungry I was becoming…that was something I was avoiding at all costs.

Over the last two weeks, I'd *decimated* my blood rationing. Between the burn Laurel had given me and the bad weather that had made for slim hunting, I was really pushing things. I'd nearly killed a cow in someone's field the week before, which wasn't advisable. People always noticed when livestock started dropping dead. And as far as the rations went, I was down to a quarter of a bag a day, just trying to drag it out.

Even Spectre was starting to look like a snack.

I was all too aware of my phone silently sitting in the window above us as the movie played. I'd sent texts to the medical student who supplied my blood, one a day for the last week, and he hadn't replied. He was reliable, at least most of the time. University was expensive in Canada, and the promise of debt repayment could make a young medical technician get themselves into all sorts of shady business, especially when it was as simple as a few bags of blood skimmed off the top of the cooler. A grand a month bought me silence and blood and kept the kid afloat. An easy arrangement for everyone involved.

But since he wasn't answering his texts…

The hunger gnawed at me. Had *been* gnawing at me all day. I'd gone longer on less to drink, but I also hadn't been spending all my time next to a walking meal the last time it had happened. I wouldn't be able to hide it forever, especially not with the swell of emotion it always brought. The weaker I grew, the worse the thoughts became. Today it was grief, but what would tomorrow bring? Rage. At some point, it always came down to rage. When the starvation set in properly, I couldn't stop the hunger. I'd kill someone, no matter how bad they tasted or how much I liked them.

And Laurel…Laurel was too good a thing in my life to end up dead because I couldn't find other ways to eat.

The hunger was stealing everything already. Laurel's legs were beneath mine and I barely felt her there, my head was drifting so far away. To my loves, yes, and the sadness that came with them, but also just…away. Half-asleep, half-awake. It would be too dangerous for her soon. I'd never pushed it much further than this and still kept my wits about me.

While swords clashed across a battlefield on the TV—whatever fucking movie I'd agreed to watch, I had no idea—I prayed to whatever gods were still out there.

Please, let that phone ring.

CHAPTER TEN

Laurel

By the next night, Spencer still wasn't out of his funk. His texts were few and far between, and before I'd left the night before, he had been a few steps away from catatonic. Hard to talk to, impossible to keep his attention.

Grief was hard, I knew. When Dad had ditched us, I'd mourned him *so hard*, despite how little good his presence had brought us. And then when Pop had passed. And cousin Becky. Having someone torn out of your life could destroy you. I couldn't imagine grieving my three most important people all at once.

I'd only realized how lost in thought I'd been when Greg started trying to get my attention from across the dinner table. I looked up, dazed and slightly annoyed. Normally it was me trying to get even a sliver of his attention. Talk about the pot calling the kettle black.

"Fuck, I hate that. You just zone out and never fucking hear when I'm talking to you," Greg snapped. He'd nearly cleared his plate in the time I'd been in my head.

"Sorry. Just tired today. What did you say?" I set to work on my food, which I'd let go cold.

"I said don't wait up tonight. I'll be at darts late. Billy's bringing a two-four and it's probably going to get sloppy." Greg got up, leaving his plate on the table along with his cup and everything else he'd brought with him.

"Of course. Have fun." I managed to keep the spite off my voice, but not by much.

Wait up? As if you would bother.

When was the last time he waited up for you?

You could die and he'd only notice when supper wasn't on the stove the next evening.

Sometimes I found myself with the stark understanding that Greg could leave and not come back, and I'd be better for it. At least then I wouldn't have to do the hard work of telling everyone what a piece of shit he'd been.

I picked at my food as he stomped back and forth around the house, grabbing things and putting them by the door. My body sat hard as rock, tense and alert, waiting for him to finally shut the door behind him.

Fucking Greg.

My phone buzzed in the window. I went to check it.

Spencer:
Good morning

Laurel:
Good evening

I hadn't expected to anticipate the moment Spencer woke up, but I found myself doing it all the time. Whiling away the hours until sundown, no matter where I was or what I was doing. I could be on a job, standing on a roof, and part of me would still be clocking the sun on the horizon. And that day I'd been thinking about what I could possibly do to help him.

I might not have been able to take away his sadness, but I wanted to do *something* for him. I'd never been one to sit around and let things be broken. It was my job to *fix*. And considering how many things around Spencer's place needed fixing, that felt like a tangible place to start.

When I arrived at his front door, it was still light outside. The nights were getting shorter as winter faded to spring, and I was careful to let myself in without throwing the door wide open. As I closed it, Spencer scoffed from the kitchen entry. "What's all this?"

"I assume you're referring to my dozens of very handy tools," I said, showing off the toolbox in one hand and the overladen work bag in the other.

Spencer leaned a little too heavily on the doorframe. He was smiling, but he looked tired. Unhealthy, like his skin was losing whatever colour it had left. "Yes, I might be referring to that. And why, pray tell, have you brought tools into my home?"

"You have a dozen small repairs that need doing, and I'm going to do them." I set the tools down and pulled out a compact jar of putty and a spackling knife.

Spencer's head drooped. "You don't need to do that."

I moved toward him. "Spencer, you're not doing well. Anyone could see that. I don't know how to help. It would make me very happy to do *something*."

He opened his mouth to argue, paused, and then waved his hand dismissively, clearly too exhausted to fight me.

"Excellent. You can keep me company while I work."

I started in the living room, covering small holes in the plaster and leaving them to dry. Then it was on to the drooping door in the library that needed its hinges tightened. On further inspection, the kitchen cupboard was too far gone for a simple fix, but I was able to rip off the black-speckled caulking around the countertop edge and freshen it up. By the time I had done all that, Spencer had improved his mood just slightly, listening to whatever stories I could come up with to kill the silence.

"So," I said, cleaning the tip of the caulking gun, "Emma, Mary-Jo, and I decided to ditch the rest of prom and walk home barefoot around the Harbour. As we were walking, the fireflies came out, and the fields were *just beautiful*. We played Mario Kart until two in the morning, and honestly, it was one of the best nights of my life."

Spencer passed me the tool bag I'd asked for. "It sounds incredibly innocent."

"I'm sure you mean boring." I took the bag from him. "It can't stand up at all to the wild adventures of an old man like yourself."

The heckling sparked life into his eyes. "Old man? How dare you? I'm only 260! Give or take."

"What?" I dropped the bag on the counter and turned to look at him. "You made a comment about seeing the Black Death! From the 1300s!"

"That was a *joke*, Laurel. I'm not *a thousand years old*. I don't know any vampires who survived over six hundred years!" Spencer crossed his arms over his chest. "I don't look a day over thirty."

"Didn't you tell me you were thirty-one once?"

"*I look young, Laurel.*"

"Right, sorry! Sorry. You're so young, yes." But I couldn't stop smiling. It was the first life I'd seen in him all night. Figuratively speaking.

I put the caulk gun in the tool bag and picked it up, but being distracted by the conversation, the strap slipped, and the entire bag came crashing down onto my sock foot, wrenches and all.

"Fuck!" I hissed and pulled my foot out from under the enormous bag. It wasn't broken, but it was going to smart for a while.

"Are you all right?" Spencer's hand was on my shoulder, steadying me. "Come, sit down."

I hopped out to the living room, heading for the couch. Spencer held my arm for balance. When I plunked myself down and pulled off my sock, a sliver of discolouration was already appearing under my skin.

Spencer sat down beside me. "Let me see."

"No way! Those aren't clean."

"Please, you have no idea what the definition of unclean is. Try crawling through a sewer to escape an angry mob." Spencer gently took my foot in his hand and touched the places near where I'd dropped the bag.

"It's bruised, but it's not too bad. I'll live." I started to sit up, but he held firm.

"Lie back. You managed to hurt yourself on my behalf, fixing my home. This is the least I can do."

I started to argue, but when he began to gently knead the pad of my foot with his thumbs, I let myself melt into the couch. "Oh, well, fuck, okay," I mumbled.

Spencer's grip was strong, but he was holding back. He could tear a door off its hinges without trying; I was sure of it. And for him to be so gentle with me…it wasn't something I was used to.

A man who could hold power over me and not use it?

What would that be like?

Spencer

The one saving grace to Laurel's injury was that she wasn't bleeding. Had that bruise been a cut, there would have been no casual massage. Just a bloodbath and an endless supply of regret.

The hunger was too far gone, eating at my gut and my mind. And the beautiful fool thought it was just grief. I couldn't bear to tell her otherwise.

Laurel was all right, of that I was sure. Tenderness but nothing broken. No true harm done. And I had to ensure she would stay that way.

Watching her lying on the couch with her eyes closed, completely trusting me to be kind with her, I knew it was time for her to go home. It should've been impossible to earn the trust of a human, and yet here she was. And I was putting her at risk every moment she was near me while I was hungry.

As I pressed into the arch of her foot, a little whimper escaped her. It drew out a need in me so deep and twofold that I had to stop and force it back down. I was starved. For blood and touch and affection.

And there she was, so close.

Right in my hands.

"Spencer?"

She noticed. Of course she did. It was part of what she did. Notice the minuscule changes in a room, aware and ready to escape at any time. That happened to people often enough, when someone else made them into prey.

I set her foot down and tried to muster an apologetic smile. "I'm sorry, Laurel. I think I've reached my limit for the day. I appreciate everything you've done here, but—"

"Don't apologize, Spencer," she interrupted. She sat up and started to put her sock back on. "You look like death. Is there anything else I can do for you? If you just need quiet company, or if I can go get something for you, just say the word."

The loss of contact with her left me cold. I'd learned to crave her warmth—not just her body, but that kindness. I didn't *want* to send her home. I *had* to.

"I'll text you tomorrow. I think I'll be going to bed early tonight. I'm just…not myself." I watched her silently as she gathered her things and went to the door. Lying to her felt unnatural now that she knew what I was.

"I hope you feel better." She put her boots on and opened the door. Night had fallen hours ago. "Call if you need me."

"I will."

She left.

I waited a full ten minutes before I grabbed my wallet and keys.

I had to eat.

If I didn't seek out someone else, it would be her instead.

The city was an hour away by car. It was far enough that people still tasted like people, even if they weren't locally convenient. At midnight, starving to the point of messy homicide and with no real fear of death, I was motivated to make the drive in forty minutes or less.

The thing about driving in this part of the world was the emptiness. As I sped down the highway, teeth gritted against the searing burn of my stomach, I saw no one. Not a car to be seen on either side. Outside of my headlights, the world was bathed in absolute darkness. The only thing in sight was the occasional animal, but given that I could see in the dark further than any set of high beams, animals weren't anything I normally worried about, neither for food nor roadkill.

I needed a proper meal.

I glanced at the dash. Half past twelve. Local bars closed relatively early compared to larger cities, but that still left me time to find someone easy to catch.

My stomach screamed out, sending gnawing, painful tendrils of hunger through my middle. If I weren't so gods-damned far from civilization, I wouldn't get so bloodthirsty that I lost control of everything I was. Trapped in the middle of nowhere because I couldn't get a handle on myself, couldn't get over the loves of my life who had been dead for decades. *Decades.* If I'd been mortal, the time I'd been mourning them would've added up to half a lifetime. What was so wrong with me that I couldn't get out of my own way for the proper part of a human life? So deep in my sorrow that I was hiding in a town where I couldn't eat, to what? *Punish myself?*

The excuses were getting too thin.

I could just leave. Leave and be done with it. Pack the car with what I didn't want to lose and move on. Go to the city. To Milan. To Detroit or Siberia, anywhere away from the sun, who fucking cared. Anything, anywhere to be able to find good blood again. Nothing was stopping me. It wasn't as if I had—

Laurel.

The woman I was trying not to kill. Who had been kinder to me than I had been to myself in decades. My mind swam with memories of the last while. How quickly she'd wormed her way into my house and my heart. Somehow, with her around, I'd figured out how to laugh again. Astra, Willem, and Violet had been *mythical.* Powerful and deadly. Beings I had spent almost two centuries worshipping. And this woman, this normal human woman, had managed to crack the ice around my soul. Stupid, really—

A deer stood on the highway, its eyes gleaming, staring at me as it stood in the other lane.

My head was swimming, my thoughts overwhelming my sense. I hadn't seen the fucking deer until I'd been on top of it, and if it had been in *my* lane…

I had to focus.

Things would be clearer once the incessant gnawing was gone. The way things were progressing, I could hardly tell if I was hungry for her blood or for *her*.

It was hardly the first time I'd gone to the city for something to slake the beast. I knew what streets the bars let out on. Where the people gathered and wandered off. And since no easy opportunities had come upon me between the car and the club, I was forced to keep my wits about me and play the game.

Which was a tall order, considering how hazy my senses were becoming.

My favourite club was easy to haunt. If I'd gone hunting frequently, I'd have to change the scenery. Keep people from seeing me there too often.

Instead, I dodged a gaggle of loud girls on their way to the bouncer, eager to get inside. He didn't even attempt to ID me—one of the perks of having been turned in my thirties.

The irony of bouncers, though. A group of burly men guarding doors, who rarely turned away actual killers just because we could conceal our weapons so neatly.

The club was half-full, which I preferred. Enough bodies to have privacy in the chaos, but not so many that it made it hard to hunt. The music thumped against the inside of my skull the moment I walked in. The contrast between my vision in the club's darkness and the flashing lights always made for an odd combination. Thrilling, I assumed, for someone who saw blackness in the dark. Less atmospheric for me, considering I could see every couple in every corner, hands all over each other's bodies. Hiding from everyone, just not from me.

A young man sat at the bar, alone and sipping on a colourful drink that looked more like magic than alcohol. The black-and-pink floral shirt and the matching pink eyeshadow he wore were a quick tip-off that he might be tempted into coming along with a pretty man flashing a wicked smile.

How fortunate for me.

I sat down beside him, an empty stool between us. A moment later, the bartender was leaning toward me.

"Sorry, what are they having?" I asked the bartender, pointing to the drink two seats over.

That got my target's attention, even with all the noise.

"Blue Galaxy," the bartender yelled back. "House special."

I turned to look at the man holding the drink, sipping it from a dainty little straw. "Is it good? Should I?" I gave him a long-practised look of doe-eyed curiosity.

Pink Eyeshadow's gaze slid up and down me, trying to figure me out. After a moment, he smiled, something just slightly wolfish in his eyes, and slid the drink gingerly across the bar. "Find out."

I graciously took the drink and sipped on the straw, keeping eye contact with him as I did. It was far, far too sweet for my liking, but I didn't need to advertise that. I slid the drink back. "Two of these, please. One to replace what I drank."

Pink Eyeshadow leaned over, his elbow propped on the bar. "You didn't have to do that. It was just a sip."

I flicked my wrist dismissively, leaning closer to be heard. "You saved me from wasting my money on a bad drink. It's the least I can do." Playing coy, staying demure, and trying to focus through my fading sense of clarity.

"I'm glad I could help." He smirked and went back to his drink.

"Well, actually. If you're still feeling generous—" I pulled out my phone and pointed to it, which drew him into shouting distance again. "My plane was diverted here and I never planned to stay anywhere. I need to find a last-minute hotel, and I just—I'm lost. Do you know which I should avoid?"

"Not local, eh?" Pink Eyeshadow shifted to move to the stool directly next to me. "Let me see."

That was the thing about small places: everyone was so eager to help, especially when it came to a damsel in distress.

It was so *easy.*

"Thanks." We sat shoulder to shoulder, bent over my phone together. His ear was close enough to speak into, and his neck was right there. The heat of him…gods, the hunger. It was too easy to imagine pushing him against the bar and drinking him right there. But that was how good vampires died. A lack of patience.

"These two are roach hotels." His breath was hot on my ear. He smelled like honeyed sweat and sandalwood. "This is right down the street. Expensive, though." He made a face. "Fuck me, these last-minute rates are horrendous."

"I know, but I have no other choice. So this one, yeah?" I tapped a hotel with rooms half-fit for royalty. It would go on a black market credit card like every other expense I had, and as long as they left me alone while the sun was up, it didn't quite matter. Two nights in a row, because it was the only way the hotels would let me sleep through the day and leave after dark. Besides, while I really would need a place to stay, the conversation was the whole point.

Pink Eyeshadow introduced himself as Marc and spent the next twenty minutes hunched over the bar with me, making small talk. Each moment felt like an eternity, the hunger biting at my patience as I listened, trying to offer enough to keep the conversation moving. When I couldn't use words to my advantage, I did my best to keep my body engaged and my expression soft. My head throbbed, and every time I lost his words in my daze, I blamed it on the music. And then, finally, a deeply obnoxious song came on, and it was time.

"Marc, I don't want to be rude, but I'm really enjoying this conversation and it's getting harder and harder to hear. Would you want to walk with me? Find a quiet pub, if they're open, or maybe just enjoy the night?" I worked hard to find an expression that conveyed exasperation, but also a hopeful pout.

Marc hopped down from his stool. "Yeah, fuck it. Let's get out of here." He settled his tab and I followed him out the door.

The cool air was blissful as we stepped out into the silence, like a sigh of relief. Marc started down the street, talking exactly at the point where he'd left off, and I trailed along beside him, barely conscious enough to hear him.

He offered to take me by a park he liked—though he'd never been there after dark, he stated—and then he'd walk me over to the hotel. "No strings attached, of course," he finished bashfully.

I gave him a shy, sidelong glance. "I wouldn't mind strings."

Marc was silent for a moment, and then slipped his hand into mine.

My empty stomach burned at the heat of his skin, knowing what deliciousness lay underneath.

The park was empty when we arrived. It was a straight shot across, with no trees or foliage cover, only snow-laden garden beds lining paths that led to a gazebo. I tried to be subtle as I scanned the area for anyone else who might have come out for a late-night stroll. My vision wasn't as sharp as it should have been, though. Nothing about me was. I needed to finish things, fast. Or at some point, the beast would do it for me.

His hand still in mine, I turned to walk backward, leading him in the direction of the gazebo. A little smirk, a little false mirth. "This looks cute. Come on."

Marc followed, picking up the pace with me. I pulled him along, up the steps. The weather-worn structure was empty; no people, no seating, nothing. I led him to one of the little half walls and hopped up to sit on the waist-high wooden rail.

"Maybe this cancelled flight won't end up so bad after all," I murmured as he got close. I needed to play coy with him for just a little longer.

He moved to stand between my legs. As it was, he was slightly taller, and his neck was *right there.* The quick rhythm of his heart thudding inside his body. The poor dear was *so* excited.

"Can I…can I kiss you?" Marc's hand had found my neck, his thumb tracing the line of my jaw.

It was so adorable when they asked. Courtship had changed a lot since I'd been alive.

I leaned in to kiss him, barely feeling the brush of his lips, despite how immediately hungry his kisses became. His pulse throbbed in my ears, so close to being mine. I lingered, struggling against the urge to act right away. I wanted him disarmed. At my mercy.

So close.

And then his hands found their way to the edge of my shirt, starting to sneak their way to my skin. And that was absolutely the limit of where I wanted his hands.

I slowly kissed down his chin and along his neck.

Restraint fell away.

My fangs slid out of their sheaths and I bit down.

The taste was *glorious.*

Blood flowed into my mouth, coating my tongue in hot, rich flavour. Thin, though. The way it always was when too much alcohol was involved. I held Marc tightly to me as I drank, and through the starved haze, I could feel him struggling against me. In any other circumstance, he might have won. Could've easily overpowered me, based on the feel of his body.

But I was a demon and he was not.

He was *dinner.*

Each mouthful made it harder and harder to stop. After rationing myself for months, I wanted to gorge. To drink until he was empty, and find someone else to empty again, no matter how bloated and drunk it made me. It was more blood than I needed, but moderation was so unsatisfying.

Marc grew slack in my grip, threatening to fall to the ground. I kept drinking, cradling him as he slipped into unconsciousness. He was emptying out, long past saving, and finally, *finally*, I could think again.

I pulled my mouth away from his neck. The two clean puncture marks oozed blood, and I couldn't stop myself from cleaning it away with a long, languid lick.

I freed a hand to wipe my lips, red smearing on my skin. Gods, I hoped I hadn't eaten too messily.

Hopping down from my seat, I gently set Marc's body down, leaning him against the wall of the gazebo. I felt bad, honestly. He seemed like a genuinely nice guy. Some people were easier to kill than others, and Marc had just been at the wrong bar on the wrong night. He seemed like someone who should have gotten to live. On another night, when I was in control, he might have. Life wasn't always fair, but I tried to be, sometimes. But food was food, and it had been him or Laurel.

As I stood, the world turned a little around me. Lights too bright, the air a little hazy. I leaned against the rail, composing myself.

Gods above and below, Marc had been far further into his cups than I'd realized. His blood had been full of alcohol and was hitting me in a rush. I laughed, suddenly sated and five rums into the night.

I pulled the hotel address up on my phone and let it guide me toward the building. It wouldn't be a far walk, but the grass seemed a lot less solid under my feet than it had a few minutes ago.

The streets were alive with the vibrant energy of young revellers as I passed through them. Bars were letting out onto main streets, closing up for the night, and my map was leading me further from the party. Along dark side streets and quiet avenues.

The daze of the hunger was gone, replaced by the buzz of alcohol, but I still felt clearer. Unfocused, yes, but in a different way. A less dangerous way. Gods, I hadn't eaten that well since the last trip I'd made to the city, months ago. If I were smarter, I would make regular trips instead of relying on rations alone.

But intelligence like that would require me to stop flagellating myself long enough to be reasonable.

As of late, it seemed more reasonable to take care of those needs instead of pushing them to their limits. Funny how things could change so quickly with the right motivation.

A noise drew my attention. Somewhere close, on the empty street of closed shops and darkened doorways, a voice cried out.

Something from a nearby alley. At the mouth of the alley was a woman, and someone in a hoodie pressing her against the wall.

"Shut up," the attacker hissed.

"Please, let me go," the woman whimpered. She was trying to keep back. Keep her stomach away from the blade in his hand.

And all I could think about was *Greg.*

Heroics were not smart. Heroics left witnesses. People to tell tales. Being a known entity was not what kept vampires safe.

And yet.

I strode over to the alley and grabbed the hooded person by the back of the neck. He practically shrieked, but his grip on the woman released. The knife still flashed in his hand, but it was hardly a deterrent. She cowered away as I lifted her attacker from the ground, holding him so his feet dangled.

I stared at her, fangs out and snarling. "Run."

She bolted.

I threw him to the ground. His body hit the concrete with a thud. A wheeze escaped his lips, the air knocked from him. "You think you're strong?" I asked him. "Cornering young girls like that?"

"It's none of your business," he sputtered, picking himself off the ground. He had the knife pointed at me, his stance poised to strike. "Stay back, pansy-ass motherfucker."

The slur cut the last bit of logic from my mind. I moved in and swung, my fist connecting with his gut. Something cracked under the pressure, and he cried out. He swung the blade in response, clumsily slicing it across my stomach. I barely felt the bite. A left hook to his face and he was down again, staring up at me, holding his jaw.

I pounced on him, straddling his ribs. I tore the knife out of his hand and threw it into the alley. "Oh, you really showed me. So tough." Grabbing his jaw, I forced him to look up at me. "You're going to taste *so gratifying.*"

He started to protest—as much as he could with his jaw clamped shut—and I leaned in to lick his face. The cry of disgust brought a wicked laugh out of me.

I twisted his jaw to the side and sank my teeth into his neck.

Messier, more ravenous than before. A hunt of rage, all teeth and fists and righteousness. Hundreds of years of the same old slurs, the same old crimes. One bleeding into the next, until it was a pile of bodies I felt entirely justified in creating.

I drank until long after his body went slack under me.

I sat up, running a thumb across my chin. Hot, wet blood coated my lips and dripped down my skin. I licked it away and then used my phone camera to check for anything I'd missed. It was the only option I had, since reflections were out of the question and I could hardly show up at the hotel drenched in red, could I?

Standing up, I brushed my clothing off. The knife had slid a clean cut through the T-shirt under my jacket. Peering through the hole, I spotted the thin slice across my stomach. It would smart, soon enough. When the adrenaline and booze wore off. But it would heal before the night was out. I zipped up my jacket and strode back into the night. My phone guided me once more, away from the unintelligent but deeply satisfying mistake I'd made. I hadn't picked a fight with a queer-fearing asshole in a long time and honestly, I'd kind of missed it.

I would be far away by the time anyone found the body. The drunk haze was fading, but slowly. That man—who had tasted more like grease and sodium than blood—had left me bloated. I'd wanted to give in to the craving and drink someone dry, and I would pay for doing just that. The vampiric equivalent of a food coma.

I looked forward to sleeping like an overfed baby when I eventually fell into that bed.

The hotel was business chic. Practical, hard edges and harsh lights. The kind of place accountants and travelling salesmen liked to stay in order to feel special. It made me miss the elegant, rich softness of so many of the places where Willem, Violet, Astra, and I had stayed over the decades. But I had no room to be choosey.

I approached the front desk and the young lady looked up.

"Oh, hello! You must be Emmett Smith." She looked chipper for someone being forced to work the night shift.

"I am. Last to arrive, I take it?" I passed her my forged ID that said I was, in fact, Emmett Smith.

"You are, but I won't hold it against you." She gave me a silly wink, typed a few things into the computer, and handed the ID back. "Two nights in a row, I see. Excellent. Here's your key card for room 706, and you're all set. Anything else I can help you with tonight?"

"One thing, yes." I tucked my wallet back into my pants. "I won't be needing any cleaning services until after checkout. I intend to sleep off some jet lag."

The keyboard click-clacked at lightning speed. "No problem at all. It's noted on your account. Have a good night, sir."

"And you as well." I gave her a smirk and her cheeks turned pink. I chided myself. I wasn't supposed to be acting memorable. And yet, here I was, feeling so much myself for once that I was casting low-dose flirtations at whoever spoke to me first.

Key card in hand, I went to the elevator. A moment later, I was on the seventh floor, looking for 706. The key slid into the automated handle with a click and a beep.

Like the lobby, the room was business fancy, all hard lines and polished surfaces. A window that stretched across the wall. One large bed, a TV, and a long wooden desk that could make a passable office. The bathroom door was frosted glass—a choice I'd never understand, no matter how many centuries I passed through. And beige. Beige as far as the eye could see.

I closed the door, locked it behind me, and began to strip. I inspected each piece of clothing for blood: the jacket, the jeans, the shirt. The shirt was lost, which was fine. I'd bought the thing for the sake of blending in, and when I wore it, it felt like wearing the wrong skin. But it had done the job.

Since I'd need them again tomorrow, once each piece had passed inspection, I folded them and set them on the bathroom vanity. A drop had found its way onto the collar of the jacket, a single spot of dried brown on the navy blue. I scrubbed it with cold water until it faded and became a problem for another day.

For all the impersonal touches of the hotel room, the shower was delightfully large. When I turned on the tap, the water gushed out from above like rain. Soon, the air was full of mist, obscuring the shower glass and the enormous mirror that reflected only an empty room.

I stepped in and turned up the heat until it began to sear. It would take a while, but eventually, the warmth would permeate my cool skin and breathe life into my undead muscles. The modern shower was easily my favourite invention. An opportunity every single day to feel heat coursing through me? And all I had to do was pay the bills? It was irreplaceable bliss.

I lingered in there long after I was clean, letting the heat pull the alcohol from my skin. Letting it ease the discomfort of overindulging. With the hunger gone, it was easy to be patient again. At ease. Finally, after days of it, nothing pulled at the edges of my attention.

I wondered what Laurel was doing, feeling unwelcoming for sending her home.

The poor dear had no idea how monstrous I was.

Telling her was a risk. She might run and never come back. I could end up alone again, whiling away the decades in solitude. She had taken the first surprise well, oddly enough. So perhaps my trust would be well placed with her. She was accustomed to monsters, after all. Wasn't she?

Anyone who would seek to strike fear into the heart of their lover could only reasonably be called a monster.

If I hid the truth from Laurel, it would only create more opportunities for me to harm her. In suppressing the hunger to spare her feelings, I could lose her to that urge to eat.

And who was I to remove her agency? To decide for her? That wasn't something done out of care. That was selfish.

My fear of loneliness couldn't be allowed to compromise her safety.

Unable to justify lingering any longer, I turned off the shower. The warmth in my bones radiated sweet comfort. As I dried off, I could feel it seeping away already. Slow and subtle, but happening nonetheless.

Having not had the foresight to pack anything, I wrapped the towel around my hips and went out into the main room. The difference in the temperature was stark, and I turned the heat up in a futile effort to hold on to the moment.

I went to the window and looked down at the city. A collection of dark buildings, sprinkled with the lights of people who refused to sleep.

I missed it. I missed *this*. The freedom of wandering and roaming. Of being part of the night, invincible and untouchable. I'd been such a quiet little thing when I was alive, and I'd grown to love being dead. Before I lost my loves, if anyone had asked if I'd ever go back to the quiet, I'd have laughed in their faces. *Why would I go back to being less than this?* I would've said. *Why would I go back to being a mouse, afraid of everything? Terrified of loving men and dressing daintily and living deliciously?*

It was easy to close my eyes and imagine having that conversation with someone across from me in a booth, inside the Irish pub that we'd loved to frequent for a while—never to cause trouble, simply because it was queer and our favourite and couldn't be replaced—with my loves littered around the room. When we'd each died, we'd fallen outside of society. No money to make, no families to tend, no norms to keep. No more excuses to deny ourselves anything. We just became what we'd always craved and could never have. Astra playing cards and smoking cigars, their maroon men's jacket hanging from the back of their chair, her short, sharp hair loosely slicked back and her biceps hard as bricks. Willem, dressed like he was sharing drinks with royalty instead of some ancient chap who kept coming back for more discussions on the horrors of England. And Violet, her delicate embroidered dress too long for dancing, but being taught a jig by another vampire all the same. A place where the accent started to slip back into my voice until I sounded like home again.

All of us, so full of life.

The moment I remembered I wasn't there, the moment my vision came into focus and I stopped living in that dream, the cold hit me all at once. If I stared out the window, I could imagine them on the bed, relaxing against each other, waiting for me to join them. I could keep staring out into the city. Keep the dream alive for another moment.

Instead, I turned and found the bed the way I'd left it. Empty. Made. Lonely.

Better not to tease myself with dreams.

I pulled the curtains closed.

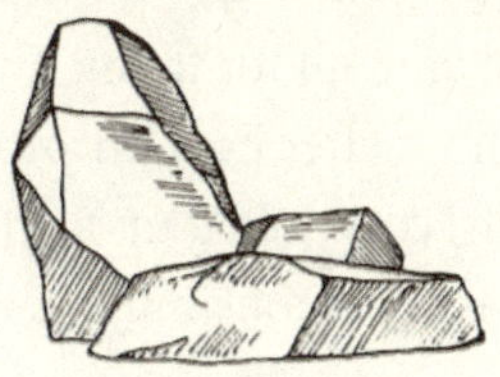

Penny Harbour

Black smoke filled the sky, blotting out the stars. Flame crawled between the beams of the house, licking in searing hot tendrils, burning hotter than the water trying to extinguish it.

The family watched from the lawn, Jared and Holly holding their daughter to their legs, as everything they knew went up in smoke.

It was the third fire in a month. The third one anyone had *noticed* at least. An abandoned shack near the beach. A half-demolished camp in the woods, tucked at the back of someone's property. And the home. Brandon and his lighter had been busy—not that anyone else knew that. All the town knew was that things were escalating. Again.

Every so many years, it seemed, someone started lighting fires.

The volunteer fire department had shown up quickly, a small fleet of cars parked along the road, with a solitary fire truck hosing down the flames. But as far gone as it was, they knew their only job was to keep the fire from spreading. Make sure no one else lost anything that night.

All across town, people were talking. They'd started right away, fingers typing on screens, speaking in hushed voices into phones. A message to an aunt, a quick word to a friend. And within minutes, everyone seemed to know. Cars were parked in yards or driving by slowly to see what had happened. Family arrived to be of use.

That was the way of things. Gathering for tragedy. It had been for longer than anyone could remember. Before the industry died, the town had gathered at the mouths of mines, waiting for news. Holding each other as their men and boys came up out of the pit—or didn't.

The house was gone by the time morning came. Jared and Holly hadn't stayed to watch. His mom had pulled up with the car and piled everyone inside. The family had room enough for them. There was *always* room enough in Penny Harbour, no matter how uncomfortable the squeeze. Couches would become beds, cots pulled up from basements. Overcrowded tables and big meals and shared responsibilities. Because that was what community did.

They showed up.

By lunch, the news was all over Tabs, as neighbours sent links.

> *New Event: Benefit Dance for Jared and Holly @ Penny Harbour Legion*
> *Admission: $20*
> *50% of alcohol proceeds go to the family, along with admission*
> *Featuring: DJ Jazzy Jazz*
> *Donations of clothing, food, and household goods can be dropped at Unity Church every day before noon*

CHAPTER ELEVEN

Laurel

That close to my face, Greg's breath was putrid. Sour. He had been out the entire night before and he was hungover and out of rational thought.

"I shouldn't have to remind you about what needs doing around here," he snarled, backing me into the kitchen table. "I don't want to get up again tomorrow to find half my fucking breakfast missing. No milk, no coffee. The fuck am I supposed to drink, Laurel?"

My heart hammering in my chest, I struggled to find the words to pacify him. "I'm sorry. It slipped my mind."

"Well, don't fucking let it." Greg slammed his hand on the tabletop beside me and I jumped, closing my eyes and leaning away from him. "I ask you to do so goddamn little around here. The other boys don't gotta remind their wives to get fucking milk. Should be a basic fucking task." He looked at the clock on the stove and spat a curse. "Now I'm gonna be fucking late 'cause o' you."

I kept my eyes down, not looking at him as he pushed off the table and went to put on his boots. Normally, but not always, if I just kept quiet long enough, he'd leave. I tried not to breathe, holding each little inhale as long as I could manage, my head getting light, waiting for him to tie his work boots. Pick up his bag. Shrug on his coat. Unlock the door, and finally, finally, walk out into the morning, slamming the door behind him.

As soon as I heard the truck squeal out of the driveway, I shrank down onto the floor in a pile. The tears burst from me in a scream of frustration. It had been too quiet for too long, and I'd let my guard down. I'd started forgetting things. I hadn't gone to the store and preempted this fucking whole morning.

I'd started to feel too safe.

I peered over my shoulder, the draw of that safety making me check the window for my phone. It was there, right where it should be, and on the other end was the one person whose voice I needed to hear. I pulled myself off the ground and went over to it, picking the phone up and opening it to hit call.

And stopped.

As easy as it was to hear his voice in my mind, asking me if I was all right in that watered-down Irish accent of his, I couldn't bring myself to hit the button.

Spencer had asked me to go so he could rest. He'd looked like garbage, which was a tall order for him, and he needed the sleep. If I called him in the middle of the day and made him worry over me when he should be taking care of himself…

Greg had yelled at me before. He'd done worse for longer, and none of this was new. I was in no more danger than I had ever been in; it was just that I'd started to get soft. Spencer wasn't someone I had to endure, and it made enduring Greg that much harder.

The itch to reach out remained, though, so I backed out of the call screen and found the group chat with Emma and Mary-Jo.

> Laurel:
> Morning ladies

Two sets of dancing dots appeared.

> Mary-Jo:
> SHE LIVES
> WHO IS THIS MYSTERY WOMAN

> Emma:
> Shhh stfu MJ

Laurel:

I know, I'm sorry. I've been busy with work and TO BE
FAIR you two aren't exactly swimming in time either.

I went back to the spot on the floor where I'd been sitting and slunk back
down. Why not? Sometimes the floor felt like the best place to be.

Mary-Jo:
You're not wrong. Which obviously means it's time to
get up to some shit

Emma:
Already speed dialing mom, what's the date

Mary-Jo:
Fuck think fast
Um
BENEFIT DANCE

Laurel:

Yes sweet baby jesus yes, let's go to a stupid DANCE

Emma:
BOOM BABYSITTER ACQUIRED
WHO'S BRINGING THE SNACKS
GET YOUR SLUTTIEST DRESSES

Mary-Jo:
You don't own those, either of you

Laurel:
Offended

Emma:

Fuck you MJ

I watched the chat banter bounce back and forth as Mary-Jo accused Emma of only owning mom jeans and Emma struggled to retaliate. A night out with them would be fun. I'd seen them so little since Spencer had become a permanent fixture, and it wasn't exactly fair to have cut them out like that.

And the chat had also done exactly what I had hoped it would. I could breathe again. My heart wasn't so thunderous, and aside from the remnants of the cold sweat, I'd more or less come through the fear and landed on the other side.

As temporary as that was, at least.

I stuck my phone in my pocket and stared across the kitchen from my spot on the tile. I had to figure out how to have both these things at once. How to be fully present in my life when the sun was up, and how to keep scratching out time with Spencer after sunset. Trouble was, the days kept getting longer and nightfall kept getting pushed further and further back. It wouldn't be long until the sun was going down after nine in the evening, and I'd have to choose what parts of my life took priority.

I knew what I wanted to take priority, but it didn't mean it could. If spending time with Spencer made me feel safe, what good was it if I was putting myself in more danger with Greg by letting go of that hard-won vigilance?

If I wanted to have both, I needed to work harder.

I got a series of texts just before dark.

Spencer:

Can you meet me tonight? We have something to discuss

Laurel:

I can come over soon, just finishing supper

Spencer:
I'm not there. I'm in the city. I can explain when I see you
Once it's dark enough to drive, I'll be back in an hour
See you soon

So, having done the math badly, I found myself on his doorstep with his Civic missing and his door locked. The evening air was chilly. I stayed in the truck, engine running, and hoped he wouldn't be much longer.

About ten minutes later, his car pulled in, heavy guitar and drums blasting from his speakers. He got out, grinning in pleasant surprise, and leaned against the car, waiting for me to join him.

I hopped out, leaning on my truck across from him. "I thought you were going to bed when I left."

"That…that was a lie." Spencer scratched the back of his head, mischief in his eyes. The life seemed to be back inside him, after so long missing. "But that's why I wanted to see you. To talk."

I tilted my head, confused. "All right. Should we go inside…?"

"I think we should stay out, actually. Take a walk."

I gave him a disparaging look. "Oh, sure. What about my poor bruised foot?" It wasn't really injured, just a little tender. But what good was it if I didn't ham it up a little?

His slight sheepishness gave way to something else. Concern. "What I need to say isn't pleasant, and I don't want you to feel…cornered."

A chill ran down my back. What exactly could he have to say that was that intense? Spencer was never the one who made me feel cornered. "Well, if that isn't ominous, I don't know what is. Okay, let's get walking, then. It's not going to get any warmer tonight."

Spencer led the way down the driveway, hands in his jacket pockets. He wouldn't look at me, just kept staring at the ground. He wasn't speaking, either.

"Something best left until we're away from the street, I'm guessing?" I leaned in and elbowed him, trying to lighten the mood. "Vampire stuff?" I asked conspiratorially.

That made him laugh. "Yes, darling. Vampire stuff."

I let him be, walking down the road with him to the entrance of the track. It only took a few minutes to get that far, but I'd created a dozen possibilities in my head during that time. He was in danger. He'd changed his mind about spending his nights with me. Or he was leaving, which was the possibility that scared me the most.

When we were safely tucked in the trees, trudging across the well-packed snow, he finally spoke up. "After you left last night, I drove to the city. I'd asked you to leave because the hunger was barely in my control."

I looked up at him, a shadow in the dark. I reached into my pocket to grab my phone, using the flashlight to guide my way, but also to see his expression. A person could tell a lot by someone's face. So much danger could be avoided by noticing the little things. Spencer seemed…resigned, more than anything. "What do you mean?"

He looked up at the sky, trying to find the words. "You know I have the blood in my fridge."

I gave him a little mhm in response.

"It's not enough. Not really. I get it from a guy in the city, and it helps keep me fed, but it's like being on a diet. Eating half of what you need and hoping it goes well."

Humming a note of disapproval, I shot him a glance. "That doesn't seem like a good idea."

"It's fine, mostly. I hunt in the woods to make it more manageable. But the blood guy hasn't been answering texts, and I've been stretching the bags further than is realistic for weeks. There's not much left, and last night you were right there…"

I blinked, the point of the entire conversation dawning on me. "You wanted to eat me."

"Absolutely not, not want." Spencer pushed back, visibly upset. "Let's be clear about that. Want has nothing to do with it. I let the hunger get too far and it's like…at some point, it's not my choice anymore. I'll eat, and it won't matter who it is. The hunger makes it so I can't think anymore."

The thought was unsettling. He'd been massaging my foot and I'd been lying there, eyes closed and unsuspecting. Nothing had felt off at all. "So you asked me to leave and went to the city."

"To hunt, yes."

The woods grew overwhelmingly silent then. He'd talked about it before, but never in the context of what could happen to me. Unlike Greg, whose possibilities I was constantly aware of, Spencer had done nothing to make me question my safety. He'd barely even touched me without my permission, let alone made a move I thought would hurt me. He'd been nothing worse than a lost, lonely kitten since I'd met him. A kitten that bites, but a kitten all the same.

I stopped walking and stared at him. "Did you kill someone?"

"Yes." He stood more than arm's length away, keeping his distance. "It's… it's part of this, Laurel. It's not pretty, not like in some of the movies. I don't have to kill people, not in most cases, but there's a beast in here." He put a palm on his chest. "It's as much a part of me as anything else, and there's very little I can do about that."

Spencer was so serious, his gaze hard and intense. The words were candid, a bared soul waiting for me to carve it up. Waiting for me to weigh my options and make hard choices I wasn't willing to make. As if I could stay with one monster for most of my life and turn someone else away at the first sign of claws.

So I did the thing I was good at: I came up with the darkest joke I could and started to laugh.

"What?" Spencer crossed his arms over his chest, his weight switching to one leg. Annoyed.

Unable to resist, I reached out to put my hand on his. "Do you have the skin of a killer, Spencer?"

He groaned, his face craning back in annoyance. "Gods above, Laurel. I'm trying to tell you something serious and you're quoting mediocre vampire movie lines at me?"

I pursed my lips, forcing the laughter back. "I know, I know. You just… Come on. When am I ever going to get to use that again? What choice did I have?"

"Well, I take it you're not afraid then?" Spencer gestured with an open hand, frustrated. "I bring you out to the woods and remind you I'm a murderer and you step closer to laugh at me? What insanity is this?"

I shrugged and kept walking. "First of all, it has occurred to me that vampires kill people." The next part had a harder time coming up my throat. "Second, I feel like I've kind of lost the ability to feel crisis. Maybe it's a lifetime of callousness or maybe it's Greg. Or maybe it's the last ten once-in-a-lifetime disasters I've watched unfold around me this decade. I don't know. Obviously, murder is bad. I just don't know what else to do with this but laugh." I gestured to him with a defeated wave of my hand. "I mean…doesn't it track that life hands me you, someone I actually feel safe with, only for it to come with a pretty dire catch? What about that is different from any other day in my life?"

Spencer's expression was deeply puzzled. "I have no idea what's going on in your mind right now. "

I tried to find a way to express what I was feeling—or not feeling. "If I tied you down and starved you, what would happen?"

"That seems like quite an escalation, frankly. But I would go practically feral and eventually die. Very eventually. It would suck, for lack of a better term."

"So you drink blood to survive."

"Yes."

"Around here, a lot of people do a lot of things to survive," I said, jamming my hands into my pockets. "Not all of them are pretty. I've known things. Heard rumours. Some people sell hard drugs. Some work under the table or have three jobs. I've known thieves, liars, cheats. Innocent people who are desperate to escape bad situations. Almost anyone would do anything to make sure their next meal was on the table, if it came to that." I took a breath, the cold seeping into my lungs. "Maybe here, we all understand that better than most. The place was built on horrors done to get by, after all."

Spencer was quiet. Snow crunched under our boots, seeming to echo in the empty space. The woods were coming to an end. As we reached the edge of the trees, the world let out onto a wide, grassy expanse. Overhead, the sky was black and dotted with a sea of stars. The path led out onto the dykes, the tall mounds of earth that were built to keep the harbour at bay during flooding season. The water that fed into Penny Harbour swept against the top foot of the banks. The moon was full, which meant higher tides than usual. Already, the water spilt over the banks in some places, creeping toward the dykes.

"No city can compare to these stars," Spencer breathed, taking in the view. Then he turned to me. "Thank you. I don't know why you're being so alarmingly understanding, but it's appreciated."

I shrugged. "Would it surprise you if I said it felt natural?"

"A bloodthirsty monster feels natural to you? In what universe?"

I gazed out over the water as we walked. "Sometimes, when I'm talking to people from Away, they look at me like I'm lying about my life. I'm not close with my extended family, but they're all over the place here. I've got a cousin who's addicted to oxycodone and is a zombie most days. I've got an aunt who goes off her meds sometimes, and when she does, she winds up in jail. My mom doesn't know who her grandmother is, not even a last name. My uncle's childhood friend used to light fires in people's barns and destroyed a half dozen lives. My father's friends were killed underground before they had a chance to build a life. Nearly everyone in my extended family is sick with something. Diabetes, burnout, a bad heart. Depression, if nothing else. The list goes on."

"Jesus Christ, Laurel." Spencer's expression was mystified. "Why have you never said anything? Those seem like things worth mentioning."

"Are they?" On the one hand, I agreed with him, but on the other, it was just my life. "It's the world I've known, Spencer. Do you know there are all these people out in the world that don't have this much tragedy in their lives? It isn't until I leave here and start telling stories to people from other places that I realize this isn't normal. But the reality is that this is just what I have to carry. It's what a lot of us carry. What relationship have I had that didn't cost me something? So for you to tell me you need to do some harm to survive… it just feels oddly reasonable. Like the next step in a series of horrors I have to live with."

Spencer kicked his foot into the dirt. "I'm not…I don't want to be another horror in your life."

"You're not. Not directly." I kept moving. Without the trees to block the wind, it would get cold quickly. "It's like the universe is saying accept this thing if you want this friend. And considering everyone I know and love around here has done something ranging from mildly wrong to horrific, I feel like I don't have much of a moral high ground here. Besides, maybe since we're both some kind of monster, you'll be able to understand the fucked-up things in me, too."

Spencer choked out a laugh. "As if you could have anything monstrous in you."

"Of course I do." His words bit at me, so counter to what I felt. But how could he know what I had never told anyone? I took a breath, working out the words. "Sometimes there's this voice. Like a second version of myself that would do anything to survive. It makes me wonder what I'm capable of, if I ever just stopped and listened. Things I'd be horrified to do, but I think them all the same. And even without that, I've killed off parts of me. How else could I get through any of this? Isn't that monstrous in its own way?"

He let those thoughts hang in the air for a long time. Long enough that I wondered if I had somehow just severed everything. Admitted to something darker than even he could handle. The crunch of our boots on ice and dirt and gravel filled the air, the wind whipping in short gusts around us.

"I'm sorry, Laurel—" His voice got lost on the wind for a moment, an appropriate pause considering the weight of what I'd confessed. When it died off, he continued, "I wish I had something better to say. It's a lot to untangle…but I appreciate knowing."

I shrugged. "It's nothing." And it wasn't nothing. Not at all. But I knew how to push things down to become nothing, and that was almost the same thing.

Spencer let out a breath, something between a nervous laugh and a sigh of relief. "I'm not sure how I thought this would go, but certainly I didn't expect this."

The words that came to mind felt too vulnerable, but I tried to pry them from my throat anyway. "I feel like this part of you just isn't enough to outweigh what you've given me."

He looked over at me, softness in his eyes, and shook his head. "Gods, that may be the most foolish thing I've ever heard. I want you around, Laurel, but I also can't change what's true for me. After centuries of it, I have very little remorse left. I need to eat, and blood is the option I have. If you're searching for innocent friends, I'm afraid you won't find that in me. I can be monstrous, darling, and when I'm at the depths of that hunger, I can't promise you anything. Are you sure?"

I stopped on the dyke and looked out over the water, the moon's reflection shimmering on the surface. The water was high enough that I could see a shadow of my reflection in it, but not Spencer's. I had to check to make sure he was still there. He was, staring out to the other side of the river, his hair brushing across his cheeks in the breeze. He was being candid with me. Trying to shock me, perhaps. And maybe it was all the practice of shutting out surprise that made it easy to swallow. I'd been on my toes most of my life, waiting for the next problem, the next crisis, the next time Greg was angry. Vampires, that had been a surprise, but this whole problem came with the package.

"It seems to me that the easiest solution is not to let you go hungry."

Spencer laughed. "That certainly would be ideal. But I've fashioned myself a delightful little prison here, which makes that harder to do than you'd expect. I don't have enough for tonight, let alone the week."

The urge to fix it roiled in me. I was good at that. At identifying and solving and repairing. And I could fix the issue myself. I'd seen it in enough movies, after all. Offer up my veins and be the one to save the day. Save him. And wouldn't he appreciate it? Appreciate me as I let him drink what he needed, so intimately?

What lengths was I willing to go to in order to ensure he valued me?

Was I literally willing to feed myself to him? To let him sink his teeth into my skin, at the expense of being devoured?

I had a sinking suspicion that the answer was yes—that it had been all my life, for everything, not just with him—and I had to look away from it before it said too much about me.

"What stops you from hunting?" I asked instead.

Spencer's voice was hesitant. "Bad weather, mostly. You, sometimes."

"How so?"

"I can't hunt if we're watching movies, can I?"

I scoffed. "Do you mean to tell me that you've been going hungry so that we can watch Only Lovers Left Alive together?"

His lips pursed, and he clicked his tongue. "It's worth it."

It was difficult not to read too much into that comment. Was it worth it simply because I was good company, or because I was his only company?

I sighed. "How hungry are you now?"

Spencer put a hand on his stomach. "I could eat."

"All right, then, let's go." I turned and started back to the woods.

"What? Go where?" Spencer caught up a second later.

"I'll hunt with you, since you won't leave me alone long enough to take care of yourself."

"Laurel—"

"Spencer whatever-your-name-is—"

"Campbell, but—"

I wagged a finger at him. "I can't scold you properly without a middle name."

His brows furrowed, his mouth agape. "Tompkin."

"Spencer Tompkin Campbell, this is not a negotiation." I turned the flashlight so I could see his face properly as we walked. "You brought me out here to tell me that I'm in danger if you don't eat, but also that you've been starving yourself in order to spend time with me. Where I'm from—" I gestured to the world around us. "—we don't sit back while other people suffer. And we certainly don't let them do it in our name. We bring them a casserole and a pot of coffee. So pick your favourite spot and let's go."

Spencer's face was the definition of confusion. Just when I thought he would fight back, he let out a groan. "Gods, how is it that I'm hundreds of years old and at least twice as strong as you, but still doing everything you say?"

I smiled up at him, pleased as peaches. "Usually that's out of spite or love. Dealer's choice."

Spencer glared at me, trying not to smile, and followed me back into the woods.

Spencer

We went back to the house first. Laurel needed extra layers if she was going to sit in the woods and wait with me. I grabbed a pile of thick blankets from the closet and filled a hot water bottle. She zipped the bottle into her jacket, and we set off down the path at the back of the house.

"This isn't necessary," I whispered again.

"I think you've proven that it is." Laurel's hands were on her stomach, propping up the water bottle. "Now shut up before you spook your meal."

She had a point.

I led her further into the trees, past the mine entrance. When we were far enough from the house, I stopped and tossed one of the blankets on the ground. I gestured for her to sit.

"Why, thank you," she teased quietly, sitting down.

One blanket at a time, I wrapped them around her, tucking her into an absurd bundle.

"Are you sure you don't want to sit in the blankets with me?" Laurel asked.

"If something comes along, they'll just tie me down. Besides, I'll leach all your heat and offer nothing in return. Best you stay in there alone."

I sat down next to her, which felt a little like sitting next to a snowman. Her hot breath misted out onto the air as she stared ahead, not saying a word. And that was it. For a long time, we just…kept each other company. Every once in a while, I was tempted to get up and tell her to just go back to the house. It was cold and it was ridiculous that she had come out for such a stupid errand. But the feeling slipped away and I was glad for the companionship. Because whether we spoke or not, I could hear her. The rhythm of her heart and the cadence of her breath. So much more than I was used to, out in the cold of the woods.

After a time, Laurel's breath began to change. Each one grew deeper and longer. I felt like I remembered what that meant. I hadn't needed to breathe in so long, but it seemed like sleep. Her head bobbed, and she stirred awake again. Then again, bobbing and startling.

Laurel shifted, trying to get more comfortable. As she inevitably dozed off again, her head fell on my shoulder and stayed there.

I listened to her breath grow deeper again, and in a moment, she was fully asleep. Her nose had turned red from the cold, along with her cheeks. I wouldn't be able to keep her outside forever. It wasn't fair to force her to endure it just for me.

But if we sat like that for a little while longer, she would be fine. She could use the rest, I told myself. Disturbing her meant she would move and the moment would die, and I wasn't ready for that. Having her there felt good. Right.

Just a little while longer.

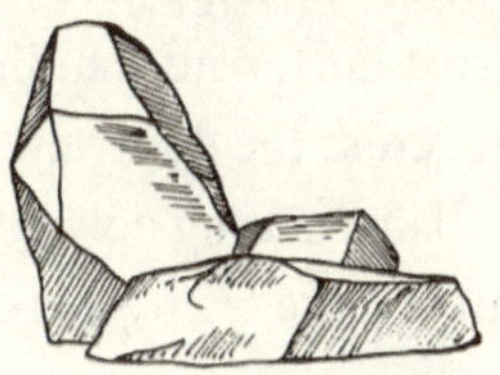

Penny Harbour

Deep in the woods, at the tail end of a piece of land, sat a cabin. The Marshes had owned that land for three generations, and over the years, they'd cut the trees to form a path, and they'd put up that cabin with their bare hands. The cabin was important. Going back to the camp was important. A place to get away—despite the house being right there, a meagre ten minutes on the four-wheeler. It was a place to gather or to be alone, depending on the weekend.

The Marshes all loved the camp, no matter if they were brothers or aunts or cousins. As frigid as it was that night, the majority of them had made their way back to the camp. The fire pit was going, blasting heat across the clearing, and the wood stove was on in the cabin. Kids and teens and adults, a fair thirty of them, sitting and running, making the best of the chill. Drinks open, stories being told, old wounds being mended.

Claire and her cousin Ben were having a great time. They were a little too old for antics, but she had gotten caught up in the joy of it all. The extended family was complicated, she knew that, but she couldn't know about the secrets among them. Dark things. She felt it emanating off some of them, sometimes. But she was fourteen; what did she know about darkness yet? About trusting her gut? For Claire, the camp was one of the rare times she got to be around everyone and it felt like the world was finally coming together. Like being part of something.

Chasing Ben out of the cabin bedroom, she tried to cut him off around the kitchen table. Ben dove under the chairs and crawled out the other side, making for the cabin door. Of course, Claire couldn't let him get away. She had things to prove.

Before she understood what had happened, Claire was on her back on the hard cabin floor. Her throat hurt. And standing in the door was Aunt Jessie, her arm stretched out across the doorway.

Aunt Jessie stood above Claire, staring down. Smug. Eyes rimmed in black.

Claire grasped at her throat, sore from where she'd connected with Aunt Jessie's arm at full speed.

"You didn't say hello to your grandparents, Claire." Aunt Jessie gestured to the fire pit outside, where Claire's grandmother and grandfather were sitting. They had both watched. Had both seen it. And were staring daggers at Claire as she peeled herself off the floor.

Claire knew better than to fight back. She knew what Aunt Jessie did to her children. Everyone did. They saw the way the kids flinched. How long she kept them outside in the cold. How she hated them.

So instead, Claire walked out into the night and said hello to her grandparents. "Hi, Nan and Pop."

They huffed and turned away from her, growling about kids having no fucking respect anymore.

Claire stepped carefully, not sure where to go next. People were staring at her, and she kept her head down, heading to the edge of the clearing. Too ashamed to know what to do.

"Hey." Ben ran up beside her. "Are you all right?"

Claire shook her head. Tears were welling in her eyes.

Ben was older than her. He had been around long enough. He knew what they were all like. "Come on. Let's go for a walk."

Claire followed him down the worn path in the woods. He held her hand as they walked and whispered. As she cried.

She was so thankful for Ben. No one else had stood up for her. Asked her if she was okay. She could get by, as long as he was with her.

CHAPTER TWELVE

Laurel

"Emma, if you don't sit down, I'm going to beat you within an inch of your life." Mary-Jo poured rum into three already once-emptied glasses as Emma puttered around the kitchen in her pyjamas, putting away dishes.

"I'm listening. I just need to finish a few things before we go; that's all." Emma rearranged the bowls in the cupboard.

"Honey, you asked us to come out tonight because you needed a night off. This—" I waved my hand at the clean kitchen that she insisted needed attention. "—isn't a night off."

Mary-Jo poured Coke over the rum and gave each glass a little stir. "This is your last chore. Wrap it up or I'm leaving."

Emma huffed and closed the cupboard door. "Oh, fine, I'm done." She sat down at the table and took one of the drinks. "It's just hard to stop. I'm not *used* to stopping."

"You got your mom to take Logan for a reason, right? Enjoy it." Mary-Jo clinked her glass against Emma's and took a long swig. "How are your classes coming?"

"How'd that test go?" I asked.

"Not a test, a history paper on outdated psychology practices. I think I nailed it, but the grades won't come back for a while." Emma stuck her finger in her drink and swirled it around. "What I wouldn't do to be on the tail end of this thing. I need to have less on my plate and the Harbour needs a therapist today, not in two more years."

I tapped Emma's foot with mine. "You can't be thinking like that. There's nothing you can do to speed things up. The town is lucky you're doing it at all. You're not obligated to set up shop here. It's not like there's going to be a lot of money in it for you."

"It's not about the money. You know that. I'm well aware of what the suggested hourly rate is and I'm going to refuse to charge it. People here can't afford over a hundred bucks a session." Emma drank half her glass at once. "Look at Jared's family. House burned, everything gone. The benefit dance tonight will help, but it's never going to replace their photos or heirlooms. It's not going to take away their nightmares."

"You're not going to do that either," Mary-Jo said.

"No, but I can try to help. I just have to ask them to wait two more fucking years." Emma drained the glass. "More please."

Mary-Jo started to pour again. "*Anyhow*, time to get changed before you're too plastered to leave the house." She stole Emma's newly full glass and started toward the bedroom. We followed her through the living room, dodging abandoned toys and half-forgotten laundry. The first door on the left was Emma's. At the centre of the room was a large bed with a floral printed quilt that Emma's grandmother had made years ago, and it had started to fray on the edges. A vanity on one wall, a dresser and a closet on the other. The room could've used a tidy, much like everything else could have, but no one was going to hold that against her.

Mary-Jo started stripping immediately, getting rid of her grey jogging pants and her band tee. Underneath, she was in a black lace bra and panties. She grabbed both of her dress options from our collection on the bed and held them up in front of her. "What do we think?"

One dress was a slinky navy-blue number with a low V-neck. The second was a thin-strapped black-and-pink floral dress that would fit snugly around her thighs.

"Pink one," I said, trying not to show on my face what I was really thinking. Ever since Spencer had asked me if I liked women, the question kept coming up in subtle ways. Things I hadn't given any attention before were suddenly creeping into my periphery. Seeing Mary-Jo nearly naked wasn't new to me—we'd been changing in front of each other since we were kids—but the *context* was new. She was a gym rat and had the muscle definition to match. And her curves…they looked really hot, actually, if I were to think about it too much.

So obviously I just was never going to think about that again.

Best not to.

Mary-Jo gets away with it because they expect her to be deviant.

Your people would rather tear your heart out than see you love.

"Absolutely the pink one." Emma had started to change as well, putting on a pair of high-waisted acid-wash jeans and a sleeveless, frilly blouse. "How's work, MJ? Kill Dave yet?"

"Ugh, no. It's terrible." Mary-Jo unzipped the black-and-pink dress and stepped into it. "Dave hired some twat of a guy who refuses to fill in his time sheets and thinks it's somehow my job to do it. So I have to harass him every week and he's clearly getting off on it. It sure gets my attention every Friday at three when it's still not fucking complete, which means he gets me all to himself, yelling at him for ten minutes."

"Gross. They're gettin' desperate over there, aren't they?" I asked.

"They take what they can get these days." Mary-Jo had started to line her eyes with thick black eyeliner, leaning over to see in the mirror. "Don't even have to be good at the job; just have to know what to do. Not many options locally and not a lot of people willing to move from elsewhere to live in town. Can't ask people to commute either. The gas money is killing me, so it's not like I can judge people for not wanting to make that trip."

I shimmied out of my pyjamas and started to change. I wanted to have things to say to Mary-Jo. Advice to offer. But we'd been over it time and time again. She could change jobs, but the options weren't plentiful. She could put up a fuss at work, but it might lead to being fired or it might make her job harder. Sometimes I didn't feel like there was much left to say, but at least I could listen.

Possibly for the first time, it occurred to me that she and I were playing the same game with each other. She wouldn't change jobs and I wouldn't leave Greg, and nothing we said made any difference.

No lack of irony there.

Mary-Jo stood up, blinking back her eyeliner application tears. "But fuck it, we're going out to have a good time, not so I can stand here and make everyone depressed. You're awfully busy these days, Laurel. Surprised we could even get you to come out tonight."

I looked away as I pulled my loose tank top over my head, not wanting my face to display any of the lies I was about to tell. "Hard to get the time sometimes. Repairs, sleeping, housework. You know, the usual."

"I've never seen you so booked up before. You've got a ton of work all of a sudden." Emma sat down at her cluttered vanity and started to apply foundation to her cheeks. "Good for you, honestly. It's not like you can't use the income."

Mary-Jo sat on the bed, in my eyeline. "Whatever happened to that Spencer guy?"

I froze for just a moment, reaching for my distressed black jeans. "What guy?"

Unfortunately for me, my voice broke halfway through the two shortest words in existence.

"Oh my god, *Laurel.*" Mary-Jo threw herself onto the bed in front of me, staring up at my face. "You're full of shit. *What guy,* as if. Have you been hanging out with your friend from Away?"

"I don't know what you're talking about." My face was burning. I was such a bad fucking liar.

"*Bullshit.*" Mary-Jo punched me in the leg, her face under mine, watching my cheeks turn scarlet. "You don't have any new repairs. You have a *fuck buddy.*"

"MJ!" Emma had turned around in her chair to scowl at her.

"I do not!" I hid my face in my hands, my cheeks burning at the suggestion. I couldn't get the words out fast enough to cover my guilt. "He's a *friend.* We hang out a lot, all right? There *aren't* new clients, but I just…It's new! And he's nice to me. He buys the snacks I like and we watch movies and play video games. He *reads.* I just—it's nice, all right?"

"Does Greg know?" Emma asked, foundation drying on her face as she stopped mid-application and stared.

Mary-Jo stared up at me, her face suddenly serious. "Of course he doesn't."

I shook my head. "You know he'd lose it."

Mary-Jo scoffed. "Greg could never stand the idea of competition.

Remember when Billy was talking to you at the bar on your birthday when we were, like, twenty? Greg nearly put him in the hospital. Last time I saw Billy, his jaw still fucking clicks when he talks."

"Yeah, I remember." I jammed my hands into my jeans pockets. "This time it's not Spencer I'd worry about. He could handle Greg if he needed to."

"But what's Greg going to do to *you*?" Emma whispered.

The room was quiet for a minute. I went to the side table and grabbed my drink, swallowing the rest of it. "Who fucking cares. I'll deal with it when I deal with it."

Emma opened her mouth to protest, concern written all over her face, but MJ cut her off. "That's the spirit." She turned on her side, resting her head on her hand. "You could always *invite* Spencer."

"Mary-Jo, stop stirring the pot." Emma turned back to the mirror, working to make the best of her makeup, even through those deep furrows of worry.

"What?" Mary-Jo sounded affronted, as if she could be reasonably thought of as innocent. "I'm just sayin'. We could meet him. I mean, if he's going to be sticking around, it's important that your besties approve, isn't it?"

I sighed, a smile creeping onto my face. Mary-Jo was such a meddler, but she also pushed me out of my shell. Sometimes I needed that.

"*Fine*, but I probably won't get a reply yet. He works a lot of backshifts." For some reason, that lie was easier. Probably because it didn't involve hiding my feelings, just obscuring the truth.

I sat down and pulled out my phone. No new texts from anyone, but I only had two bars in the bedroom. I followed the signal out into the living room and found another two. I tapped onto the conversation with Spencer.

> *Laurel:*
> *There's a benefit dance at the Legion tonight*
> *for that family who lost their house.*
> *Emma and Mary-Jo will be there and*
> *they've been asking about you.*
> *Will you come?*
> *They want to meet you.*

I hit send and waited. It was barely dark, and he wasn't always awake yet. It wasn't likely he'd respond so quickly, but part of me hoped he would. Hoped he'd reply back and say yes. The idea of a perfect night unfolded in front of me, the four of us drinking and talking, music thudding all around the Legion hall. Laughing. The three of them getting along so well that they would become friends themselves, and one dance would turn into a lifetime of moments. Movies, games, campfires. Spencer and Mary-Jo and Emma at my side all the time.

People who loved me.

I shook myself back to reality. Three minutes and no text from Spencer. I shoved my phone back into my pocket and went to the bedroom. He knew where to find us, even if the texts didn't come through. And if he didn't find us, I would live. Probably wasn't that smart anyway, being seen around someone prettier than Greg. Wouldn't want anyone to start talking.

It was fine.

I didn't need that dream of a future with more love than I already had.

I knew how to make do.

When we piled out of Emma's car in the Legion parking lot, another two dozen cars were already parked around the old, cracking pavement. Newer cars, junkers, several carbon copies of the same beat-up Sunfire. Night had properly fallen, and the music was thumping through the walls of the old building. The Legion was hardly a marvel of architecture; it was an oversized two-storey building, flat-faced and covered in windows in the front, bare on the sides. The beige siding gave it no character at all, but in front of the ramp stood a large grey statue: a veterans memorial—our village sometimes seemed to have more names on memorials than living people—with a snow-padded garden in front of it. On the front, above the doors, were enormous green words: *Royal Canadian Legion*.

I followed Mary-Jo and Emma up the steps and inside. The door opened and the music escaped into the night, an '80s classic rock song blasting out of the speakers. It wouldn't be a band—it was almost never a band—but it was one of the better local DJs. Though around those parts, a DJ was just someone with a good playlist and a set of speakers. As with every other dance, we hung our coats on the Legion's built-in coat rack and paid our cover fee at the folded-down card table near the entrance. Inside, a slew of horrible laser shapes zoomed around the high-ceilinged hall, changing in colour and pattern in some deranged budget version of a light show. The walls were painted with enormous murals of war scenery, which really made for a hell of a finishing touch on dance decor.

The place was already packed, which meant at least thirty people had shown up, half of them out dancing. And the half that were dancing were the women, of course. Men didn't dance in Penny Harbour. They sat and drank, or they held up the walls and drank.

The three of us made our way to the cash bar. The drinks were overpriced, but putting money into the pockets of the family was the point, so none of us minded. The Harbour didn't have much cash as a whole, but when someone needed it, we found a way to make it flow in their direction. No one wanted a *handout,* though, so intermediaries like dances and fundraisers were needed to soften the blow. Mary-Jo ordered a Coors, Emma got a Breezer, and I opted for a Mike's Hard Lemonade. Drinks in hand, we went to pick out an empty table.

I pulled out my phone for the first time since we'd left Emma's. I hadn't heard it ping, but a text was waiting.

> Spencer:
> I wish I could. There'd be too many people, I think.
> Too many questions.
> Have fun tonight

Disappointment rushed over me. No matter what I'd told myself since sending that text, I'd really, *really* hoped he would come. The future I'd imagined vanished in an instant. Maybe he would never meet Emma and Mary-Jo, and my lives would have to remain separate. I could understand, logically, that he needed to protect himself. In all honesty, it was foolish for me to be seen in public with him in a place where I'd grown up with every face in the Legion. In a place where it could have gotten back to Greg.

But still.

I had hoped.

I tucked my phone back into my pants and turned my attention to the table, ready to drown my feelings.

Spencer

Will you come?

The text had been waiting for me when I woke. I was used to waking up to messages from Laurel, but I'd hardly expected that. The words weighed on me as I got out of bed and went downstairs, Spectre perched on my shoulder. I carried her down to the kitchen and set out a dish of food for her. As I warmed my own meagre breakfast, I continued to stew on what I'd said back to her.

I couldn't go. I had gone years in Penny Harbour without being noticed, and it was by staying inside, not killing anyone, and not showing my face anywhere for too long. To be seen was to be remarked on, and in a place that knew all the faces already, I would stand out like an easy mark in a nightclub.

When the blood was warm, I poured it into a wine glass and went to the window. Drawing the curtain revealed a beautiful winter night, sparkling white below a starry, cloudless sky. Somewhere in that direction, Laurel was spending her time with the most important people in her life.

I wanted badly to be one of them.

When was the last time I'd been out for more than the hunt? The last time I'd had a drink with good company, staying out late to laugh and be part of something? Since my loves were taken, certainly. I had spent time drowning my sorrows in bars, yes, but that was hardly the same. I'd been trapped away from joy since then, a cage of my own making. Of *grief's* own making, if I was being fair to myself for a moment.

But this woman, *this fucking woman*, was peeling back the solitude I'd so carefully wound myself in, and I wanted to see her. I could. I could just open the door and go to her. If I did, would anyone around her know me for what I was? Would they somehow see the beast in my eyes?

It was nonsense; I knew that. For more than two centuries, I'd walked countless bars and streets and convinced countless pretty things to come dine with me, and none of those people had known me for what I was until my teeth were in their necks. So what kept me so sure that these people would?

The loss. The fear of starting over. Of running. Of going out there and opening my heart, only to have everything torn away again.

To have *her* torn away.

I drank back the glass all at once and then let the last drops slide down onto my tongue.

Immediately, all I wanted was *more*.

It was never enough.

Gods, I was constantly walking on dangerous ground. Keeping myself barely sated. Thinking of her too often. Keeping myself from texting her lest *Greg* catch us. Stopping myself from going over there in a fit of rage and ending him whenever Laurel looked even remotely sad.

I wasn't daft.

She was rapidly becoming more important to me than I'd expected.

Maybe in a different time or place, she would've been just another person. Just another meal. But here, she was everything. Constant. Always present, if not physically, then thoughts of her keeping me company. I hadn't let myself wonder too deeply. She wasn't letting go of Greg, and I certainly wasn't fool enough to think she would defy him in feeling something for me. I should swallow it down, if only because I had to.

She was hardly going to come and live in the night with me, eating people and running from the sun, after all. And if I were to scare her away by being too forthright with my feelings, I was out the only friend I'd made in decades. She was so easy to startle sometimes. It was never pain or violence that scared her but, somehow, affection.

Spectre knocked her head into my leg and I brought my thoughts back to the present. I picked her up and propped her up in my arms, my glass balanced by the stem between two fingers.

"What do you think I should do? Should I stay home?" I asked, smiling down into her yellow eyes, her pupils as large as saucers.

Without a blink, she swatted at my face, her claws raking down my cheek.

I hissed, nearly dropping her and the glass. "Damn it, you bitch. It was just a question." I could feel blood pooling along the scratches.

She began to purr, staring up at me like she'd never done anything wrong in her life.

"Fine." I took her to the kitchen to replace the empty blood glass with an open-corked bottle of red wine. "But if you want me to go, you need to help me find an outfit. What does one even wear to a *benefit dance* in the middle of nowhere?"

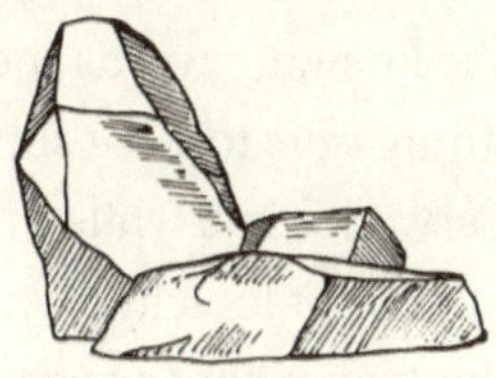

Penny Harbour

Every generation, there were a few souls around Penny Harbour whose misery followed them like a cloak of disgust, especially around the age of thirteen. That specific taste of self-hatred and loathing. An unsettledness in the skin. Disgust of the self, mixed with confusion and isolation.

Some shoved it down their whole lives.

Those who did…tended to have very short lives.

But of the few whose very specific misery fed into the lifeblood of Penny Harbour, one seemed most acute.

So many things were wrong in Jacob's life, but the most pressing of them at the moment was the cold. It seeped into her bones, and she had to suppress a shiver as she held aloft the light for her father as he tinkered at the engine.

"Here, Jacob. Not—here, damn it," her father mumbled, tapping the wrench on the spot he needed light.

Jacob didn't even know why she was out here, freezing her ass off, doing nothing but holding a light while her father worked. Especially when the light in her hand had a hook to hang off the hood currently propped open before them. But better safe than sorry, for the price of telling her parents no, in her experience, far outweighed the cost of mild hypothermia.

Her father was at least better than her mother. Less yelling, less ignoring, more getting her to try new things. Constantly pushing her to do something with her life. More present. More listening.

Trying to make her a better human, she supposed.

But the truth was she didn't care. About any of it.

Mostly because she didn't know who—or what—she was. How could you care about anything when you didn't feel like you belonged anywhere?

There was no language she knew, no words she could say. She'd never heard anything describe anything *close* to what she was. Sure, she'd heard of those drag shows they did every once in a while in town, but those were meant to be laughed at. They certainly didn't look like what she wanted for herself.

It wasn't as if she could look up what she was. She had no internet access, and when she did, she was afraid to get caught looking for answers that no one else seemed to be looking for.

She just didn't know.

She just wanted to be a girl.

But she wasn't.

And as far as she knew, that was that.

So here she was, stuck out in the snow, holding this damn light for her father, trying to play entire video games in her head to pass the time, hopping from foot to foot to keep warm.

But as always, her mind drifted. To the people in her life. Her mom. Her older sister. Her dad. Her classmates.

She shuddered at the specific memory of asking out Kelsey on Valentine's Day last week. Her words—*Are you kidding, of course not*—sat heavy in Jacob's heart as she relived the moment, the shake of her hands making her father sigh.

"Jacob. Please. You know what, fine. Hang the light there, and go back inside if you're cold."

Taking the excuse and running, she did just that, leaving her father behind and almost bolting back into the house.

Rubbing her hands together in the low heat inside, she tried to breathe some warmth back into them as the memory of Kelsey's rejection still sat in her mind, refusing to let go.

Some days Jacob didn't know if she wanted to be with Kelsey or *be* her.

Jealousy mixed with frustration in her heart. She wasn't allowed to touch the thermostat, and her desperation for warmth pushed her to the washroom to run a bath.

The water came out oily, a flickering of black dust, like it always did in the Harbour. But that was never a bother to her. That was just how the water worked.

As she pulled off her shirt, looking in the mirror, she grimaced.

Her hair was getting to the point where her father complained she was looking like a hippie, but she just…wanted it long. Maybe if it were longer, it wouldn't hurt so much to look in the mirror. She hugged herself tightly as steam simmered off the filling bathtub, trying her best not to look at her jaw, her narrow hips, or the worst of all.

How the skin of her hands was starting to harden, every day a little drier. For some reason, that terrified her. She didn't know why. That her hands, one day, might be as calloused and hard as her father's.

The bathtub full, she dipped a single leg into the hot water, breathing a sigh of relief, not caring about the film of barely noticeable black on the surface. Giving herself a few moments to settle into the water, appreciating the warmth, bit by bit.

And then, with a pink razor stolen from her sister, she did her silent rebellion. Shaving the hair from her legs, nicking them every other minute. A slow, methodical kindness, one stripe at a time.

Tiny trickles of blood seeping into the coal-soaked water.

David had tried everything to connect with his son.

He loved him.

But Jacob was just as broken as he was.

Muttering as he pulled the broken head gasket free, he tried to remember the firing sequence of the engine, but he'd lost it in thought.

In memory.

Fresh out of high school, David had done what several of the citizens of the Harbour had done and married his high school sweetheart. And when the local mill that used to supply the mine with timber shut down and laid them all off, in his desperation, he listened to his father and joined the navy.

For two years, the family prospered. David and his wife had two children. He got to see the world and loved the structure of the military.

Until his wife told him to come home, or she'd take the kids.

So he came home.

And she left him and took the kids anyway. She was just looking for an excuse.

A messy divorce followed, a lying wife accusing him of abuse to a sympathetic judge, when in reality, the kids were suffering by her hand instead. When the children turned thirteen and chose to live with him instead, David hadn't been surprised.

It made him so happy.

But it also meant his ex-wife wasn't paying the child support anytime soon, despite all the money he'd paid her when the kids were with her and her new husband. He'd starve himself for a day here and there to make sure the kids had food. He desperately needed that child support, but he couldn't afford a lawyer to get it.

But for his kids, he tried.

God, did he try.

Some nights it was hard, really damn hard. But he did his damn best.

And so far, he thought he was doing all right. Charlotte, Jacob's sister, was easy. A bit wild, but his daughter had friends, had her music, and was happy, as far as he knew.

Jacob, his younger child…Well.

Jacob had only moved in last year, and for a fourteen-year-old, he was a handsome kid. Bright, smart, did all right in school—at least as far as his grades went. But there was a lack of life in his eyes. David could see it plain as day. The kid was miserable.

David tried everything he could think of. Put the kid in hockey, but his first time on the ice he got checked so hard he didn't get back up. Watching him get escorted off the ice, David couldn't believe his son, crying his eyes out over a single hit.

Next it was music. He put a guitar in Jacob's hands, and damn was he good, but… Still, no life in it. He wanted to give up the first week, and six months later it was the same story.

David took him hunting every season, and that he liked well enough, but he took no joy in it. Nothing.

He'd hoped that maybe by being outside, watching him work on the engine, Jacob would get interested in cars, in the mechanics of the engine. Like how David had with his father. Before David was Jacob's age, he was tinkering with dirt bikes and four-wheelers. Maybe it would be the thing that got his attention. Put some life into his eyes.

But instead, the boy looked like he'd been about to cry any minute.

With a sigh, David worked away, wondering about his son as the wrenches clicked under his experienced hand, with little puffs of blackened dust shuddering off each bolt like rust.

CHAPTER THIRTEEN

Laurel

On our third drink of the night, while taking a small break from dancing, Emma, Mary-Jo, and I had settled into a row of chairs along the edge of the room. We were forced to lean close to be heard over the thumping roar of the classic track "Hot in Herre."

"Nancy does *not* look impressed," Emma said, staring at Nancy and her husband, who were clearly arguing from the other side of the dance floor.

"Obviously not. Have you met him?" I asked. Dude was a jackass through and through. Among other things, he was arrested for hunting moose out of season two years back and did jail time for it to boot.

Mary-Jo's head turned. She sat up bolt straight, looking past me. "Who the fuck is that?"

Someone Mary-Jo didn't recognize was rare. She knew everyone. I turned to look, and a smile crept on my face.

Spencer was handing cash to the lady at the card table, paying his entrance fee. He dug into his wallet and stuffed more cash into the donation jar, which earned a bright smile from Rhonda. He said something to her, returning the smile, and then strode into the room, eyes scanning the small crowd.

Spencer had clearly made an attempt to blend in. He wore a plain white T-shirt—though anyone paying attention would see it was slim fitting—without any kind of embellishment, over a pair of black skinny jeans. He wore nothing loud or out of the ordinary about him at all, unless you caught

180

a glimpse of the crisscrossing jean strips on either side of his hips that left tiny patches of skin exposed. His blonde hair was mussed and a beautiful sharpness glinted in his eyes that caught my breath.

No wonder so many people had chosen to walk into the night with him, never to be seen again.

Spencer caught sight of me. I gave him a wave and he smirked, moving toward the table.

Mary-Jo smacked my arm. "No fucking way!" she yelled. "That hottie is Spencer? Fuck *off*."

I blushed, turning my attention to him as he came to stand over me. "I didn't think you were coming," I said, loudly enough to be heard over the music.

"I changed my mind. May I?" Spencer gestured to an empty chair next to me. I gave a wave of permission. He pulled the chair closer, so that we formed more of a circle than a line, our heads together to be heard.

Mary-Jo gave me a scandalised look and then turned to Spencer. "You must be Spencer, the mystery guy who has been stealing our friend away."

Spencer laughed. "And by that comment, you must be Mary-Jo."

"It's nice to meet you," Emma said. "What brings you to Penny Harbour?"

The questions were starting so quickly, and I hadn't thought of any answers to help him cover his ass. I would have, if he had told me he was coming. Would he—?

"The Harbour seemed like a good place to get my shit together," he answered without missing a beat. "It's quiet. Easy to keep to myself."

"You must have." Mary-Jo paused to take a drink. "Otherwise all the grannies would've been talking about you."

"What do you mean?" he asked, smirking.

Mary-Jo waved a hand at him. "You're new and you're pretty. That's, like, top-tier gossip in a place like this."

Emma nodded enthusiastically. "Talking about people from Away is a nice break from talking about our neighbours." She laughed, and her eyes lit up with an ease that had gotten rare to see on her face. "What do you do for fun?"

Spencer leaned forward, elbows on his knees. "Nothing exciting, really. Reading, gaming—" His eyes flashed to mine, mischievous. "—*hunting*—"

"He collects music," I interrupted, panic flooding my chest. "Like cassettes and shit."

"Oh, that's neat. God, remember cassettes?" Mary-Jo put a hand to her mouth. "My first one. Backstreet Boys' *Millennium*. Jesus, who was I back then?"

"No thank you, none of that in my house," Spencer said, laughing. "My tastes vary, but that's far too sugar-pop for me. Though I did try Hanson once, and the damn thing got stuck in my car's cassette player. That was an unpleasant week of driving."

"Oh, do you work in town?" Emma asked. "Laurel said something about night shifts."

I hadn't expected the lying to catch up with me so quickly. I knew Emma and Mary-Jo would be curious, yes, but I didn't think they'd grill him quite so hard.

Spencer opened his mouth to answer, but I cut him off.

"You don't have a drink!" I stood up and smacked him lightly on the shoulder. "I'll show you where the bar is."

Spencer looked up at me, a knowing smile on his face. "Yeah, all right. Excuse me, ladies." He got up and followed beside me, leaning in as we walked. "You're quick on your feet, aren't you?"

I gave him a sour look as we skirted around tables and distant cousins. "It's not like you can tell them the truth."

"Laurel, I've been at this for hundreds of years. I would've just told them I work online. Hard for them to prove I don't. It worked on you, didn't it?"

Two people stood in line ahead of us at the bar. I fished out a twenty from my front pocket, mulling it over. "I guess I didn't think of that."

Spencer leaned in toward my ear. "I appreciate the concern. Don't worry about me, darling. I can handle whatever comes."

His mouth so close to my ear sent a shiver down my spine. "You didn't *have* to come tonight. I mean, I'm glad you did. But I don't want you to expose yourself on my account either. It's risky, for both of us." I fiddled with the folded bill, not looking up at him.

Spencer elbowed me gently. "You're worth the risk."

My cheeks flushed. That was an awfully kind thing to say for someone who didn't owe me anything.

The person at the front of the line moved away, drinks in hand, and we stepped forward.

After a moment standing there, I let the words crawl out of my throat, even as they tried to stay lodged in me. "You're worth it too."

When Spencer didn't respond immediately, I looked up to gauge his reaction. His gaze was soft, staring at me with this little crook of a smile on the corners of his lips. Dreamily, almost.

Then the person in front of us was gone, and it was our turn to order.

Relieved by the interruption, I leaned on the counter and craned over so Trevor could hear me. "Rum and Coke, please!"

Trevor looked at Spencer, holding his stare for a second as he tried to place him. "And you?"

"Keith's, if you've got it," Spencer replied.

As Trevor walked away to grab the drinks, I gave Spencer a curious look. "No wine?"

"Do you see any of the men here drinking wine? I'm trying to blend in!" The shit-eating grin on his face had really started to grow on me.

Trevor set the drinks down on the counter and I handed him the twenty. "Put the rest in the donation jar."

As we walked away, Spencer took a long drink from the bottle of beer. His face quickly turned to a scowl. "Gods, I need a better cover story than this swill."

"Do you want something else?" I asked, snickering at him.

"Nope. I'd rather die than admit defeat. If these men can drink this yeasty bathwater, so can I." Spencer took another long drink, as if getting it down faster would help.

As we approached Emma and Mary-Jo—who were both watching us, grinning as they spoke into each other's ears—the song faded into another, and Emma squealed.

Spencer seemed to be trying to identify the song, and it said a lot about the company in the room that we all knew it by heart and he did not.

Mary-Jo and Emma were off their feet, drinks in hand. "Okay, enough chatter, let's get at 'er!" Mary-Jo yelled. "Time to dance. Come on!" She took Emma's hand and hauled her onto the dance floor to join dozens of other women who were enthusiastically shaking their asses to the singer suggesting they "save a horse, ride a cowboy."

"Don't mind them." I leaned in so Spencer could hear me. "We don't need to join."

"Of course we do." Spencer chugged back his beer, made a displeased face, and set the empty bottle next to the chairs. He nodded his head toward the others and waited for me to make a move.

Spencer wanted to dance. *A guy.* That wasn't something that happened in Penny Harbour. Even now, the dance floor was full of women of all ages, doing the white-woman shuffle or participating in a platonic, male-gaze, girl-on-girl grind, specifically for lack of other options. The men were either looking at the women from their posts against the wall, or busy talking to their friends. To be caught dancing was to never live it down. *That shit was gay as hell*, as I'd heard said all my life.

Spencer was going to stick out like a sore thumb.

"Don't be shy," Spencer cooed into my ear. "Your friends are waiting."

Sure enough, Emma and Mary-Jo were beckoning to us from the bright laser lights–covered dance floor.

I sighed, downed my drink, and gestured to the dance floor. That brought a grin to Spencer's face.

We slid in beside the women and Emma immediately let out a squeal, slapping Spencer playfully on the arm. It wasn't far-fetched to think she'd never seen a man dance before, at least not in real life. And Spencer seemed to bask in the attention, matching her enthusiasm.

The drinks made it easy to dance. To let go of myself and get lost in the moment. The thump of the bass, the heat of the room. The chorus of excited cheers when the song changed to something else we loved.

Spencer was the best dancer of us all, and he wasn't shy about it. At one point, he took Emma by the hand and pulled her into some sort of fancy dance move, spinning her around and dipping her. She let out such a delighted noise that I couldn't help laughing. Then they were working off each other, bumping hips and directing horrible dance moves at each other. Emma even taught him the Shopping Cart.

Suddenly, that vision I'd had of a future with them all in it didn't seem so ridiculous. Spencer was still a secret, but maybe one that I didn't need to keep from them, at least.

The song changed and the room exploded into nostalgic excitement. The "Cha-Cha Slide" had been a staple of every high school dance I had attended, and practically everyone there knew the dance. Except Spencer, who was deeply puzzled as everyone in the room shuffled into a series of lines, one behind the other.

I grabbed his hand and pulled him to stand beside me. He watched as I worked my way through the lyrics, clapping my hands, stepping to the side, stomping my feet, all as the song instructed. I kept an eye on him as he tried to keep up, stumbling as unexpected steps arose one after the other. I slid right and he slid left, and we collided, and he was bent over, laughing, as the song continued to play. There was no time to stop, so I shimmied him onward. As we hopped in place, he yelled, "What in the fuck *is* this nonsense?" but the spirit of the room moving in hilarious unison was clearly entertaining him.

After three and a half minutes of mind-numbing repetitive moves, the song turned back to something more danceable, and our little circle closed in again. The levity of the "Cha-Cha Slide" had left us loose, and I had a hard time keeping my eyes off Spencer. The beat of the new song was thumping and sultry, and Spencer's eyes were closed as he moved to the beat, all long swaying hips and rippling hands. And as he danced, the hem of his shirt lifted, the strip of skin peeking out above the line of his jeans, sitting on his sharp hips.

It was *so hard* to look away from all that beauty.

Little Laurel, that kind of beauty isn't for you.

You'd tarnish it, little one.

Besides.

With teeth like those, won't he tear you to shreds?

Spencer

If I closed my eyes, I could pretend I was somewhere else. Not in a crusty old hall in a tiny little village with rainbow snowflake lights dancing on the ceiling. No, with my eyes shut, I could imagine the inside of the Berlin nightclubs I'd once loved. The same thumping bass in my chest, the same warmth of bodies around me, liquor in my blood.

Oh, for just a moment, to be lost in the music.

I opened my eyes, letting the dream fall away, and caught Laurel staring. Curious, it seemed. After a moment, she looked away, playing shy. Then the beat slowed and the music faded into a pop ballad. The room seemed to take a collective sigh, some of the women relieved for the chance to get a drink and rest, and most of the men exasperated with having to join their women on the dance floor.

I watched as people paired off and started to sway in identical tight circles, couples dotted across the dance floor. A woman's arms around a man's neck, spinning *devastatingly boringly* in place, and something about that was profoundly sad. I'd gotten such joy from waltzing with my loves in the centuries past, gliding around rooms together, leading Violet and being led by Willem or Astra. To see dancing brought down to such depressing depths…it nearly hurt.

But Emma and Mary-Jo had latched onto each other, twisting into an exaggerated, dramatic mess. They were both singing at the top of their lungs at each other. Laurel was smiling at them, standing stock-still, one hand on her arm as if she didn't know what else to do.

I held my hand out to her, and she gave me the most adorable, bashful smile before taking it. So, naturally, I pulled her into a twirl against me and swung her back out, just to hear that laugh. And then we were keeping pace with Emma and MJ, acting like fools to the tune of "Truly Madly Deeply."

Laurel was so earnest with her silly little moves, egging me on. Caught in the spirit of it, I pulled her against me, one hand in hers, the other on her waist. I sang with that same childishness, *"I'll be your hope, I'll be your love, be everything that you need!"*

And then she froze. Her face fell, and her dancing ground to a halt. A deer in headlights.

And I remembered why.

We weren't supposed to be that close. Singing love songs and dancing against each other. She wasn't mine to hold like that, no matter how deep or shallow the relationship.

She moved out of my hands and the fear on her face tore at something in me. I reached for her and she stepped back, but her eyes were apologetic. Sad.

I had to get out of there. Laurel looked like a wounded animal and I *felt* a little like one. I leaned in so she could hear me. "I'm going to get some air. Be back in a minute."

I didn't wait for her to respond. Instead, I strode through the tables without looking back, cursing myself. No one got in my way as I headed for the front doors and pushed them open, the cold bursting to life on my skin. I hadn't stopped for my coat, but I was hardly going to turn back to get it.

Walking away from Laurel was already difficult enough.

By any rational account, it was what needed to be done, but I didn't *want* to. I *wanted* to keep her with me. Be the person who kept her dancing, who was responsible for the joy on her face. But she understood more clearly than I had.

We'd both pushed our luck far enough. I'd gotten used to spotting the glares around a room when I danced or did something else *too effeminate,* and I'd gotten the attention of too many people already. It would be a wonder if news hadn't made it back to Greg, but I'd spent most of my time on Emma for a reason. Paying too much attention to Laurel alone would have been a mistake. If I'd done the same with Laurel, her husband would've been trying to kill me before the night was out; that much I was sure of.

He wasn't *physically capable* of it, not in any classical sense, but out of respect for Laurel, I figured I should leave him alive.

I kept walking out into the cold. Stragglers were already crowded around the outside of the building, grouped in twos and threes, smoking and talking. I bypassed them all and went over to my car, sitting on the edge of the hood. I looked up, the stars blanketing the sky above. Far more than any human could see, a vast, *stunning* sea of pinpoints of light. Thousands of stars, swimming in the black.

No matter how this ended, it was a good night to be out trying to live.

I thought of Willem, Violet, and Astra, and the thought of them didn't tear me apart for once. I closed my eyes and it was easy to imagine Willem putting his hands on my cheeks, pressing his forehead to mine. *I'm proud of you,* he might have said. Had said, once. Back in Italy, a hundred years ago, for some choice I had made and had lost to time, but not that action. Not those words. And I could still feel his forehead against mine.

Tears were welling in my eyes. I blinked them away and fished in my pocket for a distraction. I pulled out my phone. No reception, of course not. No browsing to distract myself either.

Instead, my thumb went to the text icon. The conversation with Laurel at the top.

Would it be counterproductive to read them over while I tried to distract myself from how much I wanted to march back inside, take Laurel's hand, and show everyone in there what a sensual slow dance *really* looked like?

Likely so.

I did it anyway.

A few dozen texts later, the Legion door creaked open in the distance, letting the overly loud music out for a moment, before containing it again as it slammed shut. A curvy woman with defined muscles clad in a slinky black-and-pink dress pushed through the crowd, stopped for a moment, and then caught sight of me. Mary-Jo.

"I was wondering where you snuck off to." Mary-Jo came to stand next to me, searching around in her clutch for something.

I looked up at her. Away from all the lights, she had a different look about her. Tired, but hungry. Like nothing in the world was enough to satiate her soul. And little wonder, in a place with limited offerings. Had she ever been let loose in a city? Would a city survive her?

"Just needed some fresh air," I said.

She pulled a joint and a lighter from her purse. "Can I offer you some less fresh air?" Putting the end in her mouth, she flicked the lighter with one hand and used the other to shelter the flame. After taking a drag, she passed it to me.

I took a pull from it, holding it in my dead lungs, then letting it out into the night. It burned in all the right ways, and promised to take the edge off all this melancholy. I took a second, smaller drag and passed it back. "Thanks."

Mary-Jo leaned on the car next to me, smoking. After a few more puffs, she offered it back wordlessly, but I declined.

She spoke, not looking at me. "She's married, you know."

Ah, it was like that.

"I know."

Mary-Jo turned to look at me, though I didn't look back. "You seem like a good guy, so I'm going to give you a piece of advice." She paused, as if waiting to see if I'd push back at that sentiment. "Don't let the ring stop you. Laurel deserves someone who will treat her right."

I adjusted my seat on the hood of the car, pivoting to stare at her. She wasn't laughing, or smiling, or anything that might give her away. She was dead serious. "You *want* someone to have an affair with her?"

"Of course I do," Mary-Jo said through pursed lips as she took a pull on the joint. "Have you *met* Greg?"

"Once. I regret not killing him every day." I made sure it sounded like a joke, despite the fact that I'd fantasized about draining him dry at least a dozen times. It would taste awful, but it would be worth it.

Mary-Jo waggled a finger at me. "If anyone gets to kill him, it's me. You haven't had to watch that shit since we were kids like I have. I've *earned* it. Laurel needed to kick his ass to the curb a long time ago, but an affair would be a great start."

I gave her an incredulous look. What an absurd conversation to be having. "And what makes you think that person is me?"

She shrugged. "I dunno. It's just a feeling." She waved a hand up and down, indicating my general presence. "You're different from what's on offer around here."

I laughed. "Was it the dancing that gave me away?"

"That and your little jeans." She reached out to poke a finger in the hole in the fabric on my hip. "If only there'd been people like you around when I was younger."

"How do you mean?"

She leaned in conspiratorially. "Like knows like, and you're not exactly subtle. I mean, I feel like you're *trying to be?* But you're not very good at it, 'cause there's obviously *something* going on here—" She waved her hand at me. "—but you're also definitely into Laurel, so the math says bi. I dunno. I suppose we're all out here, hiding in plain sight. I used to think there was no one but me in this dinky place, but here we are. There aren't supposed to be any queers around, but I've eaten a lot of local pussy."

I stifled a loud laugh. "Such a presumptuous and vulgar young lady," I teased.

Mary-Jo shrugged. "It's nothing worse than what any of them would say." She pointed at the men perched around the front door. "People just don't like it when ladies don't act pretty."

"Isn't that the truth." I reached out to request the joint again and took a long drag, feeling a little more comfortable as the conversation went on. Whatever Mary-Jo was, she was no liar. "So what would you have me do, then? You know Laurel better."

"How am I supposed to know? I've been telling her to leave Greg for a lifetime, but she hasn't listened to me yet." Mary-Jo took the last little stub back from me, finished it, tossed it onto the pavement, and ground it down with her heel. "She needs to get out of Dodge, but she's not going to do that until she's good and ready. Who knows when that'll be." She took a seat on the hood next to me. "I don't envy you, man. I mean, you do like her, right? I'm not imagining it."

"Let's pretend for a moment that I might," I conceded.

"That probably makes you a sucker for punishment." Mary-Jo laughed darkly. "If you're smart, you'd get your heart out of this because there's no guarantee she's going to change her mind about Greg. But I'm selfish, and I don't want to wake up one day to hear what Greg *did to her* while I was sleeping. He might try to kill you for it, but if Laurel feels something for you, take her and get the fuck out of town."

"*Greg* doesn't scare me, Mary-Jo." His name sounded more like a curse on my tongue than it did anything else. "I promise he can't touch me, and I'd deeply love to ensure that he can't touch her either. But once again, you've known me for five minutes, darling. What makes you so damned confident?"

Mary-Jo looked up at me. "Better a chance with you than a guarantee with him."

She held my gaze and as she did, her eyes started to glisten. Her lips pursed and I was sure she was holding back a swell of emotion. How many years had she been waiting to find Laurel dead? Waking up to find out if today was the day?

The toll of that was obvious in the set of her jaw and the tight flex of every muscle in her shoulders.

"I see." It was all I could manage to say.

I couldn't tell MJ about who I was, not the depth of it. The body count and the blood on my hands. And yet I wondered if that would sway her in another direction. It hadn't swayed Laurel, as dark as that was. Would Mary-Jo accept all the red on me in return for her friend's safety? If that was the only promise I could make her?

Mary-Jo shivered suddenly, wrapping herself in a hug and rubbing her bare shoulders. "Fuck, aren't you cold? I'm going back in, but listen. Show Laurel a good time, all right? Just don't fucking hurt her or I'll cut off your most prized appendage and stuff it in the tailpipe of this pretty car of yours."

"Fair enough," I replied, smirking from ear to ear. "See you inside."

Mary-Jo sped back to the door, her heels clicking on the pavement, up the wooden steps and into the hall.

While the threats of bodily harm were likely uncalled for, I could appreciate the need to protect your people. If Mary-Jo was a fraction of the person she seemed to be, we'd get along just fine. It was everything else she'd said that left me unsettled.

Could I even be reasonably sure that Laurel thought of me that way, let alone that she had a desire to bring that to life? Could *I* stand to open my heart to someone again?

I wasn't sure of either.

I pushed up from the car and started back toward the hall. If nothing else, I would have the night to remember, and sometimes one night was enough fuel to get a lonely little vampire through a small eternity.

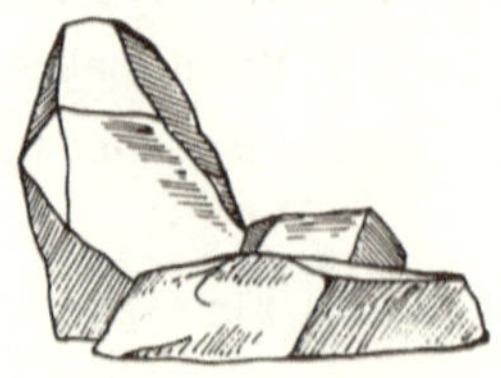

Penny Harbour

Walking the perimeter of Penny Harbour was a right of passage, growing up. For Lily and Stephanie, they'd been doing it since they were old enough to get off their parent's leashes. It wasn't as if much happened down there anyway. Nothing else to do, certainly, but also no thieves or muggers or murderers. They could walk through the night to their hearts' content, and the only thing worth worrying about was bears. But with no one talking about having *seen* bears lately, it meant the night was still theirs.

They walked and talked. About how John's family had moved to town, making the dwindling population of the school just a little smaller. About how something felt off about the time Sarah's mom picked her up from that party, looking like she was gonna beat the tar out of her daughter. Stories about who liked whom, and their favourite new shows, and the depths of their family secrets. All of it whispers on the wind, with no one around to hear.

When they heard the sound, it stopped them in their tracks.

It was hard to say what the sound *was*. So distorted by distance and the air, it could have been a crunch, or a bang. A gunshot even. Lily and Stephanie couldn't make out what it was, but as the dread settled over them, they stared across to the other side of the harbour, in the direction of the noise.

It had been so loud that it had travelled entire kilometres to get to them. Some noises were just *bad*.

"What do you think that was?" Lily asked, staring into the darkness.

"I have no clue. A transformer blowing somewhere?" Stephanie answered.

Nothing followed the sound, and soon they were forced to move on.

They walked fast after that, eager to get out of the dark. They picked up their conversation where they'd left off, but that sound stayed with them like a haunting.

By morning, news had spread.

Lily woke and opened her phone. A dozen messages appeared on her screen from Stephanie and more from people in her family.

There had been an accident.

Lily had heard her cousin die.

CHAPTER FOURTEEN

Spencer

By one in the morning, the Legion was starting to empty out. Sitting together at one of the tables, watching as groups slowly started to pack it in for the night, I turned to Laurel. "Why is everyone leaving so early?"

"Oh, this place will be open for a while still, but we're not teens anymore, Spencer." Laurel pointed a thumb at Emma. "Some people have kids and shit. Babysitters to pay, shifts to wake up for tomorrow."

"But not you," I said, leaning over the table toward her, eager to keep her to myself for a little longer. "You could stay out."

Laurel looked away. "I have a Greg to go home to, and that's basically like going home to a child." She got up and waited for us to stand, not looking at me.

"Yeah, I guess I should get home." Emma yawned. "Mom wants me to help her with baking tomorrow."

"I could stay out." Mary-Jo got up, arms crossed over her chest. "These two are boring, though. You'd stay out with me, wouldn't you, Spencer? I can tell you like to party."

I might have understood Mary-Jo to be flirting with me if she hadn't just given me a speech asking me to woo her friend just a few hours ago. Instead, I laughed and brushed it off. "I do like a party, but I tend to like more of a crowded seductive bar basement than a line-dancing parents' night off."

"The man has a point. Our party game has downgraded over the years."

Emma got up and shuffled toward the coat racks at the entrance. We all dutifully followed, including Mary-Jo, who pouted at me as she walked.

As the four of us went out into the cold, pulling on our coats, we found the parking lot half-full of abandoned cars. Some had already left, either with sober drivers or *not* sober drivers. Equal odds for either, I assumed.

A small smattering of people were still around the stairs, smoking and talking. That seemed to never change, just to be a constant rotating watch of people. Once we were on the cracked parking lot pavement, a thought occurred to me. "How do you three intend to get home?"

"Walk," Emma offered. Her cheeks were newly pink with the chill and her eyes were glazed over from the alcohol. "It's only like twenty minutes by foot to my place."

"And you?" I looked at Mary-Jo.

"I'm stayin' with Emma. The cove is too far to walk to." She burped and put a hand to her mouth. "I'd get eaten by a bear."

"Walkingggg," Laurel singsonged, dancing absentmindedly over cracks and avoiding looking at me entirely.

"You can't be serious." I stopped, looking at her as she shrugged noncommittally. "It's fifteen below, darling."

Emma squealed. "Oooh, call me darling too!"

I put on a thick accent, the purest version of the old Irish I was still capable of. "Anything at all for you, *darlin'*."

She squealed again, dancing on her tiptoes.

"It's Penny Harbour, Spence." Laurel had never called me that, but she'd also never been six glasses of rum deep when I'd been around. "This is how we do things. Drunk Walk is a time-honoured tradition."

"I know all about the glory of walking drunk, Laurel. We did that where I'm from too, but not in the middle of fucking winter *during the age of technology*." I gestured at Mary-Jo's feet. "She's in heels, for gods' sakes. I'm driving you home."

Emma's arms were suddenly around me, her cheek pressed into my bicep. "That's so nice, but we don't drunk drive, *Spence*. It's dangerous, and if you do it, you can't be the Charlie to these Angels."

I scoffed. "I think I'm offended by that, actually. Mary-Jo is clearly a Charlie and *I'm* Farrah Fawcett. I'm also not drunk. I had been *planning* to drive home, unlike you tricksy fae creatures." I pulled my keys out of my jeans—not without difficulty, considering how tight the hips were—and hit unlock. The car beeped to life. "Get in the car or I'll put you in the trunk."

I opened the back door on the passenger side and let Emma slide into the back seat. As I did, I looked up and caught a pair of men staring at me. One had a cigarette in his hand. The other had a beer. Both had long, unkempt beards and ball caps on. Neither of them had wardrobes that would wow anyone, but their glares certainly made their dispositions clear. They were *not* happy to see me.

I gave an effeminate little wave and blew them a kiss.

Laurel, who was getting in the passenger side, stopped. She looked at me, and then back at the men. "Spencer, don't. Not those two."

"Too late." I started to tell her that I'd handled worse than them—and I had—but the sharp memory of searing flames snapped into the front of my awareness, and I held my tongue. All the fun had made me sloppy, and I had recently come into possession of something new to lose.

I got in and started the car, eager to leave the two gawkers behind. I took just enough time to flip on the heat, the seat warmers, and the front and back window defrosters, and was about to put the car in gear when I realized I wouldn't be going anywhere quickly. The front and back windows were caked in thick frost, and I could either wait it out in the car, or scrape it off and leave quickly.

"I'll be right back," I said to the women before getting out of the car. The scraper was in the back seat, and when I opened the door to get it, Emma passed it out to me. I gave her a hurried smile and closed the door.

When I looked up, the men were gone.

I set to work scraping the ice off the back window, the plastic grinding and chipping at the frost. It was coming off quickly, especially with the car running, but it didn't make the warning bells in my head stop ringing. I wanted to leave, and fast.

Not for me.

For them.

I would live through whatever came next, but they didn't need to get tangled up in it. *Especially* if things got bloody.

Music thumped from inside the car. Laurel must have been playing with the dials. The tempo kept switching as she flipped tracks, one to the next to the next, until she landed on something that stuck. Then the hard thump of boots came from behind me and I spun.

A palm slammed into my chest, knocking me off balance and into the side of the car. The two men who had been across the parking lot were standing far too close to me, the reek of whiskey pungent in the air around them. Fighting them wouldn't so much as tire me, but I wasn't willing to involve Laurel or her friends in a brawl. The temptation to swing at them with the ice scraper was strong, but with vampiric strength behind the swing, I'd crack their heads wide open. I couldn't make a scene that stupendous with so many people watching, no matter how glorious it would be.

"Who the fuck are you?" The guy with the beer still had the bottle in his hand. "Ain't no fags like you around here."

I clicked my tongue, smirking at him as I leaned against the car. "Aww, there's no one for you to play with, then? You must be so lonely." The goading probably wasn't advisable, but it *was* fun.

"I ain't no cocksucker," he spat back.

I flicked my wrist toward him, simply because I knew it would enrage him. "Obviously not, or you'd know this is no way to ask me out." From inside the car, someone was banging on the window. Emma. She was yelling something, but the sound was muffled.

He swung at me, as they always did when I insulted their manhood. His fist never connected, though. I moved just slightly and grabbed his arm, twisting until he winced.

"See," I growled, doing my best to keep my composure. A slip of fangs or red eyes wouldn't help anything. "You can't start with the domestic violence. You always open with dinner and wine, sweetness." I swung at his jaw, pulling my punch to what *surely* had to be soft enough. Still, it rocked his head to the side and he stumbled back, bent over with the shock. I smirked. "You'll never get a boyfriend this way."

He was bleeding, I could smell it. Faint. A nosebleed, maybe. I licked my lips involuntarily, and then tried to push the thought of fresh, hot blood from my mind.

"The fuck, man?" The guy with the cigarette threw what was left of it on the ground and took a step toward me. "You're fucking *dead*."

Well, he was right about that, at least.

A car door clicked open. "Hey!" Mary-Jo's voice came from behind me, but I didn't dare look back. "Jeremy, what the fuck are you doing?" The door slammed and the click of heels rounded the car until Mary-Jo had positioned herself between me and Jeremy. "Are you fucking stunned? Did you fall out of the fucking stupid tree and hit every branch on the way down? What do you think your mom would say about you beating people up in parking lots because you don't like how they look? 'Cause Sheryl and my mom hang out at bingo all the fucking time, Jeremy. And I know you got that gay cousin your mom loves so much. How fast you want everyone to know you're a homophobic arsehole? 'Cause I can make sure everyone knows yesterday." By the time she was done, Mary-Jo was almost nose-to-nose with the guy.

My jaw dropped. I'd had a lot of run-ins with people like those, and sometimes others had stepped in to defend me, but I hadn't heard someone use their lineage against them like that since I was alive in the old country.

"Speak up, Jeremy. 'Cause I'm not afraid to lay you out neither." Mary-Jo's voice was gruff, the quirks of her rural accent growing more pronounced. I had a feeling she had been the cause of a few fistfights in her day.

Jeremy looked toward the stairs, where more than a few people were watching us. He looked back at Mary-Jo and swallowed hard. "You don't scare me, MJ. What are you doing hanging around with queers anyway?"

I barely registered Mary-Jo winding her arm back before Jeremy was on the ground. I'd thought she looked strong, but *phew*. The crack of her fist on his jaw was still playing in my ears like the sweetest sound I'd ever heard.

She spat on him. "Go fuck yourself, Jeremy. Next time you want to pick on someone prettier than you, I'll beat you until you've really got something to be jealous of."

Completely enthralled with the scene, I finally noticed that Laurel had come out of the car to stand next to me.

She leaned in. "You good?"

I spoke under my breath. "Normally I eat people like that for fun."

"You must be disappointed, then." Her voice was decidedly neutral, all the levity from the night of dancing gone.

I nudged her with my elbow. "Are *you* all right?"

"I…" Her mouth hung open but the words took a while to come out.

"Maybe this is why I didn't look too hard at who I was, you know? I don't think I would've been able to have people talk about me like that. People I knew." Laurel watched with glassy eyes as Mary-Jo corralled Jeremy and his friend away from the car. "I'm not strong enough to live through that."

"And you don't have to be. You never have to say a word if you don't want to." I set my hand on her shoulder. She didn't say anything back, just stared into the distance. I took both her shoulders in my hands and turned her to look at me, which seemed to startle her awake a little. "Laurel, no matter what, we have you."

She looked up at me, part of her a million miles away. Her eyes were searching my face for something, but I couldn't place what. And a moment later, she was pressing herself against me, her arms around my back and her head against my chest. The surprise quickly faded, and I hugged her in return, savouring the thudding of her heartbeat through my open jacket.

"That's right; get outta here!" Mary-Jo yelled, removing one of her heels and throwing it after the retreating pair of idiots.

Beside us, the car window rolled down and Emma stuck her whole top half out, hands on the window frame. "Losers!"

I laughed quietly into Laurel's hair. This wasn't the family I had lost, but it did feel a lot like a strange version of home.

"I think we're being suspicious," Laurel mumbled into my coat.

"By hugging?" I asked.

"It's not suspicious if it's a group hug. That's just science." Emma yanked on my coat until Laurel and I stumbled back and she threw her arms around us both. "Come on, MJ!"

Mary-Jo was walking crookedly toward us, shaking the snow off the shoe she had thrown and retrieved. She slipped it back on. "What are we doing?"

"Laurel needed a hug, and we're making it not suspicious," Emma whispered far too loudly.

"Gotcha gotcha." And then Mary-Jo was at my back, inhaling the smell of my coat dramatically. "You smell like flowers."

I laughed in surprise. "You're all fools, do you know that? And how long before a group hug also becomes suspicious?"

"Probably this long." Emma wiggled away, sitting back down on the seat of the car. "And my knees hurt." She paused for a minute. "Mary-Jo! I'm old!" she whined.

"I know, man. I'm old too. Scootch over." Mary-Jo got in the car beside Emma and let the pouting woman lean on her for comfort.

"Time to go?" I asked Laurel, who was still leaning against my chest.

"Yeah, I guess it is." Laurel moved away, sniffing slightly. But before I could ask if she was all right, she was walking around the front of the car and getting in.

I looked down. A small wet spot had appeared on my T-shirt where my coat had been open. The sight brought a wave of sadness over me.

She and I needed to talk.

I got in the car and, faking enthusiasm, picked up my phone. "What are we listening to?"

"Paddy Murphy!" Emma yelled, her head in Mary-Jo's lap.

I gave Laurel a pleading look and she took the phone, typed a few words into the app, and hit play. Surprisingly, Irish-style folk music poured out of the speakers, complete with accordion in the background.

Emma and Mary-Jo began to sing along in the back as I pulled out of the parking lot, forcing the car to purr aggressively as we left. The song quickly became a jaunty funeral celebration that was full of mischief, one that everyone else in the car knew the words to.

A verse in, even Laurel was singing again, though with more reservation than her friends. She gave me directions to Emma's house, and when I pulled into the driveway a few minutes later, they refused to get out until the song was over.

"And every drink in the place was full the night Pat Murphy died!" they screamed together, and the song ended abruptly. Mary-Jo and Emma fell onto each other laughing, and Laurel smiled at me as if she were a proud mother hen.

Once their excitement subsided, I turned off the music and tried to urge them out of the car. Gently. "Ladies, you've landed safe and sound. Thank you for tonight."

"Are you two not coming in?" Emma pouted.

"No, that's enough for me," I replied. "Don't want to stay out too long and find someone else to fight. Thank you, by the way."

Mary-Jo waved it off. "Anytime. I love punching assholes."

"Please stay," whined Emma, blinking her big doe eyes at me. "What about you, Laurel?"

She shook her head. "I'll get Spencer to take me home. I'm tired, sweetie."

"Come on," Mary-Jo groaned, climbing out of the car. "Let's leave these losers alone to flirt. Night!"

"Flirt?" Emma was aghast. "*Flirt?* Did I miss something?" Then she was climbing out of the car after Mary-Jo, slamming the door without saying goodbye.

"Let's go," Laurel said quietly, staring out the side window.

I let her be for a while. The drive back to my house would pass in the space of a few minutes, but I couldn't bring myself to interrupt the silence. We drove, cutting through the dark, and the only sound over the engine was her soft breathing.

I pulled into my driveway and put the car in park, but didn't turn it off. Laurel finally looked at me. "I'm sorry I put you through that," she said.

I arched an eyebrow at her. "What exactly did you put me through?"

"I asked you to come out and it was selfish. You got called those things because I asked you to come out. You knew you shouldn't, and so did I, but I convinced you—"

"Laurel."

She stopped talking, her gaze not coming higher than my neck.

"You can't *make* me do anything, all right? You asked, yes. I knew the risks, and they're why I said no at first. And they're why I'm going to say no next time. No more public appearances like that. I didn't see anyone with cameras, but it doesn't mean someone wasn't recording us. It risks me being found out, but most especially risks you with your husband."

"I know," she whispered, and the physicality of it was heartbreaking. She was folding into herself, her chin down and her shoulders sagging. So against who I knew Laurel to be.

I put my hand on hers. "Laurel, it was still worth it. It's too dangerous for us to do again, but I don't regret it either. I would have if something had happened to you. But it's the happiest I've been since…since *them*. Did you know I used to love dancing?"

She shook her head.

"I did. The four of us danced often. It always made me feel alive. The bass of a speaker is like a heartbeat sometimes. It's the only time I get to feel that."

I put my hand to the stillness of my chest. "I'm glad we went. And nothing those two arseholes could have done would have been your fault."

Laurel took a long breath. Watching the words settle on her, I realized I was seeing the person she was with Greg. She had been waiting for the consequences. She had never really explained in detail what they were, but seeing how she shut down in the face of the possibility fuelled a rage in me that took all my willpower to tamp down.

"Nothing is wrong, I promise," I managed to say. "You can stay here if you like. If it's safer."

"I…I told Greg I was staying at Emma's." She looked into my eyes, finally. It was hard to know what I was seeing there. It felt almost…curious. Like she was holding back a question.

"Do you *want* to stay here?" I asked, wanting to be sure the choice was hers, not mine. The way the last few moments had been, I was sure she knew too well how to acquiesce to someone else's will.

"I don't want to go home." It was all she said.

I kept my eyes on her, waiting for more, but it never came. "All right."

Shutting off the car, I got out. While I was unlocking the front door, Laurel's door shut, and she followed me inside. "You should get something to eat," I said. "Have some water. You left some popcorn and chocolate last time, I think."

I took my shoes off and stared at the room, hands on my hips. I'd never had anyone stay in this place before. What in the gods' names was I going to do with her? I couldn't put her in bed *with me*, not as drunk and pliable as she was at that moment.

But while I was thinking, she went to the kitchen, got her snacks, laid the blanket on the couch cushions, and curled up on her side.

"I'll sleep right here," she said.

"Is that going to be comfortable enough?" I asked. I'd slept on it plenty, but I was a centuries-old vampire with excellent bone structure.

"Yup." Laurel shoved a handful of cheese-flavoured popcorn in her mouth. "Could use some more blankets, though. Then will you watch something with me? I don't know if…" She paused for a moment, and then changed what she had been saying. "I think I want the company."

I ran upstairs to grab a heavy comforter and a pair of sheets from the upstairs closet. She was also still wearing jeans, and asking her to sleep in them was cruel, so I went to the wardrobe and pulled out the matching set to my burgundy silk pyjamas for her to borrow. Realizing I too would be stuck in my jeans soon, I undressed and threw on a thin zippered black hoodie and a pair of pink fleece bottoms. All of that taken care of, I went bounding back down to the living room. By the time I made it back, Spectre had found her way to the couch, curled up on her perch on the back of it.

"You go change," I said, handing Laurel the clothing, "and I'll make up the couch."

"Thanks," she mumbled, taking the pyjamas from me and peeling herself off the cushions. I began making the bed, a curious feeling settling over me. When exactly had I started playing caretaker again? I'd doted on my loves plenty, once, but I'd thought that trait was long dead. Now here I was, eager to make sure that Laurel was comfortable.

That she felt *safe*.

As I waited for her to come back, something caught my attention. Despite living within the walls of this house so endlessly, confined to it like a prison, I'd never made it a *home*. It had just been a place I whiled away the hours, waiting for something in me to change. Nothing on the walls, no touches of taste. Just the things I needed to kill time and a blank canvas where a person should be.

Maybe, since things *were* changing, it was time to do something about that.

When Laurel came back, her clothing folded in a pile in her arms, I drew in an unneeded breath. She looked tired, yes, but silk didn't care about that. Silk hung and draped and slid, and as far as I was concerned, those pyjamas should belong to her from that moment on. No matter how ill-timed the thought, she looked *good*.

On some other day, in some other life, where things were easier…

I gestured to the couch. "Your bed awaits."

Laurel set her things on the side table and crawled back onto the cushions, exactly like she'd been before. One by one, I tossed the sheets and the comforter over her, and then sat down on the furthest cushion, where she promptly stretched her toes out to touch my leg.

I handed Laurel the remote and put my socked feet on the coffee table. She took it, staring at my legs.

"Do you have clouds on your super soft pants?" she asked, reaching for the popcorn on the coffee table.

"Yes, I do. I think they're cute."

"So do I," she said, cracking a little smile, and she turned on the TV.

Laurel

Spencer fell asleep halfway through the first movie.

It was hard to tell. He didn't breathe, so I couldn't use my normal methods. That was how I knew Greg was sleeping. It also meant Spencer didn't snore either. And slouched down the way he was, I didn't notice that his head had fallen to the side, tucked into the throw pillow. When had he closed his eyes and drifted off? Even his arms were still crossed over his chest, as if he were impatiently waiting for something.

That was fine. I hadn't been paying attention to the movie at all. Instead, I was thinking about what had changed. The rum was losing its hold on me, and I was starting to see the night more clearly.

I was treading dangerous water. I'd been lying to myself pretty successfully for weeks. Telling myself he wasn't as attractive, thoughtful, or kind as I made him out to be in my head. That it was only in comparison to Greg that he seemed to be those things. I'd been telling myself I was imagining him staring at me for longer than he should.

Spencer was growing feelings for me, I could tell, and I…

I was trapped. No matter what I thought of him, he wasn't an option. Not like that. To choose him was to throw away the rest of my life. No matter how rotten things were with Greg, I had built all of that for myself, and I wasn't ready to just give it away. Because that was what it would amount to. Tossing out everything and everyone connected to Greg to play house with someone I couldn't even take outside in the daytime.

Spencer was amazing, but how could I take a chance on him when I couldn't even figure out if I was done with what I had?

What if I ended things with Greg and Spencer got tired of me? He was immortal. He'd seen the world, done things I could never dream of. How would he be content for long with a little girl from Hicksville, Nova Scotia? Who was I to assume I was anything to him, a man who knew what it was like to have everything?

And what if he *did* stick around? I was only getting older and he would never look any different than he did now. I'd wither away someday, without him. Or die to be with him, which was what everyone in the books did, didn't they? Give up their whole lives to be in the dark with their vampire love. I was still with Greg so I wouldn't lose everything. If I let Spencer turn me—presuming he even cared to put up with me for eternity—I'd still lose everything. No matter what I did, I didn't get to keep my life.

Why had he come into my life if I *couldn't* choose him?

This man who, as he slept, seemed like an angel. Spencer's face was soft and relaxed, his lips open just slightly. A halo of blonde hair, his hoodie hugging his lean chest tightly. Pink nail polish chipping on his fingernails. Had he always worn earrings? He had two sets of holes, a cluster of silver stars in the back and a dangling star in the front. Had I just never looked at him long enough to see the details?

Beautiful. Spencer was breathtaking. Like that, it was hard to believe he had ever killed anyone.

Realizing what I was doing, I pushed the thoughts away. I couldn't open that door. If I let Spencer know that what I thought he was feeling was mutual, it meant having to deal with the fallout.

No. I couldn't do that. Not to myself, not to him. Not even to Greg.

I pushed it down and begged it to stay down.

Spencer was such a very, *very* good friend.

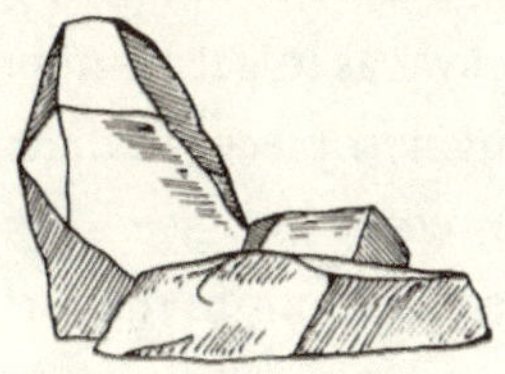

Penny Harbour

Jennifer and Rebecca had been playing together for years. Since they were babies, according to their parents. And at eight years old, that felt like forever, but mostly in a good way.

The two children went back and forth to each other's houses all the time. Sometimes they stayed in, playing with dolls and action figures and, when they were lucky, video games. Jennifer liked going to Rebecca's best, and actually, Rebecca agreed. Being at Jennifer's was *different*. Rebecca had fun most of the time, but she was always playing an extra game by herself. The game of not getting in Jennifer's mom's way while she had her beers.

Other times, they would take their outdoor toys and walk up to the trees that bordered the back of Rebecca's yard. Up there, they could pretend to be anything and go anywhere. Best of all, they had a little tree fort. Well. It was a ground fort since it wasn't in a tree, but they loved it all the same. Once they were inside, they could play for hours. They had even stashed some toys in there for good. Ones they could use whenever they went up there.

Rebecca didn't love the fort in the woods as much as Jennifer seemed to. Every time they went up there, the funky wood flooring was covered in black soot. It didn't matter how often they wiped it off. It got on their clothes and Rebecca's mom would growl at her about it every time.

But more than that, Rebecca didn't like some of the games they played while they were in the trees. Some were fine, ones she played with her friends at school too. But Jennifer played a game Rebecca didn't really understand the rules of, and she never wanted to play it anywhere but in the woods.

Now that they were back up there, Rebecca felt weird. Like her skin was crawling with ants. Today could be another day for the game. Any day could be. She didn't know why, but she *did not like the game.*

Sometimes the easiest way was to get Jennifer into a game first. Distract her with Barbies and building new pieces to their fort. But when she suggested that, Jennifer screwed up her face.

"Nahhh." Jennifer pushed the door to the fort open. The floorboards had that black dust everywhere, and the walls were so tiny that only four kids could squeeze inside at once. They had drawn on the walls with crayons and markers, and their art littered every corner of those boards. Half the roof was gone, but it made it fun to try to climb out sometimes, so they didn't mind. "I want to keep playing magic, like last time."

Magic. The game. A pretend world where all their favourite characters from TV shows were alive and real. They could run through the trees, playing with the heroes and villains, talking to them and having adventures. And that was fine, mostly. Rebecca played lots of games like that. But when Jennifer wanted to play magic, it never ended like those other games.

"I don't want to do that." Rebecca didn't step inside the little fort. It felt much smaller than usual. "If we find a bunch of good sticks, I bet we could build stairs up into the trees."

Jennifer blew a raspberry. "That never works. Come on. I can be the boy and you can be the girl."

Rebecca didn't feel good all of a sudden, but she felt less good about saying no. She never ever felt good about saying no.

"All right," Rebecca said, stepping inside the fort. She walked past Jennifer and did exactly what she knew Jennifer would ask. What she always asked at some point during the game. She started taking off her clothes.

Rebecca wished she knew who had taught Jennifer the game.

"Lay down," Jennifer said, reaching for the door to the fort. "What character do you want to be today?"

But before Rebecca could answer, Jennifer had shut the door to the fort and locked out the world. The magic had to stay inside the fort, after all. Just like the person who had taught Jennifer the game, she knew it was very important to keep it a secret.

She'd get in trouble for playing it, and so would he.

CHAPTER FIFTEEN

Laurel

The days after the benefit dance were hard. A certain amount of it could be chalked up to not being young and impervious to booze anymore. What used to leave me with barely a hangover had now morphed into three days of dehydration, fatigue, and indigestion.

The other part could be described as wasted attempts at denial. As I struggled to distance myself from any of the feelings that had come to the surface at the dance, Spencer continued to exist, galling me simply by speaking kindly to me. Mary-Jo hounded me by text for days about *Spencer this* and *Spencer that*. And the churning was made worse by having to hide it all from Greg.

I'd half expected him to have heard something from the dance before I'd even gotten home the next day. When he didn't say a word, I tiptoed around him for hours, waiting for him to pick up the phone and learn what I'd been up to. Whom I'd been with. What punishment I deserved. But the moment never came. It might almost have been better if it had; that way I could've stopped anticipating it with every breath.

Of course he didn't notice, Little Laurel.

He doesn't think you're worth the trouble.

He doesn't think of you at all.

What kind of monster doesn't notice his wife falling in love with someone else?

It would be so easy to free yourself, girl.

A little violence. That's all it would take.

Two weeks. Two weeks waiting for the sword to fall. Waiting with my breath caught in my throat, getting angrier and angrier with each day that slid by and Greg didn't notice a fucking thing.

My heart wasn't even in those four walls anymore and it should have been *so easy to see.*

If he had been paying any attention at all, I would've been easy enough to figure out.

He *made* it easy.

As time slid by, I filled it with clients and cooking and cleaning and constant worry. Because no matter how much I tried to dissuade myself from Spencer, the feelings always seemed to bubble to the surface. *Why should I have to do all the housework alone?* I would think. *Spencer would help me.* Or, *Why do I have to sit in the house in silence with Greg when Spencer would be delighted to keep me company?* Or, *If I were running around behind Spencer's back with someone else, he'd have noticed by now because he fucking pays attention!*

Not even a shift in my work hours had been enough to spur Greg along. Sunset had drifted to after eight in the evening, and that meant either Spencer needed to be up before sunset or I needed to stay late. I'd started staying away until sometimes one or two in the morning, and pushing my repair jobs further into the day. It was becoming harder to manage. I was getting less and less sleep all the time, but I couldn't help it. Half the time, being in my own home felt like the walls were closing in on me, and the only relief was to stay at Spencer's as long as I could manage.

Washing the dishes was the last straw for me that night. As the game roared out of the TV in the living room at exceptional volume, something in me grew impatient. The noise grated my soul, so loud and disturbing, as he relaxed and I did everything. Like always.

What would he say if you screamed everything you wanted to say to him?
What would he do?
Nothing needs to stop you from hurting him back, little lamb.
What other option do you have?

I dried my hands and went to the cell phone window. I stuck my thumb on the screen and found the chat with Spencer.

> Laurel:
> Want to do something different tonight?

I hit send and put the phone back in the window. Sunset wouldn't be for another two hours. I went back to my dishes, waiting for the phone to chime. Once everything was washed and I was wiping the counters, the phone went off.

> Spencer:
> What do you have in mind?

The delay in response had given me plenty of time to think about it.

> Laurel:
> Let's go to town. 8:30?

> Spencer:
> I'll drive. Meet me here.

The car was already warming when I arrived. I opened the front door to find Spencer pulling on his black boots. He looked up to greet me and my breath caught. He wore a forest-green fisherman's sweater, the entire thing made of intricately knitted knots. It was a sharp, masculine look I didn't expect on him, especially with so much of his wardrobe consisting of silks, florals, and feminine-cut pieces. It looked…downright commonplace for a province surrounded by ocean.

Spencer stood up and gave a spin. "Do you like it? It's my Blending In outfit."

"It's very good," I admitted, and then pointed over my shoulder to the car. "Ready?"

The less time I had to look at him and contain my blushing, the better.

Spencer grabbed his wallet off the coffee table and walked toward the door. "Let's go."

The car had been warming for a while, made obvious by the broil of my heated seat. Spencer got in and started to fiddle with his phone. A moment later, music began to play, a steady rhythm of an alt-rock track I'd never heard before. With that taken care of, he buckled up, put the gearshift in reverse, and stopped to look at me.

"Anywhere specific in mind, darling?" he asked, his expression far too much of a smoulder for me to handle.

"Anywhere but here," I replied, and he whipped the car out of the driveway and onto the main drag.

The world ahead of us was reduced to what I could see in the headlights, interspersed with the occasional light post. The car sped smoothly down the road, a huge difference from the constant wobble of my old truck. Spencer held the wheel with one hand, concentrating on the road. A passing car lit up his face, and his eyes seemed to flash red for a moment.

He glanced over at me, catching me staring. "So, what spurred this on?"

I slid down in the seat, pressing my boots to the far end of the mat, and sighed. "I don't know. I'm restless, I guess? I wanted a change of scenery."

"I thought you liked watching endless movies with me." Spencer smirked, teasing me.

"I like watching *a finite* number of movies with you, but there has to be something else we can do between dusk and dawn."

"You're aware the stores will be closed by the time we get into town, right?" A new song came on and Spencer immediately switched it for something else. "There won't be anywhere to go. If it were the dead of winter, we'd have hours to peruse."

"See, this problem is because you're not from here. You don't know about the single best option we have."

"And what's that?" He gave me a look of confusion.

"Getting Timmies and sitting in the mall parking lot for hours."

"Oh my gods, you weren't kidding," Spencer scoffed as he pulled into the mall parking lot, a dozen spaces away from one of the six other cars that had arrived before us. "So this is why they're always parked here."

"Yup." I blew into the small opening on my takeout cup, hoping the hot chocolate inside would come down from scalding to drinkable. "Welcome to the hippest spot in town."

Spencer put the car in park, unbuckled his seat belt, and turned to me.

"But *why?*"

"What else is there to do, man? The movie theatre doesn't let you talk, plus it costs money. The stores are closed, and there are no other indoor public areas at this time of night. This is what we've got. This and sitting at the border, but they don't have a Timmies."

Spencer chuckled and reached for the cup stowed safely next to the stick shift. "You'll have to show me how it's done, then."

"I can do that. First, you drink things. Then you play music. And then you talk. Repeat until you're bored and want to go home." I raised my cup like a toast. "Drink time."

Spencer opened up his white hot chocolate, took a tentative sip, and grimaced. "Why is it so fucking hot?"

I shrugged. "It's the law of fast food coffee. You're not allowed to enjoy anything right away."

Spencer took the lid off the cup, opened the car door, and started to dump white hot chocolate on the ground.

"Whoa, what the fuck? Don't waste that!" I stared at him, slack-jawed. "I would have drunk it!"

Spencer took the sealed travel mug that had been in the car since I got in and opened it up. He tipped it over the white hot chocolate and red poured out, changing the white to a disturbing shade of rippled pink.

"*Spencer.*" I put my hand over my mouth. I didn't remotely know what to say. "There's no way that tastes good."

"We'll find out." Spencer closed up the travel mug, then the hellish hot chocolate cup, and took a sip. He made a show of tasting it slowly and deliberately, like he was judging wines or something. "Not bad." He took a longer drink, and after a moment, he didn't seem to be interested in savouring it anymore. He was drinking it back like he had been a week without a drop of water.

"Hey, cowboy, better slow down." I had no reason to say that, really. Or a reason to think it was true. What did I know about vampire hunger? But some instinct in me wanted to interrupt the deep reverence he was showing to that cup.

Spencer stopped drinking. He licked his lips, his tongue sliding across his fangs after. When he looked at me, his eyes were that red again, the same they had been on the day I'd found out his secret.

"You good?" I asked, every muscle in my body on the defensive.

"I'm good." Spencer put the coffee cup back and took the mug of blood instead. That he did toss back in seconds. When he put the empty mug back, I noticed red trickling down his chin.

I scratched my own chin, trying to give him a hint. "You got a little…"

Spencer wiped at his skin with his thumb. "Sorry."

I shrugged. "Honestly, that freaks me out a lot less than your horror show of a concoction. I'm never going to be able to drink anything with a strawberry swirl again." I tested out the temperature of my drink with a sip. "But speaking of, how is that hunger of yours? Has the guy gotten back to you?"

"Actually, yes. I woke up to this, and he's fucking lucky, because this was the last of what I had." Spencer took his phone from the console, navigated to something, and passed it to me.

> The Guy:
> Sorry, family emergency out of country, had no phone
> service.
> Back now, pickup this week?

"Text him and see if we can get it tonight." I passed the phone back to Spencer. "May as well. We're already here."

Spencer raised an eyebrow at me. "First of all, it's in the city. Second, you want to come along on a mission to illegally obtain human blood for a vampire?"

I gave him an incredulous look. "Are you going to try to go without again? You agreed you wouldn't eat me."

Spencer started to type into his phone, absently replying, "Darling, I'd only bite you with your consent."

Something churned in my stomach and my cheeks flushed. "What?"

"Nothing," he muttered, finishing the text and hitting send. He put his phone in his lap. "What should we do in the meantime?"

He was brushing off that comment, but I wasn't sure how well I could. Especially since that undeniably vampiric part of Spencer was so visible. I had seen it so little since we'd started spending time together, and something about it gave him a dangerous sort of beauty. "You know…it's strange…"

Spencer cocked his head, curious. "What's strange?"

"I think this version of you is supposed to scare me, but it doesn't." I probably shouldn't have been saying it, but it was a truth that didn't want to stay down. "Red eyes, teeth that could tear me to shreds. But I can still think of more immediate dangers than you."

Spencer's gaze softened, and I was almost worried that that beast in him would slip out of sight, but it didn't. I wanted to keep getting used to it. Keep accepting who he really was underneath. It made absolutely no sense that I was so used to being afraid that I found comfort in his danger.

"I would never want you to be afraid of me, Laurel. You're the only good thing that's happened to me in a long time." The serious, gentle tone of his words rubbed against something deep inside me, and I felt the need to bury it further.

"Even if I'm basically no different than cattle to you?" I joked, changing the mood before he could get to the heart of anything vulnerable that couldn't be taken back.

"Even if you're basically sweet, delicious veal, yes." Something slightly crestfallen had come across Spencer's features, but it was a thing I had learned to live with since the benefit dance. Sometimes he would lean in just slightly to the relationship, and I would lean away. A kindness met with cold silence, or a touch met with empty air. Push and pull, over and over.

"All right." I needed to distract him. "If we're going to be doing this more often, we need a mutual playlist. Name it *The Lion and the Lamb.*"

"*I will not,*" Spencer groaned. "You can't keep making references to those books. I will *die* if you continue this."

"Would you be ashamed?" I made a pleading face at him.

"I would be very ashamed." Spencer showed me the title of the new playlist. *One Girl in All the World.*

Heat rose in my cheeks, despite the clear double reference. "Now I'm the one who has to veto the name."

Spencer smirked, typing something new into his phone, biting down on his lip in concentration so his fang hung over the edge. When he held up the phone again, the playlist read *Dead But Still Pretty.*

I cackled. "Okay, that only applies to one of us, but I accept this title. Now, what are we putting in it?"

Spencer began to list off tracks from all genres and eras, creating a list so eclectic that it was hard to believe an algorithm would be able to do anything with it. I added soft rock from the radio that I'd heard all my life, tracks that were apparently listed as *post-grunge* hits from the 2000s, and a list of singles that my app had exposed me to over the last few years. Within a half hour, we had eight hours' worth of music to keep us company.

"I noticed you didn't add that song from when we dropped off Emma and Mary-Jo," Spencer said. At some point during the conversation, his fangs had retreated and his eyes had gone back to that piercing grey again, though I hadn't noticed when.

"No, that's a sometimes song. I couldn't stand to listen to it too often. But if you're looking for more of that, I can arrange it." I gave him a smirk and took a drink of my nearly empty, nearly cold hot chocolate, expecting him to recoil from the idea.

"You know, it's not that different from the songs of home." Spencer looked out the window, staring at the empty street ahead of us. "My father played the fiddle. There was a lot of music back then."

"Ireland, right?" I asked.

"Yeah."

"Do you remember any of the songs?" I wasn't entirely sure if I was treading in welcome waters.

Spencer thought for a moment. "What I remember gets hazier all the time. If you think it's hard remembering what you did last week, try two centuries ago. But that song felt familiar. Not the exact song, but the spirit of it."

"Would you recognize any of them if you heard them?"

"Probably. I'm not sure. It's not as if I hear that many of them day to day."

I laughed. "Maybe not on *your* playlist. Give me that."

Spencer passed me his phone and I pulled up the entire discography for Atlantic Canada's best-known folk band. I hit play on song after song. Most were easily discarded as too modern, and a few required deeper listening and failed to be a match in the end. Then, finally, one sparked something.

"Wait. This sounds wrong, but I might know it." Spencer leaned forward, tapping his fingers with the beat. "It should be a ballad, not a jig, but—" And then the words were pouring out of him, the story of Captain Kidd rolling off his tongue with more accent than I'd heard on him before.

Excited to have struck the right song, I tapped my hands on my lap and sang along. It was a joy to hear him sing in the first place. He wasn't exactly talented, but he clearly loved to do it. And since it was a short song, it was over much too soon. But his smile didn't fade.

"That…that made me think of Father playing at the pub in the evenings when I was just old enough for work. I hadn't thought of that in a long time." He looked at me, gratitude in his eyes. "Thank you."

"Where did you work?" I didn't want to lose the opportunity to ask him about the distant past. How many people in the world could say they had spoken with a living history book?

"I was a farmhand when I was a boy, growing flax for linen. I spent my youth dreaming of sewing clothing in the city, and by the time I got there, my life was practically over. A year spent making the finest things I'd ever touched, and then I was dead. Turned." Spencer examined the fresh polish on his nails, black and glittering. "Now look at me. A dozen lifetimes later."

"That explains a lot, actually." I laughed.

He squinted. "What do you mean?"

I gestured at him in general. "The hair, the clothing. It matters to you. I guess I just have a better understanding of why now. Did you make anything I've seen you wear?"

Spencer gave me an incredulous look. "It's been a long time since 1793, Laurel. I haven't made clothing since I turned."

"Well, if you ever change your mind, my wardrobe could use an upgrade—"

Spencer's phone let out an aggressive melody, cutting me off.

"It's him." Spencer picked up the phone and scanned the screen before firing off another text. "Time to go, darling."

Spencer

"I don't think I want to do this." I looked pleadingly at Laurel. She had demanded we make a stop first, so it was her fault I was here.

"Spencer Tompkin Cambell, it's just a drive-through. You can't be afraid of a drive-through. You're a centuries-old creature of the night." Laurel was staring at me and trying to contain her laughter.

I put my hands up, frustrated. "Exactly! What am I supposed to have ordered at a drive-through? A short brunette with family trauma issues?"

"*Spencer!*" She was hiding her laugh behind her palm, but the shock was visible in her eyes. "You *stop*. Figure out how to order my nuggies or we're not going anywhere."

I groaned and put the car into gear. "Tell me how to do it."

"Drive up to the screen. It'll talk at you. You know my order."

I did as she said, pulling up to the screen and putting down the window. The box crackled to life, horrific static blasting into the night.

"*ARE YOU COLLECTING POINTS TODAY?*"

I looked at Laurel, panicked.

She sighed and rolled her eyes before leaning over me to respond to the person on the other side of the speaker.

I pressed my back into the seat as she spoke, not hearing a word she was saying. That close, she was overwhelming. Her shampoo, the scent of her skin, the thrum of her heart. It would've been so easy to slip my finger under her chin and steal a kiss. Feel the heat of her lips burning into mine. I wasn't even all that convinced she'd be angry about it.

And then she was leaning away, digging her wallet out of her overalls.

I took a breath and drove forward, trying to let go of what she'd stirred up in me.

Laurel guided me through the rest of the order, not seeming to notice what kind of reaction I'd had to her closeness. Sometimes I was sure she knew. I'd say something suggestive or inviting, and she'd lie through her teeth, trying to act as if she hadn't noticed. As if I couldn't hear her heart thundering to life each time, or see the blush in her cheeks.

I was falling and she was…what? Hanging on to the cliff's edge for dear life, by the feel of it.

With her order in hand, Laurel started to dig things out of the bag. I pulled the car out of the drive-through and onto the street toward the highway. A long fry wiggled its way into my view.

"Open up." Laurel made a chomping noise and smacked it against my mouth.

And just like that, I once again started to forgive the things she couldn't give me.

I snatched the fry out of the air with my teeth and turned onto the highway to the city.

While she ate, I turned up the music and drove, my mind too full of questions I couldn't ask.

Being with Laurel was beginning to wear me down. I still deeply desired her company, but that was the problem. Every time I let her see even the slightest drop of what she meant to me, of how much I had started to care about her, she skirted around it. Made a joke or changed the subject. She knew; that was obvious in how masterfully she anticipated and deflected. She couldn't bear to let it in.

And yet, here she was, once again sacrificing a decent night of sleep to be near me. I'd noticed the shadows under her eyes. It wasn't *just* that she was coming to see me later in the day; it was also that she was refusing to go home. Two nights before, she had stayed until three in the morning and only left because I begged her to, for her own sake.

It felt…it felt like Laurel was chasing something with no awareness of doing it. Like she was drawn to me or my home or something more intangible, but when it came up, she swore she had no idea what I was talking about. From the outside, it seemed like her tolerance for being within

Greg's reach was growing thin.

But perhaps it was just wishful thinking.

Laurel was being torn between two worlds and it was making me impatient. Giving her time was the only option, and yet part of me wanted to shake her. If she couldn't choose me, she should at least stop choosing *him*. Whether I was good for her was debatable. *He* was undeniably bad for her.

The song changed and Laurel began to shimmy in her seat, humming through a mouthful of fries. Relaxed and happy.

I sighed and put my frustrations out of my mind. Part of loving her was to put her needs first. She needed time, and what was time to me? I had eternity.

Just because *she* had a rapidly aging shell that would be dust in a hundred years didn't mean I could be impatient with her soul.

But her mortality was a problem for when she could look me in the eye without turning away.

"This?" I asked, yelling over the music. "This is what you added to our playlist?"

Laurel only responded by singing the words at the top of her lungs.

I shook my head, grinning ear to ear at the irony, before joining her in singing the gritty rock cover. As it hit the chorus, we both dramatically belted out, "Jolene, Jolene," and the moment lifted something in me, if only for a moment.

I kicked the car into the next gear and hit the gas. She squealed, laughing, and grabbed the door handle.

"Spencer!" she yelled, but her voice was filled with joy.

As the music thumped through the car and we barrelled down the highway in the dark, acting like fools, I knew I'd do most anything to make sure she never stopped smiling.

We pulled into the blood clinic parking lot close to midnight. It was a compact little place in the middle of a street lined with enormous stores. Not a home in sight, just neon lights and commerce as far as the eye could see. Despite the hour, one of the windows was lit up. A good sign. It meant he was inside.

"You don't have to come in." I unbuckled my seat belt and looked at Laurel, who was leaning over the dash, examining the building. "Wouldn't want to make you more of an accomplice than you are."

"I'm already in this deep. Might as well come with." She was up and out of the car before I could try to convince her otherwise.

I got out and approached the front door a few steps behind her. After tapping out a text to my contact, I pocketed the phone and waited next to Laurel. She was shivering, the air outside much colder than the car we'd been camped inside for the last two hours. Then the front door creaked open, revealing a tall young man in his mid-twenties. He was dressed down in grey jogging pants and a purple polo, his black hair neatly cropped. Without any facial hair to speak of, he barely looked any older than a teenager.

"Hey," I said, following his gesture to come inside. "Hoe gaat het?"

"Waarom breng je haar mee?" My nameless little student accomplice was not pleased to see Laurel, not at all.

"Whoa, whoa. You speak German?" Laurel pushed herself past the student, her mouth hanging open.

"Dutch, actually, among others. You'd be surprised what a person picks up after a while." I pulled the front door closed behind us and forced him into English. "She's a friend. It's fine. Nothing about our arrangement has changed. Nothing except you disappearing on me, that is."

The expression on his face darkened. "It couldn't be helped. Family is a good enough reason, I think, yeah?" His accent was throaty and heavy on the rolled *r*'s. He led us into the lobby, a lavender-and-white waiting room with an enormous counter behind which a secretary would normally sit, then into the back.

"You could warn me before you scamper away. I'd have made other arrangements." I could hardly tell him his negligence had nearly caused me to eat the woman walking behind me. I'd never expressly told him what I was, though I knew he had his suspicions. "Unless you want the cash to dry up, that is."

"You know I don't." The boy gave me a sideways look. "I said I was sorry. It's not that big a deal, is it?"

I groaned, irritated to be dealing with the obstinacy of youth. "So send me a text, all right? That's all I ask."

"Yeah, fine, whatever." He led us down a short hall and then stopped before opening the door to the lab. Looking between Laurel and me, he pursed his lips and switched back to Dutch. "Weet je zeker dat ze geen verader is?"

"Wait, what?" Laurel squinted at him. "What are you saying about me?"

I leaned toward her. "He wants to know if you're a rat."

"Holy shit, kid." Laurel laughed, mocking him with a look. "You work at a blood bank. I'm not sure who I'd even tattle to if I wanted to rat you out. The cops? The hospital? Doctors Without Borders?"

Unimpressed by Laurel's humour, the student opened the lab door and let us inside. The room was lined with complicated equipment, everything wall-to-wall fluorescent white. But nothing in that room mattered, not even the tall fridges that were packed with the public blood supply. It was the walk-in refrigerator at the far end that held exactly what I needed.

The student pulled the heavy latch and the door opened with the thick noise of suction releasing. Cold poured out around us.

My mouth began to water.

"How many this time?" I asked, trying to keep my composure.

The student went into the back of the fridge, dragging several boxes to the side to reveal a camping cooler. He opened the top to show me the contents. "Twenty-four. Figured I should add a few extras for disappearing."

"What a sweetheart," I cooed, pulling out my phone. A few taps inside an app and the deal was done. "Your money has been deposited. Don't forget me again next month."

A chirp came from the student's pocket. He checked his phone and nodded. "I won't. It'll be here, promise." He slid the cooler toward me. "Sometimes I wonder what you do with it…"

I winked at him. "Believe me, kleintje, you don't want to know."

I went to grab the handles, but Laurel bumped me aside and took one end, waiting for me to take the other. I could have slung the thing onto my shoulder if I'd wanted to, but helping was part of what she did, so I was hardly going to tell her no.

We walked the cooler out of the lab, through the lobby, and out to the car. With the blood stashed securely in the trunk, we got in the front seats. We hadn't even been inside long enough for them to cool down.

Laurel stared at me as I pulled the car onto the road and started for home.

"What?" I glanced at her, trying to keep my eyes on the road. "I hope

222

you're not regretting tagging along."

"We just extorted human blood out of a foreign exchange student and all it took was a pile of cash," Laurel said.

"That is exactly what I said we were doing, darling. You can't act surprised."

"That was, like, straight out of a movie. I think I'm a criminal now." Her eyes were wide, her hands over her face in shock.

I laughed. "Absolutely devious. The queen of crime, surely."

"And you speak other languages. I mean, it makes sense, but, like…what else haven't you told me?" Laurel was quickly becoming pure adrenaline, thrilled beyond measure.

I steered us out of the crowded downtown, toward the highway once again. "Endless things, Laurel!" Her enthusiasm was catching. "I've forgotten more than most people will ever learn, just by virtue of being impossibly old!"

"All right, say neat things, then. Be a parrot for me. I only get to hear other languages in movies."

"I am *not* a parrot." We hit the on-ramp, losing focus on the conversation for a moment as I merged us onto the highway, picking up speed. The car purred beneath me, even through the music.

When I looked back at her, Laurel was pouting dramatically.

I scoffed. "Ugh, fine." I paused, trying to come up with something to say. My grip on the steering wheel tightened as I said the only thing on my mind. "Schatje, we kunnen blijven rijden en nooit meer terug kijken."

"Oooh, what does that mean?"

"It means we need to get home and get you to bed, darling," I lied. Because as beautiful a dream as it would be to drive off with her and never look back, Laurel was never going to agree to that. Her whole life was in that little village, for better or worse.

All I could do was hope she would see which parts of it were really worth keeping.

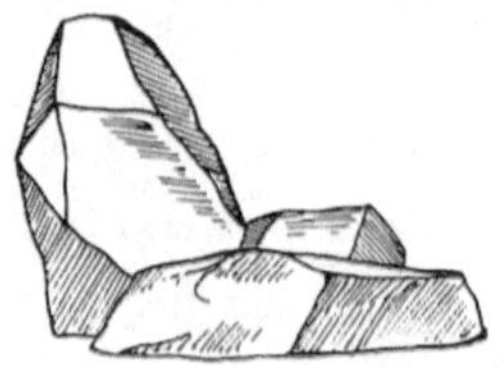

Penny Harbour

Rural Nova Scotia was made of village after village. Homes congregated in small communities, dotting the map, spread out like stepping stones between one town and the next.

The cove was only a hop and a skip away from the shore, a tiny community that was the same as Penny Harbour and not the same at all. The wind whipped off the ocean, crumbling dust from the cliffs. Homes sat on overlooks and in marshes below, and when storms rolled in, they hit those homes with a ferocity that could make their foundations shake.

The shore was a beach, but not the kind they put in movies. It was made of pebbles and sharp rocks and coal seams, and the clay that made up the ocean floor was red, which meant the water was always a muddy brown. It could dye a person's clothing rust red, and that never came out. And when the tides were out, it opened up the ocean floor for miles, leaving space for locals to walk under the cliff or dig up clams. Six hours later, the water would storm back into the bay, creeping up so fast that it had taken far too many lives of people who had just not been paying enough attention.

The ocean demanded respect, and it took what it felt it was owed.

With the warm weather coming, the kids with cars had started to get the shore in their heads. They would pile into those cars, as many as they could fit. Set up on the beach and spend the evening together. Those who dared brave the frigid water might wade in, screaming as the waves hit their skin. They'd light a campfire on the rocks—which was technically illegal, but they didn't give a single fuck about it—and roast marshmallows and hot dogs until well after dark, talking and drinking whatever someone's older brother had managed to score for them.

And if the tide was out, they would walk the shore under the cliffs, looking for sea glass and rocks that looked like bones.

Those cliffs were full of tunnels. Some still standing, some caved in. Mines, dug into the walls, where the ocean might come up and flood inside. Most were impossible to find, but one still stood. A doorway into a cliff, boarded off. Toxic-orange rust baked into the corners of the doorway, seeping out from the entrance and stained into the rocks, trickling down, down. Water running through that path, little by little, taking that coal dust back to the ocean.

CHAPTER SIXTEEN

Laurel

Holding the phone between my ear and my shoulder, I flipped the chicken cutlets in the pan. "Mom, I get it. I've just been busy, all right?"

"Are you getting more clients than usual? You sound tired," Mom chirped from the other end of the Tabs call. Without a landline, service for actual phone calls was basically impossible.

"No, not more than usual. I don't know, I'm just trying to have a little more fun. Get out and see people more. You always said I shouldn't stay cooped up."

"Good, Laurel. I'm glad. Just don't forget to visit me, eh, sweetheart?"

In truth, I wasn't all that interested in visiting. Not just because of the time I'd been spending with Spencer. Mom was off living her own life, having taken it back since Dad disappeared on us. It was hard to watch sometimes. It felt like she had climbed out of a trap Dad had kept her in, and I had willingly crawled into that same trap after Mom had left it.

A door slammed shut in the driveway. Speak of the devil.

"I won't forget. Listen, Greg's home so I've gotta get supper on the table. I'll talk to you soon, all right? Love you." I fumbled to get all the oven dials turned off.

"All right then. Love you too. Bye-bye now." The line clicked and I put down the phone just as the boots hit the steps.

The door flew open and Greg kicked his snowy boots on the outside of the doorframe, leaving most of the dampness outside.

"Hey," I said, trying to start things out on a good foot. "Supper's almost ready."

"I'm not eating." Greg scraped his boots on the mat and pulled the door closed. He didn't take the boots off and started walking toward the living room. "Gonna head to the camp with the boys for the weekend."

That was news to me. "For the whole weekend?"

"Yup," he called from the other room.

I took the meat off the burner and followed Greg into the bedroom, where his fucking shoe tracks led me. He was packing clothing into a duffel bag. "When did this get planned up?"

"This afternoon. Gonna see if we can't shoot a moose." Greg didn't so much as look at me as he jammed socks and underwear into the bag.

Something was sizzling inside my veins. I had planned supper and cooked it, and spent all afternoon worrying about having things perfect by the time he came home so he couldn't yell at me about what wasn't done or how hungry he was, and he was *taking off*? At the drop of a hat. Why was he allowed to go where he wanted with no plan or repercussions, but I wasn't allowed to have supper ready more than ten minutes late?

Because he isn't afraid of you.

But he could be.

It would only take a moment, and he'd never look at you that way again.

"You're back Sunday, then?" I asked.

"Yeah, probably. Maybe Monday. Could decide to call in sick, fuck it." Greg zipped the bag and threw it over his shoulder. "See what the boys do first."

I didn't say a word as he walked past me and back out into the kitchen. I didn't even make it out of the living room before the door slammed again and he was gone.

I went to the cell phone window and peered over the driveway. The truck was backing out of the yard. He probably hadn't even turned it off.

"*Motherfucker!*" I kicked the door, just to have something to act out an ounce of violence on. It was no good showing Greg how fucking irritated I was. It would only lead to threats and berating. Just because he was an inconsiderate asshole didn't mean he was open to hearing about it.

He'd left me with a sink full of dishes, a meal I'd made essentially for nothing, and a weekend of responsibility. Because it was *supposed* to be his job to split enough wood for the next week, but once again it had fallen to me.

I took a deep breath. Yes, he had taken off on a dime, but on the other hand…he was gone. It was six on Friday evening, and he wouldn't be back until Sunday evening at the earliest.

I was free, even just for a little while.

I had all the options in the world, for once. What was I going to do?

The smell of burning chicken brought my attention back to the stove. I scrambled to get it and the rice plated before I charred the bottoms of everything. I should eat first, definitely. And I'd have leftovers for lunch tomorrow. But what else?

Lie on the couch and watch movies until morning, with no responsibilities waiting?

Crank up the music and dance and sing, knowing no one would stop me?

Leave and not come back until Sunday?

Two full days where I could do anything I wanted. So what did I want?

I looked at my plate, then at Greg's, then at the big, empty table.

I didn't want to be alone.

Grabbing the phone from the counter, I went to the cell phone window. Once two bars appeared in the top corner, I hit call. I'd be trapped next to the window, but I wasn't intending for it to be a long call. The phone started to ring, and after the fourth ring, I heard a click.

"Are you all right?" Spencer's voice was groggy but clearly worried.

"I'm fine. Better than fine. Greg is gone until Sunday. Will you come over?"

The line was silent for a moment. "Gods, you scared me, Laurel. You never just call."

"Sorry." I bit my lip. "I didn't mean to freak you out. But will you? I don't know what we'd do but I feel like it's time to pay back all the hosting you've done."

"Yeah—" Spencer groaned, and I imagined him stretching out in bed, Spectre sleeping beside him. "Give me until the sun goes down or you'll have to sweep me off the front porch."

"I'd rather not have to do that, thanks." I found myself smiling suddenly. "Then whose ass would I kick in Mario Kart?"

"I'm centuries old, darling. Ancient. You're picking on an elderly man."

"Oh, *whatever*. See you soon."

"See you soon, love." *Click.*

Love. That was a pet name he hadn't used before. Why did it leave my heart beating out of my chest? I shoved the sensation down and checked the time. Two hours until sunset. Enough time to eat, wipe the boot prints off the floor, and shove those feelings down.

The knock came slightly after sunset. I hopped off the couch and went to the door. On the other side was Spencer, a bottle of wine in one hand, a stack of books cradled in his other arm. Once again, he hadn't bothered with a coat, and he'd chosen a long-sleeved green velvet top with black jeans.

I pushed open the screen door to let him in and then immediately went to put the kettle on. "I'm so glad you're here. Having the house to myself is cool and all, but I basically don't know what to do with it." I grabbed a mug from the cupboard and threw a tea bag in it. "How do people just have the run of their space like this all the time? Jesus."

"Laurel."

I looked up. Spencer was still in the doorway, where I'd left him, the screen door propped open with his foot.

I stared at him. "Yes?"

"I feel like you're forgetting something very specific about vampires."

I kept staring, and after a moment, it dawned on me. "Oh, holy fuck. Spencer, please come in."

Spencer sighed in relief and pushed the screen door with his hip, finally crossing the threshold. "Thank you for your generosity. Eventually."

"No need to get sarcastic on me." I went over and took the precariously tall stack of books out of his arm. "That's going to take some getting used to."

"Oh, it's real. Probably one of the only things that truly protects the living." Spencer kicked his boots off and set them tidily on the mat. "Imagine how fast you could decimate a population if they could be caught unawares in their beds all the time."

"I…do not like that thought." I laughed darkly and went back to the kettle. "Something to drink?"

"I only need a corkscrew." Spencer put his bottle of wine on the table and then made a face. "Laurel, am I losing my mind or is it far too chilly in here?"

I took a deep, annoyed breath. "Ah, yes, that *is* the other thing Greg was supposed to do this weekend. He hasn't split any firewood this week and now he's *fucking gone drinking.* I've been trying to ration out the wood until tomorrow because I can't be arsed to do it in the dark."

Spencer's hands went to his hips. The look on his face was one of contempt. His eyes flashed red, and one side of his mouth went up in an impatient snarl, revealing a fang. The tone when he spoke was beyond irritated. "And how much is left that you can use?"

I shrugged. "An armful. Might get me through the night."

Spencer's fingers went to his forehead, massaging his temples. "Have I ever told you how I feel about Greg?"

"A few times, yes."

"Good. I hope he falls off a cliff." Spencer bent over and grabbed his boots.

"What are you doing?" He wasn't *leaving*, was he?

"I'm not going to let you freeze, Laurel. It's—" He looked around, and finding the thermometer in the window, he snarled. "Gods, it's sixteen degrees in here. You should be wearing a parka."

"I can do it myself tomorrow. I—"

"*Fine.*" Spencer pulled on his second boot and held a hand up. "If not for yourself, then *I'm* not going to sit in a frigid house. For me, cold is the usual. *Warmth* is a comfortable joy that I don't pass up when I have the option. I also have no interest in watching you shiver all night."

My mouth opened and I had every intention of saying something snarky in return, but I didn't. Spencer was concerned for me. I…I didn't know what to do with that. "You don't have to—"

"And yet, I shall." Spencer gave a dramatic bow and strode back outside. "Where's the axe, Laurel?" he yelled back to me as he went down the stairs and rounded the house, out of sight.

I sighed and put on my coat and boots. The thought of accepting help didn't sit well in my gut. I'd been so self-sufficient for so long that it felt disjointed. I was perfectly capable of splitting my own wood, and Greg had left so much to me over the years that I was really tempted to tell Spencer to go pound sand. It was easier, somehow, to contend with being stuck alone with it. Letting someone help…it would hurt more when the help was gone.

I closed the door behind me and made my way around the back of the house. A pair of gloves were stuffed in my coat pocket, which I promptly put on. The lack of light in the backyard made it hard to find Spencer at first.

"Where'd you go?" I asked the dark.

"Over here." Spencer was next to the shed, though I could barely see his outline in the dark. I grabbed my phone out of my pocket and turned on the flashlight. Illuminated, it was clear Spencer had found the axe without me.

I went to the shed to grab a proper floodlight and set it up on the ground outside. I couldn't imagine Spencer would need it, but I certainly did.

The wood was stacked into a wood rack along the outside of the shed, tucked under a tarp. I had nowhere inside for us to keep it, as preferable as that would've been, so we did what we could with it. The rest of the yard was a thin layer of snow on mown grass, and far in the dark, waist-high weeds covered the ground between there and the woods way out back.

A thunk caught my attention. I looked up and Spencer had already split the first log. He leaned the axe handle against his leg, making a sour face.

"Why do I bother wearing my good shirts…" he mumbled, and then pulled his shirt over his head. Suddenly, Spencer was standing bare-chested in my backyard, folding his velvet shirt into a neat square and setting it safely aside.

I swallowed back the panic rising in my throat. He was making it hard not to stare. His fangs were gone and his eyes were back to that beautiful grey. He was lean, but not quite muscular. The beginning of definition was etched on his chest, but without the hard lines of someone who spent their nights at the gym. And the angle of his hips as they met his jeans—

I looked away.

"Wake up, Laurel. This will go faster if you throw them to me," Spencer said. "Then I can get back to that bottle of wine and you can settle for that tea."

I laughed, trying to brush off my thoughts like they had never happened. "Oh, no, if you're making me cut wood at nine at night, you're sharing that wine."

So it went for a while. I would throw him a large chunk of wood and he'd split it once or twice, depending on the size. I'd have no choice but to stand and wait for him to be done, watching. The winding back, axe overhead, then the swift strike down. The wood split effortlessly under his strokes in a way that was definitely unnatural. If I had been cutting it, the log would have given some resistance. Some sense that I was straining to do the work. For Spencer, the axe slid through the wood like butter and wedged into the dirt. It was hard not to stare at the strength in his wiry frame as his biceps flexed and loosened.

I shouldn't have been looking, but it was getting harder and harder to stop. Not just because Spencer was a pretty, powerful guy swinging an axe. He was also there, with me, taking care of what needed doing. Refusing to let me do it alone.

Taking care of me.

That alone was enough for Spencer to feel like he was too unbelievable to actually exist, forget all the rest.

Spencer

She was staring.

It was obvious. Sometimes she looked away, pretending she hadn't been. Sometimes she didn't. At points, her heart hammered so hard I could hear it, even as far away as I was.

The feeling was mutual.

Partway into the work, Laurel had taken off her coat and sweater. In just a vintage T-shirt, she was still working up a sweat, tossing me log after log. A novel concept, sweating. I had done it too, once. Back when I could still walk in the sun. When I had a pulse and a heartbeat and breath.

But watching her work filled me with a strange sort of awe. Laurel was strong and healthy, and the sight of her striving was intoxicating. Her scent was in the air, the sweetness of perspiration on her skin, the remnants of soap and shampoo, the glistening on her forehead. It filled me with questions I longed to answer. How would she feel under my hands? How would she taste if I ran my tongue along her neck? How hard would her heart beat if we were pressed so close her skin could burn me?

Gods, it was cruel to tease myself with thoughts like that.

A hiss drew me from my sinful dreams, and a moment later, the scent of blood.

"Are you all right?" The smell wasn't strong, but perhaps it was worse than I thought.

"Yeah," Laurel complained. "Shouldn't have taken my gloves off. Jammed a jagged piece of wood into my finger."

I leaned the axe against the new pile of wood I'd made and went to her.

Sure enough, though her finger was bleeding, it wasn't much of a cut.

She held her hand over the cut, angling it away from me. "Is this going to make you freak out?" Laurel's eyes were wary. She'd gotten more comfortable over time, but she was certainly no fool.

"I'll be fine. I drank before I left." But her expression didn't change. It was smart of her; I was under control but never all that far from ravenous.

I took her bleeding hand delicately and held her finger to my lips to plant a kiss. Her cheeks were already pink from the cold, but her eyes went wide. I ran the tip of my tongue across her cut. A dare.

I barely got a taste of her. She pulled her hand away quickly, examining the cut for herself.

When she was standing that close, her heartbeat was a wild thing in my ears.

"It seems fine," Laurel said, barely hiding the tremor in her voice. "I've had worse." She looked around the yard. "I think that's enough for now. We should go inside before the whole night is over and all we did was chop wood."

"Of course." I watched her move away, gathering the floodlight and the axe and then stowing them. She filled her arms with wood and went back to the house without a word.

Patience, Spencer.

After dusting myself off, I pulled my shirt back on and followed her inside. Laurel was already in the basement, the clunk of wood rising from the vents in the floor. Soon, the house would warm, and perhaps it would take some of the chill out of the air between us. Or was that just hopeful thinking again?

When Laurel came up the stairs, I clicked my tongue at her. "You're a mess. Go on, get a shower."

She looked down at herself. She was covered in sweat and wood chips, her hair sticking to her neck. She scowled at me. "That's not fair. You don't even look clammy."

I shrugged. "The bloodlust is an inconvenience, but the perks are to die for."

That startled a laugh out of Laurel. She shook her head and sighed. "Fine. I'll be back soon. Make yourself at home." She went into her bedroom, and I found myself floating back toward the kitchen.

The kettle had been long abandoned, the mug and tea bag sitting untouched on the counter. I turned the button on again, in case she wanted it after her shower. As for myself, I needed a wine glass. Well, *need* was a strong word. Polite society demanded I didn't drink out of the bottle, but at the edge of the world that was Penny Harbour, I could definitely get away with it.

I opened a few cupboards. Cans, baking tins, boxes of crackers. Things I hadn't needed in centuries. Things that hadn't been invented back when food was a priority. I pulled down a box of cereal that was laced with hard marshmallows and tried one. Sweet and oddly crunchy, and not something I needed to try twice. I put the box back and found the dishware behind the next door. Four little wine glasses, ripe for the taking. Then it was off to find a corkscrew, which she'd hidden behind the cutlery.

The cork came out easily and I poured. Half a glass of bitter red, something out of the south of France. Then, glass in hand, I was left with time and curiosity.

Pictures dotted the kitchen and the living room. I looked, taking them in one after the other, and something stood out. Laurel had photos of her mother, and of Emma and Mary-Jo. Some were more recent. Others were from more than a decade ago, judging by the youth in their faces. A photo of Laurel in a wedding dress with what must have been *Greg*. But he was missing from every other photo. And her father was nowhere to be seen.

A glint of light caught my eye. A frame I hadn't spotted before. Laurel, standing next to a very young Greg. I picked it up, staring hard at it. Trying to see something that explained their relationship. Explained *him*. They were sitting on the front steps of a building, no older than eighteen. She barely looked happy, even then. Smiling, yes. But her eyes. Had she always been so tired?

Greg's arm was slung around the back of her neck, holding her to him possessively. Even her face read *chokehold*. My grip on the frame tightened and I had to force myself to put it down before I snapped it.

I took a long drink of the wine and walked away.

I followed the hall to the first room. A bare space, except for a small bed, a nightstand, and two bookshelves. A small pile of books sat on the nightstand, and when I bent to look at the titles, they were all copies I had lent her. A smile crept onto my lips. I stood and skimmed the titles on her shelves until I found something to page through as I waited. A silly old vampire novel from the '90s. I pulled it out and went to the bed, sitting on the mattress against the wall, and opened it to the middle.

A while later, the door down the hall cracked open and Laurel's footsteps came toward the room. She walked by at first, and then backtracked into the doorway. She was in a pair of plush baby-blue pyjamas, a towel wrapped around her hair. "I should have trusted you'd find the books." She started to dry her hair aggressively with the towel, stepping into the room. "What did you—? Oh, wow, *that's* the book you picked?"

I smirked at her. "Were you always so taken with vampires? Do you have a *type*?"

She pointed at the book, ignoring the question. "That thing made me so mad."

"Why is that?" I turned it to look at the cover. It was hardly high literature, but I hadn't found anything *enraging* yet.

"Because the main character's whole issue is that she's alone while going through this horrible thing, then she meets the vampire, clearly has feelings for him, and in the end, he just *dies*? Just walks into the sun of his own free will. And she has to keep living with everything she's going through, alone. She went through *all that,* just for him to *choose* to leave her alone again. Doesn't seem fair." Laurel's lips were drawn into a fine line by the time she was done, her towel held against her chest in a death grip.

"Why did you keep it?" I closed the book, got up, and put it back where I'd found it.

"Because I thought about it all the time. Art is supposed to make you feel things." She shrugged, trying to push away whatever was going on in her head.

I stepped closer to her, lifting her chin with the crook of my finger. "I promise not to walk into the sun on you."

Laurel's eyes were glistening with tears. "You better fucking not."

It would be a lie to say I didn't think about kissing her then. So open and vulnerable with me, for just a moment. But when it happened—if it ever did—it needed to be her choice.

And instead of kissing me, she yawned.

"Oh, sorry." She rubbed her eye with her hand and turned to walk into the hall. "I guess that workout got the better of me."

I licked my lips and let out a small sigh of frustration before following her. "Maybe it's time to settle in, then? Watch something."

"Honestly, that wasn't the plan before, but it might be now." She poured herself a glass of wine, and then brought it and the bottle with her into the living room. After setting them down, she passed me the remote. "Your choice."

The TV was at the far end of the couch instead of across from it, which made for odd seating. I sat down with my back to the arm of the couch and pulled my feet up on the cushions, expecting her to sit at the other end. Instead, she wormed her way toward me until she was lying against my chest, sitting between my legs.

I stared down at her, my hands up, frozen in place, waiting for her to realize what she'd done and change her mind. Waiting for that shy denial to kick in and make her run.

She didn't. She just sipped her wine and waited for me to choose something.

The freshly showered scent of her. The cool of her wet hair slowly soaking into my shirt. The creep of her warmth against me. I barely dared to move lest she spook.

After a moment, I lowered my hands and tried to relax. If nothing else, I needed to pick a movie before she thought I'd lost my mind. Flicking through option after option, I found I hadn't been paying attention to my choices at all and hit play on the first romantic comedy I saw.

With Laurel pressed against me, I didn't care what we watched anyway.

Eventually, we were both sucked into the horrific plot. Each time the male lead would choose some tactic to woo his lady, I remarked how closely it resembled things I did while hunting. Laurel would groan and agree, and we found ourselves laughing more at the premise than at the jokes. Then, when I bemoaned a moment of *deeply* straight behaviour from the male lead, Laurel didn't say anything back.

I looked down. Her head was slumped to the side, her breathing long and deep. She had fallen asleep against my chest.

I shut off the TV, unwilling to wake her. A blanket was over the back of the couch, and I struggled to pull it up and over her body. The movement caused her to stir, and Laurel turned onto her side, curled against me.

Gods.

I was trapped beneath her, afraid to move and ruin the moment. Ruin the closeness of her, when she so often kept herself so far away.

A thought flittered into my mind. Astra's voice in my ear as I sat between their legs in the grass one night, lounging. *You long for things, Spencer. Don't*

*lose that. These lives of ours turn into eternities, but if you're always reaching
for something, it will get you through the worst of days.*

Astra. Would she have liked Laurel? Would she understand how quickly
I'd fallen for her? Astra understood loneliness, that I knew. And she would
have mourned just as hard as I had, if our places had been reversed.

Spending time with Laurel had eased so much of the pain. I had learned
to manage it, but it was only with Laurel in my life that I had figured out how
to live again.

When *was* the last time I'd thought of my lost loves?

Three days ago.

How had that happened without my notice?

I looked down.

Her. That was how.

Longing for her had pulled me out of the hole I'd been in. And maybe
that wasn't what Astra had meant, but it was working. Maybe I could finally
learn to keep the three of them in my heart, along with someone new.

The quiet of the house, dark and motionless, was far too much to sit
through for long. I carefully dug into my pocket and pulled out my phone. I
hadn't gotten the Wi-Fi from her and the reception was atrocious, but I had
several ebooks that would help me while away the night. There was no way
in hell I was planning to move, not when I could stay and enjoy the gentle
rhythm of her breathing.

Laurel slept for hours. She barely moved the entire night, so exhausted that
she didn't so much as turn over until three in the morning. I spent the night
switching my phone from hand to hand as I read, my other hand constantly
trying to find somewhere to settle that didn't break her trust. I managed to
make it halfway into the book before I realized it was five in the morning and
sunrise was coming. I had no choice but to go, which meant waking her.

"Laurel…" I ran my hand down her scalp, my fingers tracing gentle lines.
"Laurel, it's time to wake up." She sighed into my chest, trying to get more
comfortable. "Oh, no, darling. I can't have you going back to sleep, not with
the sun coming up in an hour."

She groaned and looked up at me, her eyes fluttering against sleep. The
phone gave a little light for her to see by, but not much. "It's too early."

"For you, yes. It's far too late for me. I'll be charred to a crisp soon and you already made me promise I wouldn't do that."

Laurel squinted, trying to focus. "Don't go."

"I have to, sweetness. As much as I've loved being this close with you, I don't have much of a choice."

Slowly, Laurel began to remove herself from the spot she'd lain in all night. The heat of her was gone and the chill would be back so much quicker than I wanted. "Come on," she mumbled, and pulled herself off the couch.

My body practically creaked as I moved it for the first time in hours. I followed her. She led me to her bedroom. In it, a large bed sat against one wall with a closet across from it, and a small window overlooked the bed. Laurel climbed onto the bed, pulled the shade down, and covered the shade with a homemade quilt.

"Now you're safe." She pulled back the covers. "Stay."

I watched, speechless, as Laurel crawled into the other side of the bed and waited, fighting to keep her eyes open long enough to see me lie down. Unsure of what else to do or how else to fight it, I moved to the bed. Based on the contents of the table next to it, she had given me her side. Probably for the best, since the room already smelled more like Greg than I would've liked.

Laurel covered her eyes with her hand, and I laughed. "All right, you win. I'll stay." I unbuttoned my jeans and pulled off my top. It occurred to me to put something on, since I was lying next to her, but I wasn't compelled to snoop through her things, and I would rather die again than put on anything of Greg's. In just my underwear, I crawled in beside her, making sure to keep ample space between us.

She moved her hand away from her eyes, reaching out to sleepily touch my cheek. "Good night, Spencer."

I couldn't help smiling. She was already falling back asleep. I nuzzled my face into her palm. "Good night, love."

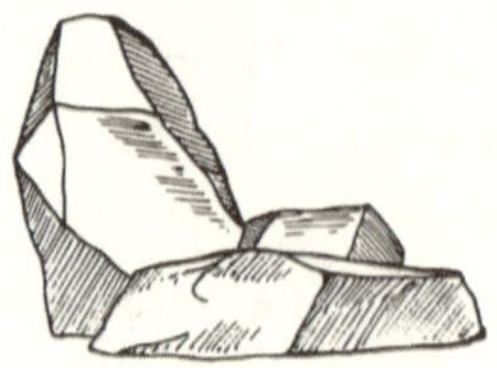

Penny Harbour

A family mourned the loss of their own, far too soon. Their home was like a mausoleum, curtains drawn and dark, eyes full of tears. Sarah had lost her son, and for days, people had been showing up who had lost the same man in the form of a nephew, a cousin, a friend. And she was so sick of it, so sick.

She didn't want words. She wanted her son back.

The doorbell rang.

She wrested herself from her armchair and went to the door. When she opened it, she put on her best face. It wasn't polite to be cruel to people who were grieving, or who wanted to help you grieve. It wasn't their fault that they couldn't *do anything*.

On the other side of the threshold was Richard Andrews, a silver fox of an old man, carrying a heavy box.

"Mornin', Sarah."

"Mornin', Richard. What brings you here?"

Richard shifted the box in his arms. "Well, I got no good words for you, but I do have a quarter of a cow from this week's batch. I know it don't do nothin', but it's what I got and if I can save you a few bucks at the grocery, well…"

Sarah gave him a pursed little smile, one that was so very tired around the eyes. "Awful thoughtful of you, Richard."

He bent down to put the box inside the doorway, and Sarah saw more than a dozen paper packages, each labelled *hamburger*, *steak*, or *liver*. Enough to do her a while, that was for sure.

"It's nothing." Though it wasn't nothing and they both knew it, because

Richard could have sold that meat for as much as any grocery store and made a few hundred from it. "I just wanted to do somethin.'"

"I appreciate it. It'll go to good use, I promise." And it would. Richard had come with something humble and grand, all at the same time, and he hadn't peppered it with useless words. Platitudes that only made things worse.

"Well, I'll leave you be. But we're only just down the road. You ever need a coffee, you just come on by. We'd be glad to see you." Richard was already stepping off the porch, making to leave.

"Will do. Be careful out there." Sarah gave him a wave, and Richard got back into his truck and was gone.

She shut the door and hefted the box into her arms. Taking it to the kitchen, she opened up the freezer and piled the packages in, one at a time. The meat would keep, at least. Until the grief was less and she could stomach eating anything again.

With the box empty, she closed the freezer and opened the fridge. Inside, food was piled high, glass containers with casseroles and salads, one, two, five, ten. Each with a little sticker and a name. Barbra-Jean, May, Grammie Sue, Doris, Rhonda. A gift. A thought. Someone who cared enough to try to make her eat.

But that was the way of things, down there. Tragedy met by kindness.

CHAPTER SEVENTEEN

Spencer

I woke in a strange bed, warm and alone. Laurel's scent was everywhere, along with something musty and masculine that I cared a hell of a lot less for. When I opened my eyes, I found myself curled in her bed and remembered where I was. I stretched, my muscles cracking and popping from the day's disuse, and then curled back on my side, pressing my face into the pillow. I breathed her in and smiled to myself.

Wouldn't that be something? To be someone who wakes up next to someone else again.

A tiny sliver of evening sun peeked through the curtains on the other side of the room. It seemed to be nearly dark, and despite it being time to get up, the comfort of Laurel's bed kept me from crawling out. It was cosy, and despite that she would have been long gone, the bed was still warm. I never woke up warm. When I explored the foot of the bed with my toes, they struck something hot and wiggling. A hot water bottle.

I pressed my hands into my face, smiling like an idiot. Laurel had snuck in and made sure I was warm while I slept. It drew butterflies up from the depths of my stomach, a well of emotion creeping to the surface. Such a small thing, and yet…*gods*, what chance did I stand? This doting on me was going to destroy every last ounce of willpower I had left to give her *time*.

A noise came from outside the room. I needed to drag myself out of bed and see her. Thank her for the kindness. As I sat up and put my feet out of the bed, I found yesterday's clothing and slipped them back on. The bottoms were a bit dirty from chopping wood, but they would wear just fine. I missed the warmth of the bed immediately, but I would live—figuratively.

Once I was dressed, I carefully peeked the bedroom door open. If the curtains were open in the other rooms, the sun might have been pouring through the hallway and living room. But the sliver of the open door revealed only darkness and electric light. She'd closed out the sun, just for me.

I'd been on her mind in a world I'd made sure had all but forgotten me.

Music trickled into the air from the kitchen. The kind of music with heavy instruments that deserved to be played loudly, but she had kept it low, presumably to let me sleep. I stepped softly down the hall and into the kitchen. She hadn't heard me yet. I had a knack for creeping, I supposed, and couldn't fault her for it.

As I stood just metres from her, she hummed along to the music, stirring something on the stove just out of view. She seemed happy. Content. *Safe*. It felt odd, in a way. I'd seen her pull her guard down bit by bit around me. At the dance, she'd been half-drunk, and that had loosened her up for a while. She had slept for hours against my chest, tucked into my arms. But this felt different. She was in her own home, unaware that anyone was watching. Being purely herself for just a moment. Affection bloomed in my chest, watching her at peace like that.

I'd been telling myself no in order to protect us. To keep her safe from Greg, and to keep myself safe from guilt and new heartache. To make sure I didn't forget the great loves of my life, or have someone stolen from me again.

But watching her, I knew I couldn't keep denying it. I wanted to make her life safe and carefree, every day. To hear her sing, off-key and happy, *every single day*.

Despite everything she did to keep me at arm's reach, I loved her, and it scared me witless.

Standing just behind her, I reached out a hand. Paused. Mustered my courage. And I let the longing win.

I stepped into her, chest pressing into her back, wrapped my arms around her waist and whispered into her ear, "Good morning—"

Laurel started, the ladle in her hand flying up and spraying soup all over the stove and cupboards. "Jesus H Christ!"

I let her go immediately, hands held up. "I'm sorry. I wasn't thinking."

Damn it. Sneak up on a woman who's afraid of her husband. *Good. Good plan, Spencer.*

"You scared the shit out of me." Laurel bent over in exaggerated fear, laughing as she tried to catch her breath. "Is one of your fucking powers *floating* or something?"

"Not quite. Stealth helps with hunting, however." I found the roll of paper towels and began wiping up the mess I'd helped her make. "I didn't mean to startle you. Just…wanted to say hello."

Laurel straightened, red rising in her cheeks. "I definitely didn't expect you to say hello like that."

"Even after last night?" I asked.

She looked away.

I leaned on the counter, standing well within her space.

She tolerated the closeness for a moment, looking up at me, her lips parted just slightly. Her hazel eyes were almost dreamy. That close, I could hear her heart drumming rapidly. See the flush on her skin. I was tempted to grab her by the hips and pull her in, but that would be a mistake. She had to choose it. Choose me.

Then she was gone, walking to the fridge.

And with the new sunset, we were starting all over again. At a distance, knowing absolutely what the other wanted, and being unable to span the divide to reach them. And like every other time, it was my job to swallow that frustration whole. To maintain the space when I was all but certain she knew what she wanted but hadn't given either of us permission to act on it.

And as I cursed myself for having reached out to her, she opened the fridge and pulled out a bag of blood.

I shook off the things that were all too large to feel and brought myself back to the moment. "Laurel, are you keeping secrets from me?" I purred, gratefully taking the bag out of her hands. My stomach was gnawing at itself just at the sight of it.

"I thought you wouldn't mind if I stole your keys and went to get it." She gestured at my keys on the table. "I didn't exactly have anything to offer you for breakfast. You can warm it, if you want." She pointed to one of the lower cupboards.

I opened it up, crouching down to find a selection of pots and pans. "You sure you don't mind me tainting your dishes?"

Laurel shook her head. "I'm just not going to think about it too hard, if that's fine with you."

I laughed and picked out a small pot that seemed least important if she did decide to throw it away. I put it on the stove, turned the dial, and set to work draining the blood into the pot.

Laurel clicked her tongue and I turned to see a strained look on her face. "You know what? That's yours now."

I put a hand to my chest. "For me? Is it like having a drawer in someone's dresser? This is my blood pot for when I stay over?"

Laurel hummed a worried noise. "I wouldn't count on being here too often like this, but yes, it'll be here."

Gods, she was still resisting, and I wondered how much longer she could stand it. I knew. I was *certain*. And if she explicitly told me to fuck off, I would respect it. It would *fucking suck*, but I would go. However, everything about her was screaming of resisting the inevitable. Shoving things down, not disinterest.

Denial.

In that moment, I remembered Mary-Jo's little speech about how long I might find myself waiting.

Luckily, I had an eternity to let Laurel sort out her feelings. There was no such thing as wasted time for me.

"Thank you for the hot water bottle. It was thoughtful." I stirred the blood carefully with a soup spoon, waiting for her to say something.

"Of course." Laurel came to stand shoulder to shoulder with me, turning off the burner. "Seemed like you might need it."

"It certainly helps." I brought the spoon to my lips. The batch was rich and young. Full of vitality, and just warm enough. "What glass can I have?" I teased, giving her a wry smile.

Laurel dug through a cupboard and found me a silver sparkly travel mug that read *Boss Bitch* in cursive along the side. I made a face at her and she laughed. "What? Don't you think you're a Boss Bitch?"

"Sweetheart, I know I am, but it doesn't mean you have to make me walk around announcing it *very loudly* like this." I tipped the pot over the mug and poured, before rinsing the pot in the sink.

I took my meal and went to sit at the table. A moment later, Laurel joined me, sitting across from me with her soup like it was any normal day and this was any normal thing we did. I drank slowly, one elbow on the table, my legs kicked out and relaxed. Then something touched my foot. Her toes settled on top of mine and stayed there. Not recoiling, just staying. A tiny, shy smile was on her lips as she lifted the spoon to her mouth. I smiled into my cup.

She was reaching out. Giving me the slightest sliver that seemed to say, *Don't give up on me.*

And I didn't plan on it.

Laurel

Despite eating nothing I had made, Spencer insisted on helping with the dishes after we ate. He chose the washing—for the warm water, he'd said—and I was drying. The sun had been down for an hour, and I found myself staring into the backyard through the window above the sink, drying each thing meticulously and enjoying the peaceful companionship. And as I watched, a deer stepped out of the darkness of the yard, into the faint light from the window. One single buck, just standing there, picking at the old weeds in my garden bed.

"Spencer, look."

He looked up from the soapy water and reached for the towel in my hands. "Oh, look. Dinner."

"Can you get to it without spooking it?" I asked.

He shrugged. "Maybe. Depends entirely on how noisy your back deck is."

The stairs from the deck were creaky as hell. "I could shoot it. Would that work?"

He raised an eyebrow. "You can shoot?"

I shrugged. "Of course I can. Like…not great, but I can. Greg hunts, and before he stopped taking me out to the woods, we'd go together sometimes. Emma and Mary-Jo know how to shoot too. Mary-Jo's better than either of us, by a mile." I put down the pot I'd been drying and went to the coat closet. After fumbling for a minute, I pulled an old shotgun out from the back corner. With a click and a check, I found a shell still inside. It wasn't *supposed to be*, but Greg was an idiot. "Is it still out there?"

Spencer turned to the window. "It is." He came toward me, and then followed me to the back door. "Now this I have to see."

I put a finger to my lips and carefully opened the door onto the porch. We stepped out in our sock feet, and immediately the snow started to melt under me. I crept forward just enough to be able to see the deer in the light from the windows, and then took aim. It had been years since I'd fired a gun, but I still remembered how.

Deep breath in. Fire on the exhale. *Crack.*

The shot filled the air, drowning out the cry of the deer as it reared up and dropped to the ground in a heap, struggling to get up.

"*Holy shit.*" Spencer stared at me, slack-jawed. "That was incredible. You just keep surprising me, don't you?"

I shrugged, blushing. "It's only a deer."

"It's fucking dinner, darling. A three-course meal in the middle of the desert." Spencer inhaled deeply, smelling something on the air; he closed his eyes, and something almost…seductive crossed his face. Longing. When he exhaled, he looked up and his eyes were crimson. His tongue ran across his fangs. Without another word, Spencer grabbed the railing of the porch and vaulted to the ground. Before I could make a move, he had given the deer's head a sharp twist, putting it out of its misery.

I made my way down the stairs to follow him, and by the time I made it to the spot where the deer had fallen, Spencer was already on his knees in the snow, leaning over it. In the light from the window, his face was partially illuminated, his mouth clasped onto the neck of the animal. He was drinking in gulps, and still, drops of blood were falling to the snow beneath him. I stood over him, watching, not quite sure what to think or feel.

I'd never watched him drain the life from something before. I had probably killed it, or had done the lion's share of the killing, and it felt no different than if I had planned to take it home to butcher and cook. It just… served a different purpose for Spencer.

In a way, I was glad I hadn't seen it up until then. It was him, and something about that changed the context. If it had been anyone else, I probably would've run for my life. And because it was him…

Maybe I would feel differently if it were a person instead of a deer.

I crouched next to him and reached out to push his hair behind his ear. Spencer watched me with those red, hungry eyes, still drinking.

"Hey!" A voice came from the distance. "Everything all right back there?"
Ed, the neighbour.

I stood and went to intercept him before he could get too close to
Spencer. Ed was just a shadow on the other side of the low fence that divided
our yards. "Sorry, Ed." I put my elbows on the fence and leaned over. "Didn't
mean to scare you. I know it's not strictly legal, but there was a deer in the
backyard and honestly, things have been a little tight in the wallet. I just
kinda thought if the damned thing was going to wander right into my yard, I
should probably take the gift. Know what I mean?"

Ed gave a little mumble of approval. "Oh, don't I know it. We're about
halfway through that moose Eliott shot in the fall and once that runs out, it's
gonna be a cryin' shame." He gave a little nod. "If you don't find use for some
of them bones, I know the dog'd really like a few, if you don't mind."

"Of course, there's plenty to go around. I'll throw in a steak for you and
the missus too." I stood up and started to head to the backyard. "Say hi to
Jane for me, will you?"

"Will do." Ed gave a wave and turned toward the house.

I walked back to the yard to find Spencer lying like a starfish in the snow,
his face the purest expression of bliss. His chin was covered in blood, as
sloppy as a toddler. I laughed. "That good, huh?"

He hummed his approval. "It's so good to be *stuffed*. The rations, Laurel.
I hate them."

"Well, once you're capable of standing again, you can help me get this
thing into the shed. I promised the neighbour a cut, and I'm going to have to
keep it cold until I can pay an uncle to dismember it."

"Gods, just…just give me a minute. I think if I move, I might throw up."

I laughed and stepped over the deer to sit down next to him.

Spencer stared at me. "Why aren't you running? You should be long gone
by now."

I shrugged. "Because you're never going to hurt me."

"No, I'm not." His red eyes glistened; then he blinked a few times and the
tears were gone. He reached up and ran a finger along the line of my jaw.

A kindness so small I didn't need to run from it.

"Thank you," Spencer sighed. "This helps more than you know."

"Of course." We fell into silence, sitting in the snow, no jackets or shoes, the chill seeping in, as I waited for him to have the strength to get up again.

Spencer stayed until after midnight. Being with him was simple. Relaxing. He knew how to sit in a room together and say nothing in companionable silence, or how to talk for hours about things both trivial and existential. We could read next to each other, sit together, cook together—that one admittedly one-sidedly. And when the chill set into his bones, I sat outside the bathroom with the door cracked, talking to him as he showered.

The fear wasn't *gone*. It wasn't that simple. But his presence dispelled something that lived in my body. In my muscles. He made me laugh, and I felt myself loosen. I breathed deeper, became settled in my body. Not free, exactly. Just like I was on my way to somewhere better.

When I started to yawn, Spencer peeled himself off the couch.

I tried to pull him back down. "Please don't go."

"I have to." He crouched down next to me, his face close to mine. "If he comes back early and finds me here, there's nowhere I can go. If things got violent…well, I wouldn't have much choice. I don't think you want that."

I didn't want Greg hurt, not really. Sometimes the temptation grew closer to irresistible than I wanted to admit. But having seen the barest of what Spencer was capable of, I knew that if Greg picked a fight with Spencer, it would be over in a few very bloody seconds.

"You're right," I sighed. "But I still don't want you to go."

"I have loved spending this time with you, Laurel. I would stay if I could." His thumb brushed my cheek, light as a feather.

I found myself leaning in. My heart thrummed against my ribs as I set my hand on the back of his neck and allowed my lips to brush against his, just once.

Spencer didn't move. Not even in the slightest. His eyes fluttered open as I pulled away. It seemed for a moment like he was frozen. Finally he stood, leaned over, and placed a gentle kiss on my forehead. Then he made his way to the front door. With nothing but his boots and keys to take with him, he opened the door and smiled back at me. "Good night, Laurel."

"Good night."

And he stepped out into the dark, shutting the door behind him.

I touched my fingers to my lips.

What in the fuck was I going to do about all that?

CHAPTER EIGHTEEN

Laurel

I woke blushing the next morning.

Greg hadn't come back, which could only mean he had decided to call in sick, which was no skin off my back. The second he walked back in that door, the change in atmosphere would end, and I wasn't quite ready for that.

I'd gone to sleep with Spencer on my mind, and he was the first thing I thought of when I woke. Curled in my empty bed, I listened to the rain pouring outside my window. The kiss *I'd* given *him* had been so much nothing that I couldn't remember feeling anything except soul-deep anxiety. But if I closed my eyes, I could still feel his lips pressing a kiss to my forehead. That had stirred up more feelings in me than I was willing to admit.

I forced myself to get out of bed, if only to check my phone. To see if I'd been on his mind as well. It was such a fucking tentative game we were playing, and while I hoped to see something waiting, I couldn't let myself hope too hard. This kind of disappointment wasn't really something I wanted to stomach.

I went to look for my phone on the windowsill. Two missed texts and a Tabs message.

Spencer:
The sun is out and I can't sleep
When you're ready, I would very much like another kiss

I covered my mouth with my hand, repressing the squeak in my throat. I checked the time. It was half past nine. Surely Spencer had fallen asleep since. I started to reply anyway, my hands shaking as I tried to get two simple words into my phone. My thumb hovered over send, and I hit it, squeezing my eyes shut, unable to look at what I'd done.

> Laurel:
> Me too

I stood there, trying to breathe, my phone clenched in my hand. What had I done? What would he say back? *What had I done?*

But no reply came. He must have been asleep after all.

Trying to steady myself, I curled up in my armchair and tried to push Spencer out of my mind. I hit the Tabs icon, where the other notification was waiting. Emma had sent a message.

> Emma:
> Hey, know you're busy but what are the odds you could
> help me out? That shelf over the couch fell on one side
> and I can't get it to hang back up. Logan's been fussy and
> I've had no sleep and it's just hanging there. Taunting
> me.
> I'm toast, Laurel. Halp.

The poor woman was always biting off more than she could chew, and the timing was perfect. I *deeply* needed the distraction.

> Laurel:
> Put the kettle on, be there soon

Emma was still in her pyjamas when I pushed my way through her front door. Like most people in town, we had a no-knocking policy. Take off your boots and make your own coffee; you basically live there too. Emma looked up from the cluttered kitchen table and breathed a sigh of relief.

"Ugh, Laurel. Thank you. You know I hate to ask." Emma stood up and gestured at a steaming cup of coffee on the kitchen counter. "Fresh out of the Keurig."

"Thanks, boo." I gave her a long hug. "Got a little too much on your plate, huh?"

She exhaled, sounding exhausted. "Yeah, maybe. Hubby is on the road this week and it's wearing me thin."

Emma's husband was on the road a lot. His job driving trucks took him across several provinces at a time, and he could be gone for a couple of weeks in one shot. It sucked for Emma, but that was the work he had. What was there to do about it?

"You could have asked for help, you know." I picked up the coffee and took a long drink.

"That's the town motto, though, isn't it?" Emma sighed, closing her laptop. "Never ask for help, not even when you're drowning. Wouldn't want to break character."

Emma brought me into the living room. Logan's crib was set up just around the corner from the kitchen table, and it seemed he had finally settled down to entertain himself for a while. Across the room from it was the couch and its hanging shelf. All the knickknacks that had been on it before were strewn across every available surface. At least one of the ornaments had met a grisly fate, cracked right down the middle.

"That shouldn't be too hard." I walked up to the shelf, hands on my hips, staring at the wall. The drywall had cracked from the weight, by the look of it. "I don't suppose you know if this is secured to the studs."

"I assume it's not, since now my funny monkey statue is dead." Emma pouted, staring up at the wall. She looked over at me. "Pop built the place and sometimes I wonder if all he did was follow do-it-yourself videos back then, 'cause he made some poor choices."

"Him and every other person in this town." I pulled the stud finder out of my bag and ran it along the wall. When it finally beeped, I laughed. "Yeah, sure isn't in the studs. Do you want anything done with the crack or just hang this bitch back up?"

Emma gestured to the other walls, most of which had visible imperfections. "Please, it'll just blend in. Leave the crack."

As I set to work taking the shelf down, repairing the old holes, and fixing to put new ones in, Emma sat on the arm of her couch, watching me work. "So what's new with you?" she asked, her chin in her hands. "I don't want to do more schoolwork; help me procrastinate."

I laughed. "I can do that. Not much, though, not really." I cleared my throat, trying to keep my composure as I lied to her face.

I could feel her eyes on me, watching like the perceptive hawk she was. "So what did you do over the weekend?"

"Greg decided to fuck off to who-knows-where to go hunting with the boys, so I had the house to myself."

"Oh, that's nice! What'd you get up to?"

I got down from the couch and crouched down to grab something out of my bag, trying not to look her in the eyes. "Nothing really."

"*Laurel Marie Lewis*, you fucking fibber, you only clam up this hard when you've got something worth sharing."

I groaned and sat back, turning to face her but still not *looking* at her. "Fuck *off*, why can't I get anything past you?"

Emma scooted down onto the couch in front of me, leaning in. "Because we've known each other our whole lives and I'm basically training to notice things for a living. Now fess up."

"It's nothing!" I tossed my tools back into the bag, knowing I was stuck on the floor until the interrogation was over. "I just…invited Spencer over for a couple days."

"*What—*" Emma started, but I cut her off immediately.

"Not like that!" I put my face in my hands. "*Nothing happened.*" Almost nothing, but it was close enough to the truth. "We just hung out and watched movies and stuff. I don't know, it was nice! I didn't have to worry about whatever Greg fucking wanted and Spencer basically never asks for anything. It's just easy, you know?"

Emma hummed a little noise. "Yeah, I think I do know. He doesn't make you feel like you're walking on your tiptoes, huh?"

I shook my head. "Spencer's not breathing down my neck, waiting to get something out of me. He keeps his word and he does things with my best interest at heart. It feels weird, in a way. Like I don't exactly trust it, but it's not that I don't trust *him*."

"Does it feel temporary?" Emma asked.

"A little?" I finally looked up at her. Her fingers were clasped together as she watched me, her face soft and compassionate. "Too good to be true."

"Maybe it's exactly the amount of good you deserve, and it's just hard to swallow that you *do* deserve it."

I groaned. "Now you're being a therapist."

"I am not." Emma reached over and ruffled my hair. "I'm being a friend who thinks you deserve people in your life who listen to you and care about how you feel. And if Spencer is one of them, *good*. You should have as many of them as you can get." Her voice lowered to a whisper. "Bonus points if they're that pretty."

"Emma!" I covered my face again. I was *not* telling her, not yet. She'd make a big deal out of it, and MJ would never let it go. I wasn't ready to face that.

"You know what?" Emma got up and went to the kitchen, then came back with her phone. "I think I'd like to take a break from school tonight. I'm going to call Mom and ask her to babysit, and *you* are going to invite Spencer over to play cards with you, me, and MJ."

"No, no, *no. Absolutely not.*"

Emma was already typing. "Personally, I want a chance to thank the person who's got you feeling safe and comfy. You haven't exactly branched out that far with friends in the last decade and it's important to me that I make an effort to support you."

Her words left me speechless for a moment. I really wanted to fight back because I wasn't sure how long I could reasonably hide all the things I was still figuring out. Spencer was flirty by nature. If he said something in front of them, I might stand to have a coronary and die on the spot. But how was I supposed to argue with what she'd said? Especially since Emma already had her phone to her ear.

"Hey, Mom, listen, I'm going to need a babysitter." She walked into the kitchen, sticking her tongue out at me as she left.

Fuck.

Spencer

Something heavy was on my chest. It pulled me out of a lovely dream about Copenhagen in the winter, and I groaned. When I opened my eyes, Spectre was sitting on my chest, staring down at me. She let out a deep meow and started kneading the sheet with her claws.

"Ow, no—Spectre, please." I picked her up and put her on the bed beside me. "That's my skin, girl."

She began to nuzzle her face into my side, *insistent*, because clearly no one had ever fed her in her whole life.

I grabbed my phone off the table. I'd slept late, the implications of that one little kiss running through my head ceaselessly. I hadn't wanted to scare her off, and I'd spent an hour coming up with the right thing to say. *When you're ready, I would very much like another kiss.* Patient, direct, accommodating. If that wasn't the right thing to say, I had no idea how to do better.

Somehow, a text had managed to find its way onto the thing without it being in the one guaranteed spot in the house where I could get service. A single text from Laurel from earlier in the morning, followed by a much longer one several hours later.

Laurel:
Me too

I stopped reading and breathed out a sigh of relief. It wasn't much to go by, but maybe, just maybe, she was finally leaning toward me instead of away. Hopefully the next set of messages wasn't an immediate backtracking of the first.

Laurel:
So Emma is insisting you come over to play cards
tonight. MJ will be here too.
I told her you work nights, so you have an out if you
want it
I haven't told them about the thing so I'd appreciate it if
you didn't either
MJ would never let it go

I laughed into my hand. No, Mary-Jo *absolutely* would never let it go, and Laurel didn't know the half of it. But *the thing*. Honestly. Laurel was so tightly wound that she was referring to a barely present kiss as *the thing*. Adorable.

Spencer:
Just woke up. Could be there after 9 tho
PS I won't tell a soul that you think I'm
cute enough to kiss

I arrived on Emma's doorstep once it was safely dark. I'd brought a fresh bottle of rosé, a quart of rum, and all the charisma I could muster, despite knowing I was likely walking into an inquisition.

I rang the doorbell and immediately the noise began. Through the frosted glass of the front door, blurred shapes sped into view. Feet running for the door, someone yelling. The door flew open and Laurel was perched on Mary-Jo's back, trying to drag her to the floor.

"Stop it!" Laurel screamed, wiggling as if to make MJ's knees buckle. Emma was staying far away from the whole thing, watching with great amusement.

"But I have so many questions!" Mary-Jo tumbled to the floor and the two of them fell into a laughing heap.

I stared, blinking, pushing back a grin. "Ladies."

"Spencer, you're on my side, aren't you?" Mary-Jo pouted. "I bet you're that kind of guy. You want to tell me how hot you think Laurel is."

I shrugged, a bottle in each hand. "I do my best to be a gentleman and that seems very unkind. It might, in fact, kill her."

Mary-Jo rolled over and pinned Laurel to the ground, driving her fingers into her friend's side. "But it would probably be worth it."

"Spencer, why don't you *please come in* and help me!" Laurel managed to say between fits of laughter.

With the invitation finally secured, I stepped over the threshold and closed the door with my shoulder. I put the bottles on the table and stood over the women still writhing on the floor. "All right, Mary-Jo, cease and desist."

Now that I was closer, I could smell the rum on Mary-Jo's breath. She stuck her tongue out at me. "What are you gonna do about it, fancy man?"

Fancy. I looked down at my outfit and huffed in disapproval. I'd chosen a black shirt and pants with an open grey blouse over it, tied at the waist to create a slimming silhouette. Sure, I wore half a dozen simple thin rings on one hand, but it was hardly worth noting. "You're in a sleeping bag–sized hoodie with no pants and you're calling me *fancy man*? I see." In a quick movement, I scooped Mary-Jo into my arms and threw her over my shoulder.

"Oh, shit!" she cried out as I hauled her into the next room to toss her on the couch. "What are you, a fucking supervillain?"

I smirked down at her, hands on my hips. "Something like that."

Laurel followed us into the living room, panting and red-faced. "Fuck you, MJ." She raised a middle finger, and then straightened to stretch her back out.

Emma joined us, my bottles in hand, playing the role of good hostess. "Do you need a glass, Spencer?"

"That would be lovely, darling."

A moment later, she came back with a glass and a corkscrew, setting all of it on the table beside the couch. "Welcome to my house. You know everyone here. Bathroom is down the hall. Ignore the clutter; I have a baby and a university degree in progress."

"It's a lovely home, Emma. Thank you for asking me here." I poured myself a glass of wine. Emma graciously took the rosé to the fridge for me. "I can't drink all this, by the way. Help yourselves."

"Yesssss," hissed Mary-Jo, who got off the couch to go find herself a glass and a bottle of Coke. "You can come over any time if you're bringing free drinks."

Laurel came to stand near me. "Hi."

I looked down at her, the pink in her cheeks and the tiny smile on the corner of her lips. "Hello."

I'd promised not to draw attention to whatever was between us, but Laurel was doing a shit job of it herself. It would be a dire challenge not to comment on it through the night, and as *fucking adorable* as it was, I'd promised her. That was more important than anything.

Mary-Jo came over to tap her glass against mine. "I hear you're being a super cool guy and Laurel thinks you're the bee's knees. Seems like a welcome to the family is in order."

I gave MJ a stern look. "You wouldn't be suggesting anything, would you?"

She put a hand on her cheek in mock surprise. "Of course not! How dare you. I would never."

I burst out laughing. "Yeah, all right. Whatever helps you sleep at night." I threw myself down onto Emma's couch and kicked my feet out, glass in hand. "Aren't I supposed to be destroying you at cards or something?"

Emma pushed the coffee table closer to the couch and sat on the floor, two decks of cards in hand. She started pulling out the twos and shuffling the decks together. "I think you'll find that you are, in fact, the one about to get wrecked."

Mary-Jo sat down on the floor near me, and Laurel joined me on the couch, but she was clearly uncomfortable. She tucked her legs up and made herself as small as she could in the other corner of the couch, her hands tucked into her lap.

"Laurel," I said gently.

She looked up at me but didn't say anything.

"Are you all right?"

She took a breath. "Yeah. I mean. This is weird, isn't it? All of this. We all know that we're, like…basically hiding out here, since I can't be seen in a room with another man. Even if it's not like that."

Mary-Jo moved to sit on her knees, setting her drink on the coffee table. "Hey, sweetie. You're safe here. No one is coming."

Laurel looked in her lap, her fingers moving in nervous patterns.

"What's the worst-case scenario?" Emma finished shuffling and shifted to dealing cards. "*If* Greg showed up—which is extremely unlikely—I would tell him Spencer is a cousin of mine."

"I also know where Emma keeps the shotgun," Mary-Jo said, not *really* joking, and picked up her cards.

I reached for my cards, and then Laurel's. I leaned over to pass them to her. "And I've got you. He can't touch you if I'm here."

Laurel took the cards from me, looking like a cat backed into a corner. She nodded but didn't seem at all convinced. I sat back, wanting to give her space.

"All right, time to bring out the big guns." Mary-Jo got up and forced her drink into Laurel's hand. "Drink this. Come on, right now. Let's goooo." Laurel did as she was told, chugging back the entire glass of rum and Coke, and passed MJ the empty glass. "Good start. You need to loosen the fuck up." Then she left and went to the kitchen.

Laurel gave me a pained look, and I raised my glass in her direction. "Santé." And I drank back the glass before turning to fill it again. That earned me the smallest smile, and I would have drunk the whole bottle at once if I thought it would guarantee me more of them.

Mary-Jo came back with her purse, fishing out a lighter and a joint. The woman seemed to be constantly carrying around a party in her pockets. She immediately lit it and passed it to Laurel.

"Hey, MJ. Chill out." Emma tapped her fingers on the table. "Let Laurel do things on her own time."

"No." Laurel took a hit and passed it back to Mary-Jo. "She's right. I don't want to spend my whole night worrying about shit I can't prevent anyways."

"That's the spirit." Mary-Jo sat back down on the floor and picked up her cards, the joint stuck between her lips. "Get fucking loved, idiot."

"You ever play Three to Thirteen?" Emma asked me.

"Absolutely not."

Laurel pried herself off the couch. "Explain it and I'll get a drink."

Emma started drawing her finger across the coffee table as she explained things. "Three of a kind or greater counts, runs of the same suit count, aces are high. The wild card for the round is the same as the number of cards in your hand, and if you get more than 200 points in a game, your name goes on the fridge." Emma pointed to a piece of paper stuck to the fridge with a magnet. The top read *List of Shame*.

The game was both simpler and more complicated than I'd expected. Laurel had played a hundred times before and kept having to guide my hand through the first rounds. I'd caught my stride by the time we hit sevens, and then Emma announced she was out after the first draw. Mary-Jo threw her hand on the ground, called Emma a bitch, and took fifty points in a single round. By then, Laurel had started to laugh and crack vicious jokes. It was good to see her come alive again.

I also learned quickly that they were very serious about their cards. Shocking no one, my name was added to the fridge with 216 points. We could instigate a rematch, however, after another round of drinks. The games were long, and by the time we'd played twice, the clock had hit close to midnight. Nothing for me, but even Mary-Jo was starting to yawn.

"As much as I'd love to keep this going, I've gotta be to work at nine tomorrow." Mary-Jo started to separate her cards into two separate decks again. "I'm not as spry as I once was and hangovers hit harder."

"You're free to crash on the couch and in the spare," Emma added, looking at Laurel and me on the couch.

We were too far gone to drive, but I couldn't get caught outside my own house while the sun was up. Not with people who were unaware of my light allergy, that was. "I'll pass. I think I'll take advantage of the clear night and walk back."

"Mind if I join you?" Laurel asked, finished sorting her pile of cards.

I caught Mary-Jo pushing down a fierce little grin as she glanced up at me.

"Of course not." I added my cards to the pile and got up to put the empty wine bottle and dirty glass on the kitchen counter. "You can harass me more about how bad I am at this game."

"Dibs on the guest bed, then," MJ said, flopping out on the floor behind where she was sitting, stretching out.

With nothing to gather and bring back home, I went to the kitchen to put my boots back on and wait for Laurel. She followed a minute later, her friends on her heels.

"Thanks for coming over." Emma hid her yawn behind her hand and then reached out to hug me.

A little surprised, but pleasantly so, I gave her a hug, trying not to touch our skin together. With all the alcohol, she was practically on fire as far as I was concerned, and I didn't want to give her any chills to think too hard about. She let go after a moment. "Is it fine if I get the car in the evening tomorrow?" I asked. "Night shifts and all."

"Sure, she's not going anywhere." Emma reached for Laurel and gave her a hug as well. "Night, sweetie."

"Good night." Laurel peeked around Emma to wave at Mary-Jo. "Fuck you, idiot."

"Love you too." She blew Laurel a kiss, and then gave me a wave. "Night, Twinkle Toes."

Grinning, I shook my head and opened the door. "I'll remember that."

"I'm counting on it!" Mary-Jo yelled as I walked out.

Laurel came outside behind me, into the cool evening air. I let the door swing shut and heard the click of a lock as we walked up the driveway. The rain had stopped before I'd arrived, but the ground was still damp under our feet.

Once we were on the shoulder of the street, I looked at Laurel. "That wasn't so bad, was it?"

"No," she admitted. "It was good."

"Good." I put my hands in the pockets of my pants and kept moving, dodging a puddle. "You have excellent friends. They really love you."

"Yeah." She was blushing, her chin down, staring at the dirt in front of her as she walked. "They got me through a lot over the years. I don't know where I'd be without them. Though MJ is a pretty hard ticket."

"An understatement. She's a delight, though. I think we're going to get on well."

Laurel pointed into the distance ahead. "Why don't we walk the dykes instead of staying on the street. Might be a bit wet, but the view will be better."

"Lead on."

I followed her as she took a sharp left into the field next to us. A well-worn, muddy path led out to the water of the harbour.

We walked in silence between the road and the water, the night filling the void around us. The wind in the grass, animals scurrying in the distance, the steady rush of water getting closer. And Laurel's heart picking up speed.

"Laurel." I reached out for her hand. "What's wrong? Your heart is beating like mad."

"Oh, for fuck's sake." Laurel sighed, frustrated. "You're not supposed to notice that."

"Of course I noticed." I stopped walking, dragging her to a stop with me.

"Laurel, darling, if you're not okay—"

"It's not that!" She pulled her hand out of mine and stepped away, closer to the bank of the dyke. "I *am* okay. That's the problem."

I stared at her, trying to figure out what she was getting at. "Explain it to me."

Laurel didn't turn around. She kept staring out over the water, glimmering faintly in the overcast moonlight. "Greg should be home by now. He should have noticed that I wasn't home at all, not even to cook supper. My phone hasn't rung. I haven't gotten a single text. I've been gone and he hasn't noticed at all. I can't even pretend he cares if I'm dead or alive anymore."

Ah. There it was.

I went to her side and set my hand on her shoulder. "I care."

"I know you do." She didn't move, just kept watching the water. Laurel's lip started to quiver. "I wasted a *lifetime* on Greg. A lifetime! They send murderers *to jail* for as long as we were together and he couldn't—" She sobbed, breaking the sentence. "You show up and buy me wine and cheese, and hold me when I cry, and *talk to me as if you like me.* I spent years pretending everything was fine because you didn't exist! And now *I know* what this is like and I can't go back. I can't!" The crying overtook her and she began to sob into her hands.

I gently pulled her into my arms, holding her head against my chest. "I know, darling. We'll figure this out."

"But this had nothing to do with you," she said, wiping her hand over her face. "You don't owe me anything. You keep coming back, even though I don't have anything to offer you. I just keep offering you *nothing*—"

"That isn't true." I nudged her, forcing space between us so I could see what was on her face. "Where is all this coming from?"

"Me." She put her hand on her chest. "I feel fucking *stuck*."

I reached out, tentatively running the tips of my fingers down her hair. Even with tears running down her face, she was so striking. "Darling, do you know what you want?"

She didn't say anything, but after a moment, she nodded. "But I can't."

"Laurel, I'm right here, waiting for you." I put my thumb under her chin, forcing her to look me in the eyes. "All you have to do is take me."

Indecision ran across her face. Her heart was beating *so fast*, and she seemed like she might crawl back into herself or run. But I waited her out. Saying nothing. Staring at her lips and hoping.

She took a deep breath, reached up to put her hand on my cheek, and pulled me down to meet her.

Kissing Laurel was like the world unravelling. I immediately pulled her against me, my hands grasping to find purchase on her body. Her warm lips moved against mine, slow and deep, and I thought I might melt under the heat of her. Everything had led up to this, and *everything* had been worth the wait.

Her hands had both found their way to my jawline, holding my face close to hers. When she stopped to take a breath, she leaned her forehead against mine. She was on her toes, I realized, as I loosened my grip on her just slightly. Then I kissed her again, and again. Claiming as many as she would let me before she decided to run away.

Then she gently put her hands on my chest, insisting on space. I let her go, missing her warmth already, but she didn't turn and run. She stayed close, looking up at me. She pursed her lips in a subdued smile. "Thanks for waiting me out."

"Of *course* I waited you out." I grabbed her by the thighs and hoisted her into the air against me. She squirmed, laughing and kicking, as I started walking along the bank with her practically over my shoulder. "You're utterly fucking fantastic."

"Spencer!" Laurel flopped over my shoulder, unable to break from my grip. "You fool, put me down!"

I stopped, craning my head back. "Only if you kiss me again. I have to make sure you don't forget how."

Her cheeks were burning pink, but she wrapped her arms around my neck and gave me a long, soft kiss. When it was done, I sighed in delight and let her down.

She started to walk beside me, closer than normal. Figuring I might as well push my luck if we'd gotten that far, I wiggled my fingers against hers. A question without a question.

Laurel looked up at me, lacing her fingers with mine.

Maybe, just maybe, the game we'd been playing was over.

Maybe we were finally on our way to something deeper.

Standing at the driveway to my house, I refused to let Laurel's hand go. She needed to go home; I knew that. But I had only just gotten her, *truly* gotten her. I wasn't ready to hand her over to someone who didn't deserve to live, let alone be allowed to breathe in her presence.

"Just another minute," I whispered, coaxing her up the driveway and out of view of the street. "You don't have to come in. Just *one more minute.*"

Laurel didn't resist very hard as I pulled her against my chest as if we were about to waltz. "Just for a minute." She leaned up to be kissed and I met her there, stealing one and another and another. Then I let my lips slide down her chin, starting to pepper kisses down her neck.

"All right," she said, urging me back. "That really is enough."

"Yes, you should go." I released her. Despite being caught up in her, I didn't want to do anything that would make her uncomfortable. Between the leftover wine in my veins and the thrill of having her at last, the best choice was for me to go inside, alone. "Good night, darling."

"Good night." She gave my hand one last squeeze and then turned down the driveway and out of view.

I let out a deep breath, swimming in happiness, and let myself into the house.

She was gone, but I had the whole night ahead of me, and I had *so much* to celebrate. Music. Wine. Dinner. *A bath.*

I turned the heat up and went straight for the bathroom. I plugged the bathtub and ran the water. Somewhere under the sink was a box I'd bought a long while back to see what all the fuss was about. I fished out a large blue ball and tossed it into the steaming water to melt. I let the tub fill while I fetched a glass of warm blood and a new bottle of wine. I set the music on my phone, letting the bathroom acoustics do the rest of the work.

I pulled off my clothes and left them in a heap on the floor. The bath wasn't remotely full, but I got in and let the bright blue water slowly float up around me, warm and enveloping and smelling like blueberries. I drank, first to feed the hunger, and then to live in the bliss of the moment just a while longer. The water had filled to the point of danger, and I turned it off with my toes, unwilling to move further.

Floating without floating, the blissful warmth carrying me away, I ran my finger along the inside of the cup, searching for every last bit of blood. I licked it away and thought of love. Of curling up in bed with Astra, Willem, and Violet. Of racing through the streets and the rush of finally living for the first time. Of giving in to that craving to kiss a man, only to find it better than I'd ever expected. Of first kisses and first touches and mornings after. Of what I might say or do if I had another chance.

And then as a particularly ridiculous love song came on, I thought of what I might do *now*, with the chance I had.

Maybe it was too soon. Maybe it was too bold. And maybe we were already loving on borrowed time.

Only a quarter of the bottle of wine was left when I got out of the bath, and a song had started playing in my head. It was so perfectly her. So perfectly us.

She should hear it.

I towelled off and went to find a pair of bottoms, the wine in my hand. I had so many songs for her, if I thought hard enough. And what if…

I made my way to the library and pulled cassettes and CDs from the shelves, one by one. I sat in front of the old stereo and stuck in a brand-new blank cassette. Spectre found me and curled up in my lap as I selected song after song. Some were too new and I would need to record them from my phone. But if I was good at it, if I chose correctly, I could take all these things living in my chest and hand them to her for safekeeping.

After all, that's what they used to do in the movies, wasn't it?

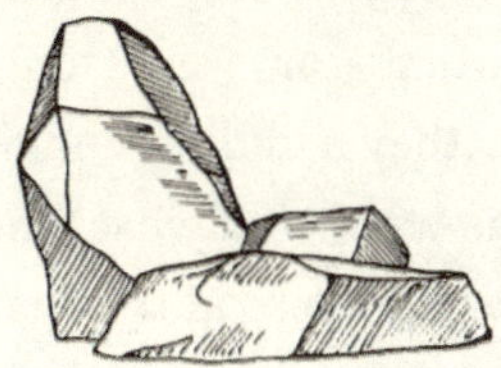

Penny Harbour

Logan had been fussy for a good portion of the afternoon and Emma had to admit she was a bit frazzled. He was maybe the best thing she would ever do, and he had come along in the middle of the *other* best thing she would ever do. A good night's sleep would fix a lot, but with Logan and her online courses, those were few and far between.

Emma yawned, Logan sleeping against her shoulder, and went to the window in his bedroom. She bounced in place; stopping often meant he woke up, especially if he hadn't been sleeping for long. As she stared out the window, she found her mind wandering.

All of the effort would be worth it, wouldn't it?

Sometimes this voice nagged at the back of her mind, asking questions that seemed to have all the worst possibilities stored up.

What if all of this is for nothing, Emma?

What if it doesn't matter, because you can't save them anyway?

Will you go into debt for people who will never change?

How can you, of all people, make a difference in the world?

Emma shook her head. Those thoughts, they rattled around sometimes, but she couldn't afford to let them take hold. Three years and thousands of dollars in the hole was no time to back out. Just because she never slept through the night and Logan had kept her nipples chapped for long enough to make her cry thinking about it…well. That was no reason to give up.

She knew she had to stop thinking of her job as *saving people*. If she was working with clients, she could only give them the space to help themselves. But still. Watching Mary-Jo struggle with substances and fighting and making good choices, and watching Laurel drowning under Greg's influence…no wonder Emma felt like she needed to fight back.

She'd gotten lucky. Her worst scars were from falling out of a tree when she was ten. MJ and Laurel…they had different kinds of homes.

As she rocked Logan, she wondered what kind of home she could give him. With Logan's father on the road so often for work, would that be enough on its own to carve a hole in her son's heart? Would she be able to protect him from whatever the world had in store for him?

She had to try.

CHAPTER NINETEEN

Laurel

Staying away from Spencer was difficult in the days after the kiss.

The one time Greg noticed I had stopped coming to bed at a reasonable hour, I told him I had insomnia. To which he shrugged and walked away. I should have been worried about being caught skulking about, especially given that I had no *friendship* excuse to fall back on anymore. The consequences would be horrific if Greg did find out, but that would mean he'd have to pull his face out of his beer and notice something about my life in the first place.

I should have felt guilty, at least. I was having an affair, technically speaking. But I found myself wondering at least once a day, how much of an affair could it reasonably be if my husband barely cared if I was alive?

But that guilt, that fear, it lived in me in a different way than I had expected. It came alive in the back of my mind like whispers in the dark.

Why should you be afraid?

You've taken what you wanted.

Finish what you've started and kill him.

The vampire can't protect you. Only you can do that.

And some moments it was more tempting than I would've liked to admit.

The truth was that being happy had become an addiction. The voice of darkness that seemed to live in my bones felt weaker when I was with Spencer. No matter what we did together, being near him closed off a part of

269

the hole in my heart that had been growing for the last decade. It was getting harder and harder to tell myself no. My body *craved* comfort. The laughter, the joy, the safety. To the point where I wondered what risk I wouldn't take to get the next hit.

All of that in stark contrast to the moment each night when I shut Spencer's door behind me to start home, the dread freezing in my veins. My body had always been ready to protect myself from Greg before. To stay in place and withstand him. That wasn't the case anymore. Since Spencer, my body was begging me not to get within ten feet of my own home.

As I rounded the corner of Spencer's driveway after dark, the porch light illuminated him leaning against the door, poking at his phone. The early June air was warm enough that I had dug out a navy blue sundress, and Spencer had chosen high-waisted black slacks and a creamy silk blouse that draped at an angle across his chest. The material shone under the light, and I found myself feeling lucky to be allowed to touch him.

The gravel under my flats drew his attention. He blinked, looking me up and down. "Well, look at you. What's the occasion?" He reached out to take my hand and pulled me into a kiss.

I gave him a dirty look. "You told me to wear something nice."

"Did I?" he mused, holding my hand up and urging me to spin around. "A dress? On *Laurel*? I never thought I'd see it."

"I do own, like…two dresses. They're just not very practical. Now, why am I supposed to be pretty today?"

Spencer reached into the pocket of his slacks and his car beeped, the doors unlocking. "It's a surprise."

He gestured to get into the car and I did. Once the Civic had purred to life, he gave me an appreciative smile as he looked over his shoulder to back out of the driveway. Then he drove us deeper into Penny Harbour.

"So we're not heading toward civilization, then." I looked in the back seat. "And there's food."

"And wine." Spencer drove through the main street of the village and past it. He steered us onto a little road that led up a hill. At the top, he pulled over and turned off the ignition.

"Wow, we drove, like…two whole minutes. You really outdid yourself on this one," I teased.

"Didn't I?" Spencer got out and then went to the trunk. By the time I got out of the car, his arms were filled with an enormous comforter, a bug lantern, and a little boombox from the early 2000s. "Would you grab the rest?"

I pulled the food and wine from the back seat and closed the door with my hip. Spencer was waiting for me at the edge of the grass. As I approached, he began to lead me further into the dark, onto the hill that overlooked Penny Harbour. At its edge, Spencer stopped, flicked the comforter into the air, and let it fall onto the grass.

"Come sit," he said, smoothing the surface out and turning on the lantern that would give me something to see by *and* keep me from being eaten alive by mosquitoes.

"Spencer Tompkin Campbell, did you plan a picnic?"

"How dare you?" He looked up at me, mock offence on his face. "I planned a gourmet snack on a hill in the middle of the night with music and ambience. *A picnic.* My *word.*"

I laughed and set the food on the comforter. Spencer sat down, arms propping himself up and his ankles crossed, and I moved to sit close to him. From that spot on the top of the hill, we could see dozens of tiny lights. Homes, streetlamps, the school. Trees and roads and quiet, all covered in darkness.

"What's that about?" I gave the boombox a nudge. It was a tiny black thing with a little antenna and a cassette slot.

"I made you something." Spencer pulled a little plastic rectangle from his pocket and handed it to me.

"That is a cassette tape," I said, taking it from him. I flipped open the case and found a cassette inside, the see-through kind that was blank and meant to be recorded on. The little label on the front read *Laurel.* "Spencer, is this a fucking mixtape?"

His mouth opened to answer, but the words seemed to get lost for a moment. He looked away, either embarrassed or ashamed.

I took his hand. "No, it's good. I just…I thought mixtapes died out years ago."

Spencer's lips pursed together and he managed a smirk. "I'm ancient, darling. Cut me some slack."

"Do I get to put it on?"

He gestured to the boombox. "If you want to."

I hit the eject button and the cassette deck popped open. I put it in, clicked it closed, and pressed play.

A soft, slow melody floated out of the speakers, the voice of a young man singing a ballad about the end of the world. I leaned against Spencer's chest and closed my eyes. The song was hopeful and melancholic all at once. It touched something deep in me, and though I didn't catch all the lyrics, the song stole my breath.

Spencer carefully reached over and grabbed the wine. The cork was already half-out, and he took care of the rest. He passed me the bottle first, and I drank. We listened, pressed together, staring out over the town. At peace.

The song changed to something I recognized immediately, and I couldn't help but laugh. I looked at Spencer. "Really?"

"What?" His grey eyes were smouldering as he gazed down at me.

"You don't think 'Kiss Me' is a little too innocent and sweet?"

"I think it's perfect for the setting, and I think we both deserve it." He placed a slow, soft kiss on my lips. "The kind of hopeful, untarnished affection people write love songs about. Shouldn't we get to taste that too?"

I swallowed. His voice had gotten lower as he spoke, until the words were just a whisper for us. "Spencer…"

"Yes?"

I could feel my mind scrambling for excuses, looking for a reason to run. He had been so patient with me for so long, while I tried to protect myself from whatever happiness he was offering me because, somehow, happiness was scarier than all the rest. "You're very good at this seduction thing, aren't you?"

"I am," he admitted. "It's…part of this life. Habit. I can stop, if that's what you want. If it feels inauthentic." He had already drawn his face away, giving me room.

"Is it?" I asked. "Inauthentic?"

Spencer turned on his side to face me, cupping my cheek in his hand. "No. You're the only real thing that's happened to me in a very long time. I want you to feel wanted, with or without pretty words."

A pinprick of light drew my attention. I turned to look down the hill. In the dead of night, tiny glowing dots were rising out of the grass, one by one. Dozens and dozens. Little stars floating everywhere. A sea of fireflies.

Spencer tipped his head against mine, watching with me.

"It's beautiful," I whispered. "Thank you for this."

Spencer took another drink of the wine, shoved the cork in, and swallowed. "Anything for you." His fingers found my shoulder, trailing his touch down my bare arm.

Heat rose in my stomach. I turned to kiss him and he met me eagerly, his lips moving in long, deep caresses against mine. I ran my hand down his chest, the silk cool under my fingers. In return, his hand drifted from my waist, up to the side of my breast, his thumb testing the limits of what I would allow. My breath caught, and without giving myself time to back away, I moved to crawl on top of him.

Spencer sat up to meet me, holding my hips in both hands. Kissing me like he couldn't get enough of the taste. I suggestively licked along his lip and he met that suggestion with abandon, his tongue searching. On my knees, sitting on his lap, I felt his body reacting to mine. Stopping to breathe, I rested my forehead against his. Deliberating.

"I want it all," Spencer whispered into my mouth, stopping to nip at my bottom lip. "The decision is yours." He pulled away, watching my eyes as his fingers walked slowly up my left thigh, threatening to creep up my dress.

My mind couldn't be trusted to let me have him, so I followed my body instead.

I pulled him in for more kisses, and he held me to him with a palm around my back, the other finding its way under my dress. It trailed up, slowly teasing its way to the edge of my panties, and my breath hitched. His fingers explored, slowly, creeping underneath the fabric, looking for places to draw pleasure out of me. I leaned my head back as his lips trailed along my neck. A shiver ran through me as I anticipated him biting down. He didn't, but part of me wished he would.

Between his lips on my neck and his finger working soft, slow circles, I could hardly breathe. How long had it been since someone had lavished that kind of attention on me? Years, certainly. But maybe never. Maybe *never*. And the thought was enough to have me leaning in to chase that rapture. I sat up, allowing him room to slide his fingers back and in, and the thrill of it—

"Like this?" Spencer whispered the question into my neck, searching for my approval as he worked.

More than the breath on my neck, more than the touch itself, it was the question that made me burn for him. The care. It *mattered* to him.

I hadn't even imagined that for myself.

I nodded, biting my lip against the waves of warmth building in me. But there *was* something off, just slightly. I adjusted my hips but couldn't get it right. It felt wrong to ask, like if I complained, the moment would end and I'd be left wanting like always. But he had asked first, so... "The angle," I mumbled, unsure of myself.

Without a word or a second thought, Spencer moved to lay me out carefully on the comforter. He knelt beside me, propped up on one hand, watching my face as his fingers returned to what they'd been doing. "Is that better?"

It was. It was *so* much better. Spencer's fingers worked and I craned my head back, basking in the heat that was coiling in my gut. I licked my lips, the pleasure escaping on ragged moans. As I started to breathe harder, my hands gripping the blanket, he leaned in to kiss my earlobe.

"Come for me, darling."

And I did, my body releasing all that coiled attention as Spencer covered my neck in kisses. Bliss ran from head to toe, and I melted into the comforter. When the moment subsided, the heat fading out of me slowly, I found myself staring up at the stars, panting. Delighted.

"Watching you is delicious," Spencer murmured into my ear.

I laughed, still high from the peak. "Holy shit."

"If you decide you want more, we have all night," Spencer purred. He reached behind him and set a container of grapes down beside us. He pulled one out and held it up to my mouth. I took it, thankful for its sweetness on my parched tongue.

"And what about you? You don't want anything?" I ran my hand down his shirt, playing with the button on his pants.

His hand found mine and he interlaced our fingers together. "If you truly wanted that, I would. But I loved getting to do that for you. That was enough for me, if it's enough for you."

I licked my lips, thinking. In theory, I wanted the whole experience. But lying with him, having nothing expected of me but my own joy...that was a new concept for me. It felt long overdue, even if it wasn't his debt to pay. I wanted to know what it was like to be given everything. To hoard it all for myself, for once.

"All right. That's enough for me," I replied, and that was that. Spencer sat up to gather the rest of the food and tuck it between us. At some point, the cassette had finished with the A side, so he flipped it and started it again. We talked for hours, and when I was ready for more, he indulged me as much as I wanted and asked for nothing in return. We played the cassette twice more, front to back, before even considering packing up.

CHAPTER TWENTY

Laurel

Despite it being days later, I couldn't keep my eyes off my phone. Spencer was asleep, but I found myself scrolling back through the texts he had sent after that night, keeping him with me even when he was in bed across the Harbour. I went back to the morning after the hill and started again.

> Spencer:
> I can't stop thinking about how you feel
> What a shame you won't be awake
> I would have told you about the very inappropriate
> things I have planned for next time

> Laurel:
What a shame you won't be awake
I could have come over and made good on those plans

> Spencer:
> Mmm, but I'm awake now
> Or is it too late to take you up on that offer?

Laurel:

It is

I'm helping Emma set up for her birthday. Sorry :P

Spencer:

But what if you skipped it?

You could be here, next to me

And attached was a selfie of Spencer lying on his stomach in bed, giving the hottest come-fuck-me eyes I'd ever seen.

"Holy fuck, Laurel. Ryan asked you something." Greg's voice boomed through the daydream.

I startled, pressing the phone against my chest. I'd already had it tucked tight to me, not wanting to get caught. Greg, Ryan, and Ryan's wife, Donna, were all staring at me.

"Sorry," I said, closing my phone and tucking it into my pocket. "I haven't been sleeping that well lately. Guess I just kind of got distracted." I laughed, trying desperately to make light of the situation.

Ryan and Donna gave a little chuckle.

"Sleeping on your feet, I know all about that." Donna waved the comment off with a swipe of her hand. "After the baby came, that's all I did. Some days I was so tired I barely knew where I was. Girl, you deserve a nap."

"Thanks. Maybe after we get home tonight I'll treat myself. Oh—" I stepped to the side as a child-sized cousin came rushing past, nearly toppling into me. Brayden ran into the garden and around the legs of everyone in his way.

Thirty people were packed into Emma's backyard on a balmy Saturday at noon for Emma's birthday party barbecue. Half of the partygoers were wearing T-shirts and shorts because if it was at least ten degrees in Atlantic Canada, it felt like a breezy summer day. Smoke was rising from the enormous barbecue, and everyone had a beer in their hands—except the children under sixteen, of course.

I barely knew Ryan and Donna, but that wasn't the case for most of the crowd. Emma had been inviting me to her family shindigs since I was a kid. When Dad disappeared, Mom had sunk into a bit of a hole for a while.

Emma would invite me for supper, or for the night, or sometimes for the week. Her family was more a family to me than most of my blood, so I could spot each of her relatives a mile off. The yard was packed with aunts, uncles, cousins. Not mine, but mine in a sideways manner, I supposed.

Donna had been talking again, and I hadn't caught all of it. I really was tired, but I also didn't care. My mind was in a dozen other places, and the most present part of my body was screaming that it didn't want to be standing next to Greg. So much so that I'd rather be caught looking at suggestive photos of Spencer from a few days ago than be in reality with Greg.

"Did I tell you we have new neighbours?" Ryan asked, his voice thick with complaint.

"Someone bought the house finally?" Greg tipped his bottle of beer up to his lips. He had cleaned himself up for once, and not that long ago I would've appreciated the effort. Found it attractive to see this rare version of him, his green plaid button-up and blue jeans looking like a half ounce of effort. Instead, I found it to be less than the bare minimum.

Spencer's best outfit didn't stop at *green fucking plaid*.

"Yup," Donna added. "Two women and their kid moved in. The one looks normal, but the other's got her hair all fucking shaved."

Greg made a gagging sound that turned my stomach. "Fucking dykes, man, they're moving in all over the place now."

I snapped my head around, staring daggers at him.

"What?" he snarled. "You got a fucking problem?"

I scowled. "You know what, fuck this." I walked away, heading across the yard, which was as much courage as I could really muster. I would pay for it later, I was sure of it. But I couldn't stand to listen to him insulting these people I didn't know and, in turn, insulting Mary-Jo and Spencer. Knowing that *if* it were me who liked girls, Greg would hate me too. Every excuse I had made for him, everything I had told myself all those years, was *finally* worn to the bone.

Next to the barbecue was a long rowboat packed full with ice and drinks. I snatched up a Breezer and used the side of the boat to pop the top off. Half the drink was gone in a breath.

"You better watch out. You keep your face sour like that and it'll stick."

I turned. Emma's dad—and in all practical ways, mine—had snuck up behind me. Tom was no taller than I was, and he was built like a welder, mostly 'cause he was one. A big grin was plastered on his face.

"What if I want it to stick, Dad? I can't scare people off if I look too pretty." I gave him a big hug. He lingered just a little longer than he needed to, squeezing tight. Those hugs. I always wondered if they were out of pity or out of fondness. Probably a little of both. It didn't matter, though. They were the best hugs I ever got.

"You didn't bring Greg, did ya? Or was it someone else got you scowlin' like that?" He let me go and took a look around the yard.

"Yeah, I brought him. Just doesn't know how to keep his mouth shut. You know how he is."

"Yeah." Tom nodded, clicking his tongue. "Never did say much that was smart."

In the past, I would have tried to defend Greg. Said he came from bad stock or that he was getting better. But he wasn't, and I didn't want to. "You know what? You might be right about that."

Tom looked at me with a raised eyebrow. After a moment, he put an arm around my shoulder. "Good for you, kid. Good for you. 'Bout time."

I hugged him back. "You get a drink yet?"

"Me? Drink?" he asked, heading for the boat. "I would never." He grabbed a beer, popped the top off, and clinked it against mine. "Oh, look who it is."

"Did you forget something, hun?" Carolyn, Emma's mom, had his guitar case in one hand, a giant bag of homemade biscuits in the other.

"Never forgot anything in my life." Tom took the guitar case out of her hand. "Thanks, hun."

Carolyn reached out to hug me as well. "I brought biscuits for everyone, but there's another bag in the car just for you. Don't tell."

"Oh, I won't, I promise." Carolyn's baked goods were practically gold, as far as I was concerned. "You gonna play us a tune, Tom?"

Tom set the case on the ground. "You get me somewhere to sit and we'll talk about it."

I snatched a chair from the patio set and put it down beside him. Once Tom had settled in and rescued the shiny black acoustic from the case, he started to strum.

Tom was particularly attached to old rock and country tunes, which made it easy for the crowd to sing along. A few minutes in, people caught on that he was playing. Some stopped talking to listen. Before long, a few of them were singing about a hotel where you can check out, but you can never leave.

Midway through the next song, Emma and Mary-Jo abandoned their conversations in the kitchen to come stand next to me. They started swinging and swaying, and before long the three of us were belting out song after song.

"You know," Emma said, leaning toward me to whisper, "you could have invited Spencer. He could've been Mary-Jo's friend this time."

"Yeah, bitch, I'd have lied for you." Mary-Jo snickered.

"He couldn't come anyways," I sighed, too empty-hearted about it to even be embarrassed. "And it's not like that."

"Isn't it?" Mary-Jo asked, her lips settling into a disbelieving pout.

"Maybe it should be." Emma pressed a kiss to my temple and accepted my silence as an answer.

Mary-Jo lit up a cigarette. She passed it to me, and I took a puff, looking for any kind of reprieve from that question. The smoke burned my throat, and I coughed. A fine black power dusted the air, fading away with the smoke. I chased the burning with the rest of my Breezer. Then Tom started to play the world's saddest song, about a man who kisses his wife for the last time in the wreckage of their car.

As we sang, swaying together, tears built in my eyes. It was a sad fucking song, and I loved all these people so much. Every time Tom pulled out that guitar, I had a full life and a good family, for just a minute. Nothing was missing. Nothing had been lost, now or ever. I'd never gone without.

Love was all there was, just for a moment.

The only thing I still needed was Spencer. And he couldn't be here with me, but he *could* see a video if I sent one. I could share the moment with him, even in that small way.

Except when I opened the phone to take the video, it opened to the conversation with Spencer, and the thumbnail of his selfie in bed.

Mary-Jo, still hanging off my shoulder, dug her fingers into my arm and hissed. "*Laurel!*"

I scrambled to put my phone away, but the jig was up.

Emma hooked her arm in mine and started to drag me across the yard and into the house. "I need you to help me get more drinks from the basement. *They're really heavy and Mary-Jo and I need help.*"

MJ was practically buzzing behind us, making the most conspicuous noises. Meanwhile, I was a solid five seconds from throwing up. Stupid. Fucking *careless.*

Emma pulled me to the far end of the house, opened the door to the basement, and then pushed me until I went downstairs. They thudded down behind me in their sneakers, slamming the door shut.

"In there, right now." Emma pointed to the door that hid the water boiler and the furnace from the rest of the house. It felt a little over the top, but given all the people and *Greg* in the backyard, I wasn't going to argue with her. When we were all inside, Emma shut the door and turned on the overhead light. The machinery rumbled around us with a steady hum.

MJ took my face in both her hands. "Laurel, get fucking talking. Why was Spencer naked on your phone?"

"He wasn't naked—"

"*Fine*, he had a blanket on. *That's not the point.*"

"It was just—"

"*Liar.*" Mary-Jo let me go and turned to Emma, grabbing her by the shoulders.

Emma's eyes were wide, her smile as bright as a 300-watt bulb. "It's happening. *It's time.*"

"It's fucking *time!*" Mary-Jo shook Emma and then wrapped her in a hug. "Ugh, we waited so *long.*" She looked at me from her hug. "Girl, *finally.* This is the best fucking news. Now give me that phone."

I rolled my eyes and obeyed, knowing she wouldn't stop until I did.

Mary-Jo hit the photo and took a long look. "Fuck, he's so pretty. Like, objectively, look at that motherfucker. But also now that I know him, it's like looking at my brother, you know? We are just on opposite sides of the queer pool, yuck." She passed the phone back. "Good for you, though."

Emma took my hand. "When?"

"Not long ago," I mumbled, trying to hide behind my hands.

"Oooh, tell us everything. Please, pretty pleeeeease." Emma batted her eyes at me.

I groaned. "Fine. After we came here for cards, Spencer and I were walking back home and I just…kissed him. Which he had *apparently* known was coming from a mile away because he's been subtly hitting on me for *a while* and then a few nights ago—"

Mary-Jo was staring at me, wide-eyed and slack-jawed. "I mean, obviously he was hitting on you. Do you not…? *Laurel*. I egged him on *at the benefit dance*. Like straight up told him to go after you. That was, like, *two months ago*. Have you not been picking up on that for *two months*?"

I tried to speak but I kept fumbling over the words. "I guess I did? But I didn't? I don't know! I'm *married*. What the fuck was I supposed to do? I just crammed it down like everything else, I guess."

"Okay, so then what? What happened the other night?" Emma was bouncing from foot to foot, so excited she couldn't keep still.

"He took me up to that hill that overlooks the town and made me a picnic," I started.

"Okay, that's pretty cute." Mary-Jo nodded approvingly.

"And he made me a mixtape."

"What, like a playlist?" Emma asked.

I shook my head. "It's on a cassette and everything."

"Adorable. Ten out of ten." Mary-Jo smirked. "Then he gave you a hot selfie."

"*Then* he…umm…" I trailed off, unsure if I could get the words out. I hadn't confessed anything intimate about Greg since we were all in our twenties. I'd listened to lots of exploits from Emma and Mary-Jo, but I hadn't added anything in years. Nothing had happened that was *worth* adding, and it felt like I was confessing something deeply personal.

"Girl. You've heard everything about the people I've slept with. Could it really be any worse than what I've said?" Mary-Jo wiggled her eyebrows at me.

I took a breath and got the words out before I could turn chickenshit. "He got me off with his hands and refused to take anything in return, and he just—" Out of nowhere, tears welled up in my eyes and my voice broke. "He took care of me."

Mary-Jo's joking demeanour dropped in a second and her arms were around me faster than I could register. I fell into her arms, sobbing, and she held my weight like the ton of muscle she was. It wasn't what Spencer had done that had brought me to tears—or not alone, at least. It was the years of absence. The lack. Realizing how long I'd lived without that kind of care had left me raw.

"It's all right, honey." Mary-Jo held me tight. "We've got you, and everything is going to be all right." She rocked me a little as I cried, and then took me by the shoulders. She looked around. "Fucking stupid closet. I'd sit you down, but we're strapped for space around here."

I laughed through the tears and stood straighter, wiping my face with the back of my long sleeve. Emma wrapped her arms around my back, the three of us hanging off each other in the middle of the dank room.

"Are you crying because of Spencer?" Emma asked.

I shook my head, wiping my eyes.

"Because of Greg?"

I nodded.

Mary-Jo started dabbing at the corners of her eyes, not quite crying with me. "Do you think you're ready to let Greg go?"

I nodded and cried harder.

"I am so fucking proud of you, boo." Mary-Jo wrapped us tightly in her arms. "I know I was hard to stomach, saying shit about him all these years. But you deserve better."

"I know that now," I managed to squeak out.

"Good." Emma gave me a squeeze. "Do you think Spencer is, like… rebound material, or is he the genuine article?"

I caught my breath, steadying my voice. "He's good. He's gone through his own shit, but…I think he loves me."

"Has he said that?" Mary-Jo's voice was sceptical.

I shook my head. "Not said it. But he makes me food he doesn't eat, and he gets me things he thinks I'd like, and he wants to see me most days. I dunno."

Mary-Jo let out a breath. "Oh, yeah, he's down bad."

"And what about Greg? Do you have a plan to leave?" It was Emma's turn to dry her tears, and it seemed we were quickly becoming a bunch of drowned rats.

"Not yet. I don't think he's noticed anything."

Mary-Jo scoffed. "I don't think he'd notice if his dick is still attached most days."

"Still. You should get out of there before he finds out." Emma's voice was stern. Worried.

"I know. I will."

We stood together for a long while, saying nothing and just holding on. And when I was ready, they helped make sure my eyes weren't too red and that I wasn't covered in snot.

"Sorry for ruining your birthday," I whispered to Emma.

"Are you fucking kidding me?" She gave me a kiss on the forehead. "This is the best birthday I've ever had."

After we came up from the basement and made a very large attempt to act natural, it only took another two hours for the beer to run dry. All things considered, the barbecue was still in full swing and it was universally agreed that someone needed to get more beer. All that was left were the girly drinks, and obviously the men couldn't be caught drinking those.

"The liquor store at the pass is open for another three hours," Mary-Jo said.

"So who's going?" Donna asked.

Most of the party had gathered around the table where all the barbecue fixings had been set out. And most of the party wasn't *really* sober enough to go anywhere.

"Laurel, you go." Greg was already glassy-eyed after probably two drinks too many for mid-afternoon.

"Absolutely not," I spat back. Alarm bells had already been ringing in my mind since coming upstairs, and as I disagreed with him, they grew stronger. *Don't antagonize him. Don't upset him. This only ends badly.* "It's not safe for me to drive." I'd been trying to kill my anxiety with Breezers and I was *not* in my right mind.

"Better than the rest of us," he snapped. "You can handle it. Just take everyone's order and go. It's not like you've got anything better to do."

"Greg, you little fucking worm." Mary-Jo was already rolling up the sleeves of her sweater. "You want to put your wife in a truck, half-blitzed, and make her go get beer?"

"Yeah, I mean, why the fuck not?" Greg shrugged, looking around for support. Ryan and Donna gave him a nod, like it was a completely reasonable request.

Mary-Jo stepped toward Greg and Emma grabbed her arm. "Nope. Nope, nope, not today. Let's go." With a little persistence, Emma pulled Mary-Jo back toward the house, where they began to whisper angrily at each other.

"It's kind of fucked up that you'd ask me to do that, Greg." I stared him in the eyes, trying to drum up the courage to stay even as every muscle in my body wanted to run. "I mean, what if something ran out in front of me? What if I got hurt or someone died?"

Greg rolled his eyes. "God, you're so fucking dramatic."

Rage roiled over me. I threw my empty bottle on the ground at his feet. Everyone was watching by that point. "You know what, Greg? Go fuck yourself. I've had it up to *here* with you."

The voice in my head surged to life as I stepped toward him.

That's right, Little Laurel.

He's pushed you far enough.

Just think what you can have once he's out of your way.

Nose-to-nose with him, I snarled into his face. "I'm *done*. I'm done with your petty bullshit, and your hateful fucking attitude, and I'm done being your fucking maid. It's not worth it. It never fucking was."

And as satisfying as it would have been to punch his lights out, I turned and stormed out of the yard instead. Through the house, out the front door. Yelling erupted from behind me. Mary-Jo. I looked, but no one was following me. A snarky grin spread across my face as I imagined her giving Greg hell.

Greg, who would fucking ask me to risk my life so he could keep getting shit-faced for the rest of the day. So he could make *me* sober up and drive him home. And maybe from there, he'd get angry, 'cause that happened a lot when he drank. Then he would want to get his rocks off, and I'd be the only convenient thing around.

My whole body shuddered at the thought. I'd let him do that, not that long ago. Like everything else, I'd made it make sense in my head. Not anymore. I never wanted him to touch me again.

I'd learned what it was like to be touched out of love, and there was no going back.

Turn around, darling girl.

Go back into that yard and show everyone what his insides look like.

Pretty and red and all over your hands.

As tempting as it was to reap violence on him, I knew I'd never win any kind of fight that involved Greg.

A dozen vehicles were parked on the front lawn and on the shoulder of the road. I walked past them, the world a little hazy around me, and set off toward home by foot. Just like the other night, I had walked back from Emma's a million times since I was a teenager. The way home was part of my blood by that point. An automatic compass.

Making my way around the far side of the harbour, nearly at a run, I thought about how much had really changed. Where it had all come from. And I only had one answer.

Spencer.

When I had been neck-deep in Greg's bullshit, I couldn't see anything else. Not even with Emma and Mary-Jo trying to pull me out. But Spencer had come into my life, and it was different somehow. Mary-Jo and Emma had always been there, and they were as immovable as mountains in my life, which meant I had taken that love for granted. They were always going to love me, whether I deserved it or not. Spencer had stepped in and chosen to stay, and he had been so *kind.* Every time he listened, or spoke up for me, or treated me to something, or happily sat next to me, it got harder to make excuses for what had been missing all along.

And I was done settling for nothing.

Fuck going home. I was never going home again.

It only took fifteen minutes to get to Spencer's doorstep.

The sun wouldn't go down for hours. He was definitely still asleep and I couldn't have cared less. I rang the doorbell, waited a minute, and rang it again. No answer. He must have been deeply asleep, but I couldn't exactly walk away. I'd burned that bridge.

I rang it again.

"Hello?" Spencer's exhausted voice came through the little speaker on the camera.

"Spencer, let me in."

"Laurel, it's still light out. What—?"

"Come unlock this fucking door," I said, my voice trembling.

The speaker clicked off.

As I waited, my body hummed and I bounced on my toes. The alcohol was still alive and kicking in me, and the adrenaline of the walk over wasn't helping calm my nerves. I wasn't sure I dared do what I had planned, but—

The door unlocked, and I pushed my way in.

"Laurel, what's—?"

I slammed the door closed and pushed Spencer into it, rattling the doorframe. He gasped in alarm, but before he could say anything, I pulled his face down and kissed him with abandon.

He quickly learned the pace, kissing me with an intensity that sent shivers to my core. His surprise turned into a growl of delight as his hands found my thighs and he lifted me until my legs were wrapped around his waist. With Spencer dressed in only his pyjama bottoms, his skin was so cool against my overheated body. When he turned me to pin me against the door, his hand slid under my shirt and up my back, holding me against him. I craned my head back as he propped me further up, his kisses starting at the low collar of my shirt and trailing frantically up my throat.

"You taste like a fucking distillery, Laurel. Why?"

I hushed him. "Just kiss me."

He did as I asked, pressing me harder into the door. The curtain moved and Spencer hissed, the sun hitting the skin on his stomach. My body had blocked all but a sliver of it, but clearly, we were playing a dangerous game.

"Spencer," I breathed, hanging my arms around his neck and thrilling at his tongue as it ran along my jaw.

"Yes?" His teeth nipped at my ear.

"Take me to bed."

Spencer

Startled fully awake by her words, I put Laurel down. It wasn't like her to be this forward about *anything* really. "Are you sure?"

She stepped around me and kicked off her shoes. "I'm sure." She shrugged out of her open button-up shirt and let it fall to the floor; then she started through the living room and toward the hall. She stopped to peel a sock off, then the other. Then her T-shirt came off.

Gods above.

I moved to follow her, need coiling in my gut. By the time I reached her, Laurel was rounding the corner to the stairs. Her jeans were in a heap by the first step, and she was walking up. Her body moved in long, languid steps, her ass covered in delicate black panties, her bra—unclasped and on the middle step—discarded.

I slowly walked up behind her, eager to rush her, but enjoying the show *so very much.* By the time she reached the top step, I'd caught up with her. She looked over her shoulder, an inviting look on her face. Then she hooked her thumbs in her panties and pushed them down. They fell to the floor, and she stepped out of them and into my bedroom.

When I turned the corner, I found her naked on my unmade sheets, her arms above her head. Next to her, Spectre was glaring, upset at having her sleep interrupted. I grabbed the cat by the middle, gently tossed her into the hall, and kicked the door shut.

Laurel was a vision, lying there, waiting for me. Crawling over her, I trailed my fingers up her stomach, around the curve of her breast, and up to her cheek. "What do you want, darling?"

Biting her lip, she breathed, "Everything."

"Good." I kissed her and then knelt on the floor at the edge of the bed, pulling her hips until her legs were draped over my shoulders. "I can give you everything."

Her skin bore the scars of a life lived, and her thighs were no exception. Soft silver stripes and raised old wounds. I'd have questions for her later. Where each of them came from. What adventures she'd had to get them. But for the time being, I could adore them while I chased her pleasure with a trail of kisses down her thigh.

I watched her face as I explored, trying to find the things she liked best. Nibbling, lapping, kissing, until she was practically singing sighs into the air. But I only indulged her for a time. She had wanted everything, and I had no reason to deny her. So I slowed and traced kisses up her stomach instead, until we were face to face and she was panting against my mouth.

"Tease," she whimpered, and I took it as a challenge.

How long could I draw out her pleasure before she just took it?

I went back to trailing my lips slowly along her strong biceps, into the tender crook of her elbow, and down to her wrist. It hadn't been my intent, but with her skin and veins pressed so close to my mouth, I could feel her heartbeat throbbing below her skin. Her blood, right there, hot and pulsing. Calling to me.

I lingered too long. She noticed. Of course she did; she noticed everything. Watching me kiss below her palm as I argued with myself. I had sworn I wouldn't harm her. Plenty of people found delight in the drinking and being drunk, an irreplaceable high, but she had to want it and I wasn't going to ask that of her. The world had already taken enough against her will.

"Would it hurt?" Laurel whispered.

I kissed her wrist again, allowing myself a reverent little lick across her veins. "A little, at first."

She drew a breath. "You can, if you want."

With the permission on her lips, I gave in to the urge. My fangs slid out and I grazed the skin of her wrist, testing her. She hissed a small inhale, but didn't protest.

I bit down gently, breaking her skin as delicately as I knew how.

Laurel's hot blood trickled into my mouth, dark and rich and *wrong*. So caught up in want, I'd forgotten. The beautiful warmth of it was at stark odds with the grit that spread across my tongue like fine sand. The not-quite-right taste. She was part of this place, and I'd known she was no exception.

I drew away slowly, swallowing the blood I'd taken from her so as not to offend. It felt unspeakably rude to spit it out. The disappointment was a lead brick in my stomach. I'd never had to tell a lover that no, actually I would not be enjoying the taste of them during sex because it was akin to licking ashes.

Laurel was watching me, suspicious. I had to say something.

I wiped my lip, leaving a small streak of red on my hand. "I'm sorry. I—"

"I don't taste right, do I?" Laurel's expression was curious, but not upset. "Like you said about this town."

"I'm sorry." I pressed my thumb against the punctures in her wrist that continued to drip. The temptation to drink still flooded my chest, despite knowing better. "If it feels good, I can still—"

"You can make me feel good in other ways, Spencer." She pulled me down to kiss me, a daring move on her part, given what I'd just done.

The care was appreciated, but I still wanted to know… "Did you like it?"

Blush filled Laurel's cheeks, and she hid her smile behind her hand. "I did. I'm not sure how I'm supposed to feel about that."

The smell of blood was still strong, and I removed the pressure from her wound. I gave my finger a tentative lick. Still bad. I sighed. "What a shame. I would've loved to take you to those places. But maybe…" I tucked my face into her neck, letting my fangs tease without breaking the skin.

A shy moan slipped from her.

That was something I could accommodate.

I let the bloodlust slip away and bit down gently without the sharpness of the fangs, thrilling at the sound of her enjoyment. Not every lover wanted to be devoured, and it pained me not to oblige her.

I pulled away. Her eyes were alight with excitement. I set to work tasting every inch of her skin, leaving bites wherever I felt like it, and basking in the sounds it coaxed from her. When I reached her hip, I nipped at the bone and she squirmed beneath my hands until I let her free.

She sat up and pushed me over, crawling on top of me. She straddled my hips and leaned forward to steady herself on the mattress. Her smile was mischievous. "I bet you're the one who always does all the biting."

I craned my face up to hers, craving a kiss. "Usually," I purred.

"And do you like to be bitten?" Her lips drew closer to mine.

Anticipation rushed through my skin. "Usually."

Laurel reached down to grasp my jaw in her hand. Gently twisting my head away, her lips found my neck and she bit down sheepishly. A shiver ran up my spine. That she would even play this game with me was thrilling, but she was being too gentle.

"Harder," I growled.

Laurel stiffened for a moment, her hesitation obvious. She placed a kiss where she'd bitten, like an apology. Then, after a few breaths, she bit down firmly. The nerves all along my shoulder and neck sparked to life, the sweet pain rushing through me until it escaped as a deep moan.

Laurel's grip on my jaw tightened in response, and she ran her tongue across the bite. "You really did like that, didn't you?"

My hands found the curve of her hips and I pulled her tightly against me, even as she held my jaw hostage. "Every vampire either has a bite kink or is a liar. If you—"

Laurel's teeth sank into the meat of my shoulder, and I found myself drawing breath simply to get through the moment. When she sat back, I gently pried her fingers from my face so I could look her in the eyes.

"*Don't* break the skin. We can't have you turning." I coaxed her into a deep kiss, appreciative of the fervour with which she was learning what I craved. I spoke against her lips. "You have too much power now, darling. I fear you'll try to use it to undo me."

"I have other ways to undo you," she whispered into my mouth. A moment later, she was reaching under my pyjamas and taking me in her hand.

I dug my fingers into her hip, one hand snaking through her hair. I let my head loll back. "Laurel…"

How lucky I was, after so long alone. This woman, who had willingly walked into the grave of my life, who had taken root in it. She'd spoiled me with kindness. Attempted to understand a grieving beast who drank blood and burned in sunlight.

Laurel, who had changed my world.

The slow movement of her hand coaxed a moan from me. All the foreplay was satisfying, but…

I fumbled overhead for my side table, reluctant to move further and hopeful that it was within reach. But we were too far away.

Laurel looked up, her hair falling over us both in a cascade. "Need something?" she asked.

"The side table—" The words broke into a gasp under her persistent touch. My eyes fluttered, the hard breaths a reflex.

Laurel grinned down at me, delighted with herself. "I think I'm going to love hearing you make that sound." She leaned forward, draping herself over me as she reached for the side table. "In here?"

"Yes," I breathed, holding her steady, taking in her body above me.

The drawer slid open. "Oh."

The shock on her face was precious.

"Spencer, how many toys did you buy?"

"In this modern century, I'm an enormous fan of three-day shipping." I couldn't help but grin as I removed what little clothing I had on. "It seemed likely we'd wind up in bed soon enough, and it's important to me that you love what we do together." I patiently ran my fingers along her skin as she touched and rummaged. Eventually, she sat back down on my stomach, her hand glistening, and started where she'd left off.

A wave of pleasure coursed through me, and I found no reason to restrain myself anymore. I sat up, holding Laurel steady, and brought my knees up behind her. Her arms wrapped around my neck, holding me close. She moved her hips down and I buried my face in her chest as I slid inside the warmth of her. Straddling me, her hips moving in a slow grind into mine, she melted me like a puddle into the sheets. I dug my fingertips into her shoulders, running a long, languid lick up her neck.

She whimpered, her body rocking in a steady rhythm. Sweat had started to gather on her skin, and she was a joy to touch. Hot enough to warm even me. Her heart beginning to beat at a gallop, alighting cravings of all kinds, no matter how ill-advised.

I nudged her to get up. I urged her toward the headboard until she was holding on to it, and then slid inside her from behind. Laurel moaned, and I leaned into her, palm against the wall. It was so easy to reach her neck. To kiss and nip. To reach between her legs and urge her on. To hear the desperate gasps each time I did something she especially liked. To be tender with her, my free hand roaming, testing. Sometimes holding her against my chest, sometimes pressing her grip into the headboard until she was white-knuckled. And when her ragged breaths began and my name slipped off her tongue, I let her guide me as she slipped over the edge.

It was beautiful to watch.

Laurel collapsed to her knees, gasping for breath. I stole a kiss from her and held her, her skin slick and hot. "Spencer…"

I pressed my forehead to hers. "Yes, darling?"

But she let out a contented little moan and let me hold her. After she had caught her breath, her gaze went to the side table. "We didn't…"

"We have all night, remember?" And I pulled her down onto the mattress into my arms, her head settled on my chest. Her heart was still hammering. I pushed the sticking strands of hair from her face, adoring everything about her. "And after that, a lifetime."

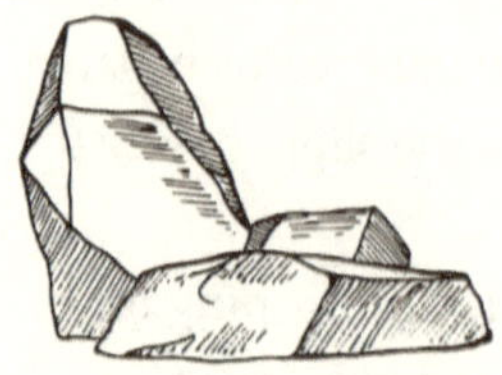

Penny Harbour

The boy, the pretty little boy. *Spencer*. He had overstayed his welcome on the planet, hundreds of years too long. And he had been tolerated in the Harbour for a time. He had touched little and been of no consequence. Then he met the girl.

Keeping things was its job. Getting inside the people, day by day. Through the water and the soil, through the wild game and the air. But mostly—mostly—through the violence. The day-to-day neglects and abuses, coiling and festering. To live in their bodies and minds, eating them up so silently that they hardly noticed it was happening. And one body would become so corrupted and vile that it would spill it out into another.

A backhand.

A gunshot.

An assault.

A lifetime of neglect.

And on and on it went. Passed down in the blood until no one escaped unscathed.

Spencer was a *problem*.

Laurel had been *so close*. It had known from centuries of experience that if it pushed just the right way, just the right times, she would break. Maybe it would have been a small act of violence. Maybe it would have been *grand*. But the boy was teaching her *love*. Undoing what it had spent so long stitching into her.

The vampire had his teeth in her. Had made himself a nuisance.

That just would not do.

CHAPTER TWENTY-ONE

Laurel

Spencer was staring, his eyes dreamy and a crooked little smile on his face. Curled under his sheets, he trailed his thumb back and forth over mine. We'd been in bed a long while, and dark had fully fallen outside. "Are you ready to tell me what brought this on?" he asked, his voice a gentle whisper.

I sighed. I was practically melting into the sheets, relaxed and tired in a way I hadn't been for a very long time. He was asking me while I was weak. "You can't get mad. This is too good to be ruined by you getting mad."

His brow furrowed and he took a moment before answering. "I don't like the sound of that, but all right. I won't promise not to be angry, but I promise I won't make it your problem. Is that good enough?"

"Considering how much of an improvement that would be from my day-to-day, yeah, that's enough."

I started to tell him about the barbecue. The story of getting caught with his picture on my phone had him laughing into his hands, until I admitted to crying in Emma's basement. He held me then, kissing my head and listening intently. And once I reached the part about Greg, Spencer's entire demeanour changed. He still held me, but he went from soft to rigid. I could tell he was holding so much in on my behalf. I had asked, and he was trying.

"And so you came here," Spencer said as I rounded up my story.

"Yeah." Part of me realized how insulting it might be, to have the whole evening come down to how I felt about my husband. "I hope that doesn't change how you feel about tonight."

Spencer reached up and cupped my cheek, his cool hand blissful on my skin. "Of course it doesn't. I want you safe, and if that means I *also* get to spend the evening touching you like that…well, who am I to argue?"

He was being flippant and I appreciated it. It helped take some of the devastation out of what I'd done at the barbecue. At some point soon, the consequences would start crashing down around me, and I wasn't ready for that.

"So what now?" he asked. "Are you…? Do you mean what you told him? Are you done?"

I nodded. "Yeah. As terrifying as that is, yes. I don't have it worked out, and honestly, I don't want to right now. But it does mean I can't go home."

"Don't." Spencer leaned in as if to kiss me, his lips so close to mine. "Stay here from now on, with me."

Feeling welled in my chest until I thought I might cry. Instead, I stole the kiss he was offering. "All right."

We lay there for a while, just holding each other, wrapped in the sheets. I took the moment to appreciate what I'd *somehow* been given. The way his lush, messy blond hair spilt around his face. The smokey grey of his tired eyes. The cut of his lanky frame. Strong, but subtly so. His fingernails were painted pastel pink, and he wore two sets of silver studs in his ears.

Now that I had given myself permission to really see him, I didn't want to stop.

I'd been tired at the start of our conversation, but after telling my story, all the emotion was running rampant under my skin. When I looked at Spencer, his eyes were drooping closed, but he noticed my change in temperament.

"Why," he whispered sleepily, "is your heart going pitter-patter?"

"I think I'm just…happy. I'm not going to be able to sleep." I looked at the digital clock next to the bed. "Also it's basically time for you to get up."

"Mmm, I know." He nuzzled his face into my neck and nipped at my skin. It sent a deep thrill down my spine, making me blush. "But someone woke me up hours ahead of time, only to wear me out again. I *could* be convinced to get up and shower with you, however. Nap on the couch after."

"Yes, yes please." I kissed his chin and slid out of bed, reaching back to take his hand and pull him up. He fought me just a little, eventually crawling off the mattress to follow me into the hall.

Spencer stopped to open a thin door. He grabbed fresh towels and a washcloth, and then followed me into the bathroom. The cream-coloured walls were bare except for a single mirror that hung over the sink, which showed me my reflection but not his. In the corner, a large tub-shower combo was waiting.

"Here," Spencer said, passing me a spare toothbrush. "Get that alcohol off your breath." He went to turn on the water, testing the temperature with his hand.

"I didn't hear any complaints before now," I teased, getting the toothpaste.

He smirked at me. "Just because you didn't hear any doesn't mean I had none."

I cracked a smile, sending muffled curses at him as I brushed. By the time I was finished, the room was beginning to steam. I set the toothbrush on the sink.

He picked up his own. "You get in. I'll join you in a second."

I stepped in and immediately had to turn up the hot water. His idea of hot enough was vastly different from mine, which might have had something to do with his internal temperature. As I moved under the water, I tipped my head back, letting the full warmth of the water wash over me, soaking my hair. I wiped my eyes, and when I looked, Spencer was joining me.

I pulled him toward me, into the stream of water. He winced at the heat but seemed to settle into it quickly. I pressed against him, trying to warm him, and in comparison to the water, his body was like ice.

When he was acclimated, I traded spots with him, the water hitting his back. He sighed, eyes closed and basking in it. He held me against him, and my heart fluttered, just to be so at peace for a moment.

Safe.

I reached up for a kiss, the cool sensation of mint on both our lips.

Spencer kissed my cheek and then ran a hand through my wet hair. "Turn around, darling."

I did as I was asked. From behind me, I could hear the click of a bottle opening. A moment later, he was gathering my hair in his hands. The soft scent of grapefruit filled the room, and Spencer began to lather the shampoo into my hair, massaging my scalp. I let my head fall back, enjoying the touch.

"Step back into the water." Spencer rinsed the soap from my hair, wiping the stray suds away from my eyes. I leaned back against him, content under his touch. Another open bottle, more lathered soap. He ran his palm from my collarbone to my jaw, gently. Then down my arms, working the soap into my hands. Between my fingers.

Kisses trailed down my neck, one after the other, down to my shoulder. His teeth grazed my skin and I drew in a little breath, only to hear him chuckle approval in my ear.

"Turn," he whispered, and I did. His fingers trailed my body, tracing each scar I'd collected over the years. More soap. As he ran his hands along my stomach, up along the curves of my breasts, he leaned in for a kiss. "Gods, you're beautiful."

I let him lavish affection on me until I was clean, and then urged him back under the water. I trailed kisses along his chest, drawing a fleeting gasp from him. I washed his hair, watching his face as I did. His eyes closed and his jaw relaxed. And as contented as he seemed, I could tell how tired he was. How spent.

As I ran the soap over his shoulders, I noticed the tension there and used my thumbs to apply pressure. Spencer twitched, but then settled into the rhythmic patterns I pressed into his muscles, trying to release whatever had gathered there. He rewarded me with a deep sigh, a smile, and a kiss on the nose.

When we were both ready, we turned off the shower and started to towel off. Despite looking half-asleep, Spencer was still playful with me, catching me in his towel and dragging me back if I tried to go too far away. He brought me to his closet to pick out something to wear, and I was astounded by the sheer number of things to choose from. I made a mental note of things I wanted to try on someday, especially knowing how *fucking expensive* some of them looked. But in the end, I chose a simple black hoodie that was cut too long for me. I brought the wrists to my face and breathed in the scent of him, like some high schooler with her first boyfriend.

We went downstairs, both of us snug in our pyjamas, and Spencer looking fit to pass out immediately. But as we rounded into the living room, he ran his fingers down my back.

"Now is probably a good time to tell you to check the cupboard over the fridge."

I went out to the kitchen and opened it up. His kitchen had always been sparse, and most of the cupboards had been bare, but since I'd last looked, he'd filled this one with actual items a human would need in a kitchen. A can opener, a cheese grater, mixing bowls, spices, cereal, mugs, cups, coffee, an electric kettle. So much more, all of it unopened and waiting.

When I turned, he was leaning on the wall in the doorway, watching my reaction.

"Spencer—"

"I wanted you to be at home here. Surprise." His voice was weary, but full of love.

I kissed him, tears brimming in my eyes. "Thank you."

He didn't say anything. He just held me, his hand on my back. I had a feeling he was listening to my heart again, this time slow and steady.

"All right, go get on the couch," I said, nudging him away. "I'll make a coffee and you find me something to watch while you sleep."

Spencer nodded and then went to slump onto the couch. Spectre had come stalking us down the stairs and quickly curled up on his lap. A few minutes later, I grabbed my phone from where I'd left my jeans on the stairs, and joined him with a cup of coffee in hand. I put a pillow in my lap, smacking it with my hand as an invitation. Spencer lay down and snuggled in, forcing Spectre to curl up next to him. He pulled the blanket down from the back of the couch and covered himself up.

I pressed play on the movie Spencer had picked out, but I could tell his heart wasn't in it. He'd chosen some random action movie that neither of us would have opted for any other day. That was fine by me. It could serve as background noise while I checked my phone for the first time since the barbecue, a coffee in the other hand, and a cute vampire snoozing in my lap.

God. When exactly did things get *so good*?

Some of that melted into guilt as I saw the messages left for me from Emma and Mary-Jo.

Mary-Jo:
Laurel where are you? Did you go home?

Emma:
Greg is fuming. Wherever you are, don't come back here
and don't go home.

The texts went on for a while, on Tabs and directly to my phone.
Voicemails that hadn't rung without service, Tabs calls I hadn't heard. Fuck.
Then one message from Greg.

Greg:
You best get your ass home right fucking now

For just a moment, fear built in my chest, realizing what I had done and
who was really fucking angry at me. I had known he'd be *pissed* and I had
spent years trying to avoid this very moment. And it was here, and—
And then Spencer stirred on my lap, nuzzling into the pillow, his hand
coming up to sit on my leg.
Safe. I was safe. *Breathe.*
Nothing would happen to me with him here.
Trying to distract myself, I started to type into the group chat with
the girls.

Laurel:
I'm so sorry I didn't tell you where I was.
No excuse for it.
I'm safe. I'm at Spencer's. I won't be going home again.
He's zonked and I'm not going to force
him to leave tonight.
We'll come see you tomorrow evening, okay? Catch you
up. Again, I'm so fucking sorry to worry you like that. I
just…lost track of time.

I was hardly going to tell them what I lost track of time *doing*. But as an
apology, I sent a photo of Spencer asleep on my lap. Within a minute, I had
responses from both of them.

Emma:
Oh thank god. You had me worried sick.
MJ punched Greg.

Mary-Jo:
I did and he's got a black eye and it was the best
day of my fucking life!!!
Glad you're safe sweetcakes. Don't fucking
ghost next time
Tell that adorable fucking twink I said to
go pound sand <3
And never tell him I said he's adorable

Emma:
Message us tomorrow and enjoy your new boo <3

I smiled to myself, looking at all the love on my screen, and then down at Spencer. The moment Greg disappeared from view, I had *so much good.* Tears welled in my eyes again. It was hard not to be angry with myself, knowing how many more years of happiness I could have had if I'd just let go of Greg sooner.

I put down my phone and ran my fingers through Spencer's hair. He was deeply asleep. If I *had* left Greg sooner, I probably would never have found this beauty of a man who had endless patience and seemed to love every part of me—so far, at least.

Maybe that would be worth it, in the end.

With my fingers still tracing his scalp, I drank my coffee and searched for something else to watch. At some point, a phone was going to ring or the movie was going to end, or Spencer would wake. The moment I existed in was finite. It would end. It was a rarity in a sea of dark years, and I wanted to enjoy it for as long as I possibly could.

Spencer

Waking up with Laurel the next evening invited more feelings than I was prepared for. Everything felt a bit like a dream I was afraid to wake up from. She had stayed up late to accommodate my sleeping habits, and we'd lounged in bed until nearly seven in the evening, taking our time since the sun wouldn't set for another two hours. And as we got up, I found I was floating along from moment to moment. Even now, staring at her as she sat on my kitchen counter in my oversized hoodie, feet dangling, coffee in one hand and phone in the other, I couldn't imagine that it was *real*.

Why would it be? She had kept herself at a distance for so long, and I had lost so much. What else could it be but some cosmic fucking tease?

I shook my head, searching for a way to attribute the melancholy to hunger. What was it people always said? If it's too good to be true, maybe you're a self-sabotaging idiot? Clearly I had mastered that concept.

I drank back my breakfast, watching her from the couch, and tried to focus on the good. The swing of her bare legs, back and forth. The little smirk as she typed in rapid-fire into her phone. And then she looked up and caught me staring, and she stuck her tongue out at me.

Setting my glass down and getting up, I stalked toward her, smirking. She sat straighter, smiling nervously, clearly waiting to see what I was about to do. So naturally I slid my cold hands along her very warm thighs.

"Oh *my god*." Laurel tried to squirm away, a shudder running down her body as she spilt coffee all over the counter.

"What?" I leaned in, smirking. "You wanted my attention, didn't you?"

She put the coffee cup and phone down and pried my hands off her legs. "You're *freezing*, you monster." Generously, she moved my hands onto the sides of her cheeks, covering them with her palms in an attempt to warm them.

"Ah, but I'm *your* monster. Isn't that a delight?" I tried to steal a kiss, but she stopped me, turning her head to the side.

"Oh, no," she said, laughing. "You've still got breakfast on your mouth. Try again later."

I licked my lips and sure enough. I could hardly blame her for not wanting a secondhand taste of human blood. I kissed her on the forehead instead and then moved to clean up the mess of coffee I'd caused.

"And? What are the ladies saying?"

Laurel picked up her phone again. "Emma and MJ are suggesting we meet in the middle and talk it out. For old times' sake."

I looked up midway through wiping the counter down. "They want to what?"

"Oh. Meet in the middle. Even when we were kids, we always lived on the other side of the Harbour from each other, so if we wanted to go walking, we would all head out at the same time and just keep walking down the main drag until we found each other." The story brought a dreamy smile to Laurel's face as she stared into her lap. "We still do it sometimes, but having a car means we go for a hell of a lot less walks."

I rinsed out the cloth and hung it over the tap. "It's a good night for it. Or it will be, once it's *actually* night."

Laurel hopped down from the counter. "I told them you had work until late, so we couldn't meet them until after sunset. At this point, I think I could have told them one in the morning and they'd still come out, just to see if I've actually ditched Greg."

I tilted her phone so I could see the time. "I suppose we should get ready then. I need to make a good first impression."

Laurel rolled her eyes. "I think you're well past first impressions."

Pulling her toward me by the hips, I hummed an unsure note. "Sure, as your new gay best friend, perhaps. Now I have to convince them I'm fit to stay in your bed."

"*Spencer.*" She groaned, her hands over her face. Gods, I loved to see her blush.

"*Fine*, I'll stop. Would you like to watch something while we wait?" I asked, leaning my cheek against her forehead.

"Yes please." She wrapped her arms around me, and despite the intention to move, we stayed like that for longer than we needed, content to just *be*.

Once the sun had gone down, Laurel and I set out, walking along the shoulder of the road along the Harbour. We had told the ladies that we'd take the road, despite Laurel worrying about being seen. I'd had to remind her that she had nothing to hide anymore, and she'd immediately asked what would happen if Greg saw us. To which I had reminded her I was easily capable of tearing his throat out with my teeth if the moment called for it. I'd told her she was safe, and the tears had welled in her eyes.

I let her try to hide them and acted as if I hadn't noticed. She seemed to prefer it that way.

We walked for ten minutes, hand in hand, before a pair of shapes appeared in the distance. Considering it was past nine at night with not another soul around, it was a safe bet that Emma and Mary-Jo had found us. Then they started waving like lunatics, which made Laurel laugh.

"Hey!" Mary-Jo yelled as we got closer. "Who are those idiots holding hands?"

Laurel looked up at me, a smile hidden under a nervous grimace. "I apologize about her in advance."

"Oh, don't," I said, squeezing her hand. "I *love it*."

Emma had her hands over her face and her eyes were glistening as she stopped in front of us. "You're so cute."

"Don't start, Emma." Laurel let go of my hand in order to wrap her friend in a hug. "You know if you cry, everyone's gonna cry."

"I'm *trying*," she whined, holding Laurel. Between the little sniffs and whimpers, even I was edging toward emotional.

Mary-Jo spread her arms and pulled me in for a hug. She was *strong*, and as she squeezed, she brought her face close to my ear. "Thank you," she whispered.

She lingered, and I held on to her, trying to give the moment what it deserved. Though I couldn't understand the scope of what it would have been like to watch Laurel suffer Greg for all those years, I could certainly understand the end of a long, hard road.

"I didn't do it for you, wench," I teased in a low voice.

"I know." She wasn't meeting my prodding, and she wasn't breaking the hug. "Just don't break her fucking heart or I'll kill you, and I don't want to do that."

I laughed and shrugged MJ off me, holding her shoulders. "I wouldn't dream of it."

"Good." Mary-Jo wiped the corner of her eye with a finger, blinking rapidly. "You smell like a girl."

"And you smell like a gym rat," I snapped back playfully. She didn't *actually* smell bad, but she smirked anyway.

Laurel was busy whispering to her crying friend, her hands on Emma's cheeks. "Everything is going to be all right now, I promise. You can stop worrying about me."

I put my arm around Mary-Jo's shoulder as we watched. "Do you think we should lighten the mood?"

MJ put a hand on my arm. "We'll give them ten more seconds. Then I'm going to scoop up Emma and race you to that light pole over there."

"Delightful."

Mary-Jo counted down in a hushed voice, and when she hit one, I snatched Laurel away from Emma, threw her over my shoulder, and started to run. Laurel screamed, her laugh interrupted by the jostling as I kept pace with MJ, who was carrying Emma in both arms. My ears were full with the excited cacophony of their hearts and the night was full of joyous laughter. And for the full minute it took to reach that light pole, something old and beautiful was alive in me again.

Mary-Jo reached the goal first and spun Emma around, celebrating her win. I could've run harder, but I didn't need to give myself away. I came to a stop next to them and held Laurel by the thighs as she looked down at me, face flushed and laughing. Gods, she was so beautiful when she laughed.

"Kiss," Mary-Jo started, putting Emma down. "Kiss, kiss, *kiss*—"

"Kiss!" Emma pumped her fist in the air with each chant. "Kiss, kiss—"

I tilted my head at Laurel, raising an eyebrow. "Kiss?"

Laurel's cheeks were scarlet, but she summoned up the courage to lean in and kiss me, long and chaste, and to the roar of her friends cheering. When I put her down, Laurel looked a little like she might happily die of embarrassment.

"Fucking adorable." Mary-Jo reached into her purse and started fishing for her cigarettes. "Cheers, motherfucker. Welcome to the family."

Family.

I could get used to that again. *Maybe.* The word stirred up such a mix of things in my chest. Longing for something I couldn't have anymore. Longing for this thing that I *could,* and a sense of confusion about how to make them exist together. The grief and the joy, all at once. To gain without losing, as if such a thing were ultimately possible.

I set Laurel down and she nuzzled against me, and the weight of that thought lingered. Because her heartbeat in my ears meant she was alive, and so were her friends, and someday, they too would all be gone. And I would keep existing without them, no matter how much of a family we became.

I held Laurel close, trying not to let those dark thoughts get their claws into me. She was here and alive, and we had time. So much time. And if someday we had a conversation about living forever, maybe we would have *more* time. I just couldn't let my eager heart jump that far ahead. If I'd been afraid Laurel would never admit her feelings for me, the fear of asking her to trap herself into immortality with me was several bridges too far. Like asking someone to get married after a first date.

A conversation for another day.

We had *time.*

"All right, enough being sickeningly cute—like, don't stop but also absolutely do stop—" MJ made a playful gagging gesture with her finger and mouth. "But I think we have sneaky fucking plans to make."

"Do we?" I asked, taking Laurel's hand again and following Emma and Mary-Jo as they started up the street. With no one at all on the empty road, we took up the entire lane, walking side by side.

"They want to go get my stuff from home." Laurel made a face and adjusted her wording. "*From Greg's.* Before he gets rid of it or does something else spiteful."

"Oh, excellent. Am I invited?" I asked, eager to take some modicum of revenge, since Laurel still didn't seem to want him *dead.*

Mary-Jo shot me a grin. "You sure fucking are. If we're smart, we wait until he leaves for darts tomorrow night, and then take all the cars at once and stuff them full. And if we're really smart, we hide a dead rat in the mattress."

Emma sighed. "MJ, that's not very—"

A horrible, deep growl pierced the night from the other side of the street, stopping us all in our tracks.

"Fuck fuck fuck—" MJ danced back. "*Bear*, that's a fucking bear."

And sure enough, a full-grown black bear came stomping out of the woods next to us, one plodding foot after the other.

"Get back," Laurel whispered, pushing me like I wasn't smart enough to back away from a bear. "Head low. Don't make eye contact."

The bear growled again and plodded out onto the road, directly in the pool of light from a nearby pole. Despite Laurel's words, I couldn't help but stare. Something *smelled* wrong.

The bear stopped in front of us, huffing thick breaths. That was when I noticed the black oozing from its eyes. It coated the fur around its snout in such excess that the black was dripping to the pavement. Pooling.

"Something's wrong," I hissed. I'd seen plenty of bears. *Drunk* plenty of bears. And none of them cried black.

Excellent deduction, boy.

The voice rang through my head, startling me.

"Did you just hear that?" Emma shouted.

Of course you did, little one. I'm in here with you.

Waiting.

"You hear the voice?" Laurel asked, panicked, her face white as a sheet. "*You can hear it?*"

"Yeah," I said, forcing her to keep moving back, away from the bear that might somehow be the least of our problems. "I think we all do."

Laurel's fingers were digging into my arm. "No, Spencer. The voice, it's—"

An old friend. Aren't we, Laurel?

"Don't listen to it! Don't—" Laurel cried out in agony and dropped to her knees, clutching her head.

So rude. We're just getting acquainted, aren't we?

And you want to ruin that.

Such a shame.

The bear kept moving toward us, its jaw open and more of that black dripping from between its jagged teeth.

"Is it the bear speaking?" Emma whimpered, holding herself as she moved back, her gaze averted but wary.

"That's no bear." I didn't know what it was, but it was nothing natural.

Come now.

Don't be upset, Spencer.

You were allowed to stay here, so long as you didn't get in my way.

Now you have.

If you'd stayed away from the girl, it would never have come to this.

This must be rectified.

"How did I *get in your way*?" I put myself between the bear and Laurel, who was still crouched on the ground, head in hands. "I don't know *what* you are."

Laurel.

Get up, Laurel.

He simply can't have you, can he?

With his fangs and his bloodlust and those stained hands of his.

What can he do but break you?

From the hands of one monster to the next, hmm?

"What the *fuck*?" Why was this thing so interested in me, and what did it want with her? "Laurel, don't—"

But when I looked down, Laurel was getting to her feet. She was rigid as she stood, and the entirety of her eyes had gone black, starting to spill out of the corners of her eyes.

"Laurel?"

She can't hear you, little vampire.

She's not yours.

"What did that thing say?" Mary-Jo looked poised to leap toward us, held at bay only by the bear, which had come to a standstill. Waiting.

"It said *vampire*," Emma muttered. "Why…?"

"Laurel." I put my hands on her cheeks, shaking her gently. Her stare was a thousand miles away, looking through me and seeming to see nothing. "Hey. Come back to me, darling. Where are you hiding?"

She blinked, her eyelashes fluttering rapidly. The black started to melt away, pouring down her cheeks. "Jesus Christ," she panted, slumping slightly. "It—it—"

What a pity.

You'll be ready someday soon, Little Laurel.

But that doesn't mean I'll let him go.

The bloodcurdling roar rose from behind me. Emma screamed and took off running into the ditch on the other side of the road. Mary-Jo called after her but didn't move. She knew better. And then the bear started to hurtle toward me.

I braced myself, the only thing between the bear and Laurel. As it reached me, I shouldered into it as hard as I could and felt something snap under the pressure. The bear cried out and reared back, standing as tall as I was. And as it came back down again, its claws struck me across the chest, ripping from my right shoulder down to my left hip.

Pain seared through me and I screamed, falling to the pavement. Somewhere in between the flashes of black in my vision, I saw Mary-Jo pulling Laurel back, away from me. Good. Because I was going to tear this bear *apart*.

I pulled myself up to all fours and threw myself toward it. My strength was just enough to send it toppling back. It hit the pavement with a grunt and a gurgling roar. Seeing nothing but red, I straddled it, grabbing two fistfuls of fur and *pulling*. The bear bucked under me as I ripped the fur from its chest. I dug my nails in, wanting to see it bleed.

"You don't fucking touch me, and you don't touch *her*!" I pressed until my nails sunk under the bear's skin, and then used the leverage to rip its flesh away. Blood flew from the wound, dripping down my arms, splashing across my face. I licked my lips and spat, noticing only then how much *black* was in it, like something had filled it to the brim. It tasted like everything else in that town.

It tasted like Laurel.

Blood was gushing out over the bear's fur, its eyes black and enraged. It swiped at me again, and I grabbed the arm and yanked. The snap of its tendons loosening from its shoulder shuddered through its body and it practically howled.

Someone was crying. I needed to end things. Make sure this beast couldn't get to them. So I reached up and snapped the bear's neck in one difficult twist. The thing collapsed under me, the life leaving it.

I fell forward, panting against the pain, my head reeling. The slashes in my chest were too deep. One had hit bone and the white was visible under all that blood. I needed to eat, and soon. My body would need more than the half measure of breakfast to get through all that healing.

"Spencer." Laurel was standing off to the side, visibly unsure if she should approach. Her face was a mess of black, as if she'd taken bad mascara out in the rain. Underneath it, she was terrified.

I moved to get off the bear, crying out as the wounds stretched and shifted. *Fuck,* it hurt. But I made it to her anyway. "Laurel, are you—?"

Mary-Jo came up from the side and threw a solid right hook into my jaw. I stumbled back, my bones shaken, pain flaring up the side of my face. "*Gods,* what is—?"

Before I could finish, her foot connected with my torn-open ribs and sent me sprawling across the pavement. I curled up, the wound searing, teeth grinding together. "MJ, stop."

"Don't fucking move." Mary-Jo stood over me, fists balled up and a snarl on her face.

I stayed very still. "I'm not—"

"Shut up."

Laurel pushed Mary-Jo back and then knelt over me. "Spencer, are you okay?"

"*Why are his eyes red, Laurel?*" Mary-Jo hissed through her teeth, staring down at us, clearly ready to tear Laurel away from me and kill me with her bare hands.

Emma called out from further away, coming back toward us tentatively. "Everyone breathe—"

"I'm not here to hurt anyone," I muttered, trying very hard to be the coolest head despite the agony pulsing through my body and the growing hunger.

"What am I looking at?" Mary-Jo gestured to me, furious. "Look at him. He has *fangs,* girl. And that fucking voice, whatever that was, it called him—"

"I know what it called him!" Laurel screamed at her. "It doesn't mean you can kick him in the chest until he drops dead."

Emma walked over cautiously. "He killed that bear..."

"With his hands," MJ added.

"To protect us!" Laurel hissed. She was examining my wounds, and her face was going green.

"He needs a hospital," Emma said, her voice growing frantic.

"*No*," I commanded, at the same time Laurel pleaded for them not to. "I don't need a hospital. It won't help."

Emma's arms went around her chest, hugging herself tightly. "Spencer, I'm going to need you to start talking."

"What would you like me to say?" I sat up slowly, both because of the pain and because I didn't want to startle Mary-Jo into beating me senseless. "Spencer. Vampire. Pleased to meet you."

Mary-Jo and Emma looked at each other. It was clear they were weighing their options. Believe this bleeding maniac or keep their little realities tidy and free of monsters. If they wanted to stand around and debate my existence, let them.

I turned to Laurel and touched her cheek. The black smeared under my thumb, gritty and chalky as it dried, like charcoal. "Are you hurt?"

She shook her head, leaning her face into my palm. "Scared, but okay. Do you need to drink?"

I nodded. "The sooner the better."

"Let's get you back to the house, get you something there." She searched my face, perhaps looking for a patch of clean skin, and placed a kiss on my cheek.

"Oh, no." Mary-Jo shifted her weight to one foot, her arms crossed over her chest. "We're not taking you anywhere."

"This is impossible, right?" Emma asked, her voice sheepish. "It is. If it's a prank, this isn't funny."

I smiled up at her, pitying the delicate thing. "Poor dears. You thought the affair was the worst of it." I took a breath, trying to will the fangs away and the red out of my eyes, but it wasn't happening. The pain was too great.

"You know what I need?" Emma's voice was high-pitched and desperate. "A drink. Yup."

"Can you give us a minute?" Laurel asked, moving to get up. "Maybe I can set their minds at ease."

"Go ahead. I'll just be here, bleeding onto the street next to the bear monster I murdered." I fell onto my back and stared up at the clouds rolling over the stars. They'd have been beautiful if everything didn't burn so fucking bad.

The three women walked over to the light pole and stood in a circle, practically shoulder to shoulder. Despite their whispers, I heard every word.

"*Laurel.*" Mary-Jo's voice was strained.

"Five minutes ago, you thought I'd made the best choice on earth." Laurel was trying to wipe the black from her cheeks.

"To be fair, five minutes ago, your side piece didn't have fangs." Emma's hand was shaking as it lingered over her mouth.

Mary-Jo huffed. "Night shifts my ass."

Laurel shrugged. "What else was I supposed to say? *I'm having an affair and actually he's a mythological creature of the night who drinks blood*?"

"I mean, you could've, yeah. That would've been good to know." Mary-Jo groaned. "It explains *so much*. The cute Irish-ish accent, the old-timey way he talks. Oh, for fuck's sake—you literally stood in Emma's house—" She gestured to the town behind her. "—and invited him in. *Fuck*."

"As if you would have believed me. I barely believe it and I know him better than you. He's still Spencer, all right?" Laurel hissed. "Can't you trust when I say he's a good guy?"

Emma cleared her throat. "You spent two decades swearing up and down that Greg was a good guy too."

They were silent for a moment before Laurel spoke. "Low blow, Emma."

"Emma's not wrong." Mary-Jo started digging in her purse for another cigarette, practically trembling as she lit it. She took a puff and let out a cloud of smoke. "*Though*, I guess if he hadn't killed that bear, you'd be dead."

"Yes, she would be," I called out. "Literally bleeding out over here. Can we please discuss this at my place after I get someone to drink? *Away* from the evil bear?"

Laurel moved first, coming to my side to help me off the ground. She let me lean on her and then started me toward the side of the road. "Emma, MJ, go get the car. We'll be here."

"I can't leave you with him." Mary-Jo's fingers were flexing in and out of fists. "What if he eats you?"

"She tastes like shit. How's that for insurance." I pursed my lips, guilt washing over me after my moment of impatience. "Sorry, darling."

"MJ, he bit me for like half a second and looked like he was going to throw up. Pretty sure I'll be fine." Laurel helped me sit on the shoulder of the road, my back against the light pole. "*Get the car* before another fucked-up bear comes running out of the woods."

Emma grabbed MJ by the shoulder and urged her to turn. I paid them absolutely no attention as they rushed in the opposite direction. Instead, I leaned my head against the pole and willed myself not to cry.

Laurel sat down beside me. "I'm so sorry." She ran her fingers through my hair and the touch barely registered through the pain of air *inside* my skin. She pressed a kiss to my lips and the tenderness brought a sob into my throat.

I shook my head as she tried to figure out what was wrong. "I just really need to eat."

"I'm here," she said, curling as close to me as she dared.

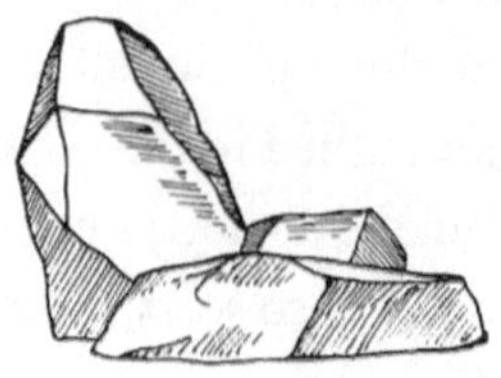

Penny Harbour

The vessel was dead. That…was inconvenient.

As all-encompassing as its presence could be, not much had ever been possible with just a body, dead or simply asleep. It had its fingers in Laurel, of course…but not quite deep enough. Not yet. Not for the glorious things it had planned for her. She had *such* potential, and it was nothing if not patient.

The sweet one, Emma…it had no tangible hold on her. Trickles of it lived in her body, but she had escaped so much of what the Harbour had to offer, somehow. Prone to laughter and acts of kindness, chasing a life that would undo so much of its work. She could become a problem, someday.

And Mary-Jo. It had taken root deep in her for years. In each drink and smoke and punch thrown. She had revelled in it, for a while. Still did, when her blood ran hot. But she was completely unreceptive to its suggestions of violence against Laurel. A flaw in the design of things. People could be twisted, however. She might have been reluctant to hurt the ones she loved, but that only meant a far greater chance that she would kill *for* them.

As it retreated to dark corners of the Harbour, to observe and wait, it knew how close at hand the end had become.

It would not let Laurel go easily.

Darkness never did.

CHAPTER TWENTY-TWO

Spencer

It didn't take Emma and Mary-Jo long to come back, but it *felt* like forever. I was certain I slipped into unconsciousness several times. As the car came to a stop in front of us, the absurdity of the situation hit me. A dead bear next to a tiny powder-blue car that they were planning to pile me into the back of so I could bleed all over the seats.

"Up you go." Laurel grabbed me under the arms and forced me to my feet. Her heart gave a thick, heaving pump and my mouth watered. Drinking her would be stomach-turning, but the hunger wouldn't care how she tasted, not in the end. I just had to keep that urge down for a little longer.

Laurel helped me into the car and then got in on the other side. I slouched against her. It didn't matter what I did. It all hurt. If it was going to hurt, I might as well get to still touch her. The world went in and out of focus around me. I knew we were moving. Knew Laurel was holding me to make sure I didn't fall over. Knew the drive was minutes. But it seemed a lifetime, fading in and out like that. A dream inside a dream inside black.

Then she was shaking me awake.

"Spencer. Come on. Almost there. Give me your keys." When I struggled to fish them out of my pocket, she went in after them. She tossed them to Emma. "Open the door."

I heard the car doors open and close around me. Heard the jingle of keys and the click of a lock. Laurel struggled to bear my weight at such an odd angle, and then groaned. "MJ, get the fuck over here."

Then they were both dragging me from the car and across the driveway. Once we were inside, they set me gently on the couch, though Mary-Jo was quick to retreat.

"Emma, sit next to him. Make sure he doesn't fall or something."

Emma's heart was racing in her chest. Sitting her next to me was a *bad idea*. The weakness would buy time, but Laurel needed to be quick. Before survival kicked in.

The world went black again, and then that darling woman was standing over me, squeezing my cheeks. "Wake up." She held a large glass to my lips and the smell of cold blood filled my senses. "Drink."

I grabbed the glass out of her hands and drank it greedily. The blood was almost sweet on my tongue, something aged but well-preserved. Sweet *relief*. Cold, not *ideal*, but fucking delicious. Vaguely, I heard the room stirring around me as I drank. Panicked voices. Laurel calming her friends. The smell of cigarette smoke. And a moment later the blood was gone. More. I needed more.

"Laurel."

She was leaning over me again. "Another?"

I nodded, and she took the glass. She was back with a full cup quicker than I could register. By the time I'd finished that one—something quiet and reserved, with a bitter note of madness—some of the clarity was back in the room. I could see properly, which meant I could make out the looks of concern and horror on Emma and Mary-Jo's faces.

So much for family.

Laurel sat down next to me and took my hand.

"Thank you," I muttered, looking over at her.

"Better?" she asked.

"I will be." I moved to adjust myself on the cushion and winced. I'd need more blood, but more pressing things were on the table.

"So this is fucking real. You just popped open two IV bags and fed them to him like a smoothie." Mary-Jo refused to sit, adjusting her weight from one leg to the other like she couldn't settle herself. She was working on at least her third cigarette of the night.

"I'm afraid so, peach." My voice was strained. I wanted to eat a pair of college sweethearts and call it a night. Curl up in bed until the world ended around me.

"But you're not going to kill us?" Emma asked.

I tried to laugh. "No. I quite like you, actually."

Emma started to pout. "That's kinda sweet."

"You've been hanging out with this guy for months. How long did you know?" Mary-Jo started tapping her foot.

Laurel looked at me, clearly doing the math in her head. "I found out somewhere after the first month. It…it didn't change things for me. Spencer has still been leagues better to me than Greg ever was, despite this part of him."

I gave her hand a squeeze. "So," I groaned, "does this mean you'll stop kicking me when I'm down?"

Mary-Jo stomped her foot anxiously, deliberating. Then she stepped toward me and handed me her cigarette. "You better be a fucking vegan."

I cracked into a laugh. "Oh, you wish." I took a drag from the cigarette and moved to hand it back to her, but my lips had left red on the filter. She immediately waved it off with a look of disgust and fished out a new one. "I promise I'm not going to hurt Laurel, nor am I going to hurt either of you. So can we please talk about the bear and the voice? I realize this vampire thing is new to you, but the rest has me pretty deeply concerned."

"Don't you need to…?" Emma waved in my direction, and when she looked, she paled again. "You're just sitting there, wide open."

"Darling, the blanket, please." I held my hand out and then covered my front with the blanket I was handed, careful to keep it from touching the wounds. "Does that help? I'll heal. It's part of the perks of being dead."

Emma nodded, but didn't say anything.

"So you…you all heard that voice, right?" Laurel was quiet. Nervous.

A chorus of confirmation, low and worried.

Laurel looked between her friends. "I've been hearing that voice for years."

"*What?*" Mary-Jo started looking around for something to tap her cigarette ashes into and settled on an abandoned glass. "The fuck do you mean?"

"I don't know!" Laurel rubbed her face with her hands. "You know how people talk about having, like…a little voice in their head? Like the one that calls them fat or ugly or whatever? I thought it was literal. This voice has been there *for years*, telling me I should hurt people. Mostly Greg."

"Oh, well, in that case, maybe the voice and I should be friends." Mary-Jo looked at Emma. "All right, psychology major, is that normal?"

Emma shook her head. "It's normal for people to have running commentaries. Not everyone does, but plenty of people think thoughts at themselves and not all of them are nice. Intrusive thoughts about doing harm to yourself or others are also common, and many people don't act on them. But it is *not* normal to have those thoughts manifest as something that shows up in *all our minds at the same time.*"

"Your eyes," I said, looking at Laurel. "Where did you go when it told you to hurt me?"

She looked at her lap. "I don't know. I was in there, but not really in control. It was so easy to imagine how I would hurt you. I hated it, but it was like…it knew where I kept my anger and it just *fed it.* For a minute, I hated you. Until you touched me and asked me to come back." A little smile on the corner of her lips. A gaze upward.

"You're fucking undead. Doesn't that make you, like, an expert?" Mary-Jo gestured in my direction and then started to move around the room, picking up whatever was in her path and examining it like she'd never seen a CD in her life.

"Living through a few centuries teaches you a lot, but no, I don't know what this is. No one is hearing anything now, correct?" I looked around the room to a chorus of shaking heads.

"It…" Laurel took a moment to gather her words. Her heart was thumping hard and her hand had grown cool and clammy. "It usually shows up with big feelings. Not always. But if Greg would—" She covered her eyes with her free hand and started again. "If he wanted to have sex and I *didn't,* the voice would show up and ask how far I'd go to *not* do that ever again. Or it would tell me not to get too close to Spencer, because he would hurt me in the end. I thought it was paranoia or desperation, but…"

That hurt. It hurt to hear specifics about what Greg had done. And what she had fought back against in order to reach out to me. I had promised just yesterday not to make my anger her problem, but I was itching to make it *someone's* problem.

"And what's the black shit?" MJ asked. "It's not *blood,* is it?"

"I've tasted plenty and I have *never* tasted anything like this outside of this area." I caught Mary-Jo's eye as she tried not to stay still. "If I bit you, you'd be the same. I'm sure of it."

Mary-Jo shuddered. "No, I'm good, thanks. More of a werewolf girl myself, if it's all right by you."

Emma swallowed hard. "If you can tell me for sure, I'm willing to be a test dummy."

I laughed. "I can guarantee it already. Laurel's swimming with it. But if you want to be sure…"

Her face grew resolute. "I'm sure. I have a baby to protect. Tell me if I'm infected with this thing or not. What do I do?"

It was impressive, honestly. How quickly Emma went from demure and shy to *please bite me, I must defend my young.* "Dealer's choice. Are you up for being bitten, or would you rather do the cutting yourself?"

Emma sat down next to Laurel and held her hand out. "I don't think I can do it myself."

I took her hand, fighting the pain to sit up. Laurel's arm went behind my back, as if to hold me upright.

Emma's eyes were squeezed shut, her heart hammering. The poor fucking thing, like a rabbit being hunted across a field.

I bit down a fang on the tip of one finger, quick and sharp. She hissed and tried to recoil, but I held her firm. With the skin pierced, I gave her finger a squeeze. Blood came to the surface, pooling in a growing red dot. I licked the tip of her finger and made a face.

"Mm, it's mild, but it's there." I let Emma's wrist go, wishing I had something to chase that flavour away with. "Not nearly as bad as Laurel's blood, but it's a hard texture to miss."

"*Fuck.*" Mary-Jo dug into her pockets and came back with a set of car keys, complete with a miniature Swiss Army knife. She popped the blade out and stabbed her thumb. "Go on. Fucking tell me."

"Don't be so *eager*, MJ," I teased. "Not in front of your friend."

Mary-Jo came over to the couch and stuck her bleeding thumb out. "Gross. Never talk to me suggestively again."

"Agreed." I hadn't thought it over before I'd said it, and it left me with a slimy feeling under my skin. But I tasted her all the same, and Mary-Jo's blood was definitely worse than Emma's.

"Bad news," I said, letting her go and lying back against the couch. "You also taste like shit."

"Fuck. So whatever this is, we're in it too." Emma's head was in her hands. She took a breath and then put her hands on Laurel's leg. "I wish you had told us. About the voices, about Spencer, any of it."

"And what would you have done?" Laurel asked, exasperated. "I sound like a lunatic."

Mary-Jo came to sit on the coffee table in front of us. She'd aged ten years, it seemed. Tired and hunched over, her elbows on her knees. "How did we go from celebrating your freedom to feeding vampires and killing demon bears?"

Laurel let her head fall onto my shoulder. "I don't know."

I kissed Laurel's forehead. "Well, I'm having an excellent time. I don't know what you're all complaining about."

Mary-Jo scoffed. "Yeah, okay, Mister Bleeding Out. I bet you're loving being eviscerated by a bear."

I shrugged, and then winced at the little burst of pain. "I've had worse. Laurel found out all this by giving me a third-degree sunburn on my arm, didn't you, darling?"

"I said I was sorry," she whined into my shoulder.

"And all is forgiven." I nuzzled my nose into hers until she met me for a kiss.

MJ sighed. "Jesus, how is this still fucking cute?"

Emma's eyes were filling with tears again. "I'm so confused, but I think this is still good."

Mary-Jo stared at Spencer again, eyes narrowed. She took a puff from her newest cigarette and blew it sideways, away from us. "So what are you, in literal terms? A demon?"

"In a sense, I suppose." I wasn't *really* up for an inquisition, but I didn't want to give them any other reasons to doubt me.

Mary-Jo's face slowly turned into a wicked smile.

"Don't ask him," Laurel warned. "*Don't do it.*"

MJ batted her eyelashes. "Do you sparkle?"

My jaw tightened, a shatteringly evil grin spreading on my face. Pain be damned, I leaned over to snatch the cigarette from Mary-Jo's hand and crushed it in my hand. "Only when I fuck your father."

Both Emma and Laurel perked up, letting out a chorus of *Oooooo*'s. Mary-Jo's face was equal parts amusement and respect.

Laurel whistled. "Burn, MJ. Burn."

"Noted. But are *werewolves* real?"

"Yes."

"Krakens."

I frowned. "I don't know."

"Zombies."

"Ugh, yes, unfortunately. Rare, but yes."

"Dracula."

"A lie written by a deeply racist asshole."

"That woman who wrote all those gay vampire books, was she a vampire fucker?"

I groaned. "Gods, woman, I don't know everything—"

"Gods. Plural?" Mary-Jo leaned over on her chair. "How many?"

"Too many."

"Do you sleep in a coffin?"

"*Laurel!*" I whined, impatience becoming the primary thing I could feel other than *pain*. "Make her stop."

"All right," Laurel said, shifting to get off the couch. "I think it's time I end this parade of oddities for the night. Spencer needs to rest and you clearly can't be trusted not to ask him the worst fucking questions."

"Can you blame me?" Mary-Jo stood, gesturing down at me. "You're banging a vampire and I'm *not* supposed to be interested?"

Laurel's face turned scarlet. "I am *not*—"

"Excuse me?" I gave Laurel a playful glare. "We are *absolutely* banging. I don't know why you'd try to destroy my ego like that."

Laurel's face turned a shade of red that I hadn't seen on her before and I laughed. Which stopped quickly, because of the piercing agony.

"Right, out, all of you out." Laurel shooed Mary-Jo toward the door, and Emma got up to follow behind her.

As she passed, Emma bent to touch my knee. "Feel better, Spencer. Sorry you had to protect us like that."

"No harm done, darling." With the couch free, I slid down onto it, lying with my knees over the arm. "I'm just going to sleep forever, or until that thing comes back to finish me off."

"You going to be all right to invade Greg's tomorrow night?" MJ asked, halfway out the door.

Emma chided her. "Obviously not, he's got a gaping wound—"

"Wouldn't miss it for the world," I interrupted. "I might not be in tip-top shape, but I'll make it work."

"See you then, Vlad," MJ called back. "And don't let anything happen to her or—"

"Or you'll chop off my dick and shove it in the tailpipe of my car. Yes, I know. *Good night*, Mary-Jo."

Laurel

With Emma and MJ gone, I slid down onto the floor next to the couch. I reached over to run my fingers along Spencer's bloodstained cheek. "How are you really?"

His eyes were closed, his head tipped back. "Exhausted."

I pulled the blanket away from his chest. Blood had soaked into it, and the wounds were still very much open, though not as bad as when we had arrived. "Can I do anything?"

"How much is left in the fridge?" he asked without opening his eyes.

"Ten bags, I think." I got up and went to the fridge. Counted. "Yeah, ten."

"Bring another. I can't stand this." His voice hitched as he spoke, and I wanted so badly to fix it for him.

I grabbed the scissors off the counter, emptied the bag into a glass—the things a person could get used to, Jesus Christ—and brought both with me. I helped him sit up and watched as he practically chugged back the whole thing. He handed it back empty and flopped down again.

He was quiet as I started to cut his ruined shirt from his chest. The fabric stuck to his skin, bloody and wet, and I was forced to peel it off in strips. When it was done, I pulled the tattered shirt away from the wounds and let it hang at his sides. He was a mess of blood—his own and the bear's—and now that the wounds had stopped bleeding, most of it was dried onto his skin.

"Do you want me to help you clean up?" I asked, running my fingers through his hair.

"No," he whispered. "Leave it. Lie down with me and sleep for a little."

I couldn't help but smile. He was so cute when he was being vulnerable.

I joined him on the couch, mirroring him with my legs over the opposite arm and my face next to his. Spencer turned to look at me, his red-stained waves of blonde hair sticking to his cheek.

His eyes were fluttering shut, but he still reached up to tangle his fingers in my hair. "You are a wonder, Laurel Marie Lewis."

"And you're a fucking dork." I scratched his scalp gently, a thing he'd admitted he loved. "Go to sleep. I'll be here when you wake up."

He nodded slightly against my hand, and I once again fell into that strange in-between, unsure if he was awake or asleep.

And as he dozed, I stared at the ceiling, remembering the moment when the voice had had its claws in me. How convincing it had been as it had whispered *what can he do but break you?*

It had seemed so real. The fear that all the strength and charm Spencer possessed would be turned against me, the way Greg turned everything against me. Spencer had never, would never, and yet…as that voice spoke, I believed he would. Couldn't imagine a world where he *didn't*.

The voice had been quiet since Spencer killed the bear, but I wasn't stupid enough to think it was gone. Somehow, it was in my blood. Inside all of us. It had been inside me since I was a girl, and it seemed invested in keeping me.

Was it paranoid to feel like I was being watched? Like it wasn't ever far away? Maybe.

I wanted to be ready for it to rear its head again, but how could I? I didn't know how to find it, or where to begin looking. How could I fight back against something I barely knew was real?

All I could do was wait.

Penny Harbour

Don had started coming home with a case of beer most nights. Geraldine couldn't make heads or tails of it. He'd always loved a beer now and again, but never like that. Don would open the door from work and immediately put his head in the fridge for a beer. He'd barely spoken to Geraldine for two weeks. Just coiled up in front of the TV, putting one bottle at a time into his gullet.

She could see him from the kitchen, but he had the TV turned up loud enough that she knew he couldn't hear. Tethered to the wall with the old corded landline, she went back around the corner, out of sight.

"I know, Ma, but I don't get it. He hasn't said a word about whatever happened. Something *must* have happened, right?" she whispered into the receiver.

"Your father went to the bottle a few years after you were born," her mother answered. "If I knew what to do about it, I'd have done it back then."

"Don isn't like Dad." Geraldine fiddled with the cord between her fingers. "Never has been."

"Honey, listen. If he doesn't come out of it himself, there's nothing you can do about a man who's gone to the bottle. It's how they drown their demons. Your Grampie was the same after the cave-in at the mines, and I'll tell you, he was a mean son of a bitch."

"He is *not* like Grampie."

"I certainly fucking hope not, 'cause if he lays a finger on you—"

"He won't."

Don could hear his wife, clear as day. Worried about him. It was sweet, in a way. But nothing touched him underneath all that haze.

He would never hurt his wife on purpose. Never.

But he had hurt someone else.

He knew what he had done. How that girl's throat felt in his hands as his fingers closed around it. And maybe, just maybe, if he drank long enough, he would forget for just a little while.

Don raised the bottle to his lips, black dirt caked beneath his fingernails.

CHAPTER TWENTY-THREE

Laurel

The clock on the bedside table read six in the evening. The sun would still have been up, but the blackout curtains made it impossible to tell. Aside from the glow of the clock and the abandoned bathroom light that crept under the door, the room was dark.

A sheet was haphazardly draped over Spencer's hips, but even in the dim light, I could see the wounds on his chest had sealed shut as he slept through the day. His skin was clean again, freshly washed before bed, and I ached to touch it. I'd been staring at him for over an hour, watching the stillness of him broken by little movements as he dreamed: a sniff, or a twitch, or a turn. His hand resting on his chest. His bare hip exposed from beneath the sheet. The temptation to touch him crossed my mind, if only to have his attention again. After so long feeling abandoned by love, I didn't want to go another minute without it.

But I needed to let him sleep. He had to heal.

Wide awake and not wanting to move from Spencer's side, I found my mind wandering back and forth between two possibilities. Stay with him and wait for the others, or go back to my house while Greg was at work and steal my things alone. They all had enough to worry about without doing me favours. I did *need* my things—some of them were irreplaceable—but it didn't mean I needed to bother them with it.

It gnawed at me, knowing I was so close to having this—having

Spencer—each day, without Greg's shadow over my shoulder. He had been texting, demanding I come home, but he didn't know where to find me, and I could keep it that way for a while yet. Once I had my stuff, Spencer and I could choose anything. I wanted to take everything that was mine and transplant it into this new life. To finalize it.

Spencer's bathroom was now mine too. *Our* kitchen, which he had started to make into a place capable of producing actual food. *Our* couch, where we had spent countless evenings together. *Our* bed, where I was learning how to love bodies again, mine and his.

It was difficult to register how much had changed, just by choosing Spencer.

Greg didn't believe in my job. He didn't believe in my friends. He would never have accepted any attraction I felt to women, a thing that kept creeping into the corners of my visions now that it had been unearthed. He didn't believe in kindness or empathy or that I was worth listening to. And here was Spencer, offering me my choice of food, protecting my friends, taking care of my mind and body.

What chance had I stood against someone who wanted to give me the world?

All that in such deep contrast to what Greg had offered. Even as safe as I was in that moment, next to Spencer, the fear crept in. As much as the itch sat in my bones to have everything over with, I knew I could never go over there alone. If Greg caught me, I might not get to leave. If ever I had done something that he felt warranted getting physical, shaming him publicly and leaving him was probably it. I had spent all those years in fear and I had no reason to start being naive about it now.

I needed Spencer with me for this.

I reached out to touch his cheek. His eyes fluttered open and he looked at me sleepily, as if just remembering I was there. A little smile spread on the corners of his lips and he leaned in, searching for a kiss. I met his lips, and even though he was half-asleep, he gave me more love in that kiss than I'd felt most of my life. It melted some piece of ice that had been frozen in me for a long time.

Spencer's head settled next to mine and his eyes closed. He didn't stir again, which I assumed meant he was attempting to go safely back to sleep.

"Ah-ah," I whispered. "We have work to do."

Spencer let out a long, sleepy moan. "But we could sleep."

I looked at the clock on the bedside table. "Greg will only be at darts for a few hours. We need to time this right."

"*Fine*," Spencer sighed, stretching out on the mattress. He winced as his hands went too far over his head for his wounds to accommodate.

I sat up and leaned over him. Much like with the burn, he had healed remarkably well. It had turned into a vicious set of red welts, but nothing like it had been last night. I ran my fingers between the marks. "How are you feeling?"

"Good enough." He sat up with just a little difficulty and leaned in for a sweet, tender kiss. The tips of his fingers trickled down my bare stomach, light as wings. "Better now that I get to wake up with you."

"You fool," I whispered against his lips. A small shiver ran through me, either from his cool touch or from the way his words sank under my skin. Both, maybe.

Spencer nipped at my lip, coaxing a giggle out of me.

"*Spencer*," I chided, but before I could say anything else, he had pushed me back onto the bed. His mouth found my throat and started to trail kisses along it.

"What?" he whispered.

'We have places to *be*." But I didn't fight back. We had *a little* time. I wanted to buy another moment to let him lavish me with attention. I'd gone long enough without that.

Everything else could wait *just a little*.

Once we were out of bed and getting ready, I went to brush my teeth in the bathroom and examine my skin. The mirror revealed shallow red marks. One on my neck, one on the inside of my thigh; another two on my upper arm; and, when I turned, an especially red bite on my ass. I flushed, following them across my skin, remembering the sweet rush each had given me.

I'd hardly expected to find any of that alluring, and now I found my mind wandering far too often. What would it feel like to have him *really* bite me? The single time he had was such a quick, fleeting moment that it didn't count. Spencer had talked at length more than once about how it felt, and I didn't like knowing that avenue was closed to me. Maybe I would never know. Never share that with him.

He made it sound like something divine.

Staring myself in the eyes through the mirror, I tried to gauge what all of it meant about me. I was tempted to let him break my skin and drink my blood. Had my life desensitized me to it? Was it years of monster fiction? Or would the heavy reality just creep up on me later when I least expected it?

Or did I simply feel safe with him?

I spat toothpaste into the sink, rinsed my mouth, and decided to file that away for another time.

Spencer was already downstairs when I went to get my phone from the good window. He was dressed and I was not, and his eyes lingered as he finished breakfast.

"I do need to remember that your marks don't disappear quite so fast," he said absently, if not a little appreciatively.

"You do. You can't just leave these where anyone can see them. Mary-Jo will never let me hear the end of it."

He came over to kiss my forehead. "Steal a turtleneck or a scarf from the closet. They'll be none the wiser."

I opened up my phone and scanned the group chat before tapping in a reply. "The girls will be here in half an hour. You ready?"

Spencer went back to the kitchen and returned without the glass. "To have you all to myself? Of course I am."

By the time I was dressed and fed, Mary-Jo and Emma were walking through the door.

Spencer looked up from the couch, surely having heard them coming up the driveway, but looking slightly affronted. "No one knocks in this place."

"Oh, I'm sorry." Mary-Jo put a hand to her chest, mocking him. "Should I have waited for an *invitation*?"

"Ha ha." Spencer rolled his eyes at her, but he had the grin of a prankster plastered on his face.

Emma was clearly uneasy, her arms around her and one hand tapping its fingers nervously on her forearm. "You seem all right," she said softly.

"Mostly." Spencer pulled up the side of his loose button-up blouse to show the wound. "Nothing to worry about, sweetling."

Emma let out a breath, visibly relaxing. "I mean, that's fucking weird, but I'm so glad. I was thinking about it all day."

I looked between Emma and Mary-Jo. They both seemed tired. Worn around the edges. "Did you not sleep?"

MJ looked at me with a sincerity that was rare for her. "Hard to sleep when there are monsters in the world, Laurel. Here in this town, even."

I let out a long breath. "There have always been monsters here, MJ. They just happen to also be kin."

She sniffed, turning just slightly so I couldn't see whatever expression she was trying to bury. "Fair enough. As long as we've got a vampire on our side, we're golden, right?"

I checked the time. "It'll be fine. Greg will have left for darts by now, which means we've got, like…three hours. He won't even notice we were there."

"Oh, he'll know," Spencer said ominously. He shrugged on a thin leather coat, then exchanged a sly low-five with Mary-Jo.

She did a little dance and followed Spencer out the door. "Fucking right, let's *go*! I got the shotgun in the back of the Jeep, just in case."

"Shotgun?" Emma baulked. "We're not shooting Greg."

We followed them out the door, and Spencer locked it behind us. "Emma, darling. Don't be a spoilsport."

"Get in, losers!" Mary-Jo said, hanging out of the front of her Jeep. "We're going to ransack a house!"

Emma raced to get in the front as MJ revved the engine, speakers blaring, and Spencer pulled me along after him. He was clearly enjoying himself, and I tried to let that levity sink in for me as well. My life was about to start, and I wanted to begin it carefree like they were. Not like *Emma*, no, but she was always a different case.

Spencer urged me into the back seat and crawled in after me. By the time I got in, the lyrics to the song caught my attention and I leaned into the front seat, slack-jawed. "You fucking didn't."

"Didn't what?" But Spencer paused and listened. "Oh, I see. That's a little too *yeehaw* for my tastes."

Emma and Mary-Jo were singing, and I felt the words coming up my throat. It was an irresistible song, no matter how personal it was, and the car filled with the lyrical story of one woman's freedom from her abusive husband via a little itty bitty poisoning.

Mary-Jo kicked the Jeep into reverse and off we went to steal back my life.

From the top of the hill, I could tell Greg's truck wasn't in the lane and all the lights were off in the house. If we played our cards right, we could be in and out before anyone noticed a Jeep had parked in the driveway.

A hand slipped into mine as I stared out the window. The music was too loud to talk, and Spencer put his hand over his heart, mimicking a beat with his fingers. I nodded, taking a nervous breath. *Again*, my heart was giving me away. This one last thing was perhaps the scariest thing I'd ever done, right next to letting Spencer love me.

Mary-Jo pulled into the driveway and skidded to a stop on the lawn. Like a wild beast, she turned the engine off, threw herself out of the Jeep, and slammed it shut. Emma followed her with slightly less enthusiasm but a grin on her face.

Spencer cupped my cheeks in both hands and kissed me. "Come on. It's almost done."

I nodded, took a deep breath, and got out.

The house was silent as we went up the front stairs. MJ was bouncing on her feet like a boxer, the shotgun in both hands. "Can I kick it in? Pretty please, can I kick it in?"

"Fuck it. Kick it in," I said, trying to remember why I was there in the first place. Fuck Greg. Fuck everything he'd ever done to me. Fuck the voice that wanted control of my head.

No one was going to dictate my life *ever again*.

Emma held the screen door open and MJ gave the wooden one a hardy kick near the deadbolt. It cracked but stayed put. With another kick, the door flew open, splinters flying everywhere.

"Fuck you, Greg!" she yelled, barrelling inside and turning on the light.

The plan I'd been cooking up in my head for days spilt out in commands. "Two duffel bags in the bedroom closet, garbage bags under the kitchen sink. I need everything out of the filing cabinet downstairs, as much clothing as you can carry, Nan's ceramic rooster, the photo albums, and at least the top shelf of books. Take whatever you can carry. Fill up every seat in the Jeep; the rest of us can walk back." I smirked, feeling the rush of this small bit of justice under my skin. "Oh, and break what he loves."

Emma went for the garbage bags. Mary-Jo immediately went to the living room and smashed the butt-end of the gun through the big-screen TV. Glass rained to the floor and she whooped. Spencer and I went down the hall, and he dipped into the bedroom. I pointed to the duffel bag above the wardrobe and he tossed it to me. Which left me alone and heading for the basement. It was for the best that it was left to me; the filing cabinet was in the back corner and disorganized from years of lax filing. But if I stood a chance in a divorce, I needed my birth certificate, the deed to the house, and a dozen other papers that defined the important pieces of my life.

I hurried down the stairs and flicked the basement light on. I still *hated* that room. The lack of natural light. The smell of smoke that permeated the dingy furniture from all those boys' nights. The dartboard on the wall was surrounded by chipped drywall from a thousand stray darts. At the back, practically forgotten, was the storage. Seasonal clothing, holiday decorations, and the filing cabinet.

I unzipped the duffel bag and sat it down in front. Four drawers of papers. A lifetime of tangled assets, mortgages, bank accounts. I opened the top drawer and started piling them in the bag. I'd have time for care later, when we were safe at home. On to the second drawer, and then—

His cologne.

I whipped around to find Greg behind me, seething. "Finally came back, did you?" His fist struck so hard and fast the skin split over my cheekbone.

His hand was around my throat before I could move, throwing me against the open drawers of the cabinet. Pain burst from my back, the thick metal ringing in my spine. I let out a muffled cry, and above me, Spencer called my name in panic.

Through the vents, I heard Emma scream, "The truck! It's in the backyard!"

And the sound of boots racing across the floor above me.

"You brought your friends." Greg lifted me up by the throat, his fingers digging into my windpipe. Choking me. His eyes. Full of malice and spite, but growing blacker by the moment. The voice—did it live inside him too? Playing both sides of the game, waiting to see who would kill the other first? "You should have stayed gone, whore. You reek like him. Did it feel good, fucking someone else? Breaking your vows?" Black oozed down his face, out from the corners of his mouth. "The vampire can't have you. We won't *let him* have you. This place *owns you*, Laurel. You can't run."

I gasped, trying to breathe through the crush of his hand.

No air came.

Spencer

Flying down the hall and skipping steps into the basement, all I could hear was the panic in Laurel's heart. At the bottom of the steps, I saw him. Greg. Holding Laurel by the throat as she gasped for air.

The rage took over and my fangs slipped out. I snarled, and Laurel's eyes darted my way. She was terrified, going paler by the second and her heart—

Slowing.

I ran at Greg and pulled him back. Laurel dropped to the ground, gasping raggedly. "Help her!" I screamed, knowing Emma and Mary-Jo hadn't been far behind. My fingers wrapped in Greg's shirt and I threw him across the room. "I've been waiting for an excuse to kill you."

Greg rolled, smacking into a shitty old armchair midway across the room. Emma and MJ passed me on their way to Laurel, their faces distraught. But I would take care of *dear old Greg*.

Except when he sat up, the black was spilling down his face.

Fuck. That would explain how he'd kept Laurel off her feet.

I had to keep him away from Laurel at all costs. Greg was strong— whatever was inside him was, at least. I bent over him and threw a fist into his gut. "She's not yours," I snarled. "Either of you. And I'll tear you apart to see her walk free of *you*."

"*Vampire.*" Greg's mouth was full of liquid black as he spoke. His voice was wrong, something hissing and bestial. Grinding. "You're putting your nose in things that don't concern you again."

I smirked. No matter how much or how little of Greg was in that shell,

I was more than pleased to beat him senseless. "That's my *very* favourite thing to do."

Greg swiped at me, trying to catch my shirt in his grasp, but I danced back, waiting for him to get up. The second he was on his feet, he charged at me, his shoulder connecting with my chest. I'd been ready for him, bracing for impact. I grabbed his throat, pressing my thumb into his windpipe until he croaked a gasp. His fist connected with my gut and I dropped him. I curled over in pain, yesterday's claw wounds suddenly burning from the impact. I wasn't used to fighting anymore, certainly not against someone who actually stood a chance.

"Spencer!" Laurel's voice was raspy and pained, coming from somewhere across the room.

Sharp pain shot through my scalp as Greg grabbed my hair, yanking my head back. I clawed at him blindly, skin catching under my nails. He hissed and dragged me across the floor by the hair.

"What a shame the sun isn't out, leech." Greg stood over me and pressed his palm into my cheek. Between his inhuman strength and the cement floor, the pressure in my skull was unbearable.

I dragged my nails down his bare forearms, but he barely seemed to notice. He pressed down harder and a scream tore from my throat.

"Get off him!" Laurel cried out. "Spencer!"

I couldn't tell where she was. I reached out to grab Greg by the neck again, but he was holding me at arm's length. I couldn't—

Something collided with Greg, sending him off balance. I scrambled away from his grip, rolling out of his reach.

Laurel was standing next to Greg, looking positively feral, Mary-Jo's shotgun clasped in both hands. She was coughing, black running out of the corners of her lips.

"Get the fuck off him!" Laurel swung it again, forcing Greg back. "I swear to Christ, I will end you!"

A gurgling snarl bubbled up from Greg's throat, black soot oozing from his mouth. Dripping on the floor. Then the light flickered back into Greg's eyes, burning the black away. His posture changed, growing timid and confused. "You." He pointed at me. In the absence of clarity, his anger was swarming to the surface. "You think you can just come into my house and take whatever you want, you fucking *queer?*"

I snarled, grabbing Greg by the throat and throwing him against the wall. That monstrous strength of his was gone. He hit the wall and buckled, and I picked him up again, snapping my fangs at him. "How does it feel, *Greg?* To spend all your life hating me, and to still lose your woman to a *soft little queer?*"

"Spencer, don't!" Emma was crying near the stairs, terrified.

"Put him in the fucking hospital," Mary-Jo snapped.

Laurel's hand was on my arm, pulling me back. "Let him go, Spencer. Please."

Looking down at her, the pity and worry in her eyes, my guilt overpowered the rage. I wanted him dead, but I was accustomed to being a killer and she wasn't. It wasn't my call to make. She had shared a lifetime with him, for better or worse. "*Fine,*" I snarled, and then turned back to Greg, my fingers digging into his jaw. "*Leave*, before I change my mind. Your monster isn't here to protect you, and the only thing keeping you alive is her. Her mercy buys you today, but if you *ever* show your face again, I'll be happy to skin you alive."

I tossed him across the basement, toward the stairs. Emma shrieked and jumped out of the way. Mary-Jo was beside her in a moment, staring Greg down as he scrambled to his feet and clumsily scampered halfway up the stairs.

"Fucking freak. She's mine, and I'll make sure you fucking know it." Clearly feeling safe with a measly few metres between us, he stood straight and laughed. "Don't wait up, fuckface. We know where to find you."

He ran upstairs. The side door slammed shut and his truck roared to life behind the house. Another moment and he was tearing out of the driveway and driving into the distance.

The three of us shifted toward Laurel, who seemed ready to fold in on herself. She was shaking, the gun hanging loosely in her hands. Mary-Jo took it from her, watching her carefully. I didn't wait for Laurel's permission; I just scooped her into my arms and headed for the stairs. With her cradled against my chest, her rasping breaths were hot on my shoulder. I brought her upstairs to gently sit her on the bathroom sink. In there, with better light and running water, I could help.

"Let me see," I whispered, nudging her to put her hands down.

Laurel's skin was split on her face, blood coating her cheek. She allowed me to examine her throat. It was already turning colours, and the bruises would probably be horrendous. Nausea bubbled in my stomach, as well as regret. Regret for not watching over her, but just as much for letting that fucker live.

Mary-Jo stood near us, her hand over her face as she tried not to cry. A moment later, Emma was with us, a first aid kit in hand. She set it on the counter and opened it up.

"I'm all right," Laurel croaked. Her throat was raw, her voice shredded. Hardly convincing.

I ran the water and fished inside a drawer for a clean cloth. The trail of blood ran all the way into her shirt, staining the fabric.

"Oh, Laurel," I whispered, helping her take the shirt off, leaving her only in her black bra. I started washing away the trail of blood, rinsing and squeezing the cloth into the sink. Emma was crying quietly again, pulling out disinfectant and gauze.

"What are we going to do?" Laurel asked, leaning her head on the mirror behind her. "You heard him. He's coming back. And I have a funny feeling that the thing knows where you live."

"We'll be okay, no matter what he does." I dabbed the skin around her cut, trying to wash the blood away, along with that trail of black in the corners of her mouth. "I won't let him lay another hand on you. He's just one fucking guy, even if that thing is inside him."

MJ cleared her throat. "What if he's not, though? Do we know what this thing is capable of?"

No. No, we really did not.

Did this thing live inside us all? What did it know about us? In my heart, I knew to expect the worst. Any amount of rationalizing was a mistake. If it was inside us, even me, it knew everything. Could get to any of us. It knew how to find us. Had always known. When it wanted us, we wouldn't be able to hide.

"We should finish what we started and get out of here" was all I could manage to vocalize.

"Not without the stuff." Laurel choked a laugh. "To think, I almost came over here by myself."

Mary-Jo scoffed. "Why the fuck would you do that?"

"To get it over with—" Laurel started to cough, her throat too raw to speak for long.

Scenarios ran through my head, one after the other. Images of him hurting her. Pinning her down. Killing her. Of finding her body. Losing her in a dozen different ways, all in a moment. Despite knowing she was right in front of me, the panicked thought that I might lose her washed over me. Darkness. That was what it would bring me. Another decade of grief that I might not find my way back from.

Too many old feelings were surfacing again.

I cupped her cheek in my hand, desperate to say *something* that would keep her from taking another risk like that. "If he had killed you, I would have walked out into the sun."

I could feel the confusion from Emma and Mary-Jo, but Laurel understood me perfectly.

Her face soured. "Don't you say that. Don't you ever say that. You know how I feel—"

"Then don't fucking take risks like that and *get yourself killed*." My eyes were welling with tears. It was cruel to say, I knew that, and the fear in my chest— "I've lost *so much* already, Laurel. Please. Losing you would destroy everything I've gotten back. I don't think I could survive that again."

"You don't have to do anything alone," Emma whispered, wiping her face with her hands. "Not ever again. *Either of you.*"

"Absolutely ridiculous, Laurel. I'm livid just thinking about it." Mary-Jo was working her fingers into her temples.

Laurel's lip started to quiver. "I know. I didn't."

"Damn right." I pressed my forehead against hers. "I can't lose you."

"I'm not going anywhere." Laurel's fingers found their way into my hair. "I promise."

I blinked away the tears before too many could fall into her lap. Wiping them away, I looked up. The cut needed tending, and I was being too sentimental. I reached over to take the disinfectant from Emma. "I'll finish this. Get what we came here to get. Then it's time to get her safe."

Penny Harbour

If one thing could be said about Greg, it was that he never went down without a fight.

When he tore into the driveway and parked the truck crooked across his cousin's lawn, he already knew things were about to come to blows. Sure, Laurel was a boring, shitty-ass wife, but she was *his* wife. No one could come in and take what was his, *especially* not some fucking pretty boy from Away.

Greg had earned his life. He wasn't about to let that fucker take it away.
Good.
He deserves what's coming to him, doesn't he, Greg?
Sleeping with your wife.
A freak of nature.
Red eyes and fangs, throwing you around like some little girl.
Are you going to let that stand? Are you that weak a man?
Are you just like your daddy said?
Weak?

As soon as he was in his cousin's house, he started sending texts, talking to Johnny between each one. A group chat, with as many cousins and friends as he thought he could count on. Telling them about the guy they needed to set to rights. Taking what wasn't his. And sure, if the tale was a little tall, who could blame him? Wouldn't any man be within his rights to raise a mob and get what was his? It was a matter of principle.

Greg went to the fridge and pulled out a beer as the messages poured in. People looking to help. Looking for a fight. He knew Jimmy had a vendetta against newcomers, and Peggy-Sue wasn't one to say no to a brawl.

They could go get her any time they pleased.
Tell them to wait.
We have things to do, first.
The freak isn't going anywhere, and if we're patient and careful...
Everything will be yours again, Greg.
Just you wait.

CHAPTER TWENTY-FOUR

Laurel

Everything fucking hurt.

My back, where I'd been slammed into the filing cabinet. My throat, where Greg had wrapped his hand around it. My cheek, where he had split it wide open. And just a little, my heart. It made sense that when I was so close to the end, that was exactly when this part of Greg would show its ugly head.

As Spencer came back with one of my shirts and helped me put it on, Mary-Jo and Emma yelled to each other across the house. They were in a hurry to get everything we'd come for and get the hell out of Dodge. I wished I had that kind of enthusiasm. Unfortunately, most of that had been beaten out of me already.

"Time to go, love." Spencer took my hand and helped me down from the sink. He stayed close to me as we walked down the hall, as if he was afraid to go more than a foot from me again. I could hardly blame him. I'd been out of his sight for, what, two minutes? That's all it had taken to get the tar beaten out of me.

When we got into the kitchen, MJ was already busy carting bags and totes out to the Jeep. Emma was passing them out the front door, and she looked up as we came around the corner.

"Just about set," she said. "We'll have to hoof it, though."

"Absolutely not." Spencer put his arm around my back. "That was before

Greg and that thing came after us. Laurel isn't walking anywhere."

MJ stopped on her way to get the last bag. "Well, what the fuck else do you want to do?"

Spencer left me to push past Emma and MJ, peeking over the rail and gesturing to the Jeep. "The fucking monstrosity has a step up to the cab. It's two minutes. Roll the windows down and we'll hang on."

Mary-Jo looked at Emma and then at me. "Yeah, fuck it. Why not?"

Emma started out the door to follow. I stopped to look around. This would likely be the last time I set foot inside the home I had tried to make for myself. Everything I loved seemed to be picked clean, and it looked as if someone had robbed the place. Still, I hadn't really gotten the chance to do any of it myself. It had been done for me and around me, and it felt *wrong*.

I reached into the coat closet, all the way to the back, and felt the long cold steel of Greg's shotgun. I pulled it out and then fished around the top rack for the shells. I loaded one into the gun, tossed the box to Emma, and took aim. Above the TV was the oversized photo of the day Greg and I got married.

I looked fucking miserable. I did in every single photo.

I turned off the safety and fired.

A chorus of exclamations sounded from outside. Spencer leapt back into the house to find me lowering the gun. He took one look at the wall where the photo had been and the decimated drywall that stood in its place and *laughed*.

"All right, Rambo, let's go." He took the gun out of my hands and led me out the door.

Mary-Jo had already started the Jeep and rolled the windows down. The tiny thing was stuffed to the brim with what amounted to everything I'd ever owned.

Emma was propped up on the passenger-side door, holding on for dear life. "I want it said for the record that I do not like this."

I climbed up on the back of the driver's side, and Spencer tucked the shotgun inside through the window. He climbed onto the step and put an arm around me, as if shielding me.

I looked up at him. "I'm fine, you know. I can hold on without you having to babysit me."

"Laurel." Spencer's voice was calm, but very much take-no-shit. "Don't

343

fight me on this, please. You can assert your independence with me all you like when you're not bloodied and bruised."

"Listen to the man," MJ said from the seat in front of us. "Don't want you blacking out halfway down the road. Is everyone holding on? Good. Let's go."

She started the Jeep forward with a small lurch and then brought it down to the end of the driveway. With no cars in sight, she turned onto the road gently. The night was quiet, the sparse collection of streetlights dotting the black emptiness.

"Fuck." Spencer's voice was sharp in my ear.

"What?" I turned to look over my shoulder, to see what he was seeing, but it was far too dark.

"People. A bunch of them."

I squinted, and as we crawled up the road doing a solid twenty clicks, shapes started to appear in the shadows. Doors opened on houses, and neighbours came out onto their front steps. Some were already standing next to the road. The Jeep's lights hit the face of someone just ahead of us, out in the middle of the street.

Their eyes. Their eyes were black and seeping.

"You guys fucking seeing this?" Mary-Jo called out.

"Clear as day," Spencer answered. "Hit the gas, MJ."

We sped up and Mary-Jo brought us up the hill, into Spencer's driveway. We hopped down, but Spencer stood stock-still, staring into the bushes.

"They're coming." Spencer tossed the keys to Emma, who was closest to the door. His eyes were darting from one direction to the next, hearing things I couldn't. "Get the guns and get inside, now."

MJ grabbed both guns from the Jeep and sprinted toward the door. Emma pushed the door open and we followed, Spencer last. He slammed the door shut and locked both bolts, but if any of those people were as strong as that *thing*, a couple of locks wouldn't matter.

Spencer whipped his phone out of his pocket and tapped until the app for his doorbell camera came on. We stood at his side as people stepped out of the bushes around the property and onto his driveway.

"That's Greta Roberts from down the road," MJ said, pointing at the screen.

"That's Ed from next door," I added.

Emma squinted. "I can't tell. It's dark and they're just…standing there."

She went to the front window to peek out and immediately jumped back with a screech. "There's someone right against the window, *what the fuck.*"

Spencer walked over and pulled the curtain back. Sure enough, Greg's cousin Daryl was just *standing there*. Staring. When Daryl didn't move, Spencer gave him the finger and walked away, letting the curtain drop.

"Can you not fucking do that, please?" MJ barked. "Unlike you, I don't think they need invitations. Rule number one, don't antagonize the death machines."

"Sweetheart, *I'm* a death machine. Body counts for miles." He waved a hand at her, attempting to look more careless than he was. He had started to tell my mood by my heartbeat, but I could see the worry in his twitchiness and the way his eyes darted around the room, looking for threats.

Emma blinked, shifting her weight to her toes and back again. "I don't know how I feel about that."

"Feel how you want about me after we get away from the crowd of mad hillbillies, but it's a blessing tonight," Spencer said. He walked out of the room and into the kitchen, where he pulled back the curtain there. More people, grinning and covered in soot. He came back and went down the hall to the library. The big picture window also had someone in it, staring right back at us. "That's at least fifteen."

Emma seemed to be growing smaller by the moment. "Why haven't they come in to get us? They know we're here."

Patience, Emma dear.

We all jumped, the voice ringing in our heads out of nowhere.

Of course I'm here. Of course I'm waiting.

There's nowhere for you to go.

I have all the time I need.

"What do you want?" I snapped, holding the heels of my hands to my temples.

You, dearest.

You have such promise.

"Well, you can't fucking have her." Mary-Jo shoved one of the shotguns into Emma's hands and readied her own, even though she had nothing to shoot at yet. "Why don't you come out here and fight us if you want her so bad?"

"What happened to not antagonizing the monster?" Spencer hissed.

I was going to wait until sunrise.

Burst open the door and let the sun take care of all my troubles.

But if you insist.

The front door rattled.

"*Shit*," Spencer cursed. "Good fucking job, MJ."

But Mary-Jo was grinning. She popped the gun open, checked the ammo, and slammed it shut again. "Anytime, Twinkle Toes. Emma, you ready?"

"Nope. That's…I know those people, MJ. Those are *our people*." She was shaking, watching the door as it started to rock with greater intensity, from a slow rattle to a vicious thudding.

"It doesn't matter, Ems. They're not themselves and they're not going to take mercy on *you*. If you want to be home to see baby Logan tomorrow, you'd best get your fucking Mama Bear out." MJ took aim at the door.

A thought swam at the back of my mind, something I couldn't give voice to. Was Emma's mother infected with this *thing*? Was Logan safe? If Emma hadn't thought of it already, I wasn't going to introduce the idea to her. Making her panic wouldn't do anything to get us back to her son faster.

Emma swallowed hard and braced the shotgun against her shoulder. "Yeah. I'm going the fuck home."

"Absolutely not," Spencer said, pushing us all toward the library. "We're going out the back, *right now*."

Something flew into the door, a shudder rippling through the house. It startled a scream out of me and I bolted down the hall, into the dimly lit library, Emma and Mary-Jo directly behind me. That lone sentry that had been at the window before was gone.

Without missing a beat, Spencer grabbed the enormous old stereo and tossed it through the window. The glass shattered, spilling to the ground like rain. Mary-Jo leapt through, her shotgun at the ready the moment she landed. As I was climbing out, she took aim and fired a shot in the direction of the driveway. When I looked up, the people who had gathered at our front door were heading toward us.

"Get the fuck back, Ed!" she screamed, loading the next shell.

"Emma!" I reached for her hand and pulled her through, trying to keep her from cutting herself on the glass. Safely on her feet, she turned to cover our backs, shaking but determined.

Then Spencer was jumping out, and the crack that came from inside the house told us the door had burst open on its hinges.

"Go!" Spencer pushed us into motion. "The shaft, go!"

I knew what he meant. The mine shaft in the back of the property. We could hide, get something at our backs so we could focus on the people in front of us.

I started to run, barrelling into the dark without much idea of what was in front of me. Spencer was nearby, and I made the effort to follow him, knowing he could at least see better than I could. Emma and MJ weren't far behind, the sounds of their hurried breathing and their footfalls filling the night.

My heart was racing, my blood pounding in my ears. When we reached the cover of the trees, I looked back. Shapes in the dark, heading toward us. They were still coming.

Of course I am, Little Laurel.

You're worth every effort.

I will have you.

The fucking voice in my head pushed me onward, as if I stood a chance of outrunning something that followed me everywhere.

"Laurel!" someone called out from behind us.

"Laurel," came another voice.

"Laurel, get back here."

Get back here.

I screamed, the voice in my head too loud, too *everywhere*. Mary-Jo called out to me as we pushed forward, but I hardly registered it. The goddamn thing lived inside me. It just kept making itself *known*.

I heard a click. A far too familiar one.

The click of a shotgun being loaded.

I looked over my shoulder, but Emma and Mary-Jo were still running, shadows in the dark of the woods.

"Go!" I hissed, forcing my legs to work harder. Spencer's arm pushed me forward, just as a shot exploded the dirt in front of us.

"They're beside us!" Spencer cried out.

I shielded my face from the spray of earth and kept moving, dodging trees as we pushed further into the woods. Some of them were close behind, their boots heavy as they ran.

Another click.

Another shot.

Searing pain, cold and racing up, up my leg.

I screamed and fell. The world turned black at the edges. Faded in. Out. I was face-first in the dirt. My leg was cold. Too cold. Wet—frigid—Spencer. Arms and floating and suddenly up. Against him.

Run.

Please.

Spencer

I heard Emma scream before I understood what had happened.

Grinding to a halt, I turned to find Laurel in the dirt, dragging herself forward. Mary-Jo stopped beside her and turned to face the house, shotgun raised. Emma fell to the ground over Laurel, and I smelled it. The tempting metallic scent of blood filled the air.

Laurel wasn't getting up and they were getting closer.

I ran to her, bullying my way between Laurel and Emma, and scooped Laurel into my arms. "We have to keep going," I hissed, settling her against my chest and turning to run. I couldn't wait to see if they would follow. Laurel was bleeding and—

Her leg. Someone had shot her in the leg.

The urge to turn around and slaughter *everyone* ran deep, but Laurel couldn't spare the time for me to do it. I had to get the wound tied off.

Another shot. Too close, but it spoke volumes about their lack of skill with a gun. In the distance, the boarded-up mine shaft appeared. I just had to get her there.

I ran as hard as I could, Laurel jostling in my arms. The blood—the smell was getting too thick. If I didn't cut off the flow to her calf, she was going to bleed out.

"Hold on, darling," I begged. "*Please.*"

I couldn't lose her. I couldn't, I couldn't.

Not again.

A wave of grief flooded over me, imagining returning to who I'd been. Lost. Alone. Full of rage. If Laurel died, I wouldn't hesitate to tear the throats out of everyone within reach. Leave the place a proper ghost town.

She moaned, drawing me back. We were almost at the shaft.

As soon as I reached it, I set Laurel down, leaning her against its wall. "Don't move, love. We're almost inside."

But she didn't say anything. I wasn't sure she could even hear me.

Mary-Jo and Emma had followed after all, and now they stood at my back, keeping guard as I tore at the planks across the open entrance. Five in total, wide across and bolted in place. It was a hard job, even for me, but as I pried at them, the nails gave and burst away. I threw each to the ground, one after the other, and then picked Laurel up again. Her head lolled back. She was barely conscious.

Looking behind us, I expected to see a row of furious locals closing in. But they hadn't. At best, some of the shadows between the trees *might* have been them. It gave me pause. Where had they gone? I wasn't *that* fast. Had they lost us? It had been a straight shot from the house to the mine.

Laurel moaned.

It didn't matter.

I needed to get her settled and do something about all that blood. And when it was done, when she was alive and better and we were out, I was going to show her *everything*. Take her dancing at the clubs in Berlin. Feed her sweets in Denmark. Walk with her at night in Cairo. Sit in the hot springs outside of Reykjavík.

I just had to save her first.

I ducked inside the mine shaft. The air was oppressive. Stale and wet. If I had needed to breathe, it might have felt suffocating. The walls were black on all sides—metal at first, and a dozen paces in, it shifted to rock. The shaft was tall enough to walk upright and wide enough for six of me, but it still felt closed in. Dank. Musty and dark and black. Soot lined everything. And the further down I went, the blacker it got. The light from the entrance died away quickly, until it was just me and my blessed eyes that could see in the dark.

Emma and Mary-Jo had followed us inside, but they were clinging to the side wall, unable to see in the pitch black. Their laboured breathing only became worse in the stale air, and I could see the regret on their faces. Neither of them wanted to be down there with us.

Reflexively I took a deep breath, and my body tried to choke the air back out. I coughed, hacking up whatever had gotten in my mouth. It…it tasted just like what I had tasted on the blood of everyone I'd eaten nearby.

It tasted just like hers.

I stopped. Looked around. The only place to go was straight down into the earth, but suddenly I felt trapped.

The thing that was living inside everyone lived down there as well.

And it had us right where it wanted us.

CHAPTER TWENTY-FIVE

Laurel

Was I dreaming? Asleep? Everything was black. So black. But the pain—

I broke into sobs, screaming and trying to breathe. The air was disgusting, so thick and wet in my lungs. The movement kept jarring my leg, sending bolts of lightning into my body.

"Stop!" I managed to cry out.

"Laurel, it's all right. We have to—"

"No!"

Spencer came to a stop. I couldn't see him, couldn't see anything, but I could feel his chest, his arms. Whatever came next was disorienting. So black and colourless and lightless that I had no concept of where we were going. But suddenly there were rocks beneath me and I was sitting on cold, jagged ground.

I heard a zipper. The rustle of clothing. I jumped as something touched my leg, scaring me so badly that I screamed again.

"Is she okay?" Emma cried out. "I can't *fucking see!*"

"Does someone have their phone?" MJ asked.

"Spencer? I can't see you. I can't see anything!" Panic was rising steadily in my chest, and I felt myself growing faint again.

"I'm going to make a tourniquet and tie off your leg so you can't bleed out." Spencer's voice was disembodied, floating somewhere in the dreamless darkness. Then his hands were on my body. Something slipped around my thigh. The tight, painful pull of fabric.

I cried out.

"Shh, I know. I'm sorry. It has to be tight."

My head didn't want to stay up. My arms didn't want to support my body. I slid down, laying my face on the rocks. "I'm tired, Spencer. I want to rest."

"We can't, darling. We're not safe. It's so much worse than we thought." His hand was on my face. "I have to take you out of here, no matter what's waiting up there."

"What do you mean?" Mary-Jo's voice asked from somewhere nearby.

"Think," he said. "They surrounded the house, but just let us get away? It knows where we are, but somehow it couldn't predict what I was about to do? Or is all that black shit coming from *down here*?"

"*Fuck.*"

"It was the coal." Emma's voice was distant, dissociated. "All this time, all these years, it was burning through us from the inside. Centuries, breathing it in."

Voices rose from somewhere far away. The surface, maybe. Spencer's hands were gone, and I wasn't sure if he was gone too, lost somewhere in the dark.

Lying there, I wanted to sleep. Float away on a dream.

Something was on my tongue. Gritty. Ashen.

More, and more, and more.

Filling my mouth.

Choking me, until my lungs were nothing but soot.

Hello, Laurel.

What do you want, my dear?

The voice again. Inside me. Part of me.

Rapidly becoming all of me.

You came so far, didn't you?

Got so close to escaping everything that was tearing you down.

But those people, those stupid, ignorant people, they stole your chance to be happy, didn't they?

Do they deserve to be happy?

Don't you want what's yours?

What you earned?

Hasn't Greg put you through enough?

He's out there, right now, trying to force you back into his arms. But with me, you could put an end to that.

Put an end to him.

The voice. It was so familiar, but instead of the whisper it had always been, it had become a deafening roar. The voice that told me to stay. The voice that told me Greg would come around, eventually. The one that fueled dark thoughts and spite and grief. That made me stronger when I was angry. It lived in so many of the people I knew. In the ones who burned things and hit people and screamed at their children. It had taken them deep into their darkness and made them act.

And now it was my turn. My turn to let it take control.

To take what I deserved.

If I couldn't know peace, none of them would.

Spencer

Watching the dim spark of outside light in the distance, I waited for someone to come in. To come after us. The voices were there, talking amongst themselves. Loud enough to hear, but not at all hurried.

They weren't coming, but why?

What had we willingly run inside of?

I turned my attention back to Laurel and immediately sank to my knees. She was lying down, her face against the ground. Her eyes. They were wide open, even though she wouldn't have been able to see a thing. Her face was filthy with soot. It hadn't been a moment ago.

"Laurel."

She didn't respond.

"Sweetheart, answer me." I shook her shoulder, but she gave me nothing. Panic swelled in my chest. Her heart was beating and the blood flow *seemed* to be slowing. But the sudden catatonia—I had no idea what to do.

"Laurel?" Emma's voice was quivering. "Why isn't she speaking?"

"I don't know…"

I had nowhere to take her. Nowhere to run. We could go up, where they were waiting, or down into nothing. Nothing but coal and corpses and death.

"Darling, please." I shook her again. "*Please.*"

Laurel's head turned, her eyes catching mine. As if waking up from a trance.

Without a word, she started pushing herself up.

I tried to urge her back down gently. "Don't. You can't put your weight on that leg—what are you doing?"

"Girl, listen to him. You got *shot*. Why would you get up?" Mary-Jo was feeling around in the dark, looking for Laurel. "Sit the fuck back down."

Laurel was fighting me, and I *could* push back, but it would hurt her. Then Laurel was on her hands and knees, getting ready to stand.

"*Stop*," I begged. "You're going to make it worse!"

But she wasn't listening. One leg. Then the next. Her body unfolded, standing straight, staring up at the entry to the mine. She shouldn't have been able to put weight on that leg, let alone stand.

"Laurel." I stepped in front of her, and only then did I see it. The black in her eyes. "*Gods.*"

"Spencer." Her voice was a rasp, thick and primal. "I'm going to fix everything."

I took her shoulders, holding her in place. "Don't let it in."

Her head cocked to the side, staring at me with curiosity. She reached up, caressing my cheek with her finger. Closing the space between us. On her toes, she pressed a kiss to my lips. That grit was in her mouth. On her tongue. She tasted like hundreds of years of horrors, of pain and fear and turmoil, trapped in the earth.

"You're too late to take her," Laurel whispered against my lips in that disembodied, haunted voice. "I just wanted to know what you taste like first. Why she was so enamoured with you."

Her hands collided with my chest and I flew back, cracking against the mine wall. The shock spilt through my body, ringing my bones. Dust fell from above, stinging my eyes like I didn't think was possible.

When I looked up, Laurel was making her way to the surface, walking like she hadn't had a hole blown into her leg.

CHAPTER TWENTY-SIX

Laurel

Compared to the dark of the mines, the night was almost illuminating. The dark had been *so dark,* but it had shown me the way. Shown me what I needed to do. And the people waiting for me on the surface had known that. They had stepped away from the mouth of the mine, out of my way, like a sea parting.

Penny Harbour was made up of two types of families: the kind who had been here for generations and the kind who had just arrived. Those of us whose grandparents had been old blood on this soil, whose pain had travelled from father to son to grandson, I could feel them connected to me like a spiderweb. The coal—the timeless beast that had been born of such enormous collective suffering and had seeped up from the ground— connected us. We were kin.

The others, well. I could see it on their faces. The ones who had healed their wounds years ago, I could respect them. They'd fought back. Earned their moderate freedom, though they'd never be *free* of the monster.

The ones who had barely been here long enough to breathe the air, they were scared. They weren't part of us. They'd come along, convinced by angry words and righteousness. But those people weren't filled with that darkness in the same way the rest of us were. They had come to Penny Harbour too late for the centuries of pain. Moved in after all the hardship had been over, to take advantage of the things that had been put in place by pain and strife and blood.

Had bought our houses for more than any of us would make in a lifetime.

They hadn't been part of what made the Harbour what it was, our families crawling into the earth and digging its soul out, bit by bit. They hadn't breathed the black air and licked the soot from their fingers. Dug their brothers out from the rubble.

Not everyone could be part of what bound this place together. Hundreds of years of striving through hardship and death, passing pain from one person to the next. In their bones. Their blood. The strands that made them who they were. Through the words they said and the hate they carried and the ways they allowed themselves to suffer instead of change.

The coal didn't live in them the way it lived in us. It was a problem.

"Where's Greg?" I asked.

"Bitch, how are you even walking?" One of them backed away.

Don't let them get in your way. One of us or not, he deserves this.

Make him pay for what he took.

"Where is Greg?" I stepped forward, toward him.

Ed stepped into my path, his lips rimmed in soot. One of us, yes, but cooperation mitigated pain. If we didn't tear each other down, how would the beast feed? "Don't," he said. "Just go home, Laurel. Greg only wanted you to stop your nonsense with this *guy* you've been running around with. It doesn't have to end like this."

"End like what, Ed?" I took his jaw between my fingers. "Like you finally staying on your side of the fence? Like you gossiping every fucking thing to the neighbours *except* what my husband was doing to me all those years? *Watching Greg through the kitchen windows for a decade, doing what he did, and saying nothing, Ed*?"

Good girl, Laurel. Show him an ending he deserves.

I squeezed his jaw until it cracked under my hand. The scream was delicious. It ran a chill down my spine until I was shivering with glee.

The black on his lips oozed from his mouth, making its way to my hand. It was mine. A little more of my birthright, seeping its way under my skin. Becoming part of me.

I let him drop. Let him scream and squeal on the ground.

Not everyone ran, but most did.

Billy, a friend of a cousin I'd once done a repair for, lifted his shotgun from a few metres away and fired a round. It hit me in the shoulder, rocking me back. Static buzzed in my ear. When I looked down, black and red were spilling out of the new hole in my skin.

That fucker.

Kill him, Laurel.

Spill his blood like he spilt yours.

Feed the earth his pain.

I want to feast.

The voice was right. So right.

He wasn't one of us, not really. He could've been, though. I saw it, through the voice, the sliver of influence the voice had over him. How Greg had called him and he had come. Brought his gun. He thought women ought to obey, and if they wouldn't…well. A person could be talked into just about anything at the end of a gun muzzle.

His rage didn't come from our earth, but it had been born in him somewhere. Tended and stoked until he couldn't help but spill it out into other people's lives. He would have made a beautiful asset, but at least he could still be a delectable meal.

As he panicked, trying to get another shell into the chamber, I closed in on him. Grabbed the gun and cracked him in the head with it. He reeled and I stole it away, turning it swiftly until the barrel was pointed at him, the butt pressed against my wounded shoulder. Daddy had taught me to shoot, once. Before he'd disappeared and stolen my heart away. Taught me how to love the worst kind of men.

Click.

Kaboom.

Blood and brain and flesh coated the grass.

Would his wife even mourn him? Or had I done her a service?

Good girl.

Such violence.

Show them no mercy.

No black came up to join me from that pretty corpse. Not even a little.

But he had a knife in his belt, and that could be of use.

I stole it and started toward the house. They were waiting at the edge of the woods to see who would live and who would die. But I was made up of so much pain. What was mine and what I had stolen. It had bled into me while I was below, unlike them. They had drunk the coal in the water and passed it down in the blood, but I was bloated with it. Stronger than they would ever be.

No one would ever, *ever* hurt me again.

Spencer

I had to gather my senses. To peel myself off the ground and convince my body to move. Laurel had *thrown me* across the shaft. She'd already been strong as a person, yes, but *that*? Before this, she could barely move me against my will, and suddenly she was throwing me into walls.

That *fucking* voice.

"Spencer?" Mary-Jo was calling out, stumbling blindly around in the pitch black, heading down the shaft and into the ground. "What's happening?"

"Back here. Follow my voice." I staggered to my feet, using the rock to support me as I fumbled my way up. It wasn't just the impact that was setting me off balance; something was wrong with my rib. Had she cracked it? If I'd needed to breathe, it would have been deeply inconvenient. "That thing has her. She's gone back out."

I reached out and grabbed MJ's fumbling hand and brought her to Emma, who had stayed securely against the shaft wall.

A scream.

I stopped, frozen in place. But the scream had been deep and gruff. A man, most likely. Not her. Anyone but her.

"Come on." I grabbed Emma's hand and forced us up the incline, needing to get to Laurel even with the *deep* pain in my chest.

A shot exploded into the air above.

We were almost at the surface. The night sky and the canopy of trees were above us, drawing closer with each step. Then we surfaced, and I grabbed on to the metal wall of the shaft and hauled myself out. At my feet was a man, sobbing and holding his face, his jaw moving in ways it *absolutely should not.* But he was no concern of mine.

"Oh my god, Ed." Emma started to reach out, but then stopped, seeming to remember that these people had just been trying to kill us. "Do you think Laurel—?"

"She's not Laurel, not right now." I stopped talking, listening for some kind of sign of where she'd gone. Voices in the distance, near the house.

I broke into a run. I had to get out ahead of whatever Laurel was about to do. Whatever *it* was telling her to do. A body lay in my path, with a shredded mess instead of a face. And then her laugh rose in my ears. *Mostly* her laugh. As hearty as her most carefree moment, but laced with something dark and menacing.

The edge of the trees came, and she appeared, crossing the grass toward the house. Laurel's fist was wound in some woman's hair, dragging her across the ground behind her. The scent of blood was everywhere. A hole had been torn clean through her shoulder to match her leg, and she was *still walking.*

"*Laurel!*" I cried out, trying to get her attention.

She turned her head for a moment, a wide black grin crossing her lips.

Behind her, all six of the people just beyond the trees stopped to grin with her.

"*Too late, lover,*" they said in unison. "*She has taken so much in my name already.*" One by one, the grin dropped from their faces, all except Laurel.

"You would not *believe* the rage she carries," Laurel said, pulling the struggling woman up by the hair.

"Don't do this! Laurel, please! Come back to me!" I stepped toward her, hands out and approaching cautiously. I didn't care about anyone else. If their blood was spilled, it wouldn't hurt me a bit. But it would hurt *her*. She wouldn't be able to live with herself. If I could just convince her to—

Snap.

Laurel had twisted the woman's neck until it broke.

She had killed and maimed three people in a matter of minutes. If I couldn't get that thing out of her, how far would she go before she stopped?

And as focused as I was on her, I hadn't heard them approach.

Something grabbed me from behind and pulled me to the ground. A crack to the face and the world was spinning. By the time it righted itself, some fucking neon-orange-and-camouflage-vested waste of breath was dragging me out of the trees and into the yard. I fought against him and it barely registered as he dumped me face-first in front of Laurel. The corpse she had just made was staring me in the face, its head on crooked.

"Laurel—" I rasped, and a boot stepped onto my back, pressing until the words choked from me.

From the edges of the yard, more shadows appeared. Faces I'd seen in passing, on the road or in stores. More of them, a dozen, black running down their skin.

"Did you think she was yours?" a mother holding a baby asked.

A teenage girl stepped forward. "Did she make you feel alive for once?"

"When she held you close?" A man in a suit jacket and tie. "When she helped you lick your wounds?"

I struggled, trying to get the boot off my back, but it wouldn't budge.

"She thought she could trust you, Spencer." An old woman in a flannel shirt.

The man whose boot was on my back crouched down, twisting my head so I could see him kneeling there with those horrid black eyes. "Do you know what she thought while she fucked you?" Coal dust seeped out of his tear ducts. "She thought she was safe with you. *Finally safe.* That she would be, forever. She let her guard down. She started planning a *future* with you, little leech. And look at her now."

He twisted my head until I was staring at her. Laurel was covered in blood and coal, torn apart in two places. It made me sick to see her like that. She shouldn't have been walking, not with two bullets in her.

And Greg, making his way to her, his eyes soulless, trained on me.

"She's barely even in there now. But the parts of her that are? Oh, Spencer, you'd be so proud." Greg's words were a gargle, black spewing out of him. "*The violence in her.*"

Laurel approached Greg slowly, holding her hand out to him. The black spilling down his face dripped into her hand. It seemed to soak into her as fast as it fell. Then she cupped his cheek in her palm and kissed Greg's coal-covered mouth. My stomach turned, watching her tongue flash into his mouth, as if searching out every last bit of that black.

Fingers yanked on a fistful of my hair, pulling my head up until I looked at the man above me. "It's only me inside her now, vampire."

Penny Harbour

Emma ran through the trees, tears streaming down her face. She wasn't built for things like this. She wanted to be a *therapist*, not a shotgun-toting maniac trying to save her friend from one monster so said friend could keep kissing *another monster*.

She was too fucking old for this shit; that was what she was.

The only reason Emma or Mary-Jo could see anything was the light coming from the shattered library window. The backyard was full of people, some who looked poised to run. Others were so covered in soot that they couldn't be anything but *that thing*.

And Laurel. *Fucking Laurel.*

Emma stepped closer to the crowd, listening as they spoke. Different voices but one mind. And then Greg, speaking to Spencer in that disgusting croak, his mouth black and oozing.

Then Laurel started to kiss Greg.

MJ immediately doubled over and made a gagging noise.

"*Shoot him!*" Spencer was pinned under Mary-Jo's neighbour's uncle. The vampire's face was a mess of blood and dirt, but the red eyes and fangs were a dead giveaway.

Emma hesitated. She knew the guy holding Spencer down. Well, *knew* was a big word but—

"Woman, *now!*" Spencer choked out.

Emma aimed quickly and fired a round high. It clipped the man's shoulder and he staggered back. Spencer used the opening to climb to his feet, only to be swarmed by three more of those things. She reloaded and shot again, trying her best to graze whoever got in her way.

She didn't want to kill anyone.

Especially not the people she'd known her whole life.

Mary-Jo stood up, wiping her mouth, and then started forward, the butt of her gun ready to swing. "Oh, hey, it's Robert. *Hey, Robert!* Remember that time you ran my cousin off the road?"

And she swung.

CHAPTER TWENTY-SEVEN

Laurel

Won't he be delicious, Laurel?
You always liked Greg's eyes.
You could keep them.
Store them in a jar next to the bed.
Won't his stomach fit like a glove, hot and sweet?

Around me, the world had turned to chaos: Emma and Mary-Jo trying
to corral our neighbours out of the yard by fear of being shot; Spencer
striking and biting and clawing toward me. Even with all of that, I kept
kissing Greg. Mary-Jo and Emma wouldn't hurt me. I could feel the darkness
trying to take hold of them. Make them ours. Even if they fought back.
Emma was a lost cause, holding back the dark with a life of love and patience
and hope. MJ was different. She had made use of the dark to protect me. It
would feed the beast all the same.

And Mary-Jo had said a hundred times she wanted Greg dead, hadn't she?
She was going to be so proud.

As the coal dust leaked from Greg's mouth, soaking into my tongue, his
eyes became clear. Conscious. More himself.

More afraid.

Greg stumbled back, out of my reach. "Laurel, what are you doing?"

"I've spent years trying to tell you how I feel, Greg." I stepped toward
him, ignoring the burn in my leg where the tissue was coming apart. "You

didn't want to hear any of it. I loved you and you used it to keep me in place. Keep me stuck and obedient and afraid. You only saw me long enough to soak me in disappointment and use my body like it was yours to take."

"I don't know what you're talking about—"

"But you do." I could see it in that small connection we still had left. The voice had shown me. Greg had known what he was doing every step of the way. He had found me as a young girl, someone who would dote on him. And when he grew to resent that part of me, when it started to make him feel less like a man, he made it my problem. "I'm going to be free without you," I hissed.

Greg turned to run and I ran too, faster than he could hope to. I pounced and landed on top of him, slamming him into the ground with enough force to knock the wind out of him.

He tried to get away, squirming beneath me like the worm he was. All those years of making sure I only cried when he couldn't see me, and now he was face-down in the dirt, sobbing. Had there ever been anything to *really* be afraid of? Or had he always been the kind of man to talk a big game and fall to pieces when someone struck back?

I grabbed his wrist and forced him to turn over.

I wanted to see the life leave his eyes.

He has taken so many years of your life.

Take all the rest of his.

My hands went around his throat, squeezing slowly. Tighter and tighter.

His breath turned to rasps. His nails, cut to the quick and useless, clawed at my hands. I didn't falter, not for a second.

I deserved it. I deserved to be free from all this. From him.

Spencer

Everything hurt. Between the *definitely* fucked-up ribs and the beating I'd been taking from seemingly *every fucking person in Penny Harbour,* I was tempted to lie down and let them have me. I was *trying* not to kill anyone. I didn't know which of those freaks were someone's relative and the last thing I wanted was to kill someone Laurel loved. But pulling my punches was beginning to have a cost.

The erratic beat of a dying heart drew my attention as I rolled a woman onto her back and knocked her out with a fist. From the corner of my vision, I could see Laurel on the ground with Greg. Her hands clamped around his throat.

Fuck.

As much as he deserved it, she wasn't the one choosing to do it. If I didn't stop her, she might never forgive me.

I scrambled up and fell to my knees behind her. Wrapping my arms around her waist, I tried to drag her off him by force. Laurel paused and turned her head toward me. Without so much as a word, she pried my fingers off and shoved me back.

Gods, that thing was strong.

Fine.

I leapt at her, knocking her off-balance, and wrestled her to the ground. The *fury* on her face was heart-wrenching. If I hadn't known that something had taken root in her—I hoped she *never* looked at me with that much loathing again.

"Spencer—" Laurel swung a hand at me and I caught it, pressing her wrist into the dirt. Her voice wasn't hers, full of spite and bile. "*Fuck off.*"

I straddled her waist, hooking my feet between her thighs to try and keep her down. Her shoulder—what I could see *inside* her shoulder—tore a hole in my heart. "I'm not letting you have her."

Her lips moved into that horrific grin, her teeth coated in coal dust. "If you loved me, you'd let me go, *darling*. Or would that make you walk out into the sunlight?"

Rage shot through me. I grabbed her jaw and squeezed. "*Get out of her.*"

Laurel winced, but that grin stayed where it was, her eyes staring back at me, pure black. "*Never.*"

If it wouldn't leave on its own…

I bared my fangs and bit into Laurel's neck.

My teeth broke her skin easily, and the rush of her blood into my mouth left me with the overwhelming urge to vomit. The *taste*. Before, she had been gritty—chalky, even—and the flavour had been like living charcoal. The depth of it now…it tasted like pain. Scorching desperation. Images flooded my mind as I forced myself to drink deep, crowding out everything else.

Laurel, just a child, getting scolded by family members.

Laurel, a few years later, watching her aunt be carted off to jail.

Laurel, a little older, waking up to find her father gone.

Laurel, in her teens, losing interest in everything but the void in her heart.

Sixteen, meeting Greg.

Seventeen, he makes her beg for the words *I love you*.

Twenty, they're married and he tells her she belongs to him now.

Twenty-five, she can't find her way out.

Thirty, she can't find herself in the mirror anymore.

Thirty-four, she—

Hello, Spencer.

I forced my eyes open, trying to come back to the moment. Laurel was limp under me. Her heart—still beating but weak and erratic. I'd drunk so much.

All that pain she carries, Spencer.

You could take that from her.

Save her.

All you need to do is keep drinking.

Take me in.

You'll never hurt again, darling boy.
You'll be safe and so will she.

I wanted to save her from the things the world had done to her, and for just a moment, I believed the voice.

My stomach lurched and I fell to the side, vomiting up the vile black evil I'd taken out of Laurel. Heave after heave, the air around me turning rank with the smell of it. I couldn't let it settle in me. Its voice was already so strong. The compulsion to act faded as I emptied my stomach, but it had been inside me already.

It would be there still.

"God damn it, Spencer." Mary-Jo stood nearby, the butt of her shotgun covered in blood and the scent of gunpowder hanging around her. "That's disgusting. Is Laurel—?"

Emma sank to her knees next to Laurel, shaking her. "Laurel!"

I looked around, trying to get some bearing on what had happened. Half a dozen bodies lay strewn through my backyard, some moving and some not. Blood and black were splattered across the grass. Everyone else had either come to their senses and fled, or had been pulled away by that *thing*.

The only other person still there was *Greg*. His eyes were locked on the body of his wife. He was trembling.

Good.

As I righted myself and pulled Laurel into my arms, I glared at him. "*Go,*" I snarled, fangs bared. "Because someone ought to kill you, and I'd love to be him."

Greg scampered away like a rodent running from a cat.

"Laurel." I ran my hand across her forehead. She was cool. Fading.

The smell. In all the chaos, I hadn't caught the smell.

Death and sweat and damp rot, emanating from her wounds. She smelled like the mine shaft.

Laurel coughed, violent spasms rocking her body. I turned her on her side and the black poured out of her mouth in a rush, coating the grass. More of it than I thought possible. I held her tight, praying for her to stop. And when her body stopped shaking, she fell limp into my arms again.

Her heart was slowing.

CHAPTER TWENTY-EIGHT

Laurel

The warmth of the sun soaked into my skin, blissful. A tiny breeze shook the trees at the edges of the hill, but it wasn't cold. Just enough to keep the sun from scorching. Lying on the blanket, eyes to the sky, we were enveloped by the grass. Tall green strands flowed back and forth around us. Bees and butterflies flitted by, on their way somewhere. Dandelions and daisies and buttercups.

Spencer's face nuzzled into my neck, the cool of his nose tickling me. I reached up to pick a buttercup from the grass and held it under his chin. A tiny reflection of yellow shone on his pale skin and I smiled.

"You like butter," I whispered, as if it were a secret. Maybe it was, to him. Would he remember liking butter after so many years of not eating?

"I want you to stay, Laurel." Spencer's voice was pained. I had no idea why. It was such a beautiful day.

He sat up, tucking his hand under my neck. He moved me until I was cradled in his arms. So upset. Tears ran down his face, splashing onto my nice sundress.

I curled up against him, tucking my face into his chest. "Don't cry, Spencer. I'm not going anywhere."

"I love you," he choked out, growing more and more distressed. "You can't go. You can't leave me here."

It didn't make any sense. Why would I go anywhere when I could stay forever on the hill over the Harbour with him?

Spencer

Laurel wasn't waking up.

"Please." I shook her, railing against the reality of what was happening. How she'd been on her feet with two bullet holes in her, killed *so many people*, and had been stuffed to the brim with poison *before* I'd stolen her blood. I'd thought I was helping her, trying to force that thing out, but it was a mistake. It had only made things worse.

If Laurel died, I wasn't sure I'd come back from it.

Their faces flashed into my vision and I recoiled from it. Astra. Willem. Violet. Watching them burn. Hearing their screams. Feeling the crushing weight of that for years. Would I ever be able to think of Laurel again after this? Would her face haunt me like theirs did?

Her pulse was weakening. I had no time to get her to the hospital, not as far away as it was. Even if the volunteer paramedics arrived quickly, *even if* they knew what to do for someone as bad off as she was, she would never survive the drive to town.

I had two options.

Let her die.

Or turn her.

But we'd never talked about that. We'd never discussed what she'd want, someday. If immortality would be a gift or a curse for her. She was young and healthy, and we'd only known each other for a moment. Why would we ever have talked about how she wanted to die?

"*Spencer!*" Mary-Jo smacked me on the shoulder. I hadn't been listening. Hadn't heard anything they were saying to me. "Wake the fuck up. What's wrong with her?"

I looked up at MJ, her eyes darting around the space as she stood guard, shotgun in hand.

"She's dying," I managed to choke out. The fear was washing over me in waves until I could barely think.

Loss. Loss, loss, loss.

Yes.

Let her go.

She's already gone.

All you have to do is sink back into that grief.

Doesn't it feel like home?

That fucking voice. I shook my head, gritting my teeth. If I'd figured out anything, it was that nothing it said was worth a damn. She wasn't lost, not yet. But if I waited too long, the alternative would cost her everything.

Emma looked at Mary-Jo, shaking her head. "There has to be something. She'd never make it—"

"She's *not* dying. That can't fucking happen, not when she just got out." Mary-Jo's face was stone as she crouched down, dropped the gun, and looked Laurel over, trying to find something she could do. But her hands hovered over her friend's body, so helpless.

I shook my head. "It's not a guess, MJ. She's got minutes and we're down to one option."

"What option, Spencer?" Emma's eyes were locked on mine, and I saw an impressive ferocity there.

"I turn her, or she dies."

"Like the movies?" Emma asked. "Make her like you?"

"Yes. Close enough. But I can't just do that to her—"

"Why can't you, man?" Mary-Jo's voice was panicked, practically screaming. "If she's dying, just *do it*!"

"You don't understand!" I shot back, holding Laurel tightly against my chest. "It's not a gift! It's not some easy, uncomplicated thing you want me to give her! It may save her life, but she'll spend the rest of her days hunting humans. Hiding from the sun. She won't be who you think. She'll spend years practically feral. It's going to tear her out of this life!" I looked down at Laurel. "She may not forgive any of us."

"Then it's on me, Spencer." Emma leaned forward. "If she wakes up and hates what she is, I'll be responsible for that. It'll be on *me*. I'm not going to lose her by being too cautious, not when there's a chance."

I took a breath, trying to steady myself.

Her pulse was quieting. We were out of time.

When I had died, hadn't it been the thing that freed me to actually live?

Couldn't her death be the start of something new for her? Even if it made a monster out of her too?

I let her legs fall gently, bringing my wrist to my teeth. With a clean rip, red came rushing from the fresh wound. I pried Laurel's mouth open and held my wrist to her lips. She didn't move. Didn't respond at all to the blood dripping onto her tongue. Down her throat.

The three of us waited in silence, fear thick in the air.

It might already have been too late.

"This won't be pretty." I kept my wrist where it was, wanting to be sure she had enough for the change. "If she wakes up—*if* she isn't too far gone already—you still may wish she had died. She—"

I stopped talking. Focused on the sound. The missing sound.

Laurel's heart had stopped.

A sob worked its way up my throat, choking me. "She's gone."

Emma fell into Mary-Jo's arm, sobbing. MJ…she stared at Laurel hard, her teeth gritted as if she expected her to wake up any moment. But it didn't work like that.

I stroked Laurel's hair, trying to straighten the loose, blood-soaked strands stuck to her face. "Now we wait and see if she gets back up."

It was a cruel twist of fate. To have spent months fearing Greg would decide to kill her. In the end, it had been me who drained her to the brink of death.

It had been me she should have feared.

Penny Harbour

Losing Laurel to the vampire was a concession it hadn't been willing to make. The prize, however, had been delightful.

She had done such good work.

It had poured power into her until her violence made it *sing*. Most of the tribute and glorious pain it received was a trickle. A spiteful word or a shattered spirit. But every so often, someone in the Harbour grew so full and dripping with darkness that it exploded into something *delicious*. But rarely had it been as satisfying as what she had done. What she had set in motion.

They had collectively spilt so much blood and created so many scars. Their actions had fed the thing living beneath the Harbour until it was bloated. It would rest, practically splitting at the seams, content to while away at the slow threads of future pain. It would hardly be dormant, no. It would live in the people as it always did, in their little actions and the hate they poured into others. But it would have *time*. Time to craft new avenues to the next big event.

After all, the people never came down to see it anymore, walking right into the maw of the earth. Instead, it needed ways to soak into them, wherever they were. And once it was inside, it wouldn't just *leave*.

Laurel had done it *such* a service.

CHAPTER TWENTY-NINE

Spencer

Emma's house, for all intents and purposes, had become a mortuary. Laurel had needed such care. Filthy, head to toe. Full of wounds and soot, her hair ratty. We'd taken her out of my yard and wrapped her in blankets, and that had helped keep her alive in their minds. Treating her body kindly. Mary-Jo and Emma had insisted on helping. Setting her in the back of the Jeep with me. Holding doors as I carried her into Emma's house. Sitting with me as I ran the water shallowly in Emma's bathtub and peeled away the ruin of Laurel's clothing. But the moment she saw the hole in Laurel's shoulder, Emma had her head in the toilet.

They didn't need to see their friend like that.

I sent them away to grieve.

Which left me alone with Laurel. I ran streams of warm water over her skin until the dirt was gone. I picked debris from Laurel's leg so it wouldn't heal inside her. It killed me to see the damage done to her, but it was nothing worse than I'd done to someone else with my own hands. Nothing I hadn't seen a hundred times.

It didn't stop me from crying as I spent time with her body, getting her ready.

For a new life or a casket, I didn't know.

When she was clean and dry, I picked her up and brought her into the guest bedroom, where the sheets were turned down and waiting. I laid her out and Emma covered her up. Emma's son had a baby monitor, and we put it in the room, so we could watch over her at all times.

If she woke, she would need to be kept from hurting someone.

If she didn't…well, we'd smell it soon enough.

Mary-Jo was chain-smoking again, and since she kept offering me the second half of each cigarette, we'd gone through a pack before dawn.

The sun was getting ready to rise, and Emma had another pot of coffee on. Mary-Jo had gone to her house around midnight and come back with foul-tasting but effective energy drinks. Between the nicotine, the caffeine, and the sugar, I had managed to stay awake through the night. It was paramount that I did. If I was asleep when—*if*—Laurel woke up, she'd kill Emma and Mary-Jo as soon as she smelled them.

Standing on Emma's back porch with Mary-Jo as the sky started to lighten, I took one last cigarette from her. I cupped my hand over the end and lit it, dragging the smoke into my lungs.

"How much longer, do you think?" Mary-Jo asked, puffing smoke out into the humid air.

"By nightfall, I hope." I stared off into the distance. I rarely lingered outside so close to dawn, and watching the sky lighten was full of beautiful danger.

"And if she does…she'll go back to normal, won't she?" Mary-Jo asked, a quiver in her voice.

"Someday. Mostly." I pressed a finger to my temple. My head had started throbbing mildly, though from the exhaustion or everything else, I wasn't sure. At least my ribs seemed to have healed enough. I'd left the last of my blood rations at the house, and the hunger would be a problem soon enough. Whatever I'd taken out of Laurel had left my insides practically acidic. I couldn't be sure how badly my body was in a state of disrepair.

Mary-Jo looked at the baby monitor clutched in her hand. Laurel hadn't moved an inch. "This is fucked up. I'm waiting for my best friend to not be dead anymore by keeping a close eye on her corpse."

I took another drag. "I told you it wouldn't be pretty, and it's only just started. I wish Emma would get back already. We have a lot to talk about and I'm running out of steam."

Mary-Jo turned her wrist to check her watch. "She's been gone almost an hour. Should be any time now, if she didn't run into trouble."

"Good." I held up a hand, feeling the tremble in it. "Gods, this may finally be the death of me if I don't sleep soon."

Mary-Jo scoffed. I looked at her. The bags under her eyes were dark, worry creasing her face. "You and me both, brother."

Brother. Was it the exhaustion that made that word hit so deeply?

"I haven't…" I paused, unsure if I really wanted to say what was on my mind. But weariness had turned me into a vulnerable sap, so I said it anyway. "I haven't thanked you. Neither of you needed to have anything to do with me. And as short-lived as this has been, between the dance and now…being with the three of you was the first I felt like I belonged anywhere in a long time."

"Aw, Jesus, Spence." Mary-Jo seemed slightly uncomfortable, despite the smile quirking at the corners of her lips. "I didn't realize you were such a suckup."

I reached out to pull her into a hug, the cigarette placed carefully away from her hair. She squeezed me back, her grip tight and unrelenting. Perhaps she needed the hug more than I did. "You're all right, you know," I muttered. "For a surly backwater human."

"You're not so bad yourself, Twinkle Toes." She let me go, holding my arms in her hands, examining me. "You know what? I've got a mauve leather jacket you'd look *really good* in—"

The crunch of gravel came from the other side of the house, along with the engine of a car.

I took three quick drags and stomped the cigarette underfoot. It was for the best anyway; I was only a few minutes from earning a full-body burn when the sun peeked over that crest.

By the time Mary-Jo and I came back into the kitchen, Emma was unloading two large bags and a crate onto the table. I started to close the blinds on all the windows, trapping the sun outside. Emma closed the door and dropped into the nearest chair.

A desperate, angry yowling was coming from the crate.

"Spectre!" I ran over, opened the wire door, and scooped her into my arms. She scrabbled against my chest for a moment, but then sniffed my clothing and settled in. "I'm sorry I left you there, you darling little girl."

Mary-Jo stood next to me, scratching Spectre's head and making kisses at her. "So *soft*," she cooed. Then she looked up at Emma. "How'd it go?"

"It's done," she said, emptying her keys and wallet onto the table.

"Logan is fine, slept the entire night for one. Left more clothes and diapers at Mom's, drove by Spencer's place to see what was up, and picked up everything you asked for."

"And?" I tossed Spectre over my shoulder and held her as I rummaged through the bags one-handed. "What did you see?"

"Nothing. Not a fucking thing." Emma shook her head. "The bodies are gone. There's blood and coal dust everywhere, but all those people…just gone. Animals, maybe? Or that thing?"

"You were able to just walk into the house?" Mary-Jo asked, taking the items I gave her and putting them on the counter.

"Yeah. That's maybe the most fucked-up part." Emma got up and went to the sink, beginning to scrub furiously at her hands with soap and water. "All those gunshots. You'd think someone would have called the police. Did no one see anything? No one? They all just, what…turned their heads and looked the other way?"

"Wasn't that what they did for Laurel?" I asked, unable to keep the bile out of my words. "Watched her live with her neck under Greg's boot?" Emma and Mary-Jo's faces fell, and I held up a hand, immediately regretting my choice of words. "I don't mean you. You know I don't. I'm just tired and…"

"I get it," Mary-Jo said, filling the space where I'd trailed off. "And you're right. We love to say fucked-up things don't happen here, because we've gotten really good at turning away from the things that do."

The room grew far too quiet.

I went back to looking through the bags and finally found what I needed. Four litres of blood in four little bags. I stowed three in the fridge and held the last up. "I can go somewhere else, if you'd rather. But I need to eat."

Emma blanched. "I'm gonna put my head down." She did just that, pulling out her phone and starting to scroll through Tabs, her hand shielding her eyes.

"Anything online about it?" Mary-Jo asked Emma, watching me intently as I let my fangs out and bit down on the bag, too tired to even think about warming it.

Emma kept scrolling the feed. "Nothing. Christ. It's like it never happened."

Mary-Jo's voice was oddly disconnected as she stared at me. "Either it's the best gossip anyone had heard in months, or we all refuse to acknowledge anything went down. Mom used to say that about when she was young, too. The things this town agreed never to talk about."

"I doubt that monster wants a bunch of cops floating around the Harbour," Emma added, her voice resigned. "Probably not that hard to keep it under wraps if you can control half the town."

I drained the bag dry by the time she was finished talking and wiped my mouth with the back of my hand. But MJ's intense stare was still on me. "Something you need to get off your chest, or what?"

Mary-Jo took a breath. "No. It's not that. It's…Laurel will be doing that, soon. If everything works." Her voice was so dark. Disapproving, almost.

I laughed, spiteful and barely keeping my eyes open. "You said I might be good for Laurel, once upon a time. That I had something to offer her that couldn't be found around here. Changed your mind yet?"

Mary-Jo let out a little huff and went to the liquor stash on top of the fridge. She poured herself two fingers of Jack Daniels and drank it back in a gulp.

"Maybe." She poured another two fingers and swirled it in the cup. "She's dead right now, one way or the other. The only thing keeping me going is that I believe any minute now, this fucking baby monitor is going to go off and she's going to get out of that bed. And if you weren't here, and Greg did eventually try to kill her, we wouldn't have had that option. Maybe she'd have lived a lot longer, but I don't think she was ever going to leave Greg without you. I don't think she'd ever have been safe, or happy. If she dies, you gave her those things for a while. And if she lives? You gave us a second chance with her. What more could I ask for?"

I wanted to have *something* to say, but I didn't. What could be said in response to that? I could hardly stand to acknowledge how generous she was being with me, and I was sorely tempted to say *you're welcome for making your friend into a bloodthirsty killer.* But I didn't. They were being kind, and they had no idea yet what they'd agreed to do to Laurel.

I didn't think I could explain it in a manner that would connect for them, not without seeing it.

I looked away, letting out a sigh. "Whatever you say."

The room fell into silence, and when it was clear no one was going to add anything, I started to rummage in the bags again. "Did you get the kit?"

Emma nodded, peeking up between her fingers before she straightened her head. "In the green bag."

I reached in and held up the IV line and the set of mason jars. "All right. Who loves their friend the most?"

Laurel

I slept the deepest and darkest I had ever slept. No dreams. No consciousness. Simply there and gone. An absence of so much, on and on and on.

The world came back all at once.

I had never known how *loud* living was.

The static of electronics. The hum of an air conditioner in the distance. The tick of a clock. Birds outside. The wind hitting the house. A dozen mundane sounds that hadn't been there a moment ago, suddenly so very present.

A dull, deep burning.

In my stomach, and all across my body.

My body. It felt so much and so little. Bone-deep cold. Sharp pain in my shoulder and my calf, pulsing, *screaming*. An unsettling stillness underneath it that felt wrong.

So wrong.

And the hunger.

The hunger was overwhelming.

It stole my concentration. Eat. I needed to eat. More than I wanted the pain to leave. More than discomfort. More than *anything*, I needed to *eat*.

I groaned and tried to sit up. I couldn't *remember*. People, everywhere. Screaming. Blood. When I tried to touch my face, my shoulder ignited, white-hot pain. I cried out, looking for a mirror to see myself in. What had happened to my shoulder?

But the mirror above the wardrobe showed me nothing. A bed. Blankets. And no one.

Footsteps, moving quickly down the hall, toward the room. Emma's guest room. That was where I was.

But how?

The door opened.

Spencer stood there, his eyes brimming with tears.

He came to the bed and took my head in his hands, staring at me as if he hadn't seen me in weeks. "Laurel. Thank the gods."

My throat was raw. Trying to speak—it hurt. I drew a breath and—

Had I *been* breathing?

"Spencer?" I whimpered.

"Shh, I know." He held me close, his hand on the back of my head. "How do you feel?"

"Everything hurts," I cried out. "I'm cold. Why am I so cold? And I—" The hunger burned my gut and I curled into him with a groan.

His hand. In his hand. Something I knew I wanted *badly*. Didn't want to *know* I craved.

He held the jar in front of me, the lid still on. "Laurel, I'm sorry. There was so much blood. You…you were going to die. You *did* die, darling. I hope you'll forgive me."

But he was opening that jar and I didn't care what he was saying. The smell. It hit my nose, metallic and sweet. I licked my lips, staring at him, trying to concentrate but I couldn't. I just—

"Drink." He put the jar in my hands.

I tipped it to my lips without hesitation and drank it in thick gulps. It was like nothing I could remember tasting before. The more I drank, the clearer my head became, but the jar was empty too soon.

I shook it, trying to get every last drop out. Spencer had to pry it from my hands.

He pressed his forehead to mine, holding my arms tightly.

As the hunger began to subside, I noticed things. Crying from the doorway. Mary-Jo holding Emma as she sobbed—and their heartbeats so loud I could hear them thrum-thrum-thrumming.

The bandage on Emma's elbow.

The *colour* of the liquid in the jar.

My canines, long and sharp.

The stillness of everything in my body.

"Spencer." I searched his face for some kind of answer. "What did you do?"

Guilt washed over his expression instantly, and his grip on my arms tightened. "What I had to."

My eyes fluttered. The room was going hazy around me. Sleep was taking over, dragging me down into the black again, so heavy I couldn't resist. I collapsed against Spencer's chest. His fingers stroked my hair, and as I fell asleep, I heard him say it again.

"I'm sorry."

Spencer

After tucking Laurel back into the covers, I closed the door on her again. Emma had raided her medicine cabinet for sleeping pills and had come up with the remnants of an old oxycodone prescription. Considering the label called for one pill at a time and I had four to work with, I had dissolved the rest of the bottle into the blood, praying it would be enough to knock out a fledgling vampire who wouldn't know her own strength and could tear a bloody streak through the village if she got past me.

If she had tasted the drug, she hadn't cared. Not that she would've had anything to compare it to in the first place.

It would buy us time.

Emma and Mary-Jo were already back in the kitchen, Emma's head buried in Mary-Jo's shoulder.

I put the jar down and leaned on the counter. "That was monumentally stupid, following me into the room."

Mary-Jo's face furled into a snarl. "You can't—"

"I understand why," I interrupted. "But you can't do shit I tell you not to. Not if you want to live through the next few days. She's back with us, and that is *deeply good*. I know you want to see her. I know you care. But you need to understand something *very intimately*. You haven't seen me hungry. You don't know what I'm capable of." I pointed toward the bedroom. "She'll kill you, and she won't know she's doing it until it's done."

"She drank it so fast," Emma whispered. "Like a wild animal."

"That's what she is right now. Nearly feral, at least when she's hungry." I was itching for a smoke, a drink, something to numb the whirlwind of things

I was feeling. I tried to choke out the craving, forcing it down. "From where I'm standing, three paces away, I know how fast your hearts are beating. I can hear them and *not* think of you as dinner because I've had centuries of practice. Laurel is going to hear your blood and think only about how she can get it out of you. If she calls to you, don't go. Let me handle her. If she tries to jump you, you won't be able to stop her. *I* might not be able to."

"What can we do?" Mary-Jo asked.

"Keep her fed. She's going to need to drink more frequently than I do. I don't know for sure, but I think it's got to do with removing the weakness of humans and building up everything we become. The filtering out and repairing." I put my head down, massaging my temples. "We don't have enough. I wanted something fresh for her first meal, to help with the healing, but she could easily drink you several times over in the next couple days. We need another way."

"Where do you get your blood?" Mary-Jo was motioning for Emma to stand on her own, straightening up.

"I have a guy in the city who trades it to me under the table."

"Call him."

I looked up. "I can't leave her with you to go *to the city*."

"I'll go." Mary-Jo opened her phone, created a new contact, and passed it to me. "Add him, and tell him I'm coming. We'll work it out and I'll be back with as much as I can carry."

I stared at her, knowing I shouldn't be remotely surprised, but all the same… "MJ, you would jump off a cliff for her, wouldn't you?"

"Fucking right I would." Mary-Jo scooped up Emma's keys, chomping at the bit to move.

"Wait." We still hadn't discussed something vital. Something that gave me no pleasure to tell them. "You both understand Laurel isn't going to be able to stay in Penny Harbour, don't you?"

Their blank, frightened looks said all I needed to know.

"She won't be safe with anyone she loves, not for any extended period of time. When she knows how to eat without killing and she can control her impulses, then she can go where she pleases. But I can't ask her to stay here when doing so means she'll inevitably hurt someone she loves." I put my hand on the counter and sighed. "Aside from that, it would get very difficult to explain why she can't go out in the day anymore, won't eat anything, and why her eyes turn red at the slightest annoyance."

They didn't say anything, just looked at each other.

"Again, I'm sorry." I looked away. Spectre was slinking around the kitchen, sniffing everything in sight. I scooped her up just to feel her purr against my chest.

"It's fine," Mary-Jo said, sounding deeply unconvincing. "We have the internet. We can call her. Have supervised visits. How…how long, do you think?"

I thought back to my time with Violet, as she took me under her wing and taught me how to stop surviving as a beast and start *living*. "A few years, at most. I hope."

Emma's arms slid around herself, holding her body like a shield. "We had so many things planned together. Years of adventures we never got. Things I wanted her to be here for."

"Honestly, if you're smart, you'll both leave," I said. "Not with us, but anywhere this *thing* isn't. You can't want to *stay here*, not knowing what's under the ground."

"I…" Emma's back straightened, and something in her shifted. "I'm not going anywhere. I made a commitment to help people here, and I'm going to help them. Our families have been here for a long time. I'm not just going to give up and run."

Mary-Jo shook her head. "And I can't just let you stay here alone. So I guess that's decided." She shifted her weight. "Well, fuck. We're staying; she's going. It is what it is. A few years is how I'd sum up my longest relationship, and that shit went by *fast*." Mary-Jo sniffed, her joking falling flat. "We'll figure it all out. We have to."

Emma looked at me. "How long do we have before you take her?"

"Two nights from now." The pain in their eyes was more than I wanted to witness. "I can't risk more."

"Yeah. Yeah, okay." Mary-Jo fumbled with the keys, brushing the front of her pants nervously. "We'll figure it out. That's what we've always done. That's what we'll do now." She pointed at me, turning to walk out the door. "Make the call."

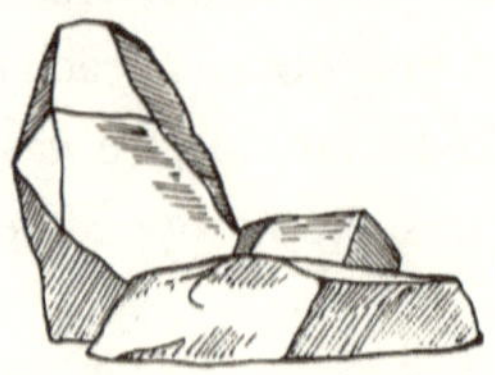

Penny Harbour

Two days.

That was all Mary-Jo could think about as she sped to the city in her Jeep. How little time that was. How much had to be done before then. Collecting the blood, getting the supplies Spencer had asked for, racing back to the Harbour. And when it was done, Mary-Jo was going to stay as close to Laurel as she could, for as long as she could.

If Spencer thought his little speech could scare her off, he had another think coming.

Mary-Jo had seen her fair share of horrors, and she wasn't about to let this one get the best of her. Laurel was alive—figuratively speaking—and that was something to celebrate.

The road blurred as Mary-Jo drove through the woods. She blinked and a pair of stray tears ran down her face.

She'd always thought Laurel would be there. Even in the futures she had imagined in which Laurel left Greg, she'd never imagined her friend would leave the Harbour. Laurel loved her clients and her friends. Her mom. Her job. Aside from Greg, she'd had no reason to go anywhere.

And now she was practically gone.

No more late-night drinks. No more begging Laurel to tell Greg to go pound sand over a cup of coffee. No more expensive trips to bulk stores in the city. No more thousands of things big and small that they had done together since they were kids.

Sleepovers.

Trips to the beach.

Dinner invitations.

Walks around the Harbour.

Gone.

And it would burn like a son of a bitch, even if Mary-Jo knew it was the right thing for Laurel.

Forget the bloodlust. Laurel deserved to get out and see the world. Especially if it meant doing it with someone who *cared* about her. Spencer could give her things that no one in Penny Harbour could. If Mary-Jo pictured them walking through old cities at night, hand in hand, that helped the ache a little.

She had always wanted happiness like that for Laurel.

Wiping the tears from her eyes, Mary-Jo sniffed and refocused. She turned up the music until the boom of it overwhelmed her thoughts. She had two big red empty coolers in the back seat and places to be.

CHAPTER THIRTY

Laurel

Spencer was already sitting in bed when I woke the next evening, a book in his hands. The covers were pulled up to his waist, his chest bare. A faint purple bruise ran across his ribcage. He must have slept next to me through the day, but I could hardly recall a thing. Vaguely, I knew where I was. Emma's guest bedroom. Had we stayed the night? Gotten drunk? Was that why my head—

My tongue tasted like stale copper, and the hunger came rushing back.

The gnawing filled my stomach and I curled into myself, crying out with the pain of it.

Blood. Blood blood bloodbloodbloodblood—

A hand on my shoulder. I snapped around, leaping onto the body next to me. Spencer. His eyes full of concern and his skin holding in what I needed.

I needed.

Spencer hushed me, holding my face in his hands as I straddled him. "It's all right, darling. I have blood here for you—"

I shoved him into the headboard. Pain ripped through my shoulder and calf, but it wasn't enough to stop me from sinking my teeth into Spencer's neck. The blood gushed out and I drank deeply, but it wasn't like last time. Cold. It tasted like food without salt or spice. Perfectly fine, but not *good*.

Spencer held my shoulders as I drank, his head craned back. Containing himself. He let out a little sigh, and it reverberated in the muscles of his neck.

He was enjoying it, but trying not to show me. His fingers dug deeply into my skin, and the longer I drank, the stronger his grip got. His nails pressing into my skin were alighting some sense in me.

"That's enough, Laurel." Stern. Commanding.

I swallowed and removed my mouth from his neck. Red dripped down his shoulder and into the line of his collarbone. I leaned in and licked it off.

Spencer shivered under my tongue. "Enough."

He reached over the bed and popped something open. A cooler. Inside were bags and bags of blood.

"Can I?" I asked, trying to find the capacity for words. "I'm so hungry, Spencer."

He picked one out and passed it to me. "It's all for you. Drink up. Your friends want to see you."

I bit down into the bag, just like I'd seen him do before.

This. This blood was better. Cold, yes, but full of depth. Flavour. I could hardly pinpoint it before it was gone. The bag was bone-dry, all wrinkles and tiny lines of leftover red.

I stared at the bag in my palms for a long time as the hunger began to fade and I could think again.

I dropped it to the bed, curling over Spencer, my palms on the mattress.

The loss of control.

The hunger.

I'd hurt him without a thought.

Who was I?

I started to sob, and Spencer pulled me into his arms. His skin on mine didn't feel cold anymore.

It just felt like more of the same.

Spencer spent more than an hour telling me about what happened. I remembered some of it. Some came back to me as he told the story. I knew he wouldn't lie to me, and it *felt* true, but not all of it was sticking in my mind. According to him, I'd killed people. I believed him. I remembered the bodies. Remembered the smell and the voice. But the killing…maybe if I just held it at arm's reach, it wouldn't be my fault.

Maybe it could have been someone else who had done those horrors…

Not that I would stay innocent for long.

Not anymore.

I had hurt Spencer without any conscious effort. Not even the pain of my wounds had been enough to stop me. I wasn't sure what would have, and it scared me to my core. What if it had been Emma or MJ? Would I have torn their throats out just to have a taste of that hot, coursing, sweet—?

I shuddered. The thought filled me with such desire and such revulsion, all at once.

No.

I couldn't think about it. I couldn't.

I couldn't.

And all that paled in comparison to what he said next.

That we had to leave.

The thing I'd feared about leaving Greg had come true after all. That in getting rid of him, I'd have to leave everything else in the dust. And this was different; I knew that. Different reasoning. *Good* reasoning. But it was loss all the same.

Everything, just…gone. And no time to grieve it, not until long after we left.

I had no reflection—*I had no fucking reflection*—and as he removed the bandage, the air hurt. He took a photo of the wound in my shoulder to show me how it was healing. But the photo showed the muscle stitching itself back together. Better than what it had been, he said. And when that was done, I made him show me my face.

Two long, sharp fangs and eyes as red as blood. No matter how hard I tried, I couldn't get them to hide.

It had taken all my willpower to keep my nausea at bay.

He helped wash the blood from my face and brought me something of Emma's to wear. When he came back in the room, all I could focus on was the vicious bite I'd left on his neck. Healing, yes, but raw. My fault.

Spencer helped me dress, to keep from straining the tissue around the holes in me—*I had fucking holes in my body*—and after a while, when I was ready, he held my hand as we left the bedroom.

Emma and Mary-Jo were sitting at the kitchen table. Mary-Jo's leg was bouncing as she sipped at a cup of coffee, her brows knit tight with worry. A baby monitor sat next to her on the table.

It was Emma who looked up first. "Laurel." She stood up, her fists clasped in front of her chest. She looked ready to bolt or pounce. Or maybe both. Her face had a question on it, and she was staring over my shoulder at Spencer.

I looked back. He stared into my eyes for a moment, and then nodded to Emma.

Emma and Mary-Jo were on me in a flash, wrapping me in their arms. Their tears fell and I could smell them. Smell everything. Skin and sweat. Lavender and pomegranate. Coffee on their breaths.

"God, never fucking die on us again," Mary-Jo whispered in my ear.

I relaxed into their arms for the space of a few breaths, but the quick thrum of their heartbeats was pulling my attention.

Th-thump.

TH-THUMP.

TH-THUMP.

Spencer must have noticed that change in my body. "Ladies, give her space. I know, I'm sorry. But I don't want to clean you off the floor either."

"I…" I put my face in my hand. "It's so hard to hear anything over your hearts. How—?" I looked up at Spencer. "How do you do this every day?" Tears were welling in my eyes again.

He took my hand. "Do you need some air?"

I nodded, my head full with the scared racing of their hearts.

"All right." Spencer pushed me toward the front door, where shoes were waiting for both of us. We slipped them on. Spencer looked up at Emma and Mary-Jo, apologetic. "We'll be back, and we'll all sit. I promise."

It didn't make me feel any less guilty as we went out the door, into the night, leaving my friends behind.

The sky was clear, and when I stepped out of the house, the oceans of stars overhead stopped me in my tracks. The night was so much *brighter* than it had ever been before, and I could see more of everything. I didn't have the words for what I was seeing. Nebulas? Milky ways? I wasn't a fucking astronomer, but suddenly all that space was more enthralling than it had ever been before.

Spencer stood next to me, staring up. "Is it stupid to say I've gotten so used to it that I forgot how beautiful it is?"

Tears welled in my eyes. I looked away, trying to find somewhere else to stare. The streetlights on the road that I barely needed anymore. The depth of the shadows between trees and bushes, where nothing could hide from me. Even the sound of animals in the grass, from who knew how far away. "I had no idea. Everything is so *much*."

Leading me onward by the hand as I stared in awe, Spencer started to talk. "It's overwhelming. I remember being confused for days. I didn't have anyone to help me when I needed it, but I'm not going to let that happen to you."

I focused, turning my eyes away from the world and toward him. "I don't know how I'm going to survive this, Spencer. They were *so loud.* If they'd been in the room when I woke up…" I pulled him to a stop on the side of the road and looked at his neck. The wounds were still only half-healed.

He put his hand on the bite. "It'll be fine. I've had much worse. Hey—" He took my face in his hand as I started to turn away from him, distraught. "You didn't hurt me. At least, not in a way I haven't *asked* to be hurt before. And as far as your friends, they weren't allowed near you, for their safety. I took care of it. I'm not going to let you do anything you would regret."

I nodded somberly, and he motioned for us to walk on. Just up the road was the path into the grass that would take us along the dykes, the place I'd really kissed him for the first time.

We said nothing for a while. The peaceful hush of the world around me was a balm for the anxiety I'd been feeling inside the house. I let it wash over me, listening to the rush of the wind in the grass and the crickets somewhere in the distance.

"Are you angry?" Spencer asked. "About what I did?"

I looked up at him. "For turning me?"

Spencer nodded, and his face was full of concern.

I took a moment to answer. I'd barely had time to figure out what had happened, let alone how I felt about it. Apparently, depending on the moment, I was either level-headed or a bloodthirsty monster, so it hardly seemed fair to ask me what my thoughts were.

But I was alive—or still existed, rather. And that was something.

"I'm not angry," I said, finally. "I don't know what I am. But I'd rather not be dead. Even if it means everything is about to get harder now. Even if I have to leave like you said."

"Not everything will be harder," Spencer answered. "You're still Laurel.

You won't have changed overnight. You're still the bashful, sweet woman who plied me with kindness until I adored you. You're just…more now. And not all of that will be easy to stomach."

We walked toward the water, and as we reached the edge, I looked down. The moon was a thin sliver that night, but our reflections still should have been there.

This time, neither of us looked back from the surface.

"Does that ever stop being strange? Not seeing yourself where you should be?" I asked.

"At this point, I feel like it would be strange to see myself in a mirror at all."

"Pros and cons," I said, turning to him. "Con, I do have to disappear off the face of the earth, I guess. Pro, I don't think I have to go to work anymore."

"Con," Spencer mimicked, "you *will* crave the blood of living things until you perish. Pro, you'll never pay for another astronomically costly grocery order again."

I laughed, since that was a *very* helpful pro. "Con, I'll never stand in the sun again. Pro, the night is so much more beautiful now."

Guilt washed over Spencer's face. "I'm sorry for stealing the sun from you."

"I do think I'll miss that. A lot, actually. But I would have missed it if I were dead too, so I guess I'll figure it out."

Spencer's guilt turned to a genuine smile. "You're handling this arguably too well."

I shrugged. Yes, a lot of things were weighing on me, but I'd gotten very good at carrying too much on my shoulders. It was easier to package it all up, store it in the back of my head, and try to ignore it. "I don't know. An eternity with you? It could be worse."

"About that." His gaze went to his shoes. "I don't want you to feel bound to me because I turned you. On the scale of endless time, we've known each other for a *second*. If you decide you want to disappear once this is done, I understand. You don't owe me anything."

"Now it's my turn to call bullshit." I put a hand on his hip, carefully teasing a finger under his shirt so I could touch his skin. "I don't plan on running off."

"And I'm glad for it. But you need to know I'm not going to trap you with me. I don't want to be another Greg in your life." He looked up at the sky.

Anywhere but at me, it seemed. "Maybe we'll do this for a while and discover our time has come to an end. Or maybe we'll be side by side until the world falls down. Whatever comes, I will *never* hold you here."

"I know that, Spencer." A memory floated to the surface, and I smiled. "I had a dream about you. When I was dying."

Spencer's eyes finally met mine. "Oh?"

"I dreamed you said you loved me. You wouldn't stop crying."

Spencer pulled my hand up to his lips. "You heard that, did you?"

Butterflies rose in my chest. "Did you mean it?"

His face was incredulous. Insulted. "Of course I meant it." He drew me in by the waist, holding me tightly against him as he stole a kiss. Our first since I'd died. And despite the lack of a heartbeat in my chest or blood flowing properly in my veins, that spark wasn't lost. The hunger for him that had nothing to do with blood and everything to do with how he'd shown me in such a short time how to actually live.

"Pro," I said, breaking the kiss, "no breathing means endless making out."

He gave me a little *mmm* and stole another. "I love you, Laurel."

I froze. I wanted to say it back. I felt it. But saying it out loud was too intimate. Too new and raw. Too much of me exposed at once. More than anything, I wanted to protect my heart, and I couldn't get past that, not even with his fingers laced in my hair. Not even if he made me feel safe. Nothing could have made me more scared in that moment than putting my heart on display.

"You know I do, right?" My words were sheepish. Shy. It was the best I could manage.

He snickered. "Imagine, you having your guard up. So unexpected." His tone changed to something serious. "Laurel, you've loved me for months. You were showing me over and over, long before you realized what you were doing. I waited for you to understand, and I can wait for the words."

"I'm sorry..." While what he said didn't *cut* exactly, I did feel foolish.

"Don't be. You were always worth waiting for." And looking in his eyes, seeing the warmth on his face...I knew he meant every word. That he could be patient with me as I crawled out from under all that weight.

Not for the first time, his generosity left me grateful to have him.

Spencer kissed the palm of my hand and a shiver ran down my arm.

He had bitten me there before, on that wrist. Tasted what was inside me long before any of us knew what lived under my skin.

"Do you think it's still there? In my blood?" I asked, staring at the artery on my wrist.

"I don't know." Spencer shook his head, thoughtful. "I pulled a disgusting amount of that bile out of your body, but I don't know what stayed."

I held my wrist up to him. "Would you tell me? Taste me?"

Spencer smirked. "So eager already. I told you all vampires were like this."

I gave him a light tap on the shoulder in jest, only to discover it wasn't so light.

"Ow. Be careful, love." Spencer rubbed his skin where I'd smacked him. "You're a lot more dangerous now than you think." He took my hand gently and lifted my wrist to his mouth. He bit down and the nerve lit up my whole arm. I held back a gasp and watched him drink.

After a moment, a tiny, content sound came from his full mouth. He swallowed and pulled away, pressing his hand over the wound.

"And?" I asked.

"It's not gone." He licked his lips and something roiled in my gut— jealousy or hunger, I wasn't sure. "It's less potent. Drinkable. Maybe it'll be washed out of your system as your body heals, but I don't know. The bullet holes will disappear by tomorrow, but the grit…I've never seen anything like what happened here. I don't know if it will let go of you."

"It will," I said, more confident than I actually felt. "It has to."

Spencer smirked at me. "I can't tell if you're lying anymore."

I squinted at him. "And why is that?"

"Your heart used to give you away."

I laughed and leaned in to kiss him. "Maybe you'll find it still does."

He rested his forehead on mine for a moment and the world stood still. Just…being there, together. Then he let out a sigh and moved away.

"Are you ready to go back?" Spencer removed the pressure on my bite and slid his hand into mine. "We need to give them time with you before we have to leave."

Ah, that was where that sadness had hidden away to, suddenly back with a vengeance.

"Yeah. I think it's time to have a wake for my life."

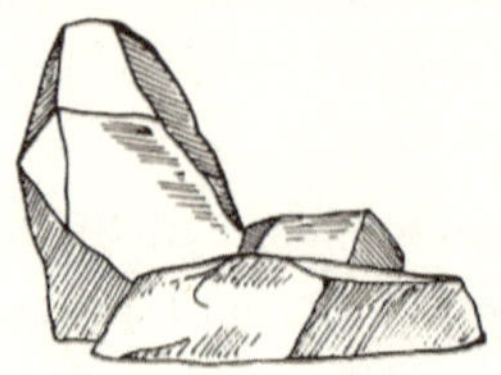

Penny Harbour

While Laurel and Spencer slept their final day away, Emma and Mary-Jo had work to do. A few last-minute errands. Some of them would be delightful surprises, and one…well, one had been a long time coming.

The two tired women pushed back through the front door and into Emma's kitchen, not bothering to unload the trunk of the car yet. They would have time to finish up those errands in a bit. For the moment, coffee was calling to Emma, so she went to brew a cup.

"When does he get off work again?" Mary-Jo asked, setting her shotgun down on the table.

"I think we got out of there just in time, honestly. Probably shouldn't have stayed as long as we did."

Mary-Jo chuckled. "I don't know, I feel like we could have done Greg dirtier."

Emma flashed her a smirk. "We definitely could have."

They had their coffees and talked, whiling away the minutes. Waiting for it to happen. By the time the car door slammed in the driveway, Emma was contemplating making supper.

A shit-eating grin spread across Mary-Jo's face. She stood, taking the shotgun with her. "Showtime."

Emma opened the door to find Greg stomping down toward them, his truck parked behind her car. They met him outside. No way in hell was he going in that house. Not just because Laurel was in there, but because she probably wouldn't let him out again. That was fine by MJ, but Emma had taken a stand against it.

"You fucking bitches." Greg's lips were curled in a snarl, the vein in the side of his head bulging. *Furious.* "I know it was you."

Mary-Jo shrugged. "I don't know what you're talking about."

He stopped a few paces away, seething. His face was beet-red, the veins in his neck popping. "Someone trashed my house *again*. Can't see how it wasn't you."

"What reason would we have to do that?" Emma batted her eyelashes at him.

Greg started to cough violently, like his lungs were full. When his back straightened and he looked up, his eyes had gone black.

"Oh, no," Mary-Jo crooned, raising the shotgun. "Not this shit again. You get off this fucking lawn, Greg."

"Where are you hiding my wife?" Greg hissed. "Send her out here! All her shit is gone! *I know she's here.*"

"Laurel is long gone, man. Off with someone who knows how to treat her right, unlike you." Mary-Jo couldn't help but smile. It wouldn't be a lie soon.

"For your sake, you need to let her go." Emma sounded almost pitying. But she had always been kinder than Mary-Jo.

Greg didn't listen. He started toward them, fists at the ready, jaw clenched.

Mary-Jo clicked the safety off and aimed. "I was hoping you'd choose violence."

She fired a round into the dirt in front of Greg, who immediately spooked and jumped back.

"No, no," Mary-Jo taunted as Greg backed away. "You came here looking for trouble. Now you got it." She reloaded and the sound made him twitch. "Stay, please."

"You're fucking crazy." But that black haze was fading from his eyes, leaving him as the scared, emasculated piece of shit he'd always been.

"You laid hands on my girl, you shitstain," Mary-Jo growled, following him as he backed away toward his truck. "I'm gonna blow your fucking dick off."

That was finally enough to send him hightailing back to his truck. He fumbled for the door handle, missed the step up to the cab, and cracked his knee. Cursing, he tried again, managing to get inside and slam the door.

"I know who you are, you rotten son of a bitch!" Mary-Jo screamed.

"Every woman in this town is going to know by tomorrow! You ever come back here, you're a dead man. You hear me?"

He was already starting to peel away. Mary-Jo took aim again and fired into the bed of his truck. The metal screeched as the bullet pierced it, and then Greg was gone, dust flying up on the road behind him as he fled.

Mary-Jo clicked the safety back on and propped the gun against her shoulder, beaming at Emma. "I dunno, something to remember me by, I guess."

Emma shook her head, smiling at her. "You're kinda scary, you know that?"

Mary-Jo put her arm around Emma's shoulder, walking her back inside. "Only when I have to protect my own, girlfriend. Otherwise, I'm a fucking saint."

Spencer

The next night, as I packed our things into the duffel bags Emma had dug out of a closet for us, Laurel sat in the bedroom. Her voice carried into the hall as she spoke to her mother on the phone.

"I know, Mom." Laurel was crying, and it broke my heart. "I don't want to go without saying goodbye, but I have to. Greg…it ended badly, Mom. But I promise I'm not going to leave forever."

I took the half-filled bags and went to the kitchen, in part to give her privacy, in part to alleviate how fucking horrible the conversation made me feel. Just because I had no choice but to turn her didn't mean I felt good about ripping her life to shreds.

Emma was cleaning up the dishes from their late breakfast. Despite our insistence that they not upset their lives for us, they'd both switched their sleeping schedules to match ours, staying up all night to make sure they saw as much of Laurel as they could before we left. Emma had called in more favours from her mother to keep Logan at a distance, and Mary-Jo had said she'd *called in dead* and wasn't going back to her job.

I couldn't blame either of them.

"Hey, Spencer. Do you have everything you need?" Emma asked, hanging up the brush she'd been using to wash the frying pan.

"The gods only know, sweetness." I put the bags on the table. "It's a fucking shame, honestly. I'm terrified to take Laurel back to that house, either because of that fucking thing in her veins or because it might break something in her mind to see the blood she spilt." I braced my hands on the table, seething. "Do you know how long I spent collecting books, music, games, *everything* in that house? Clothing I *love.*" I picked at the shoulder of the two-sizes-too-large Guns N' Roses T-shirt Emma had taken from her husband's closet for me. "I'm wearing this, but I have a velvet jacket from Düsseldorf just sitting across this harbour. Emma, it's infuriating."

She nodded. "You have save files too."

I let out a wail. "My *farm*! I had so many chickens in that file. Life isn't fair."

Emma dried her hands and came over to pat me on the back. "I know. But it's going to be all right. We won't let your books and clothes disappear."

"You're too good to me, but the pain is still too fresh."

Mary-Jo walked into the kitchen, freshly showered and dressed only in a large towel, Spectre following on her heels. Something about MJ in a towel was like seeing a sister naked, and it felt both neutral and a little off-putting.

"What's our little twink whining about now?" Mary-Jo started making herself a second cup of coffee.

"He's sad about leaving his stuff behind."

"*And* Laurel's things." I took my phone out of the pocket of the cruddy old jogging pants I'd forced myself into. "They're just sitting in boxes in my house, but again, I can't leave her and I can't bring her back there."

Mary-Jo set the coffee maker to brew and leaned against the counter, smirking. "I dunno, man. If you want your stuff, have you tried looking in your trunk?"

"My trunk? Why would—?" But Emma was hiding a smile behind her hand and Mary-Jo was grinning like a lion. I whipped around to swing open the front door to find my car sitting in the driveway. When I turned back to MJ, she was already tossing me the keys. I snatched it out of the air and hit the trunk button. It swung open, revealing a full trunk of boxes that hadn't been there before.

I turned to them, my jaw hanging open. "That isn't…?"

"It's some of it," Emma said. "We tried to choose carefully."

I ran outside and started to pry the boxes open. The first was Laurel's. A photo album, a pile of papers, and neatly folded clothing. The second was stuffed to the brim with fabric I recognized. Overjoyed, I pulled out my white silk blouse and held it to my face. "Ugh, *yes*. I'm so sorry I almost left you."

I dug around, and between the final three boxes I found a pair of high-waisted black pants to go with the top. They'd chosen a selection of books, and wrapped in a knit sweater was my Switch. *My farm.*

Pulling out a change of clothing for Laurel, I closed the trunk and went back inside. Mary-Jo and Emma had been watching me from the door, smirking.

"Gods, I'm not spending another *second* in this shirt." I pushed past them and started to change, not caring who was watching. If they were bashful, they could look away. "Thank you for this."

"Don't sweat it," Mary-Jo said. "There's a lot left and probably I missed something important, but I plan to get someone to put in a new window so you can just come back for everything else later."

I'd just pulled the blouse over my head when a door creaked at the other end of the house. We all stopped, looking as Laurel walked into the living room. Her eyes were bloodshot from crying, but they were still hazel. She didn't come closer than the doorway to the kitchen.

"I'm hungry, Spencer," she said, sniffing.

Instinctively, I snatched Spectre up off the floor and tucked her into Mary-Jo's arms. Then I opened the fridge and got a bag of blood. She'd already used half of the reserves that Mary-Jo had brought back, not including the few I'd needed for myself.

I held it up, testing her resolve. "Can you wait until it's warm?"

Laurel was holding her arm with the other hand. After a moment's thought, she nodded.

"Good." She hadn't been able to wait to feed yet, not once. If she made it this time, she might not again for weeks. It required a lot of resolve to keep the hunger at bay that early on.

I set to work at the stove, pouring the blood into a pot. I kept my eyes on her. If she moved, I would have to be faster. But she kept her distance, her tongue slipping over her lips just once as she trained her focus on her meal.

It only took a few minutes to slowly bring it up to body temperature, but I knew too well how much of an eternity that could feel like.

Meanwhile, neither Emma nor Mary-Jo moved a muscle.

Once it was ready, I brought her the cup. She took it, drinking greedily, all noise and mess. She had done *so well*, waiting. I kissed her on the forehead when she finished, and then took the empty glass from her. After wiping the blood from her chin, I held her against my chest. A look at Emma and Mary-Jo and their bodies relaxed. Pity was written on their faces. It had been horror, the first day. But by last night, they understood Laurel wasn't in control of any of it.

"It'll pass," I said, as much to them as to Laurel. "Today, and then someday, it'll be a thing that only happens when you're at your worst. And I'll be here for all of it."

Laurel stepped out of my arms and slowly went to the sink to wash her face. When she looked up and reached for a paper towel, she scanned the faces of her friends. "Sorry," she said simply.

"Think you can handle a living-person hug, bestie?" Mary-Jo asked.

Laurel nodded, and let herself be cradled in MJ's arms.

As they held each other, my body tensed for a moment, waiting to see if Laurel could handle the proximity of both MJ and the cat, but nothing came of it.

Fuck. *The cat.*

I sighed, my heart unprepared for what I was about to ask. "Mary-Jo?"

She looked up at me. "Yeah?"

"I…it's not safe for Spectre to come with us. She'd be too tempting to have around. And she deserves a home, not a blanket in a car while we skip from town to town. Clearly she loves you." I gestured to the cat, who had nuzzled herself into MJ's chest. "Would you keep her for me, until Laurel has this under control?"

"Fuck yeah, I would!" Mary-Jo pulled out of Laurel's arms and lifted Spectre up to stare her in the face. "You're coming home with me; yes, you are. We'll get you a nice bed and some cat litter and you can hunt the mice in the backyard until your daddy comes back to get you, yeah. Who's a good meow-meow? You are! Yeah!" And then MJ was dancing with the cat, her whole face shoved into its fur.

I couldn't help smirking. What a delightful idiot. I would miss that cat, but it helped, knowing how loved she would be in my absence.

"You're off soon, aren't you?" Emma asked quietly, bringing me back to the mood of the moment.

"We have to be." I unzipped the bags, double-checking for phone chargers, changes of clothing, and the few things Emma had been able to steal when she'd gone by the house. "We have a hotel in Port John that we need to get to before the sun, and she's going to need to stop at least twice to eat."

"Yeah, that makes sense." Emma's cheeks were going pink, tears welling in her eyes. "You should get going."

And just like that, all three of them were crying. They curled into each other and slowly drifted to the floor, their limbs tangled. They said nothing, just held each other as the emotions overwhelmed them.

I'd done that to them. I'd torn them apart. Yes, me and the monster made of coal, and the people who had hurt Laurel all her life, but it was my finishing blow. And now I had to stand and watch her say goodbye to the people she loved most.

My vision blurred and I choked back a sob.

Someone hit me in the leg. Mary-Jo was grasping for my hand, inviting me to join them and be held.

I got on the floor and fell in with them. I rested my head on Laurel's knees, and both Emma and Mary-Jo reached out to pull me in.

I closed my eyes, and for just a moment, I drifted back. Back to being held by the loves I had carried in my heart for the last two centuries. And that warmth, in the past and present, tore me wide open. I had given Laurel so much care that I'd had no time to think of them in days. And for once, it didn't burn as much as it had.

Eventually, the crying stopped. I wiped the tears from my face and tried to laugh. I felt a bit of a fool. Too old to be sitting on the tiles, sobbing about the future and the past.

"I feel like that's our cue to go." I peeled myself off the ground, stretching my newly kinked back.

"Get out of here before Emma starts again." Mary-Jo helped Laurel up with one hand, the other trying to keep her towel in place. Despite her words, she had probably shed more tears than any of the rest of us.

"Here." I handed my phone to Emma. "Add your number. If you need anything, call. Just because we're leaving doesn't mean we want to stop hearing from you."

Emma sniffed as she tapped her number into my phone. "There," she said, passing it back.

The contact read *AAEmma,* sitting firmly at the top of my contacts list.

A notification popped.

Mary-Jo:
Go fuck yourself, hag

I looked up to find her grinning, her phone in her hand.

I scoffed. "I'm the hag? You're in a towel. I can basically see your appetite from here."

"*My appetite!*" Mary-Jo cackled, smacking her palm against the counter. "That's something my grandmother used to say!" She stopped laughing and took a deep, centring breath.

With the sadness in the room broken for the moment, I gave the bags to Laurel and stuffed the last of the blood bags into the cooler. With that in hand, I urged Laurel toward the door. "We'll leave a message from the hotel. Don't bother calling until dark, but we'll answer when we're awake."

Laurel opened the door and walked out, refusing to look back as she made her way to the car.

I closed Emma's door behind us, leaving them and their broken hearts inside.

I popped the trunk, shoved the bags inside, and got in the driver's seat.

Laurel buckled in, staring out the front window with an intensity that scared me.

I started the car and set the music. Something from her side of the playlist, a little Our Lady Peace. "Are you all right?"

"No," she said, looking over at me. "But this isn't even the hardest thing I've done."

"No? Do you mean the leaving, or the hunger, or the being dead?" I shifted and pulled out of the driveway, leaving the lights of Emma's house behind.

"All of it." Her voice was full of cold resolve. "I've done harder. I'm not about to let any of this get in my way."

I seriously doubted she had done anything more difficult than resisting the killer that now lived under her skin, but I didn't say that. I hadn't lived her life. I had no idea what she'd endured in that town before she'd stumbled on me in those woods. Knowing what had happened since, though, left me open-minded to the horrors that could've been inflicted on anyone there.

It wasn't for me to say.

Laurel watched out the window as we drove up the main drag and around the harbour. Then up the hill, where the house stood with a deed still in my cover name. The house where we had watched a thousand movies and shared wine and slept together, and where she had killed for the first time.

I didn't imagine she'd miss it.

Then down the hill, past her house.

We hadn't been that way at all since everything had happened. Greg's truck was in the driveway and the lights were on in the living room.

The urge to stop and kill him just for *existing* was hard to push down. But it would also make a very bad example for a fledgling vampire.

Instead, I reached for her hand and squeezed.

I picked up speed, racing to get out of Penny Harbour. We hit the woods, darkness flooding out around us. It would be a long drive to Port John. Frankly, I had only the vaguest notion of where we would go after that. A city, certainly, where Laurel would have the backdrop of chaos and crime to make mistakes in. She'd need that. Gods knew I had made my fair share of trouble at the start. Perhaps we could find more of us to lean on. She'd need community. Someone other than me who knew what it was like to live in the shadows. For all I'd tried to cover it up, I barely knew what I was doing, and Laurel deserved better than that.

But that was tomorrow. For now, we had music and the road ahead. I had her, and we had an eternity to figure out what came next.

Laurel and Spencer's Story Continues.

For updates, visit CatRector.com

Reviews are critical for the success of indie books. Please
consider leaving an honest review of this book and any other
you read via whichever review platforms you use. You'll
make a lot of indie authors very happy.

If you want the latest news about upcoming books by Cat
Rector, including any upcoming books,
join the mailing list at CatRector.com

MY SUPPORTERS

As an author, it's impossible to have a career without the support of amazing people. This list represents a collection of readers and colleagues who have gone above and beyond to champion my work in the last several years. Some have purchased ungodly amounts of books from me, while others have helped in the reading and creation process. Some of them simply listen to me gripe about never having enough time in the day.

To each and every one of you, thank you. Your support means the world to me, and without you, I wouldn't get to do this amazing job. Sorry I have to destroy your heart all the time, but if you didn't like it, you would read something cuter I guess *BIG SHRUG*

Rowan Liddell
Kaea Branch
LotteH
Carballo
Gabriela Florea
Jolien Nijns
Cheyenne Brammah
Allie B
Casey
A.J. Torres
Lisa H.
Aleksander E Petit
Alex Rae

Tanushka
Fem Lippens (looníeslibrary)
Erin Kinsella
Tanni
Amanda Diegan
DC Guevara
Michaela
Dina B.
Vanessa R.
Brinley
Audrey
Matías Ruelas
Analiza
Becca Leigh
E. L. Pagès
fi
Suzanne Fraser-Martin
Nox T.
Lien drst
Esther
Elisabeth
Hannah Decock
Jules
Aiden
Cath
Alice
Rachel Kasparek
Alicia Ann
Tessa Hastjarjanto
Brea Helgard
Ash Helgard
Sheridan

ACKNOWLEDGEMENTS

This book turned into a self-fulfilling prophecy in ways that I didn't expect. In writing Laurel and Spencer, I thought I was addressing an old wish to have more love in my life, but well before the end of this writing process, I found myself with a new abundance of just that. New people came into my world and filled it with so much joy. More than I may have ever had before. With that came a sense of security and safety that I hadn't imagined for myself, and I'm grateful to have it.

First, to the village that raised me, thank you. My relationship with that place might be complicated, but there's a reason I came back in the end. As a kid, it gave me a place to spread my wings, walk the roads safely, and be close to nature. It let me connect with people who have a warmth and generosity of spirit I haven't found anywhere else. The area is growing away from some of the things that soured it. When I left, I understood that I could never be queer there. When I came home, there were tiny pride parades, and flags in windows, and I had queer colleagues. I had travelled across the world looking for community, and was never prepared to find it at the place I'd started from. It moulded me into who I am, for better or worse, and it will always feel like home.

Jessica - I did the math a while ago, and at this point, you've been a rock in my life for longer than the years I didn't know you. You've taught me so much about living well and my body, and how to keep myself healthy, body and spirit. From telling me to slow down and find balance, to asking me to think of myself, to teaching me how to eliminate my debilitating headaches, I owe you so much. And in the last few years alone, you always came to the table with wisdom, patience and security. When I stepped into new avenues and took new risks, you accepted that with open arms. Things are on the cusp of changing in so many ways, but I know you'll be in my corner every step of the way.

Vincent - This year has been a wild ride. I've asked a lot of you, and you met that with compassion and understanding. You've taken a bunch of difficult steps and I'm proud and grateful that you'd decided to take this journey. I'm excited to take on all the challenges coming our way, from finding a place to settle down to crafting a life that suits us, finally. We have a lot on the horizon and by the time this book is published, I imagine our lives will have shifted drastically. So much has changed and will continue to change, and we're just two silly humans trying to get this right. Whatever we choose, I'm excited to do it alongside you.

Leslie - Fate kept us apart at least ten times and brought us together at exactly the right moment. I'm so thankful that a single night at a library conference led to such a deep and fulfilling partnership. I didn't expect to walk away from that weekend having been set on a path to the happiest I've been in years. Your work is incredible, your mind is delightful, and you've brought me such peace and companionship. From writing retreats at the beach to nights spent watching the stars to countless moments where you just understand me, you're the perfect change I never saw coming. I can't wait to spend so much more time creating vast worlds and walking the woods with you. How lucky am I that I get to love you.

Not A Horse - You've made space in your life for me, and I'm eternally grateful. You're an amazing ray of sunshine and getting to know you has been a delight. I'm sure there are moments where you look up to find two weirdos perched on the couch talking about characters that only live in our heads and wonder what you got yourself into. I look forward to more evenings of horsing around playing Magic and demolishing tree stumps in the future <3

Sheridan - It's hard to believe that we met on Tiktok at random because you asked to buddy read a book with me. Now you're someone I share so much with, and you've done such incredible things since we met. I'm so proud of you for everything you've accomplished, but more than anything else, I'm proud of how you've grown into yourself. You have so much love and care to offer, and I can't wait to see where that takes you.

Erin - Even though our careers have taken us down different paths, I can always count on you to be in my corner. You have such an incredible eye for this job and always know what will bring out the best in a story. I wouldn't be anywhere without you, and I hope that our paths keep crossing for years to come, no matter where we end up in this wild industry.

And to you, dear reader. Thank you for following me on this journey. If you've been around a long time, you probably know I stepped offline to find myself this year. The fact that you stuck around means the world to me. I hope this book brought you some mixture of entertainment, catharsis, and joy. I write about dark things, I know, but I believe in hope as well. In finding your people and creating light, even when things are dark. I wish nothing but light for you in the days ahead.

CONTRIBUTORS

Written Contribution by Leslie Allen
leslieallen.com/
linktr.ee/leslieiswriting

Edited and Proofread by Ivy L. James
authorivyljames.com
Twitter.com/AuthorIvyLJames
Instagram.com/authorivyljames

Cover Art by Scherville
scherville.com

—

Cover Text, Interior Formatting and Design by Cat Rector

ABOUT THE AUTHOR

Cat Rector grew up in a small Nova Scotian town and could often be found simultaneously reading a book and fighting off muskrats while walking home from school. She devours stories in all their forms, loves messy, morally grey characters, and writes about the horrors that we inflict on each other. After spending nearly a decade living abroad, she returned to Canada to resume her war against the muskrats. When she's not writing, you can find her playing video games, spending time with loved ones, or staring at her To Be Read pile like it's going to read itself.

Coals Gets In Your Veins is her fifth book.

Find her on Twitter, Tiktok, and Instagram at @Cat_Rector
Or visit her website, CatRector.com

www.ingramcontent.com/pod-product-compliance
Lightning Source LLC
Chambersburg PA
CBHW021922220726
48287CB00019B/1256